In The Spotlight:

Fame's Temptation

RACHAEL STEWART

SOPHIE PEMBROKE

ABBY GREEN

MILLS & BOON

First Published in Great Britain 2025
by Mills & Boon, an imprint of HarperCollins*Publishers* Ltd
1 London Bridge Street, London, SE1 9GF

www.harpercollins.co.uk

HarperCollins*Publishers*
Macken House, 39/40 Mayor Street Upper,
Dublin 1, D01 C9W8, Ireland

In The Spotlight: Fame's Temptation © 2025 Harlequin Enterprises ULC

Beauty and the Reclusive Millionaire © 2021 Rachael Stewart
Slow Dance with the Best Man © 2017 Sophie Pembroke
When Da Silva Breaks the Rules © 2014 Abby Green

ISBN: 978-0-263-41860-6

This book contains FSC™ certified paper and other controlled sources to ensure responsible forest management.

For more information visit: www.harpercollins.co.uk/green

Printed and Bound in the UK using 100% Renewable Electricity
at CPI Group (UK) Ltd, Croydon, CR0 4YY

BEAUTY AND THE RECLUSIVE MILLIONAIRE

RACHAEL STEWART

For my mum and dad,

For sparking my love of Greece – the food,
the people, the stunning islands...

Yamas!

xxx

CHAPTER ONE

'WOW!' CATHERINE WILDE pushed her sunglasses back, sweeping her fringe away as she squinted against the rays of the sun and took in her home for the next month. A Greek island surrounded by crystal blue waters with a golden cliff face that curved before her and seemed to hug and welcome in one. 'It's incredible.'

'The most beautiful island, *nai*?' Marsel grinned as he lugged one of her many bags off his small sailboat that she'd chosen to hitch a lift on. Her PA had thought she was crazy—*'You know I can sort you a nice speedboat, right?'*—but she'd wanted to start this holiday as she meant to go on. Relaxed, laid-back and under no circumstances rushed. So when she'd learned of Marsel's regular trips to the mainland to source supplies she'd jumped at the opportunity to climb aboard.

It had nothing whatsoever to do with delaying her arrival at said island and coming face to face with its owner.

Nothing at all.

She stopped herself from shaking her head emphatically as she threw her focus into the beauty of the island. This trip was about relaxing in authentic Greek hospitality. No security detail, no flash vehicles, no celebrity fuss.

And it was a good plan…if only her bobbing feet and drumming fingertips would get the message.

She'd *tried* to relax on the journey. She'd *tried* to focus on the beauty of Greece, to let the heat of the midday sun warm her, the sea breeze soothe her. She'd tried really hard…and maybe that was the problem. Relaxing didn't come naturally, not to her.

And neither did nerves. She was an award-winning actor after all. It didn't pay to let nerves get the better of her. But this kind of unease was different, uncontainable, and she couldn't deny its source—Alaric de Vere.

Her best friend's older brother. Her friend once too, many moons ago.

And this was his private island, his place of solace, cut off from the world and civilisation, just the way he liked it…

Until now.

Was she truly as welcome as the curving cliff face made out?

Or had his sister, Flo, worked the same persuasive magic over him and left him no choice but to welcome her? A burnt-out celebrity, reeling from a breakup and in desperate need of isolation, if the press were to be believed.

And though they didn't know the half of it, they weren't far wrong…

But she wasn't here just to fix herself, she was here for him. As a favour to Flo and to appease her own worries too. She was here to do everything she could to help Alaric. To remind him of his life beyond the island, of those who missed him and needed him to return.

Her stomach churned it over, her head thinking the worst, her heart…too tender. Was he really as bad as Flo had made out? The media even? Was she going to make it worse coming here when she was hardly a picture of mental health herself?

'*Nai?*' Marsel's brows nudged skyward, his brown eyes dancing and bright.

She frowned. *Nai? Yes. Yes, what?*

'The island?' He gestured to it as he leapt back onto the precarious gangplank with another of her bags.

'*Nai*. Very beautiful.' She gave him an unrestrained smile, thinking only to hide her worries, and immediately regretted it.

His knees seemed to buckle beneath him, his body leaning precariously overboard, and she flung her hand out with a yelp, too far away to reach. She held her breath and was forced to watch as he swiftly regained control and hurried to land, his eyes averted, his tanned cheeks sporting a flush he wouldn't want her to notice.

She wanted to apologise. She knew the affect she had on people, but she'd hoped her and Marsel had moved past that after several hours in one another's company. Her efforts to show him she was just another person, a person capable of carrying her own luggage, capable of laughing over the fact he'd run her suitcase over her foot in his haste to get to it before she could herself, paying off.

But it seemed he was still as star-struck, and after a decade in the film industry, she should be used to it… and she was…

It didn't make it any easier to live with though.

She loved acting. She loved projecting another life on the screen and moving people to tears, to laughter, to joy. To provide the kind of escapism people needed when times were tough or to pass a few pleasant hours of downtime.

But fame came with its pedestal and a lonely one at that.

Not that she was being all woe me. She knew how lucky she was; she just wished at times to be able to blend in, be normal, to have her personal affairs kept just that—

personal. Her hand went to her stomach, her fingers idly stroking as the pain of the recent past threatened to invade.

The future would be different; she was determined to make it so. One step at a time. First, a change in career. She wanted to make a difference on the other side of the screen. She wanted to write her own tales for others to perform. Something this trip was supposed to aid with by giving her the space, the freedom and the time to get her first script finished.

Time to work and time to grieve, Flo had said. Time to help Alaric, and time to help herself.

She lowered her gaze to where her fingers stilled over her flat stomach that showed nothing of the slightest baby bump that had once been and swallowed the bubble of pain that threatened to shake her anew. She thought of the soft smile on Flo's lips as her friend had bade her a teary farewell, her own palm resting over her well-pronounced bump. A sight that had brought both pain and happiness, the reminder of what she'd lost contending with her joy for her friend who deserved every bit of happiness.

She pulled her phone from her bag. She'd promised Flo she'd message when she arrived safe and now was as good a time as any. It would also free Marsel to go about his task without another mishap courtesy of her and her world-renowned smile. And though she'd offered to carry her own baggage off the boat, she was relieved he'd insisted on doing it. She really didn't fancy her chances of making it across, bags in hand, not with the way the flimsy gangplank was shifting with the boat. She had to wedge her body against the rail just to text Flo.

She kept it short and sweet, pocketed the phone before she could drop it in the rolling waters and breathed in her surroundings.

It really was beautiful, beautiful and isolated and...quite

unexpected. With the simplest of wooden jetties forming a safe path over the rocks, its white painted railing distressed and peeling away, it was hardly luxurious and so unlike the family to which it belonged.

Or more specifically the man…but then what did she know of Alaric after all this time?

The boat lurched with the waves and her stomach took another roll. A roll she knew had nothing to do with the waters beneath her and everything to do with him. She grasped the handrail to steady herself, wishing she could steady her stomach and her nerves just as easy.

She'd known Alaric her entire life. They'd played together as children, hung out together as teens, got drunk and disorderly even… He'd been her first real crush too, in an intensely forbidden best friend's older brother kind of… A ridiculous bubble of laughter cut off her mental spiel—*not helping, Catherine.*

But so much had changed since she last saw him. His entire life had been upended, and here she was waltzing right back into it…surely it was too little, too late?

Was she deluded to even try? To believe Flo when she'd insisted Catherine could help, even when his own family hadn't been able to?

Her phone buzzed in her bag and she lifted it out, glanced at the screen as it buzzed again and again with more messages arriving in quick succession.

You're on the island?

You've seen Alaric?

Is he okay?

Her brows drew together as she tapped in a reply.

Yes. No. Don't know. Calm down, Flo. Xx

Her friend's response was just as quick.

Sorry! Where is he? Xx

Her frown deepened. Good question. Where was her host? Surely it was polite to greet a guest at the dock… especially one that you hadn't seen in for ever?

She typed back.

I don't know. We've just moored up. He's probably at the house.

Three dots appeared to show that Flo was typing…and typing…and still typing.

The hairs on Catherine's nape prickled, her anxiety aggravated with every prolonged second…

She glanced up to see Marsel landside with all the bags, his phone to his ear as he spoke in rapid Greek. She looked back to her phone, tapped her foot. *Come on, Flo, spit it out…*

Okay. Keep me updated, yeah? Xx

That was it. That was what had taken several minutes to type?

'Way to go in helping me relax, Flo,' she murmured under her breath as she fired off her reply.

Of course. Xx

She shoved her phone back into her bag and lowered her sunglasses, moving before she changed her mind about the whole affair. She needed this break and Alaric needed to get a life, to use Flo's words. It was a win-win.

Marsel saw her approach and quickly cut his call, hurrying to the end of the gangplank to offer out his hand in aid. Gladly she took it, careful to keep her smile to the ground.

'Kyrios de Vere is aware that we are here,' he said once she was safe on land.

'Great.' Though her stomach didn't feel great.

She reached for one of her cases and as Marsel tried to stop her she waved him down.

'I think it will be quicker if I help. It looks like there's a walk ahead?'

She eyed the worn and dusty pier, the sandy pathway through the cliff face, the small cove that looked like it had no decent exit point…it wasn't as though a car was suddenly going to appear. And there were the food supplies Marsel had brought back from the mainland to carry too.

'Is Alaric—Kyrios de Vere—on his way?'

Marsel didn't eye her as he took her other bags in hand and started off down the jetty. 'He says that we should head on up. The jeep isn't too far away.'

'Oh…' She peered into the picturesque distance and saw nothing remotely vehicle-like. She'd just have to take his word for it.

Brows drawing together, she followed him, her mind pondering Alaric's whereabouts. It was perfectly reasonable, she tried to tell herself, that he wouldn't want to greet her at the dock. She didn't have to think the worst. And besides, she was here for her space too, having rejected her security detail and her PA's pleasant company. This was just another element of getting all the space she desired.

Perfectly reasonable. Perfectly fine.

Only…

No one had seen Alaric in a year. The public hadn't

seen him in nearly three, and she…well, she hadn't seen him for almost ten…and she *knew* he was suffering. She got that. But did that mean he really didn't want her here, in spite of the invite?

Her heart ached for him, even as the urge to run nipped at her heels.

'Wait here, Miss Wilde!' Marsel called back over his shoulder. 'The jeep is just a few yards away, tucked into a cave out of the sun. I'll bring it to you.'

She blew out a relieved breath, releasing her case with a nod and fisting her hands on her hips. Not that she *couldn't* carry on up the steep incline ahead. She trained daily. She had to. She wasn't one of those actors who depended on body doubles, stunt or otherwise. If the character had to do it, then she had to—it was important to her. Though her agent and the extortionate fee for her insurance told her she was foolish to insist on it.

But a jeep was good. It meant she wouldn't arrive face to face with Alaric for the first time in years feeling exposed and in desperate need of a shower. She'd at least have her trusty armour—her make-up, her clothing and her composure—all in place.

Shielding her eyes with one hand, she took in the sandy cove, the dusty path ahead, the sprouts of green and flora jutting out of the golden cliff face, the trees looming over the edge high above…and then she saw it—a figure… someone in between the trees… *Alaric?*

She went to wave, but the silhouette vanished as swiftly as it had appeared.

Had she imagined it? Was it a trick of the light, of the haze caused by the heat of the sun?

She wiped the sweat from the back of her neck, flapped the front of her vest top to let in some air…

Yes, it had to be the heat playing tricks on her, or it wasn't Alaric, because Alaric would have at least waved.

But then the Alaric she remembered would have bounded down the path and swept her up into a bear hug the second she'd hopped off the boat.

The Alaric she remembered would have made sure she felt welcome.

The Alaric she remembered wouldn't leave her feeling like this…

This was a mistake.

Alaric had known it the second his sister had asked.

Had known it even as he'd said yes and instructed Dorothea to make up the spare room. For his use, not Catherine's, because Catherine had to have the best his house could offer and that meant his suite.

He cursed, raked a hand through his sweat-slickened hair. Catherine. *Here.* On his island. This was madness.

He'd tried to run off the apprehension, the unease, had ran and ran in the ridiculous heat with no destination in mind, until he'd found himself at the cliff edge and spied Marsel's boat on the horizon.

And then, as the boat had loomed closer, it had been her hair, captivating as it shone like spun gold in the breeze, her presence like a hit of sunshine straight to his frozen core, its warmth far more powerful than the blazing heat of the day.

It had always been this way with Catherine…or was it Kitty now?

Kitty. His fists flexed at his sides. He didn't know her as Kitty, but the world did—Kitty Wilde, Hollywood A-list and idol to millions. Would there be any of Catherine left in the movie star she was now?

And why did he even care?

He shouldn't. Just as he shouldn't have agreed. He clenched his jaw, fighting back the chaos rising within. He'd made his bed so to speak…the time to turn her away was long gone. And he could hardly leave the island himself. Where would he go? Where would he *want* to go?

Nowhere. That was the cold hard truth. His island was more than just his home; it was his sanctuary, his protection from the past, his haven for the future.

But thanks to his sister, he now had a guest, and one he wasn't ready to face, no matter what good manners dictated. He watched as she walked down the jetty, every step bringing her that bit closer, her walk so elegant even as she lugged what had to be a heavily laden suitcase…

He dragged in a breath, battling the sudden light-headedness. No, he'd wait for nightfall, for the harsh light of day to be gone. In the darkness he could find some protection, something to obscure his scars when she set her infamous blue eyes on him and that picture-perfect smile that had captured the hearts of millions, if not billions.

If she would muster up a smile at all when she saw what he had become…

She glanced up at that precise moment, her eyes behind her shades colliding with his and the world stilled, his heart the only thing capable of movement as it leapt, strong and wild. The most he'd felt in years.

He choked on his own folly as he spun away and broke into a pace that was all the more fierce for the feelings he was trying to outrun. He pounded the trail, through the trees, the landscaped gardens, the burn in his lungs nothing to do with exertion and everything to do with her. He startled Andreas, who was tending to the flowers beside the front door, and almost took out a bustling Dorothea when he burst into the hallway.

'Kyrios de Vere!' She clutched a hand to her chest, her

brown eyes wide, wisps of grey hair escaping her bun as she rushed about getting everything perfect for their guest. 'You startled me!'

He came to an abrupt halt, sucked in a breath. 'Marsel will be here shortly. Can you show Catherine around and I'll join her this evening?'

'But don't you—'

'I'm busy.' He was already moving off, heading for the stairs, and he sensed her frown follow him.

'But—'

'No buts, Dorothea. See it done.'

Yes, he was being discourteous, his manners tossed to the wayside in his desire to avoid facing her, but what did they know of it, what did any of them know of it… This was his house, his domain, and he could act however he damn well chose.

He only wished he could dismiss the nagging guilt as easily.

CHAPTER TWO

Right, so she was here, and he wasn't.

Unease rippled through her as she followed Marsel's directions to the kitchen, grocery bags wrapped in her arms. She felt like she shouldn't be here, that she was invading Alaric's home. A man she no longer knew.

All she had to go on was second-hand. Not the hyped-up, titillated news the world's media reported, but the heartfelt version from his sister. And not just the horrific details of the accident three years ago that had taken the life of his best friend, but the mark it had left. How it changed him both inside and out. How he'd cut himself off so completely.

Would he let her in? Would he talk to her? Would he even make himself known or was she going to spend a month alone?

She tightened her hold on the grocery bags as the hollow ache inside resonated out, her own loss compounded by her fear that whatever bond they'd once shared was over. And in that moment, she didn't know who needed it more…her or Alaric.

'Aah, Miss Wilde, it is so good to meet you!' A woman bustled towards her as she entered the kitchen, her brown eyes sparkling with warmth, her flour-dusted cheeks giving off a glow. 'I'm Dorothea, Kyrios de Vere's housekeeper, and you really shouldn't be carrying those—that is a job for my son!'

Catherine laughed at the woman's flurried greeting. 'It's so good to meet you too, and it's fine. I insisted on helping. Where shall I put them?'

Dorothea hurried across the stone-walled kitchen to the centre island, shoving various ingredients and cooking utensils aside to clear some space on the worn wooden surface. 'Thank you, Miss Wilde.'

'You're welcome.' She placed the bags down and eyed the concrete countertop behind her, its glazed surface covered in flour with a fresh mound of dough at its heart.

'I'm so sorry, Kyrios de Vere's not here.' Dorothea wrung her hands in her apron. 'You see, he is—well, he is rather busy with his work, and—and he did say he was sorry and that he will join you this evening.'

She nodded, though Dorothea's obvious discomfort failed to reassure her and, seeking a distraction, she gestured to the dough. 'What are you making?'

'Fresh pitta to go with souvlaki tonight. It is Kyrios de Vere's favourite.'

Catherine smiled. 'Soon to be mine, I'm sure.'

Fresh baked bread—her weakness. But it was okay, she had a month without a camera on her. She could afford to eat a little luxury so early on in her break.

'Excellent!' Dorothea's cheeks rounded with her smile as she paused before the Belfast sink to wash her hands and Catherine glanced around the room.

It was a rustic delight, all wood and concrete with a splash of colour from the copper handles and pans, and the herbs that hung along one wall creating a pleasing, natural scent. It was a proper kitchen. Well-used, homely and tasteful.

She couldn't stop her thoughts going back to her host…

had he designed this space? Did he cook here too? Or was it all Dorothea and the skill of a talented interior designer?

'Now you should get yourself settled and relaxed.' Dorothea gently shooed her to the door. 'I'll show you to your bedroom.'

'No—no, it's fine. I'll help unload the jeep first.'

'You will not.' The commanding way she said it had Catherine grinning. Not only was she unaccustomed to being bossed about when she wasn't on set, she actually found the older woman's manner quite endearing. 'My son is more than capable, as is his father. You are a guest.'

'Nonsense.' As endearing as it was, Catherine wasn't backing down. 'It's the least I can do for hijacking Marsel's trip to the mainland, and I won't be waited on hand and foot while I'm here.'

'There's no talking her down, Mama.' Marsel bustled into the kitchen before they could make it to the door, his arms laden with bags as he shook his head and gave his mum a sheepish smile. 'I've already tried several times over.'

'It's true, I insisted.' Catherine rested her hand on Dorothea's shoulder. '*Please*. I want to help.'

'You might as well agree, *agápi mou*.' In came Andreas, Marsel's father, his eyes crinkling at the corners with his grin. 'I've already had the same argument with Miss Wilde outside. She's as stubborn as you!'

That earned a huff out of Dorothea and a laugh from the rest, including Catherine, her nerves readily disappearing in the company of their easy banter.

She followed Marsel back out to the jeep and this time he didn't quibble as he handed her a brown paper bag filled with groceries and took one up for himself. 'That's the last of the food.'

As they headed back inside, she surveyed the grounds

once more, this time taking in its beauty rather than trying to spy her elusive host. The house flowed over several storeys built into the hillside, its stone walls blending into the surroundings and giving the impression of a century-old farmhouse rather than the luxury villa she'd been expecting. There were pale blue shutters at every window, terracotta pots with flowers flourishing and well-tended rock gardens with a variety of plants and olive trees offering up some verdant relief to the dry terrain.

The sound of running water came from the lowest tier and she could just make out the edge of an infinity pool that dropped off into the ocean, and rattan-covered seating areas positioned to make the most of the far-reaching view with distant boats and islands appearing as tiny specks on the horizon.

'Stand there much longer and the food will cook itself.'

She spun to face Marsel waiting in the doorway and grimaced. 'Sorry, it really is quite captivating.'

He grinned as he carried on his way and she followed him inside, the cool air of the house an instant relief to the oppressive heat of the day. It wasn't just the soothing temperature either, it was the earthy tones of the décor, the exposed stone and mortar in the walls, the interesting theme of forged cement, wood and rattan flowing both inside and out.

It was calming, Zen-like, and as she breathed it all in, she realised she could be quite happy here. That if any place could teach her to relax, it was this one. So long as her and Alaric were okay…

She wriggled the bag higher up her chest, righted her shoulders and bolstered her resolve. They *would* be okay.

Helping him wasn't negotiable, helping herself on the other hand…well, she was trying.

She walked into the kitchen and straight into the back of a stock-still Marsel.

'Mama! Papa!'

She peeked around him, her frown of confusion lifting as she took in the scene before her—a blushing Dorothea batting away a now flour-covered Andreas. Catherine didn't need to guess at what Marsel had walked in on.

'It's amazing anything gets done here,' their son admonished, shaking his head and dumping the bags on the island.

Andreas pounded his son's back. 'Says you.'

She laughed at their teasing, the speed with which they succeeded in lifting her from her worries such light relief.

She placed her bag down beside Marsel's and brushed off her hands. 'Is there anything else I can help with?'

She eyed the dough and Dorothea hurried over to her. 'Not today. You should get yourself unpacked and settled in.'

'I really don't mind.' Especially when she felt in desperate need of a distraction to fill the hours between now and dinner when she would finally get to see him. Sticking around the family and their pleasantries definitely appealed more than being left to her thoughts.

'But I do.' Dorothea started to shoo her to the door again. 'Now come, I'll show you to your room.'

'Okay. Okay.' She gave a soft sigh and followed her, pausing briefly to speak to Marsel. 'Thanks again for the lift, I really appreciate it.'

'Yes, Marsel.' The very air seemed to still as all eyes swung to the open doorway and the man now filling it. 'Thank you for bringing Catherine here.'

Alaric!

At least…it had to be…but ten years…the accident and the scar it had left. Her gaze caught on it, the way his bronzed skin pulled together along his cheek, tugging at the corner of his eye and mouth, creating a jagged line in the dark layer of stubble.

Her heart twisted. The sight of the scar in the flesh bringing with it the pain he'd endured, the agony, the loss. It felt like minutes passed when it could only have been seconds, her pulse kick-starting, her eyes blinking away the tears that would have formed as she stepped forward and stalled. He'd said nothing more. Hadn't even moved. No welcome, nothing.

And he was so very different. Taller, broader, the hard cut to his jaw more pronounced as he clenched it tight, his mouth full even in its grim line. His dark hair, neither short nor long, dripped water onto his white T-shirt, the fabric fitting snug to his chest and biceps before gathering at the hips, his loose linen trousers and bare feet far more relaxed than his posture.

Had he been in the shower—is that why he hadn't come to greet her?

It was a nice thought, a relief, but somehow she doubted it, and as she forced her eyes back to his, her thoughts emptied out. It was his eyes that spoke to her the most, those breathtaking blues that conjured up so many memories and seemed to suck the very oxygen from the room. There was no denying who those eyes belonged to. Even devoid of the light, the humour, the love, they were undeniably his, and undeniably cold.

She lifted her chin a fraction and swallowed, her smile so very forced. 'Alaric?'

'Catherine.'

He dipped his head, the movement stilted as his body tightened against the chill spreading within, rapidly taking over the warmth that had assaulted him the second he'd entered the doorway and set eyes on her up close.

She'd twisted her hair up into a knot high on her head since he'd seen her on the jetty, her sunglasses nestled in the golden tresses and unveiling her startling blue eyes that he didn't want to appreciate up close. They made his heart race, his body warm with too many memories, too many feelings. Even when they were filled with the wide-eyed horror they possessed now, her glossy mouth parted, her cheeks flushed pink.

He tried to swallow, tried to regain control, but everything about her made it impossible. Even the simple hairstyle provoked him, the way it exposed the arch of her neck, her delicate collarbone, escaped tendrils teasing at the skin there. Skin that he'd once admired, tickled, caressed even…only not in the way he'd craved.

And now she was here with far too much of that skin on show. Her vest top hanging from two of the skinniest straps, her animal print shorts lightweight and short. Much too short as they exposed her long legs all glossy and bronzed, and…and he really needed to keep his eyes up.

But then he was looking straight into her wide-eyed gaze, her abject horror freezing over his veins once more. And in a way that was better, far safer. It kept him at a distance, reminded him of how times had changed, how they'd both changed.

'Or is it Kitty now?' He couldn't prevent the bitter edge to his voice, didn't want to, and Dorothea's narrowed gaze told him she'd caught it. Caught it and was warning him to behave. To do better.

'I'll answer to either.' Her smile wavered about her lips, a fresh bloom of colour rising from her chest to her face, highlighting her angled cheekbones and the button-like tip to her upturned nose. Features he remembered all too well and bringing the strangest sense of relief that she hadn't succumbed to the surgeon's knife in her quest to achieve Hollywood perfection.

And why would she change when she's perfect enough already?

His jaw pulsed as he buried the unwelcome thought. 'Catherine, it is.'

'It's good to see you.'

Was it? Or was she just being polite. He hadn't mistaken the horror he'd glimpsed, he was sure, so was it regret he could see now? Regret and…curiosity?

Did she want to see for herself the man he had become? The beast even…

The tabloids were rarely kind, and his sister alone knew enough to condemn him.

Dorothea's brows were wagging on his periphery, telling him to respond appropriately, and he cleared his throat, gave a curt nod. 'I trust you had a good journey?'

There. That was polite. That was thoughtful.

'I did…thank you.' She stepped towards him and he fought the urge to back up, fought even harder as her hands lifted— *God*, was she going to embrace him? Hell, no. He spun away. 'I'll show you around.'

He strode down the hall, not daring to wait, not able to breathe until there was enough distance between them. He had no interest in being all touchy-feely. He didn't want her to see him up close. In the face of her perfection, he felt ever more scarred, ever more damaged.

'Hey, Alaric, slow down.'

He didn't. He raked his fingers through his hair and continued on, hearing the soft pad of her footfall behind him. Even the American twang she'd gained over the years riled his blood. Hollywood may not have forced her under

the knife, but ten years of living and breathing that world…
was she even recognisable underneath?

Unlikely.

Did he want to find out?

No.

Did he care?

Did *he*?

He couldn't even mentally deny it. Truth was he
shouldn't care. Caring led to feelings that he'd long ago
denied himself. He didn't deserve to care for another, just
as he didn't deserve another's care.

Further reason he should have refused this crazy visit.
Refused Flo and not risen to her emotional blackmail.

Flo. His meddling little sister. She'd known what strings
to pull, she'd known how to crack his trusty composure—
Catherine. She'd been his Achilles heel back then, and no
matter how he tried to convince himself that was in the
past, that she wasn't his to care for, he hadn't been able
to say no.

And what exactly had Flo told Catherine over the years?
He knew full well his sister's thoughts on how he lived
but just how much of a beast did she think he was? He
certainly looked it and Flo herself had tossed the abusive
label at him in this very space two years ago when he'd
refused to return home to visit their mother after her diag-
nosis. Called him worse last Christmas when he continued
to refuse. But to have those looks of pity, of sadness, from
those he loved, those who'd once seen him as strong, successful, invincible…no, he couldn't stomach it.

But then last month, when she'd begged him to take
Catherine in, he'd cracked. *'Please, Alaric, she needs to
hide away from the media storm brewing before it breaks
her.'*

A media storm triggered by Kitty Wilde's high-profile breakup with her co-star and fellow A-lister, Luke Walker. A man who was everything Alaric wasn't and never could be…

He raised a hand to the right. 'The dining room is here.'

He was surprised he didn't choke on the words as he fought a misplaced surge of jealousy and didn't turn as he sensed her pause to look inside the doorway.

'It's nice.'

'It opens onto the veranda and makes the most of the view. I often eat here but you can choose to eat wherever you like.'

He moved off, making sure his point hit home—that he wasn't expecting her to dine with him; in fact, he'd prefer it if she didn't—and he could practically sense Dorothea's disapproving look should she overhear.

'Alaric?'

She was hurrying after him again, but he refused to pause.

'To the left is my study which you won't need. The next door takes you to the gym. It's fully equipped with a tread-mill, bike, cross trainer, rowing machine, weights… If you need any help getting to grips with anything let Marsel or Andreas know.'

'Not you? Can't you…'

He gave her a quick look over his shoulder, careful to give his unscarred side. 'I'd prefer it if they helped you.'

'Oh…'

It was soft, filled with disappointment, and the pang in his chest of undeniable guilt almost had him taking it back.

'There's also a steam room, sauna, jacuzzi and outdoor shower.' He was already moving again. 'There are steps down to the pool too.'

He gestured to the right, to the last door. 'The rest of the floor is made up of the library which you can access here. The bookcases are well stocked, so you should find something to interest you. If not, let Dorothea or Andreas know and they will see it sourced.'

'I'm sure that won't be necessary.'

He waited as she peeked inside, her smile lighting up her face. She'd always loved books. It was an interest they'd once shared and the vision of them together on the U-shaped sofa, book in hand, the glass wall before them with the backdrop of the Aegean Sea, was too quick to form. Clear in its imagery, strong in the alien sense of longing it dredged up.

'It's so tranquil.'

He grunted, *actually grunted*, and continued on his way, heading down the stone steps to the mid-level as she hurried to keep up with him. He really was being a jerk. He knew it. Knew it but couldn't stop. Because stopping meant looking at her again. Looking at her and recalling that fleeting imagery and knowing it may be clear, it may be strong, but it was wrong. Because in it, he too was perfect. Unscarred. Happy.

And it made him angry. He could feel it bubbling in the pit of his gut. There was a time he'd dreamed of them being together. Believed it possible even. That one day he'd walk into her world of glitz and glamor and sweep her off her feet. That he'd be good enough. Successful enough.

But the accident had destroyed that dream…not just destroyed it but taken away his ability to want it. Thoughts of his best friend and the wife and child he'd left behind. The guilt of it cutting as deep now as it had the day he'd learned of Fred's death, and he clenched his fists as his fingers shook.

'Wow!'

The exclamation came from Catherine as she entered the living room behind him and he turned to see her all aglow, her eyes taking in the room, her sigh all breathy and alluring as she walked into the middle and twirled on the spot. 'This is something else.'

He cleared his throat to say something, but all he wanted to admit was that it wasn't the only thing that was. And he wasn't about to let out the obvious. She knew how attractive she was; she courted the cameras day in, day out. Knew how to pose, how best to angle her features…but he found himself lured in by her genuine delight. She had to be accustomed to the best the world had to offer, so why did his home impress her so much.

Unless it was an act?

She did it for a living after all…

'Did you design this space?' Before her eyes could reach him, he headed to the bar at the opposite end of the room.

'Yes.' He took two glasses out from the cupboard beneath the wooden countertop. 'Can I get you a drink?'

'Water would be lovely.'

'Sparkling, still?'

'Sparkling, thank you.' She continued to stroll through the room, her fingers brushing over the furnishings, the neutral-coloured recliners, the distressed wooden sideboard, her eyes lifting to the brightly coloured paintings above. 'I like it.'

Did she like the pictures too? Did she know—

'Did you paint these?'

She turned to look at him and he lowered his gaze, bent to pull a chilled bottle of sparkling water from the under-counter fridge. 'Yes.'

'Recently?'

'No.' It came out gruff. Too gruff. He hadn't painted anything of substance in years. He still didn't have the fine motor skill required in his left hand to do anything close to something he could be satisfied with, let alone hang.

He placed her drink on the side and carried his own to the glass door, sliding it open enough for him to walk out. The instant hit of the midday sun battled with the cool air-conditioned room and he sucked in a deep breath.

He wanted to be able to hold her eye. To hold a conversation. More than anything, he realised, he was at war with himself, because he *wanted* to enjoy her company. All things he would have done—could have done once.

But now, now he felt inadequate, unworthy, broken. Living the life of a hermit with a body that didn't feel like his any more.

He heard her come up behind him and kept his eyes on the ocean, the ripple of the waves, the sailboats all peaceful and serene. 'It was a derelict farmhouse when I bought the island. I had it renovated and extended.'

She walked ahead of him, out to the edge of the balcony, and he followed, comfortable that her eyes were on the view. He paused beside her, keeping his good side facing her.

'I can see why you bought it. I love that you left the stone exposed. It gives the place a soul even as it blends into the land.'

He gave a soft huff, both surprised and pleased that she could see his reasoning so well. 'Part of this floor and the ground floor have been carved out of the cliff. It stops it dominating the landscape and also means the bedrooms on the ground floor tend to stay cool even when the air conditioning is off.'

'You have an upside-down house?'

His lips quirked as a surprising laugh flickered to life. 'I guess it is. And having the pool outside the bedroom is convenient when you like to swim before the day kicks off in earnest.'

'Is that what you do?' She turned to look up at him.

'Yes.'

'Every morning?'

'Yes.'

Her eyes were still on him and he breathed in through his nose, trying to ease the anxiety her continued attention triggered, but it brought with it her scent. Floral and vanilla. Subtly sweet and tempting. He could feel it swirl within his bloodstream, a teasing warmth that he hadn't felt in so long.

It was debilitating to feel such a powerful attraction, unsettling in its gravity, and he reached out for the stone balustrade, gripped it tight. But then he wasn't accustomed to social interaction, social interaction of any sort. He saw Dorothea, Andreas and Marsel. That was it. He hadn't seen another soul in a year, and even then, it had been a visit from his sister that he hadn't even agreed to.

And now here he was, with Catherine. Temptation in its truest form, and it hit him full force once more—his sister had known exactly what she was doing and he'd played straight into her hand.

He was a damn fool.

She turned beside him, resting her elbows on the balustrade and angling her face to the sun, her eyes closed. 'I can see why you moved here.'

She sounded content. Happy. So very different to the chaos raging inside him and he risked a look. He shouldn't have. Ensnared, that was the word for it. Ensnared by the sight of her up close and so at ease.

There was no horror now and he was starting to question whether it had been there in the first place. He couldn't even recall the look as he took her in anew. Her hair shone in varying shades of gold, her thick lashes forming dark crescents over blushing pink cheeks, her lips parted as she breathed out, the hint of tongue glistening between perfect white teeth.

It wasn't *au naturel* though. Her make-up had been expertly applied, the hint of eyeliner following the curve of her lashes, the mascara thickening their lengths, the shimmer across her skin creating what appeared to be a natural flush. Her lips were pink and glossy, as though she had just wet them, when in reality she'd coated them in some expensive product.

She epitomised Hollywood.

And he wanted to hate it. He wanted to use it to keep his distance. To beat back the feelings of old that were threatening to surface and had no place in the now.

'So, the bedrooms, then?' She shifted so quick, her eyes landing on him and narrowing so quickly, he knew she'd witnessed too much.

He cleared his throat, held her eye with more strength than he felt. 'We can get to them this way, or head back inside and go down.'

'I'm easy.'

His pulse spiked, blasted innuendo, and he headed back through the open door, welcoming the chill of the air con that he desperately needed now. He placed his drink on the bar and continued to the stairs.

Was this how it was going to be for the next—how long did he say she could stay? A month? He could hardly think straight and the sooner he got this tour over with the better. His duty as host would be done and he could find some space, some equilibrium, again.

Until dinner at least…

CHAPTER THREE

CATHERINE FOLLOWED IN his wake, an awareness thrumming through her entire body. She wasn't an innocent, she knew desire when it hit her, but this…it had her skin alight, goosebumps prickling in spite of the heat, in spite of his obvious displeasure at her being here too.

And what the hell was that about?

Desiring someone who could barely bring themselves to look at you…

Was it teenage lust coming back to the fore? Was it old feelings trying to find a place in this new arrangement where she couldn't even call herself a friend any more?

A friend would have been able to gain access to the island by now. A friend would have eased him back into the land of the living and not lost the rapport of old. Not that any of his friends, his family even, had succeeded to date.

Was Flo mad to think she could?

'They miss you, you know.'

His shoulders flinched and she paused, her breath catching as she waited for something, anything, but…nothing.

He continued on his way and she knew she'd overstepped already. It was day one of thirty. Waiting at least a week before going in with the whole guilt trip might have been better. Or maybe, not at all?! She wanted to clamp her hand over her mouth, and blamed her emotions that were running high, not to mention the fact that his presence made any coherent thought virtually impossible.

The change in him was so marked. Not just his appearance, but in the way he behaved. He couldn't bring himself to look at her when they were alone and averted his gaze as soon as he spied her looking. He created distance between them at every opportunity.

He was either insecure, or he truly hated having her here, and she didn't want to believe the latter.

But Alaric—insecure, shy, nervous. He'd always been sexy, confident, fun. He was the man that had produced the wild splashes of colour on the paintings adorning the walls in the living room. The man who had once made her laugh so hard she'd almost been sick. The man that had stood up at her sixteenth birthday party and sung her a song full of wicked innuendo and tease.

They'd always had that kind of relationship. That unspoken bond. One that they'd been comfortable enough to joke about but never once risked crossing that line. And then life had intervened, her career taking her to LA, his own across Europe. And after the accident…well, no one had been welcome.

She frowned at his back, the obvious tension still pulling at his shoulders. Her chest ached as she considered the man he was now, and the man he'd once been, even as she took in his visual strength. His shoulders that were so broad, his muscles rippling beneath the light fabric of his T-shirt. He'd always been trim and toned. Now he boasted the kind of muscle you'd find in a heavyweight boxing ring, his frame speaking of a strength that would send her mouth dry, if not for the pain she glimpsed too.

She sipped at her drink, needing it to cool and soothe as she watched him turn on the bottom step and point out the first door on their left.

'This is your room.'

He didn't turn his head; instead he pushed open the door and gestured for her to walk around him.

She eyed him, frustrated, demanding his attention— did he really not want to look at her? Or was he so afraid of her looking at him?

She opened her mouth to say something, but what could she say? She was still Catherine, the same Catherine she had always been.

She caved and walked on in, trying to think up her next move, a way to change the dynamic, but the room took over. *This* was her room?

She eyed him, eyed it. Torn between the impressive vista beyond the glass wall and the room itself. It was stunning. Luxury-spa stunning. From the huge bed that seemed to float on air with its fluffy pillows and crisp white linen, the stone walls and earthen floor, set off perfectly by the infinity pool beyond the glass, the thatched cabana and the turquoise sea.

She was accustomed to presidential suites, penthouses, the best accommodation a hotel could offer, but this was his home and all that paled in comparison.

'You approve?' He came up behind her, his close proximity making her back prickle to life, wishing him closer still.

'It's incredible…'

She spun to face him and instantly regretted it as he moved off, pointing to a display panel beside the door.

'You can adjust the temperature here should you need to. Each room has its own thermostatic control. And if you'd rather have breakfast delivered to your room, a quick buzz to Dorothea with the phone beside your bed and she will see it arranged.'

He strode off to the left, through a stone archway, and the lights beyond came on automatically, illuminating what she assumed were wardrobes. 'Your dressing room leads to your private bathroom.'

She followed him, unsure what captivated her more, him, the room or the amazing ocean view that greeted them in every room, the bathroom no exception.

'The glass allows you to see out, but no one can see in.'

She nodded, silent as she took in the freestanding slipper bath positioned to make the most of the view, the double walk-in shower that seemed to be carved out of the rock with its copper dials and oversized rainwater heads, the twin copper sinks that sat like bowls atop a glossed concrete vanity unit.

'There are facecloths, towels, toiletries, everything you should need. The controls for the shower are self-explanatory, but if you need any help, call—'

'Call Dorothea, Andreas or Marsel.' She quipped, rounding on him. 'I've got the message.'

He didn't look at her. Not that she was surprised, and she opted for another approach. 'If this is the guest bedroom, I'd *love* to see what the master suite looks like.'

It was part tease, part vent, and his eyes flicked to her, so very briefly, and then he was striding back into the bedroom and she was hot on his tail, ready to press further until her eyes met with the painting straight ahead. She was held captive by it. The figures entwined, the vibrant colours, the ardent mood, the artistic flick of the brush that she recognised like a signature...

'This is your room, isn't it?'

He didn't respond as he headed to the glass and flipped a switch on the wall beside it. 'You can use this to draw the blinds and slide the doors open, and the controller slotted beside the bed does the same.'

Tentatively, she closed the distance between them, half scared he'd spook again as he re-flicked the switch to stop the blinds that had started to lower.

'I get it, Alaric.' She was referring to the controls, but as she said it, she felt it run far deeper. To him. To what had happened. To how he felt having her here.

He gave a curt nod and moved to go around her, but she reached out to touch his arm. 'Alaric?' She felt the hard heat of muscle flex beneath her fingers, the zip of electricity that ran through her as she wet her lips. 'Stop a second and just look at me…please.'

He eyed her on his periphery but didn't turn.

'This is your room, isn't it?'

'Does it matter?'

'I don't want to come here and kick you out of your space.' *Especially when I know I'm not welcome*, came the unhelpful inner voice.

'You're not.'

'I am.' She wet her lips again, edgy and unsure. 'I don't want that.'

'Believe me, Catherine, the guest room is perfectly adequate for me, and I don't make use of the dressing room as it is. Judging by your luggage, you will…' He gestured to her bags that were piled up beside the entrance, breaking their eye contact as he hastened in their direction, taking away whatever hope she had of getting through to him. 'I believe Marsel has brought everything down but if you are missing anything or you require anything else, just call.'

'Call anyone but you…' She folded her arms across her chest, fought down the rising sadness.

'I have work I need to get on with, Catherine.'

She nodded, knowing full well it wasn't work that was taking him away.

Or maybe it was, and she was being unfair?

'I'll see you at dinner.' He was already out the door. 'We eat at seven.'

We eat at seven. No, *Is that good for you? Would you prefer to eat earlier?* He seemed to give with one hand and take with the other. She opened her mouth to say something but, too late, he was gone. Not even a *Goodbye, enjoy your afternoon*—nothing.

And now she just felt weirdly…discombobulated. A word she couldn't remember ever using, let alone feeling.

The vibration of her phone coming from her handbag proved a grateful distraction and she dipped to pick it up. It was another message from Flo.

Have you seen him now?

Yes—

She stopped typing and bit into her lip. What else could she say? What else *should* she say? Her friend was already worrying enough…

He was here when I got to the house.

How is he?

She swallowed, she couldn't lie to Flo, especially when she was put on the spot.

Different. Distant.

Did you coax out a smile at least?

Had she? No. There'd been the glimmer of one when she'd referred to his house as upside down, but that was it. The rest of the time…

Not quite.

Was he rude? If he was rude, I want to know. I didn't send you there to be mistreated.

'Mistreated?' she blurted out loud, surprised at her friend's dramatic choice of words.

Don't be silly, Flo. It's a huge adjustment for him. You know that. Isn't that why you sent me?

True. I just hoped, with you being you, he'd at least pretend to play nice.

He's playing just fine. Now cut him some slack and leave him to me. Xx

She hoped her confidence would reassure her heavily pregnant friend, who was under strict doctor's orders to rest, and was relieved when Flo's reply finally came in.

Sorry, honey. I know he's in the best hands. If anyone can help him, it's you, Cath. Thank you. X

She smiled. Now all she needed was to have the same faith in herself.

She turned to the glass, took in the pool and the inviting little ripples in its surface…it looked so calm, so appealing.

Yes, a swim, some sun and some time to lose herself in her script before dinner…

Anything to stop her thinking on Alaric and the tricky path that lay ahead.

Alaric couldn't get away fast enough. Being in his bedroom, having her demand his attention, it had been too much. Too tempting to forget how he looked, too easy to succumb to the feelings that should be ancient history and to allow that connection back in.

He headed back upstairs to his study, collecting his drink on the way and contemplating something stronger. Even though he had hours to go before he'd have to face her again, it wasn't enough.

Flo and her blasted interfering ways. This was all her fault.

His phone chimed with an incoming text. He pulled it out of his back pocket and checked the screen. His mouth twitched. Flo.

Did she have some weird telepathic connection going on?

Her message was short but effective.

Play nice. Please!

He grimaced—had Catherine already reported back?

He dragged a hand down his face and blew out a breath. 'You don't ask for much, little sis,' he murmured, typing his reply: I'm trying.

And swiftly put his phone on Do Not Disturb.

It was enough that he had said yes to inviting her. His sister should just be happy and back off. Did she have no idea how hard this was for him?

He shoved open his study door, took one look at the multitude of displays all curved around his desk and changed his mind. There was only one way to rid himself of the tension—the gym. Gym, then work.

Hours later, he'd succeeded in physically avoiding her, but mentally his head had been filled with her. Her smile, her voice, her eyes as they tried to probe, her lips as she'd wet them with unease. An unease that he'd put there, the gesture upping his guilt every time he recalled it.

Because she wasn't Kitty Wilde the movie star when he glimpsed those weaknesses. She wasn't the woman projected on the big screen, in a magazine, on the internet, all confident and untouchable and unaffected by him. She was Catherine, his childhood friend, a girl he'd once have done anything for and a woman so very real and nervous enough to show it.

And that didn't just make her vulnerable, it made him vulnerable too.

He'd spent hours working out, pounding the treadmill, rowing, weight training, cycling…nothing worked. Nothing could shift her from his mind.

By dinner time, he was no better off—his stomach starving through exertion, yet sick with her unavoidable presence.

Play nice, Flo had said.

Did he know how to play nice?

He hadn't always been a social pariah. But then it wasn't the world that had done the casting out, he'd done it all by himself.

Could he at least *pretend* to be comfortable in company again?

For Flo? For Catherine? For the friendship they'd once shared…?

It was temporary after all, a few weeks, and then he could go back to his carefully controlled existence with a sister who owed him rather than berated him.

The peace alone had to be worth it…

CHAPTER FOUR

Two things struck Catherine at once.

She didn't know what to wear to dinner.

And no mirror existed in Alaric's master suite for her to evaluate her outfits in.

What was a dressing room without mirrors?

Flawed.

She scanned every wall like one would miraculously appear, checked inside the wardrobes, everywhere, and was forced to accept that she wasn't imagining it. There was no mirror. Unless you counted the one above the double vanity unit in the bathroom and there was no way she could check her length in that.

It was all she had though.

Gripping a fluffy white towel around her, she strode up to it and puffed her damp fringe out of her face. She was glowing like a beacon. It didn't matter that the air con was cranked up, and she'd chilled herself off in the shower not ten minutes ago. She could still feel the burn of her run which she'd been forced to do outdoors.

Forced by a sweat-slickened rowing machine, also known as Alaric.

A fresh wave of heat assaulted her as she remembered the view that had greeted her upon opening the gym door. Him, half naked, and rowing as though his life depended on it. His skin glistening with exertion, his muscles flexing with such power. He'd been so far in the zone he hadn't spied her gawping—thank heaven!

She'd done a sharp U-turn and hit the trails that weaved through the olive groves surrounding the house. The heat had been unbearable, but it had beat the thoughts of Alaric that every other activity had let in, her script writing included.

And at least the extra calorie burn would keep the guilt at bay as she enjoyed Dorothea's pitta bread that evening… if only she had a decent mirror to get ready in.

Who didn't have an abundance of mirrors in this day and age? She'd been so caught up in him and the beauty of the house she hadn't picked up on it earlier. But now that she thought about it, she'd seen none. Not even in the gym and all gyms had mirrors to check your form…

She puffed at her fringe once more, eyeing her reflection. She was already running late and the flush to her skin wasn't going to miraculously disappear.

She reached for her make-up bag and froze. No mirrors. No reflection.

Never mind others seeing him, *he* couldn't bear to see himself.

The realisation worked like ice over her skin, dousing the heat as tears pricked. He wasn't just hiding from the world, he was hiding from himself.

She inhaled through her nose, breathed through the chill and the sadness as she bolstered her resolve.

'You don't need to hide, Alaric,' she whispered. 'Not from me, not from you, not from anyone… I'll show you.'

Alaric checked his watch and adjusted the collar of his shirt.

Why he'd even donned a shirt was beyond him. He was

in his home, he could wear what he liked, but he had a ridiculous desire not to feel any less than he already did in her presence. Against her notoriety, he didn't just feel ordinary, he felt every one of his scars and more.

Which made him feel even more foolish now as he waited and waited…it was half seven. How was it possible to be half an hour late for dinner when all you had to do was climb two sets of stairs and walk out onto the terrace?

Maybe she too was struggling over what to wear.

Unlikely, but…

He waved Dorothea over as she hovered in the wings. 'Do you want to go and see—'

His question trailed off as he caught sight of movement behind her and his jaw dropped. She hadn't struggled over what to wear, that kind of outfit one didn't struggle over…

Where the devil did she think she was? Some prestigious awards ceremony being broadcast to the masses? A fancy soirée?

Her hair was once again twisted high on her head, only this time the tendrils that fell were purposefully there, smooth and sleek as they framed her face and brushed against the bare skin of her shoulders. The dress was a daring red, its V neckline dipping low between her breasts and unveiling the curve to each before skimming over her waist and stopping mid-thigh.

She was all confidence and poise, and he was undone.

He could swear his heart had stopped beating, the ability to swallow, to speak, to move from his semi-twisted position, evading him as his head remained angled up at Dorothea, his eyes resting on Kitty—Catherine.

'Ti?' Dorothea pressed, turning to see what had caught his eye and giving a breathless, 'Ah! Miss Wilde!'

She was already hurrying towards her and Catherine

smiled, her eyes flitting between them both as she stood in the open doorway, the sunset bathing her in gold.

'I worried you'd flushed yourself down the toilet.' Dorothea was all laughs and smiles, her tease bringing out a chuckle from Catherine herself as she raised a hand to her glossy red lips. Sinfully stunning.

'I'm so sorry I'm late, I—'

'Better late than never.' With some effort he forced himself to stand and ignored the look Dorothea sent him, Catherine's less so. Her eyes flicked to him, her lashes lowering, her fingers fluttering to her updo like it needed any more teasing to stay in place.

'Sorry.' It was quiet, demure, her grimace guilt-filled, and so he felt it too—guilt. Guilt at making her feel bad when it was more directed at himself for not being able to control his reaction to her than it was to do with her tardiness.

He looked away and rounded the table, pulling out her chair before gracing her with a smile that felt as alien as it did awkward.

'Would you like to take a seat?'

The nip she gave her plump red lip was swift and disconcerting. Did she truly feel guilty? Surely she was well accustomed to leaving people waiting—wasn't it just the way of things in the world she dominated?

'I will go and bake those pittas.' Dorothea's declaration broke the heavy silence and, thankfully, Catherine came alive. Less of the cute and demure, and more the composed movie star as she walked towards him, her high heels clipping the stone floor, their beat as pronounced as the uptick in his heart rate.

He clenched his jaw shut, dropped his gaze to the chair as he gripped its back and steeled himself for her arrival. He could feel her watching him, her eyes far too curious.

Did she know how much she got to him? After all these years, he should be well versed in dealing with his feelings, especially those sparked by her.

But then he'd spent the last three suppressing any kind of emotion and cutting himself off from the world had made that so much easier. Now he was no longer alone, and he was being tested by the one person he'd never been able to refuse.

'What's the matter, Alaric? You look like you did that day you rescued me from your pool.'

She laughed, the sound and the memory she evoked coaxing out a laugh from so deep within it shook him to the core. As though it were a release, a vent for the choked-up feelings in his chest, in his heart.

Life had been so different back then. *They'd* been different.

She'd been a vibrant wannabe, carefree but innocent too, and deserving of so much. And he'd been a boarding school tearaway with a chip on his shoulder, angry and frustrated by the constant pressure to succeed.

Was it any wonder he'd been so hooked on her?

'You scared the life out of me that day.' He waited as she lowered herself into the chair, her perfume reaching him and making his eyes close for the briefest moment.

'Well, lucky for me, you were there to be my knight in shining armour.'

She looked up at him and he moved before she could read it all in his face. He dragged in a silent breath and navigated the gap between her chair and his, careful not to brush against her. It was madness. Fourteen years ago, when he'd rescued her from the family pool, he wouldn't have thought twice about the contact. She'd been four years younger than him, sweet sixteen, and the way she'd clung to his neck and looked up at him like he was her true saviour…he'd wanted her to be his. He'd wanted to keep her safe, protected, adored. Before she had become a star, before the accident that had left him scarred inside and out.

But now she was here, on his island, seeking protection from the outside world, and that feeling, the sense of being her saviour, flooded his veins with meaning, with warmth, and he knew the danger of letting it in.

The danger of dreaming again for a future he could no longer have.

He sunk down into his seat, took up the bottle of chilled white from its bed of ice and filled both their glasses. It didn't matter what risk it posed to him; she needed this time. Or at least Flo had convinced him that she did, but looking at her so composed, so perfect before him, he found it hard to believe.

Was she really on the run or had his sister exaggerated the situation to give him no choice but to accept her presence here and to socialise once more?

'Why are you truly here, Catherine?'

Her smile flickered on her lips. 'You know why.'

'Because you want to avoid the press?'

She took the drink he'd poured, fingered the condensation forming on the glass and savoured a drawn-out sip. Was it so hard to think up an answer?

He studied her face, trying to read her; instead he was held captive by the way she pressed her glossy red lips together, her hum of appreciation for the wine teasing at his senses, the way her throat bobbed as she swallowed.

'There's a little bit more to it…' he lifted his eyes to hers, a sense that little was an understatement '…but essentially, yes.'

'More to it?' He didn't release her from his gaze and he saw how her lashes fluttered, a flash of pain that he couldn't miss.

She lowered her hand to her stomach, her eyes too, and he wanted to press further, he wanted answers, but he was also scared she'd break, and seeing her break would in turn break him.

He cleared his throat. 'Flo mentioned that you have a script you're writing?'

'Yes.' Slowly her eyes came back to his, her smile small. 'It's something I've wanted to do for a while.'

'And you're here to get it done?'

'That's the plan.'

'So why can't you do that at home?'

She flinched as he brought the conversation back to the heart of the matter.

'Because home is too distracting.' Her fingers trembled as she reached for her wine glass, provoking his concern, his need to know the truth too. 'I'm sure Flo explained.'

'She explained that the press are hounding you over your breakup with…with what's his name…?' He waved a nonchalant hand through the air.

'Luke.' Her eyes narrowed on him. 'As I'm sure you know.'

His smile lifted to one side. 'Guilty as charged.'

Did she also know he couldn't bring himself to say the guy's name without letting the jealousy take hold? Without pondering exactly what went wrong in their relationship and whether there was some truth to what the tabloids were saying? Flo had suggested it was a load of rubbish, and he didn't want to believe it, but… 'Is it true?'

'Is what true?'

'What the press are saying?'

'Is it ever?' She threw back a larger swig of wine. 'Though some of it is, I guess.'

'So, you did have an affair and call off the engagement?'

She choked on her drink as her eyes shot to his. 'No! No, I didn't have an affair. *Damn it*, Alaric.'

'I'm only repeating what the media are saying.'

'And you should know me better than that.'

'I don't know you at all, Catherine, not any more. That's why I'm asking.' Even as he said it, it didn't feel strictly true. And he'd hurt her in saying it, but he needed those walls in place, he needed to keep that distance between them as he pressed on. 'And, regardless of whether you did or not, wasn't it Oscar Wilde who said that it's better to be talked about, than not at all? Surely that applies ever more so in Hollywood. I'm sure your PR people are working it to their advantage right now, using it to build up the hype before your film launches. You are co-stars with an on-screen relationship after all...'

She cocked her head slightly, curiosity sparking in her eyes. 'You seem to know a lot about my work *and* my dating life?'

He ignored her astute observation and directed her back to his remark. 'So, it's a good thing, is it not?'

She pursed her lips and was quiet for so long he wondered whether she'd refuse to comment.

'I'd rather they didn't...'

'Because you don't like the picture they paint?'

She laughed harshly. 'No, Alaric, of course I don't, would you?'

No, and that's why he was quite happy to hide away. Not that he'd admit it.

She blew out a breath. 'At the end of the day they can do and say what they like. The reasons for our breakup are personal to me and Luke. We understand what—what really happened, and that's all that matters.'

He didn't miss the way her voice faltered. 'Even when the suggestion is that you were unfaithful, that the engagement was his way to stamp out the talk and you left anyway.'

She shrugged. 'It's what the press do. It's the nature of the beast and I'm past caring about the media.'

'Why, Catherine? When we were younger you dreamed of fame, you wanted this, you craved it…in fact, I'm rather surprised you didn't keep the relationship with Luke going purely for publicity's sake.'

Her eyes flared, her cheeks flushing beneath the make-up. 'Do you really think so little of me, Alaric?'

He reached for his wine, burying the stab of guilt as he let the chilled liquid soothe the heat that had formed around his words and contemplated his answer—what he wanted to say versus what he thought she wanted to hear.

'Look, let's not pretend…' The words flowed from him with more assurance than he felt. 'You have a successful career that demands you spend your time in the sun so to speak. You want to tell me now that you wish it all away, that you're tired of it?'

Her frown was more of a scowl. 'Is that so hard to believe?'

'But why? You worked so hard to be a media star, to look the part, to act the part, and it comes with the territory.'

'And don't you think a person has a right to some degree of privacy, regardless?'

'You chose this life, Catherine, you chose to step into your mother's shoes and then some. What did you think would happen? That you would miraculously escape the constant attention she revelled in. Strikes me that you're being all woe is me when you only have yourself to blame.'

She bristled, her shoulders rippling as she shifted position. 'If you think so low of me, why let me come and stay?'

'Because the woman I once knew wouldn't need the sanctity of this place unless it was absolutely necessary.'

'And because Flo asked, you couldn't say no?'

He shrugged. 'That too.'

'Seriously, Alaric, if I thought my presence was as un-welcome as this I wouldn't have come.'

Something jarred him deep inside, his eyes snapping to hers. 'You're not unwelcome.'

Liar.

Or was it the truth?

Underneath it all, was he blaming his sister, blaming Catherine, when really what unsettled him the most was the fact that he *did* want her here. That he wanted that glimpse of life off the island. That, above all, he *wanted* to see her again. Regardless of the fact they belonged in separate worlds. Hers was lit up Hollywood style, con-stantly in the limelight whether she wanted to be or not. And he wanted to stay in the shadows—he worked hard to stay there.

He'd lowered his guard once and a photo of him had ap-peared everywhere. The pity, the horror, the open commen-tary on how the heir to the De Vere empire must feel to have not only lost his best friend, but his famed good looks too.

He clenched his fist, his gut rolling with the mem-ory, the image front-page news…and for Cherie, his late friend's wife, to see him still walking the earth when Fred wasn't able.

'Not unwelcome?' she repeated, dragging him out of his pit of despair. 'You could have fooled me.'

Her eyes burned into his, misreading his reaction so en-tirely, and a small smile touched his lips as a single thought succeeded in breaking through the pain—she would have come anyway. Welcome or not.

He was sure of it.

She frowned. 'What?'

He gave a small shake of the head.

'What, Alaric? Why are you looking at me like that?'

'Because something tells me that even had I said you weren't welcome, you still would have come…eventually.'

Her carefully styled brows drew together. 'What makes you say that?'

'Because, like me, you can't say no to Flo either.'

Her frown eased into a smile and he chuckled because he liked that he knew that about her. He liked her for being so susceptible to Flo and just as weak to her whims as he was. He liked that it exposed the old Catherine beneath the carefully crafted Kitty Wilde shell.

'My sister is the master of getting what she wants.'

Her smile was full now, her blue eyes softening with affection. 'She is…and she wasn't the only one. You once were too.'

A silence descended, their gazes locked as memories rose to the fore, of good times, bad times and everything in between. The air filled with the sound of insects, the rush of waves, and he wished time away. He wished to be back at that pool rescuing her from her tumble and the torrent of abuse from her mother for being so clumsy, to have her look up at him with the same adoration she had then.

'But I won't lie to you, Alaric. I wanted to see you.' She wet her lips, her eyes alive with her honesty, her…concern? 'I wanted to see where you lived. I wanted to understand why you've cut yourself off from the rest of the world, your family. I wanted to see for myself if—' she sucked in a breath '—if you were okay.'

He was drowning in her gaze, trapped within it, her concern teasing at the very heart of him and tightening up his throat, his chest. 'I'm fine.'

'Are you though?'

He clenched his jaw, dragged his eyes from hers to the sun disappearing behind the sea. The glow casting everything it touched in shades of orange and pink. A small sail-boat bobbed in the distance, alone, solitary, and he wished himself upon it. Anywhere but here.

She always saw far too much. She'd always been able to get to him. And wasn't that the true reason Flo had sent her…?

'They *do* miss you, Alaric. We all do.'

He swallowed, his locked jaw aching with the effort to keep it all trapped inside.

'*We?* That's pushing it a bit, don't you think?' Now he looked at her, his derision giving him the confidence to face her off. 'You had no time for us after you made a name for yourself, so forgive me if "we" doesn't ring quite true.'

She visibly flinched, her hand reaching across the table. 'Alaric, you know that's not how it was. You can't mean—'

'Can't I? How many celebrations did you miss over the years? Celebrations that Flo invited you to, only to find you couldn't make it?'

'I was busy—my schedule was full on for a long time and I couldn't just bail on it, but Flo understood. We always made up for it after.'

He nodded, taking in her words but remaining silent. He wasn't about to point out that *he* didn't see her though, that her claim to have missed him was nonsense.

'Just because I was busy, it doesn't mean I didn't miss her, that I didn't miss you. All of you.'

'No? And yet it's been ten years since I saw you last.'

'I tried to come and see you…after the accident.'

His chest spasmed and he fought back the memories trying to invade, the pain as raw as yesterday.

'But you refused to see me. You refused to see anyone.'

'You soon gave up trying.'

'What choice did I have?'

He gripped the table edge, pushed back from it as he

tried to beat it all back. And he knew he was being unfair. He'd been just as busy in the years before the accident, travelling the world with work, rarely in one place for long.

'I'm here now, Alaric,' she said softly, her eyes not releasing him. 'And I want to be here.'

He searched her dizzying blues, seeking a lie, seeing the truth and needing to deflect. 'Was it worth all the sacrifices you made?'

'What do you mean?'

'To be crowned queen of Hollywood—was it worth cutting yourself off from all those who cared about you?'

'Me, cutting myself off? That's a bit rich coming from you.'

He didn't even flinch as he ignored her gibe, accurate though it was.

'There's nothing wrong with prioritising things in your life,' she blustered.

'No? Even when your mother behaved in the exact same way?'

'Alaric, don't…please don't compare me to her.'

'Why, Catherine? She was the one who told you, day in, day out, to put your career first, don't let anything get in the way—your relationships, your friends, your family.'

'Alaric, please…'

She avoided his eye, but he was too riled to back down.

'Do you remember how it was back then? Why you were always at our house when we were younger? Do you remember the reasons that were given, all variations on the same?'

'You've made your point, Alaric. You can drop it.'

No, he felt too close to something, a realisation, not so much for him, but for her…

'Is that the real reason you turned Luke down?' He could almost feel sorry for the guy now. 'Was he another sacrifice that needed to be made in order for you to remain focused on your dream?'

Her eyes flashed. 'You know, it pays for the press to think and print the worst of me, Alaric. What's your excuse?'

He started, surprised at her direct hit, surprised even more by the strength of his answer that he couldn't admit aloud. It paid for him to think the worst because it protected him, stopped him from falling in deep with the girl he'd once cared for deeply and now could never have.

He wanted to dislike her. He wanted to dislike every perfect inch of her that lived and breathed the superficial world of Hollywood. But he couldn't.

'Tell me what really happened between you both—give me your truth.'

She paled beneath her make-up. 'Do you want to talk about what happened three years ago?'

'No.' It was abrupt, immediate, forced out on impulse. Could she honestly think that whatever had gone on between her and Luke came close to what he'd been through? Had she loved the guy so very much that it was equal to the grief of losing someone? 'I can't see what that has to do with you and Luke. It has no relevance, no...'

His words trailed off as he watched her throat bob, her chin nudging upwards. She was in pain. She was suffering. But she'd ended it, hadn't she, so why the pain? 'What really happened?'

She shook her head, wet her lips. 'It doesn't matter. What matters is that I'm not all that different to the girl I was ten years ago...' Her anguish was there in her voice, tangled up in a softly spoken plea for him to see her as she was. 'We were friends then. Can't we be friends still?'

'Friends?' It was so gruff, so messed up with the warning siren in his brain, in his heart. 'A lot has happened since then, Catherine.'

'And?'

'Dinner is served!' Dorothea's voice carried across the terrace, saving him from himself and the answer he didn't want to give.

Catherine spun to face her, her eyes like saucers as she took in the heavily laden tray of food. 'Are you expecting more guests, Alaric?'

Dorothea gave a hearty chuckle as she approached and lowered the tray to the table. 'I believe the key to happiness is a pleasantly full stomach.'

Catherine didn't look capable of arguing as she continued to stare at the dishes Dorothea placed on the table, reeling off a description of each. 'Pork souvlaki. Fresh pitta. Tzatziki. Greek salad with kalamata olives, feta, red onion, cucumber, tomatoes, an ample sprinkling of fresh oregano and, of course, a healthy drizzle of olive oil.'

He'd forgotten how hungry he was, but Catherine looked positively panicked and old memories flickered to life, of her eating like a bird beneath the watchful eye of her mother and him sneaking her extra when the dragon wasn't looking…until she'd stopped taking them.

'I should have warned you—' his voice was colder than he intended, the memory making him suspicious of her slender figure now '—Dorothea will see it her mission to feed you up while you're here.'

She looked from him to Dorothea, a smile forming that he couldn't gauge. 'Thank you, Dorothea. This really does look lovely.'

'And it will taste even better, I promise!' She spun away, the empty tray to her chest. 'Make sure she eats, Kyrios de Vere. It won't hurt to add a little meat to those bones. Now enjoy!'

Catherine's smile faltered as she watched her go and he tried to dampen the age-old concern, the anger at her mother and the mark she'd left on her daughter.

'She treats everyone this way,' he assured her while telling himself he was overreacting. 'Don't take it personally.'

But as she turned back to him, her eyes were alive with laughter. 'It's fine. I think she's wonderful!'

He relaxed back into his seat. 'That's one word for it.'

She laughed. 'You love her really… I can tell.'

She unfolded her napkin and placed it over her lap, unaware of how captivated he was by her. Her pleasure bringing her to life and flooding him with a warmth he couldn't contain.

'She certainly has a way with people.'

'She does. It's refreshing to be around someone who says exactly what they think and doesn't try to dress it up for me.'

'Unless it's me doing the talking.'

She gave him a warning glare but her eyes still danced, her lips twitching with continued laughter, and he picked up the basket of bread between them, a peace offering of sorts. 'Pitta?'

'Please.'

He felt himself smile as she took a piece and watched as she lowered her gaze to the dishes spread out between them.

'As much as this looks lovely, Alaric, you'll need to help me. There's no way I can eat anywhere near half of this.'

His smile grew, he knew better. Dorothea's food had a habit of making you come back for more. 'We'll see, you haven't tasted it yet.'

CHAPTER FIVE

'I'M SO FULL!' Catherine groaned, gripping her hips as she leaned back and took in the food still on her plate. She couldn't eat another bite. She seriously regretted that last mouthful as it was, but she'd been unable to resist its mouth-watering goodness. Dorothea truly was an exceptional cook.

Alaric's soft laugh reached her across the table, its husky edge making her very full stomach quiver as she met his gaze.

'Something funny?'

'You, groaning. It doesn't quite fit the perfect princess you project.'

'The princess?' She arched a brow at him.

'That's what I said.' His hand was resting on the table between them and he turned it over, raised it. 'What can I say, it's how I've always seen you.'

Her temper spiked—a *spoilt* princess?! She rose to the taunt, her lips parting to give him what for, but she stopped. There was something else at play in his eyes, in the smile that touched his lips. Something that looked a lot like *affection*…had he had too much wine along with the food?

'Is that so?' She sounded breathless, she felt breathless, which was utterly ridiculous. She didn't get breathless—

unless she was working up a sweat the good old-fashioned way. And by that she meant in the gym, on the trails, so why was her mind now conjuring up images of her and Alaric, entangled in the sheets, legs akimbo. No. No. *No.*

She was the queen of composure. But as his gaze fell to her lips, projecting the same heated rush she felt inside, that crown was rapidly slipping. Hell, who was she kidding—it had hit the ground the second she'd stepped foot on his island.

'You were always destined for great things, Catherine.' He relaxed back into his seat, and when his eyes lifted to hers, the heat had gone, replaced by…not quite the cool detachment of that day, but something else. A defeatism, a resignation, and it left her as speechless as the swift heat that had preceded it.

Their pre-dinner talk may have taken a difficult turn. The questionable light he threw over the way she lived her life, her priorities these past ten years stirring up a cocktail of guilt, anger and confusion. The way he'd probed into her recent past, Luke and the—the baby she'd lost. She pressed a hand to her lips, the sudden swell of nausea making her truly wish she hadn't eaten so much.

Not that Alaric knew. No one knew but Flo and Luke.

'Are you okay?' He frowned not missing a beat and she nodded swiftly.

'I really shouldn't have eaten so much.'

She took up her glass of water, praying he'd let it go as he glanced at her plate.

'It's hardly much.'

'It is for me.'

His eyes hardened. 'Is that Hollywood talking, or your mother?'

She took a slow sip from her glass, used it to calm the current within. 'It's me talking.'

He nodded, but his expression didn't ease.

Let it go, Alaric.

Her mother may have instigated her carefully controlled diet, but she was the one who had chosen to continue it. A strict diet and exercise regime were hardly rare in her line of work and she wasn't prepared to battle it out with him.

Especially when it hadn't been the true cause of her discomfort.

She shifted her gaze to the horizon as her hands fell to her stomach, pressing into the tender flesh as she tried to push away the pain and focus on her breathing.

She craved the ease they'd gained through dinner. The smiles, even the laughter they'd managed to share as they'd stuck to safer topics. Like his island, her new movie, her script, Flo…

But they'd just been skirting around the past, his and hers, and she knew there was more he'd wanted to say, more he'd wanted to confront her on when he'd pressed: *'Do you remember how it was back then?'*

Of course she remembered.

How could she forget when she'd been made to feel like the unwanted hanger-on by her own parents? Her mother spending more time away than at home, filming, partying, living the life of a singleton when she wasn't one. And how the De Veres would welcome her in, filling her time with playdates, as her father would take to the bottle, the gambling tables, anything to fill his time until her mother returned. Then the almighty arguments would kick off, after her father had got over his joy at having her mother back, and she would escape once more to the house of De Vere, Anastasia de Vere treating her like one of her own.

'Do you ever wonder how our mothers became friends?' She looked back at him with her question, and he shrugged.

'They grew up together.'

'I know. But when you think back, they never really did anything together? It wasn't like they confided in one another, and when they were together, I don't know... I always got the impression Mum was trying to benefit from your mother's contacts as opposed to...'

'Actually caring?'

She nodded, biting her lip as she saw the relationship for what it was and felt the guilt of it.

'Isn't it obvious? Mum did it for you. She knew how your life was. She wanted to keep you close and that meant keeping your mother close too.'

She felt the invisible warmth of Anastasia wrap around her, so many memories coming forth. 'She stayed friends to protect me...'

'We were all protecting you, Catherine.'

Her heart fluttered with his soft-spoken confession, with the way his blue eyes warmed with the compassion and the affection he'd once had for her.

'Be it Flo with her urgent home study requests; my father when he insisted on yours joining him on some social affair just so you could come and stay; me when I came between you and your mother when she was berating you, sneaking you cake when she wouldn't let you have any, making you laugh when she'd have you cry.'

She shook her head, her eyes welling with the depth of feeling in his voice, the memories he recalled. She knew it all, and yet hearing it from his lips now and wishing things were the same, that he could still look at her like that, that he could still feel for her like that...

'I'm sorry,' she managed eventually.

'Why are you sorry?'

'For being such a burden.'

He scowled. 'You were never a burden, Catherine. We

all cared about you. If anyone should be sorry, it's your own damn parents for how they treated you.'

Her throat closed over. He sounded so angry, so vehement on her behalf, so protective. She wanted to reach for him, she wanted to wrap her arms around him, thank him for it all, but she knew he wouldn't welcome it. That for all the progress they were making, they weren't in that place.

She had ten years to make up for—the accident, a bridge to still cross... As for her own truth...once he knew that, he wouldn't want to know her at all.

'How about a walk?'

She started at his sudden suggestion, the surprising normality of it. 'A walk?'

'Yes.' He raked his fingers through his hair, looked out to the ocean glinting in the moonlight. 'It'll help the food go down.'

'Isn't it a bit—' she eyed the start of the trail that weaved through the olive grove '—dark?'

He took in her apprehension with a small smile. 'There are lights that follow the path. I just need to turn them on. I'm sure without the heat of the day, you'll find a tour of the island quite...pleasurable.'

She was surprised to feel her pulse skitter, surprised even more by her own hesitation. What was it about the way he said *pleasurable* that made her blood fire? And why did the idea of going off with him alone feel more intimate than the dinner they'd just shared?

And if it was intimate, why did it bother her so much?

Because your feelings for him are already running away with you...feelings that you can't afford to let in.

This past year had brought with it enough pain, and this could only lead to more. Her aim was to help him return home, clean and simple.

Anything more…she wasn't in the right place for it. Mentally or physically.

'I've already seen it all.' She took up her wine glass, hiding behind it as he raised his brows at her. She took a sip and smiled to offset the pitch to her voice. 'I took a tour this afternoon.'

'You did? With Marsel? Andreas?'

'No. On my own.' She took another sip of the chilled liquid. 'I went for a run.'

'But it must have been thirty degrees.'

'Thirty-one, not that I'm counting.'

He shook his head. 'Do you often run in hot climates?'

'It's not a favourite pastime of mine, no. But then…'

She stopped as the memory of why she had came back to her, in all its muscular, blazing hot glory. She sipped more wine, praying her pulse would calm, the nervous flutter to her stomach would ease and the heat…she really needed that long gone.

'But then?'

She hummed into her glass.

'You said it wasn't what you wanted to do, but then…?'

Oh, dear…

'When I went to use the gym, you were already in there…' She forced herself to hold his eye, even as her cheeks burned with the admission, and it wasn't the only part of her continuing to warm. 'I got the impression you didn't want to be disturbed.'

His eyes raked over her and she was convinced he could read it all. Where were her acting skills when she really needed them?

'So, you took to the trails?'

'I did.'

'I hope you wore sunscreen.'

She wriggled in her seat. 'If you're referring to the fact

that I'm looking a little pink, my skin…it just does that.'
It wasn't the fact that the heat of desire currently had her
entire insides aflame.

'You should be more careful.'

The severity of his tone jarred her and she frowned.
'Okay, Mum.'

'I'm serious, Catherine. The sun isn't safe, and with
your skin tone—'

'I know that, Alaric, I'm not a child.'

He fisted his hand upon the table, his tension palpable.
What on earth…?

Anastasia. His mum. The cancer. Oh, God, she was an
insensitive idiot. She reached across the table, her hand
covering his before she could stop it. 'I'm sorry… I'll be
more careful, okay?'

Slowly, he unravelled his fist and, for the briefest of
moments, their palms touched. She wanted to keep him
there, hold his hand in hers as she addressed the real cause
of his concern.

'Anastasia…' She cleared her throat, settling back into her
seat as he did the same. 'Flo tells me she's doing okay now.'

'She is.' His eyes glinted back at her, the lines bracket-
ing his mouth cutting deep. 'But cancer's cancer. You live
in fear that it'll return.'

'I know.' She chewed the corner of her lip, a second's
hesitation as she debated whether to say more and knowing she had to. 'Which is why your refusal to go home is
all the more concerning, don't you see?'

'Clever, Catherine. Very clever.'

'What is?'

'Turning this around on me.'

'I wasn't, I was just—' He started to rise and she
frowned up at him, her stomach plummeting. 'I thought
we were going for a walk.'

'I'm not so sure it's a good idea after all.'

'Seriously, Alaric.' She stood to face him. 'I'm sorry I brought it up but...'

'You promised Flo?'

'Even if I hadn't—' she held his eye, determined '—I would still be asking you the same.'

They stared at one another, locked in a battle of wills. She wasn't ready to call it a night now. She didn't want it to end with him running from her.

'Here's the deal—you keep those thoughts to yourself and we can have our walk.'

She managed the smallest of smiles. 'Or we can run if you like?'

He rewarded her tease with a soft laugh. 'After all that food?'

'Good point.'

But neither of them moved.

An invisible cord seemed to wrap itself around them, urging their bodies closer and closer. Her breaths shortened as his smile evaporated, his eyes falling to her lips that she had unconsciously wet, their depths darkening and full of...want.

He wanted her. Alaric de Vere wanted her.

He wasn't keeping his distance now. He wasn't pushing her away. And then his eyes flickered with some silent thought.

'Though I suggest you change your shoes.'

She swallowed the remnants of lust choking up her throat. 'My shoes?'

'Yes, your shoes.' He pocketed his hands, his mouth a tight line as he looked away. Had she misread the desire there, had it all been in her own head? 'If you've been for a run, you know how rocky the terrain is.'

She glanced down at her impractical heals. 'Of course.'

'And perhaps a jacket? The sea breeze can make it quite chilly at night.'

'Jacket. Shoes. Sure.'

She wanted to cringe. What did she sound like? But then his eyes returned to her, trailing over her front, taking in her exposed skin and the goosebumps now rife, and she forgot her shame. How could a simple look feel like a caress? And why was she craving it so badly?

'Alaric…'

'Yes?'

What would he say, what would he *do*, if he knew the goosebumps had nothing to do with the chill in the air, and everything to do with her body responding to him?

A dangerous question to ponder, Catherine.

She sucked in a breath and forced her legs to move. 'I'll be right back.'

This trip wasn't about reigniting old feelings, it was about the future, his with his family, hers with her work…

And here she was letting her teenage fantasies run away with her as though he was an everyday hot-blooded male and not Alaric. A man who'd been through hell, a man who she wanted to help, not confuse further by…by…

It was selfish, inconsiderate…not happening.

She blew out another breath, trying to let out the pent-up desire with it. She'd barely kept a lid on her feelings for him in her teens. Now she was older, wiser and a world-renowned actor, she should be able to do better.

But saying it and doing it were two different things and the one thing this trip had already proved—her acting skills were non-existent when he was around.

Alaric focused on clearing the table, ignoring Dorothea's protests that she would do it and the probing stare that followed. She was far too attuned to him and his ways and she knew Catherine had some hold over him. A hold he wasn't willing to succumb to.

'She is even more beautiful in person, I think.'

He grunted his response as he helped her load the dishwasher and cringed as she gave a little chuckle.

'I don't need you to say it's so, I see it in your face.'

'Dorothea, may I remind you I pay you to look after this house and my needs and not—'

She fisted her hands on her hips and stared up at him, the action enough to shut him up as quickly as his own mother would. 'Yes, you do, but I know you, and I think she is good for you. It's about time you brought somebody here.'

'I didn't bring her here, my sister did.'

She smiled at him, her eyes welling up—*oh, God.*

'And your sister knows you even better. You mark my words—this is a turning point for you.'

'There is no turning point for me. Catherine is here to write, and in a month, she'll be gone.'

Dorothea gave a little hum, waving off his severity. 'If you say so, *kyrios*. Now go, I have this in hand.'

He hesitated, needing to convince her he was right. Not that he could. Dorothea would maintain her own counsel regardless, but still it nagged at him.

Or was it more that he needed to convince himself?

Convince himself and delay his return to Catherine because he wasn't ready to face her yet. And it was madness.

He'd cut himself off from the world because he couldn't stand to be in the presence of others, of people who saw his scars and pitied him. Felt sorry for him. Or worse, resented him for surviving the plane crash when Fred hadn't been so lucky. He gulped down the surge of emotion—no, he resented himself enough for that.

But Catherine didn't look at him in any of those ways.

That wasn't what he'd witnessed across the table, or when she'd stood before him and looked up into his eyes…

And he'd come so close to succumbing, so close to pulling her into him and kissing those lips that she'd softly parted, subtly wet…

It was the force of that need that had scared the hell out of him.

'Go, *kyrios*!' Dorothea woke him from his stupor, shooing him to the door, her cheeks aglow, her eyes alive. 'Now enjoy your walk.'

She was off her dear sweet mind if she thought he'd let something happen between him and Catherine. Yes, they had a past. Yes, he had feelings for her. But she was a movie star with a life that demanded attention. He, on the other hand, belonged in the shadows and the sooner those around him realised it the better.

Those around you? He could hear the inner voice laughing at him. *You mean you. You're the one getting carried away under her attention, you're the one who wanted to kiss her and forget all else, you're the one losing sight of reality.*

He thrust his fingers through his hair. To even think someone as beautiful and as perfect as Catherine would want him was foolish. To want to act on that thought, foolish still. So why couldn't he shoot it down?

Perhaps because here, on his island, there were no observers, no one to judge a moment's happiness and provoke the survivor's guilt that kept him here.

You don't need others to judge you, you judge yourself enough.

He strode back out onto the terrace far sooner than was wise. He wasn't ready to see her, and yet there she was, a small shawl over her shoulders, the red dress that he'd been unable to take his eyes off and—his lips twitched—

white trainers on her feet. To his mind she'd never looked more beautiful and more endearing to his disobeying heart.

She wasn't his. She would never be his. So why was his heart beating to a different tune entirely?

'I thought you'd got lost.'

His smile spread. 'In my own home?'

'Crazy, I know. But the thought was there.' She smiled up at him as he joined her, her arm slipping through his like it was the most natural thing in the world. 'So, lead the way…'

He reached into his pocket for his phone, accessed the app that controlled the lighting for the entire island and lit the trail.

She clutched him closer with an excited gasp. 'Oh, Alaric, it's stunning!'

Ahead uplighters in the path glowed soft white, complemented by the fairy lights that weaved through the trees in the olive grove.

'When you said it was lit, I wasn't expecting this…since when did you become an old romantic.'

'Romantic?' He gave a choked laugh. 'It has nothing to do with me, I can assure you.'

'No?' She was looking up at him and he kept his eyes on the trail, one foot moving in front of the other. She was too close like this, too comforting, too easy to relax into and forget every worry.

'It's all down to Andreas and Dorothea.'

'Do they live on the island with you?'

'Yes, but Marsel lives back on the mainland. It's far too quiet here to keep him happy.'

'I can believe it. Whereabouts do they live?'

'They have a small house set back from the trail on the other side of the island. You won't have seen it on your run. It's hidden away and gives them privacy from me and vice versa.'

'Sounds perfect.'

They walked in silence a few steps, her gaze taking it all in, and then she said quietly, 'It makes me feel better knowing that you're not alone, alone.'

He scoffed. 'I'm thirty-four, Catherine. I'm quite capable of living alone.'

She opened her mouth to say more and he got there first, taking the conversation back to where it was safe. 'They started small the first Christmas I moved in.'

'Started small?'

'The lights,' he clarified. 'I wasn't interested but Christmas is a big deal here in Greece and it didn't seem fair to let them miss out, so when Dorothea asked...' He shrugged.

'You gave in.' Her voice was as soft as her smile.

'Pretty much. I gave them a budget and have done every year. As the land has matured, the number of adorned trees has grown and, to be honest, taking them down only to put them back up each year feels like more trouble than it's worth.'

'Plus, it's beautiful and you love it really.' She squeezed his arm and he couldn't stop the smile that touched his lips.

'It certainly makes the landscape more interesting at night.'

'Admit it.' She nudged him with her hip. 'It's beautiful...and romantic...'

He felt his lips flicker, felt the warmth creeping through his middle.

'It's okay to appreciate them,' she murmured, her eyes back on the track as they weaved deeper through the olive grove, the sound of the insects increasing around them. 'I promise it won't ruin the cold-hearted hermit you've worked so hard to project the past few years.'

'The what?' He froze, frowning down at her.

But she's not wrong, so why are you so upset?

'You heard me…' She slipped her arm from his. 'Or do you deny that you've been hiding here ever since the accident?'

He stared at her, his teeth grinding. She was the master of switching topics to cause the most effect.

'You don't socialise, you don't see the family. As for friends…when was the last time you saw one?'

His brows drew together as he refused to answer.

'You were the life and soul of the party once, Alaric. And now what? You don't want to be around people? You're happy in your own company, is that what this is? You, happy?'

His teeth continued to grind, his hands forming fists at his sides. 'We agreed to let this go. *You* agreed.'

Her eyes glimmered with something, some emotion he couldn't identify, but he didn't like it. It had his gut twisting, his heart pounding too loud in his ears. 'I did, and I'm sorry.'

He tried to take a steadying breath, but it was filled with her perfume, caught up in the scent of the earth as the sprinklers came alive at ground level, dousing the sun-burned earth.

She reached out, both palms soft on his chest as she nipped her bottom lip in her teeth and gazed up at him, the fairy lights twinkling in her darkened blues and he couldn't look away, couldn't step back.

'I'm sorry to press you, Alaric, I really am. But I'm doing it because people out there…they care about you… *I* care about you.'

His heart squeezed in his chest, his eyes falling to her lips. He only had to bow his head and he could taste them, taste her. How many times had he dreamt of it? Of kissing her, of forking his hands through her golden hair and holding her to him. And now she was pressing closer, or was he moving in?

'Alaric?'

He swallowed past the wedge in his throat. What was he doing? What were they doing? She smoothed her hands up his chest and he knew he should stop her, but he couldn't make his body obey as it thrived on the human contact, not just anyone's but hers.

'Is this what keeps you away?' She cupped his cheek, her thumb not quite sweeping over the scar tissue there—was she afraid of hurting him?

His heart pulsed. 'Leave it alone, Catherine.' It was a growl, a plea. He gripped her wrist and still he couldn't pull her away. It felt too good be touched, to be caught up in her spell.

'I don't want to leave it alone.'

'I'm perfectly happy here.' His voice shook, his body ached. The years of abstinence, the years of not being around people, and now he had her, hypnotising him with her touch, the look of want in her eyes. But she can't want him. Not now. No one could.

'Are you though?' She raised her other hand, cupped his other cheek. 'Truthfully?'

'What are you doing, Catherine?' He tightened his hold on her wrist, brought his hand up to grip her other, her eyes teasing at him, her lips so close, her scent…

'Kiss me, Alaric.'

Kiss me, Alaric…

His ears burned with her breathy request, need sparking so fierce inside, and he needed to quash it. He needed this under control, he needed her to know this couldn't happen. It would never happen. He didn't deserve the happiness she could so readily bring.

But one taste, just one fleeting moment…to know how her lips felt, to know how she tasted…

'What is it you're so afraid of?'

He didn't answer. He couldn't. And so he did the one thing guaranteed to silence her. He kissed her and lost sight of everything—the accident, the past, the reasons this shouldn't happen—all in the brush of her lips against his, the warm sanctity of her mouth, her whimper…oh, that whimper. It was like heaven to his tortured soul, balm to a wound he never thought he'd see gone.

'Catherine…' It was pained, desperate.

'Yes, Alaric,' she moaned against his mouth, her teeth nipping at his bottom lip, her body curving into him. 'I want you.'

I want you.

Only it wasn't Catherine he heard, it was Kitty Wilde. Those same words to her on-screen lover in a recent movie—yes, he'd watched them all, like some twisted fool who wished to taunt himself with her presence when he knew they could never be. Only…

He opened his eyes, saw *her*, and felt everything he knew to be real shatter.

He shook his head, trying to clear the lustful fog, to separate reality from fantasy. 'We can't do this. It's wrong.'

She stepped toward him and he backed away.

'Why? I know you wanted that kiss as much as I did.'

He couldn't look at her. He wanted it more. He was certain of it. And he didn't deserve to get what he wanted. He didn't. Especially with her.

'It's late, we should get back.'

'We've barely stepped out.'

'It's enough.'

He started back towards the house. He needed space

between them. Air to breathe that wasn't filled with her perfume, her temptation.

'Alaric.' She raced up behind him, touched a hand to his shoulder. 'Please!'

He stopped, unable to deny the plea in her voice. 'What?'

'I don't know what's going on here, what's happening between us, but I didn't imagine the way you kissed me back.'

His head dropped forward. He was a selfish fool, an idiot. He hated himself for it. A moment's weakness, a lifetime of guilt—is that how this would go?

'Why are you running away from me?'

'I'm not running away, I'm…'

He was what? She was right. He was running, as far away from the messy feelings she had stirred back to life and the guilt that was swallowing him whole.

'What is it you're so afraid of?'

He spun to face her, uncaring that she was so very close and that the light of the house illuminated every ugly inch of his facial deformity as he used it as a weapon now. A weapon and a defence.

'Look at me, Catherine.' He gripped her arms to hold her close. '*Look* at me!'

'I am looking!' She was just as ferocious, just as angry. 'I still don't see your point.'

He felt her tremble in his hands and released her, sucking in a breath. It wasn't her that trembled, it was him. His entire body quaked. He'd suppressed it for so long, the resentment, the guilt, the anger, and here he was letting it out on her, and she didn't deserve it.

'I'm sorry, Catherine.'

'I don't need you to be sorry. I want you to explain what's going on with you. I want you to stop pushing me away.'

'Just because we were friends once, Catherine—' he recalled her question from earlier, using it to inflict the most damage '—it doesn't mean we can be again.'

Her eyes widened into his, the pain he'd wreaked obvious in their swimming depths, and he reeled away, picking up the pace.

'What the hell happened to you, Alaric? Stop running away and just talk to me!'

'*This* happened, Catherine!' He spun on his heel, flung a hand at his face. 'This!'

Her eyes glistened up at him. 'Is that truly a reason to push us away? You're hurting and we want—we want to help you. Please let us help you.'

He stared at her, struggling to find the words. 'I'm fine, Catherine,' he forced out eventually. 'Why can't you just accept that?'

'Because you're not. The man I knew would never be happy like this.'

'The man you knew doesn't exist any more.'

'Maybe he doesn't…' She wet her lips. 'You can't go through what you have and remain unchanged, but you can embrace the man you are now and accept it.'

'What?' he scoffed. 'Broken, damaged?'

'No.' She shook her head vehemently. 'That's just it— you're choosing to be those things, you're choosing to let your scars define you, to cut yourself off when all we want is for you to come back.'

'I don't belong out there any more.'

'Of course you do and, deep down, you know it too. You *want* it too. I see it when I look into your eyes, I see it when you talk about Flo, I saw it when you kissed me just now…the longing.'

She was stepping towards him again, her hand reaching up to lightly touch his cheek once more. 'We don't see this, Alaric.'

He swallowed, trying to quash the rising tide within. 'We see *you*.'

'But I don't—not any more.'

He pulled away, thrust his hands through his hair as he made for the house—he had to get the hell away from her.

'You can blame the accident and your scars all you like.' She hurried after him, desperation clear in her voice. 'I know Flo does. But you want to know what I think? I think you're scared to live again.'

He shoved open the front door, praying Dorothea and Andreas had called it a night already as she entered hot on his tail.

'I think you're scared of enjoying life and having the rug pulled out from under you again.'

He clenched his fists, kept on going as he hit the stairs at a pace.

'I won't stand for it, Alaric,' she called after him. 'You need to stop feeling so goddamned sorry for yourself and get out there and live.'

He stilled on the next set of stairs, her words striking through the very heart of him as he turned to stare up at her. 'You think this is about me feeling sorry for myself and fearing what life wants to throw at me next?' He shook his head, his smile cold. 'Fred doesn't get to worry about any of that. He doesn't get to wake up next to his wife each morning and watch his own child grow up. He had so much to lose and I… I had nothing. Yet, I'm the one that survived, not him.'

She pressed a hand to her throat, her mouth parting but no words emerging, and he was glad of it…he'd heard enough.

'Goodnight, Catherine.'

He turned away, leaving her stood there as he raced down the remaining steps.

'You had your family, Alaric.' Her soft murmur reached him over the blood pounding in his ears. 'You had us.'

Pain ripped through him and he shook his head, refusing to acknowledge that she was right, relieved at the silence that swiftly followed—no footfall, no more incriminating words…he was free to be alone.

Just the way he wanted to be.

So why did it leave him so very cold?

CHAPTER SIX

THREE DAYS LATER, Catherine was staring at her laptop screen having tried and failed to concentrate on her script. She'd managed it for two days, ploughing her restless energy into the words flowing on the page, telling herself it was best to give Alaric some space after all that had happened, all that had been said...

But she couldn't shake it now. The haunted look in his face when he'd spoken of Fred, of his guilt at living when his best friend didn't. Worse still, that he saw Fred's wife and child as a reason to feel unworthy of living. Did he really wish it had been him?

She'd spent the night after their showdown searching up survivor's guilt, trying to understand as much as she could. The various symptoms that were so very similar to PTSD—flashbacks, anger, irritability, feelings of helplessness, disconnection, fear of the world, sleeping difficulties, headaches, social isolation, thoughts of suicide...

Just how many did he suffer?

The list felt endless and she, helpless. How could she begin to understand how he suffered, how could she begin to help him, if he wouldn't talk to her? Wouldn't even be in the same room as her any more?

At first, she'd wondered if the impossible had happened and he'd left the island but one look at Dorothea's flushed cheeks when she'd enquired as to his whereabouts and she'd known he was very much here and very much avoiding her.

Guilt had been her initial response. Guilt that she'd gone too far in her quest to get through to him and had succeeded in hurting him.

She'd been far too quick to spout off and gone in all guns blazing.

But he'd got to her, angered her hot off the back of their kiss that had stirred up so much inside. And yes, she shouldn't have done it, pleaded with him to kiss her, but then she hadn't been able to stop herself. Not when they'd been so close and that look in his eyes had seared the very heart of her. Even now it coaxed her body to life, the persistent restless energy rushing through her veins and leaving the words on her screen an indistinct blur.

She closed the lid of her laptop and swung her feet from the bed. It was time to confront him, and if she had to play on his good manners that had been instilled in him from birth, she would do. She wasn't expecting him to spend all day, every day, with her, but they could at least eat together.

She knocked on his bedroom door—not that she expected him to be there, but it was the closest place to look first.

No answer. She pressed her ear to the door. No sound.

She headed up a floor—the living area was deserted—up another and checked the gym. No sign. In fact, she hadn't caught him in there since that first day either. Was he working out at night just to avoid the possibility of running into her?

Of all the ridiculous, desperate...

She was just about to barge into his study when Dorothea appeared from the kitchen ahead.

'Miss Wilde!'

She smiled at her as she took hold of the door handle. 'Afternoon, Dorothea.'

The woman hurried forward, her eyes widening. 'What are you—?'

'I'm just going to see what's keeping Alaric so busy he can't see fit to dine with me.'

'But I—'

Catherine pushed open the door before Dorothea could stop her, strode in and halted, her mouth falling open.

She hadn't known what she expected, but it wasn't this…this *tech den*?

Huge flat-screen TVs descended from the ceiling, at least ten, fifteen even, forming a curve before a sunken platform with a desk at its heart, and there he was.

'Catherine! What in the name of—?' Alaric thrust his headset off and tossed it to the desk as he stood, the speed of the move sending his plush leather chair spinning.

She stepped closer, her eyes scanning the huge screens and the moving lines, the constant flicker of numbers…

Dorothea hurried in behind her. 'I'm ever so sorry, *kyrios*. I couldn't— I—'

'What she means is I wasn't stopping for anyone.' She gave him a small smile—*my bad*. She hadn't even considered knocking. It wasn't like his bedroom where he may have been naked after all. She swallowed, forcing out that particular image as she swiftly went back to the screens. They were the focal point of the entire room, the rest of it taken up by his desk, a water cooler, a fridge, a glass wall that led off into what looked like a meeting room with another flat-screen TV and enough seating for ten.

The entire space was white, clinical, businesslike. There was none of the exposed stone and mortar here, the rugged warmth, the relaxed lines of the beautiful building, and she shivered, wishing for the sun again.

That's when it struck her. There was no daylight either. Outside the sky was blue, the sun was bright, it was glorious. But you'd never know it in here. Not a single window existed. Or if they did, they were hidden by cleverly concealed blinds.

Wishing she was dressed in more layers, she wrapped the flimsy fabric of her kimono closer to her bikini-clad body and folded her arms to keep it there.

'It's okay, Dorothea,' Alaric assured the woman who was now wringing the tea towel in her hands. 'You can go back to whatever it was you were doing.'

'I was prepping dinner.'

'Oh, lovely.' Catherine turned to beam at her, hoping the kind woman would see her apology in her face and not the anxious churn in her gut. She hadn't wanted to upset her by barging in here, but her host had hardly given her a choice. 'Your food is always heavenly. What is it tonight?'

Dorothea smiled, her brown eyes softening but not enough to hide her continued concern. 'Lamb kleftiko, another of Kyrios de Vere's favourites.'

'Even better…' she drawled, turning to eye him. 'I assume that means we will finally be dining together again?'

She pinned him with her overbright smile and sensed Dorothea do the same. Two women staring down the giant of a man before them who looked like he'd been caught in a trap. She watched the little pulse working in his jaw and smiled wider. She liked putting him on edge…she liked it a little too much. But it brought out his character. It made him less robotic and more like the Alaric of their youth.

'Yes.' He didn't look at her as he said it. He was rigid, his back so straight she wondered if he might do himself an injury and how amusing would that be? Okay, not amusing, but it did distract her from dwelling on how incredible he looked. What was it with tall, broad men, with dark hair, a tan to envy and muscles that strained the arms of their tee? Especially when the said tee was white with a V neck that gifted a hint of dark hair and was worn with stonewashed jeans slung low at the hips. He was downright edible and—

And you're supposed to be focusing on dragging him out of his cave, not eating him with your eyes!

'Ah, that is wonderful to hear. Company for Miss Wilde at last!' Dorothea clasped her hands together.

Yes, company at last. At least she wasn't alone in thinking his behaviour rude.

Says you, who just barged into his office...

'Indeed,' she spoke over the inner gibe, her voice saccharine sweet, 'it will be lovely to have a dinner companion again.'

His eyes flickered in her direction, his smile more of a grimace.

'Of course it will,' Dorothea spoke up, 'and as it's especially hot today, I will aim for eight-thirty, time for it to cool off a little more.'

'Great.' He sounded like it was anything but great, and it only made Catherine want to laugh. His eyes darted in her direction again and she wondered if the teeniest hint of her laugh had erupted. But at least he looked alive and vibrant in his anger. It beat haunted and lost and...

She tore her eyes from his. 'I'm really looking forward to it, Dorothea.'

'Well, with that agreed, I will leave you both to it.'

And off she went, light on her feet now. Happy.

As the door closed, Catherine turned back to Alaric, trying and failing to prepare herself for how it felt to be around him again. Alone.

'Anyone ever teach you to knock?' He returned to his desk, his eyes scanning the screens.

'Anyone ever teach you how to look after a guest?'

'Thought we'd already been through this. You're Flo's guest, not mine.'

'This isn't Flo's house—island even.' She kept her voice level, refusing to rise to his dig as she sought to play on the goodness within him. 'It's yours and, as such, you are the host.'

'Lucky me.'

She wanted to laugh. She really did. No one spoke to her in this way, not any more. Since she'd hit it big, people fell over themselves to please her, to pander to her…it didn't matter that she didn't want them to, they did it anyway.

Not Alaric though.

He was giving her zero attention as he hunched over his desk, his fingers making light work of the keyboard as he studied the screens. She wanted to ask what he was doing, she wanted to ask what the screens were showing, she wanted to know it all. But while he was distracted, she was free to study him. To watch his muscles flex as he moved, the scarring to the underside of his left arm catching the light.

She wondered how many more scars his body bore and wished she could trace them with her fingers, reassure him as she did that he deserved to live, that he should let her in, let her help him…

The cool air of the room fluttered past her lips as she inhaled softly, her gaze lifting to his eyes that were narrowed in concentration, the grooves either side of his mouth deep as he pressed his lips together.

Sexy didn't even cut it.

'You just going to stand there and stare, or are you going to tell me what it is you want?'

He didn't look at her as he asked and she didn't answer, unless you counted the teasing murmur of a hum that escaped. It was pleasing enough to know that part of him was still so attuned to her, convincing her all the more that she wasn't alone in feeling the way she did.

She descended the steps into his pit, pausing alongside him and mimicking his stance over the desk.

'So this is where you've been hiding?' she said softly, careful to keep the emotional undercurrent out of her voice. The mix of concern, need and pain. It hurt that he'd been avoiding her, it hurt that he'd dismissed their friendship too.

'Just because we were friends once, Catherine, it doesn't mean we can be again.'

Even now those words echoed around her mind and jabbed at her heart.

'I've not been doing anything of the sort.' He flicked her a look and she caught his eyes dip over her length, the move swift but not swift enough. She had her favourite bikini on, a vibrant rainforest scene across the teeny triangles of fabric, set off perfectly by her sunny kimono. The fire was undeniably there, as was the anger at himself for feeling it. She could read it in every taut muscle, the twitch to his jaw, the way he looked away so quick.

'You could have fooled me…' She let her eyes drift back to the screens. 'What is all this?'

'Work.'

'What kind of work?'

'The kind of work that keeps my father happy and my life free of interference.'

'Are you trading?'

He dropped his head forward. 'Are we really doing this?'

'What?'

'Talking about my work.'

'Why not?'

'Because it's work and it's complicated.'

'Too complicated for me, you mean?' Now she really was affronted, and she knew her eyes were shooting daggers as she stared at his bowed head.

'No—though, yes—kind of.'

'Because I'm just a pretty face, right? Incapable of more than just repeating the words fed to me and adding a little Kitty Wilde pizzazz?'

He turned his head, a frown forming. 'Are you serious?'

She wished she'd stayed up on the platform now, missing the height advantage as he glimpsed the vulnerability she worked so hard to hide.

'Maybe.' She made it sound light and breezy, like it didn't bother her in the slightest. Yet the script on her laptop downstairs said otherwise. She was determined to change the world's opinion of her and show them she was more than just looks and make pretend.

He straightened, folding his arms across his chest as he continued to frown at her. 'I don't think you're stupid, Catherine, if that's what you're thinking.'

'You don't?' She gave a short laugh. 'You could have fooled me.'

'I didn't mean it like that.'

'Hey, don't trouble yourself over it, I'm fine. You wouldn't be the first man to treat me like a bimbo.'

'I'm not—' his frown deepened '—is that really what you think I'm doing?'

'You're the one who won't even try to explain this to me.' She gestured to the screens and he surprised her with a real laugh.

'Believe me, that has nothing to do with you! I don't understand the half of it. I can spot an anomaly, something amiss, an opportunity perhaps, but as far as the day-to-day trading goes, I have programs that do it for me.

Genius programmers who work for me and write those genius programs.'

She tilted her head, her shoulders easing just a little. 'So, you're like a glorified facilitator?'

His face softened into something of a smile. 'You could say that. And lucky for me, I'm good at it. It keeps my father happy and off my back.'

'Flo told me you head up the investment side of the business.'

'Exactly. It means aside from the odd conference call, I can keep myself to myself, just the way I like it.'

Her shoulders were hunched once more. 'Is that why you're avoiding me? You're keeping yourself to yourself.'

'I wasn't avoiding—'

Her raised brow cut him off and he tried again, 'Look, I think it's for the best if we keep some distance between us.'

She held his eye as she turned and rested her behind on the edge of his desk. 'Why?'

'I explained that perfectly well the other night.' His eyes dipped to her lips, the roughness to his voice and the vague flush of heat in his cheeks mirroring the rising warmth she felt in the pit of her stomach.

'No, you tried to thrust your viewpoint on me. But newsflash, Alaric, I have my own mind. I make my own decisions.'

He shook his head. 'Don't I know it.'

'What's that supposed to mean?'

His eyes creased a little at the corners, their depths turning wistful with his smile. 'You always did, even when we were young. Once you set your mind to something, you were going to do it regardless.'

She smiled, nostalgia adding to the budding warmth, the growing connection, between them. 'No wonder you saw me as a princess...a spoilt one at that.'

'Spoilt. No. I admired you for it. Envied you even.'

'You *envied* me?'

'Yes, I envied you. I envied you your freedom. My parents were always on at me, checking on my grades, pushing me to do better, to quit messing around with my paintings, to quit the partying, the fun.'

'Ha! You did go and get yourself suspended from boarding school on at least two occasions.'

'For the record—' he cracked a grin and it surprised her with both its sincerity and the chaotic flutters it set off deep inside '—neither of those occasions were my fault.'

There was no angling of his face away, no hiding the scars as he continued to grin at her, and she craved more of him like this, the need like a desperate ache inside.

'No—' her grin was just as wide '—of course they weren't.'

'They *weren't*. One was a science experiment gone wrong—'

'The fire in the boys' changing room?' she proposed, remembering that story very well.

'Yes! And the other...' His smile lifted to one side, transporting them back almost two decades as she remembered the exact same look often appearing with a glint of mischief in his eyes. 'Well, I can't be blamed for that one either.'

'Sneaking into the girls' school after hours—yeah, I'm sure that had nothing to do with you.'

Her laugh was soft, shadowed with pain. That one had stung back then, discovering he'd been caught with a girl and wishing it had been her.

But not now. Now, she'd give anything to see that spark back in his eye, to get a hint of the fun-loving guy that didn't take himself—take life—so seriously.

No wonder Flo had been so desperate to get her to come.

Though what Flo hoped she would achieve and what Catherine's own imagination was proposing were two very different things. Because when Alaric eyed her like he had not one minute ago, want as obvious in his eye as it was in her bloodstream, he was closer to the man he'd once been and she was fully prepared to tease out more of that, if it brought him back to the land of the living.

'It was more of a combined effort—Fred was forever leading me astray.'

His smile turned weak, the haunted look creeping back into his eyes. Fred and Alaric had been thick as thieves, Catherine knew that. Right up until the accident that had taken his friend's life and almost killed him too.

She swallowed down the lump in her throat as she straightened and reached out, her hand gentle on his arm. 'You must miss him.'

He pulled away from her, his hands shoved deep inside his pockets.

'I…' He cleared his throat, the thickness to his voice clawing at her heart. 'He was a big part of my life. But Cherie, she was his wife, and his little girl…to see me return and not him… It had been my idea to go on that lads' weekend. He wouldn't have been on the private jet if not for me.'

He shook his head, unable to continue, and she forced herself to hold still, to give him physical space.

'It wasn't your fault, Alaric. It was an accident. It could have happened to—.'

'To anyone!' he threw at her. 'I've heard it all, Catherine. Nothing you say can make it any better. Every night, I go to bed and see Cherie—Cherie and his daughter stood at his graveside, their lives ruined, and mine—mine—'

He stalked away and she watched him, his pain so palpable she could feel it tearing through her.

'How is Cherie?'

'I don't know.' His voice choked. Guilt. Pain. His shoulders shuddering with it all. 'I haven't spoken to her, not since the funeral.'

'But it was an accident, Alaric,' she tried again, softer. 'There was nothing you could have done.'

He angled his face towards her. 'I should never have suggested the trip.'

'But you did, and it's done, and nothing can change that it happened.'

He scoffed and she could taste the bitterness, the resentment, in him. 'Life goes on regardless.'

She nodded, hearing his words, understanding what he meant, but at the same time…

'Your life needs to go on too, Alaric.'

'That's what I just said.'

'No, you said life goes on regardless…you mean around you. Not for you.'

He shook his head. 'Same difference.'

'No. It's not.'

'Don't stand there and tell me I owe it to him to live my life, Catherine.' He spun to face her. 'I've heard it all, from my mother, my father, Flo, my bleeding counsellor. It's not that simple.'

'I didn't say it was simple, it could never be simple, but have you tried speaking to Cherie, talking to her about how you feel?'

'And put her through that? Put that on her? How selfish do you think I am?'

'You're not selfish, Alaric, you're in pain and until you face it and move on you will always suffer.'

He stared at her, long and hard, but she wanted to show him she wasn't going anywhere, and she wasn't backing down from this.

'It's been three years, Alaric. You can't hide here for ever. Your family miss you. Flo misses you. She's—she's *pregnant*, for heaven's sake.' Her voice quavered, her hand clutching her abdomen in an impulsive gesture as it brought with it the reminder of her own loss. 'Are you really going to miss out on meeting your niece or nephew, spending time with them?'

'Why do you even care so much?' he lashed out. 'You've been so busy the last ten years, pursuing your career, why come back now and interfere? Why pretend you give a damn?'

Her eyes stung, her chest ached, but she refused to let the hurtful words he threw at her in his desperation deter her from pushing further. 'What did your family do to you that was so bad you'd rather hide out here?'

His laugh was harsh. 'Aside from my parents trying to control my every move.'

'Now you're just being melodramatic.'

'*I'm* the dramatic one. Kitty Wilde is stood in my study telling me *I'm* over dramatic.'

She ignored the jibe. 'This isn't a joke, Alaric.'

'I didn't say it was.'

'Then tell me what they did that was so awful for you to turn your back on them, because the way I see it, you survived the crash, but they lost you anyway.'

Alaric stared at her, tormented by the truth of her words.

'What I would have given—' she continued so very quiet, and he wanted to cover his ears like a child as he feared what was coming '—to have a smidgen of the care and attention your parents bestowed on you growing up.'

He felt her pain spear him, his hand reaching out on autopilot, reaching for the vulnerable girl she'd once been and the woman she was now. Neither having had the option of returning to a loving family, and as she backed away, he wanted to howl at the world for its cruelty, its unfairness…

'No!' She held her palm out to ward him off. 'Don't you go softening now because you feel sorry for me. That freedom you envied, I got because my father was too distracted by my mother's absence to care what I was up to. I could have flunked every subject and I don't think they would have noticed. Run away even. But you…you had parents that cared, a sister too…you still have them.'

He folded his arms, hardening himself to her words as he acknowledged her clever orchestration of the entire conversation. Well, no more.

'And after all your family did to you, you still followed in your mother's footsteps. Of all the paths to take, Catherine, I'd hoped you'd do better.'

'I am *better*.'

'Are you?' He felt sick saying it, challenging her when he knew it was deflection, but…

'Just because I became an actor, it doesn't mean—it doesn't mean…' She broke off, her eyes glistening anew as she clutched her abdomen tighter, and he frowned over the move. Her reaction so much stronger than he could have predicted.

She'd been so fierce, so unbreakable, seconds before.

'My mother and I are nothing alike,' she whispered, broken, distraught, and any attempt to deny it died on his lips. 'For one, I don't have a family to let down. There's just me and my career. No competition. No one to neglect.'

'No one to care for?'

She stared at him.

'That's what you mean, isn't it?' he probed, a light-bulb moment leaving him feeling oddly bereft. 'Is that why you broke it off with Luke? He was getting too close and you didn't want to risk him becoming a distraction or someone you could let down?'

'Don't presume to understand what happened between me and Luke. You don't get to pass judgement on something you know nothing about.'

'I can read between the lines well enough.' He felt energised by the realisation, his defensive walls rebuilding as he realised that whatever existed between him and Catherine, whatever the connection, there was no future.

And it wasn't because of how messed up he was. No, it was because Kitty Wilde would never have room in her life for another.

'You may not have had an affair, Catherine, but I can easily imagine that Luke got too serious, and you ran. My guess is you were scared of becoming your mother, scared of having your priorities skewed, scared of abandoning—'

'Stop it, Alaric. Just stop it!' Her entire body trembled, a tear rolling down one cheek and torturing him with its journey. Had her breakup hurt her so very much? Had she loved Luke *that* much and still loved her job more?

He shook his head, shock stealing the breath from his lungs as his jealousy of the man was obliterated with pity.

'Tell me something?' he breathed. 'Is it really worth it?'

'What?'

'Your career, your fame?'

She frowned, swiping the tear away with the back of her hand. 'You don't know what you're talking about.'

'I know that you're alone, that for all you dig at me for living here alone, you're as bad. In fact, for you, it must be worse. Surrounded by people day in, day out, and standing alone…'

'And I repeat, you don't know what you're talking about.'

'No? Tell me, then, do you ever get lonely?'

'Asks the man who lives on his own bleeding island!'

'And I'm happy that way. You're not. You're stood there crying over a man that you chose to leave.'

Her breath shuddered out of her. 'You don't understand.'

'Then explain it to me, make me understand.'

She shook her head. 'I can't.'

'Why?'

'Because—just because.' She wrapped her arms tight around her middle.

'Then let's agree to leave each other's lives alone. You don't want to speak about Luke and what went wrong. And I sure as hell don't want to talk about my reasons for being here.'

'But, Alaric—'

'But nothing, Catherine, you keep your nose out of my business and I'll do the same in return. Now I have work to be getting on with.'

She stared at him, quiet for a moment, and he felt a sickening thud in the pit of his stomach. Had he gone too far? Would she bail on dinner? Would she pack up and leave entirely?

She wet her lips, sucked in a breath through her nose.

'I'll leave you to it.'

She started to walk away, and he called out. 'I'll see you at dinner?'

It was definitely more of a question and she stilled, looked over her shoulder, a second's hesitation and then the smallest of nods.

'Good.' His shoulders eased, his breath leaving him as he watched her go. Taking all the warmth, all the light, with her.

He looked back to the screens and saw nothing but the pain in her eyes, the tears, the sorrow…all over a man she had chosen to leave. A man who had at least managed to earn a place in her heart, and still it hadn't been enough for her to put him first.

Goosebumps spread across his skin, a chill shocking him to the core. This wasn't jealousy, or anger, or guilt, this was fear. Fear of how he felt towards her…how he could feel if he let himself get caught up in her again.

Had that been his sister's plan? Throw temptation in his face and use it to lure him out?

Had his cunning little sister been aware of his feelings towards her friend all along and never let on?

And if that was the case, how would she feel to learn that no matter how he felt, or how much Catherine may feel for him in return, she would always put her career first? That, ultimately, she'd break his heart if he let her…

All good reason to maintain his distance…instead they were having dinner together that evening.

And he shouldn't be looking forward to it.

But this was Catherine, and his heart was overriding his head.

'We care… We don't see this… We see you.'

He ran a hand over his scarred cheek as her words chipped away at his defences.

Not once had she intentionally made him self-conscious. No, he'd been the one seeking to hide it, to not let her see him in all his ugly glory, fearing her pity, her repulsion even. And instead she'd given him her warmth, her attention, her kiss. And that kiss… *Wow*, that kiss. A moment of madness, of weakness, that had left him feeling starved and desperate. He couldn't stop reliving it, over and over.

And in the face of such temptation, such acceptance, he wasn't sure how long he could play dumb to the attraction, especially now he was done hiding from her, physically at least.

CHAPTER SEVEN

CATHERINE WAS PLAYING with fire, but she was angry.

Angry at the way he'd thrown her mother at her, angry at the way life had construed to ruin his and stopped for her the second her baby had been taken from her.

She didn't know how dinner was going to play out, but she'd sure as hell made sure she felt invincible. Flawless make-up, glossy skin and a dress to die for. She wasn't going to let Alaric break her again.

If he didn't want to talk about the past, then fine, she'd let it go. On the proviso that he let hers go too.

She couldn't bear thinking on it, let alone talk of it. The pain, the guilt, the shared suffering with Luke over a baby…a baby they hadn't—*she* hadn't wanted, hadn't planned and miscarried mere weeks after the test result.

But in those weeks so much had changed. She had swung from panic, from fear, from wishing it away to feeling a new life growing inside her, of feeling its importance, its unparalleled importance. Her vision for the future changing so completely because she wouldn't be her mother, she wouldn't…

And just when all had felt good again, better even, it had been snatched away.

The ultimate punishment for her selfishness.

Her hand went to her stomach as she froze on the stairs,

her other hand clutching at the handrail to fend off the fresh wave of grief, of remorse.

She wasn't her mother. She *wasn't*.

Yet she'd failed her child before they'd even been born.

She sucked in a breath and let it out slow. Not even Flo knew the whole truth. The fact she refused to believe it at first, then the resentment…

How could she even begin to tell Alaric that when he already had such a twisted view of who she was?

No, putting words to it would only confirm what he already suspected.

What he already suspected and what she feared.

That she was as bad, if not worse, than her mother ever was.

No. She wanted to forget and she owed him the same consideration over his past too. No matter what Flo had asked of her, what she had set out to achieve in coming here, she needed to respect his decision.

Taking another breath, she combed her fingers through her hair and shook out the waves she had carefully crafted as she'd opted to leave it down, free of restraint as she wished to be free of the past.

Tonight at least…

He was already on the terrace when she got there, a drink in hand, his eyes on the view. She came up behind him, surprised when he didn't detect her approach, and she cleared her throat. 'It's a beautiful evening.'

And it was—the sun casting its soft glow as it sunk into the sea, the heat of the day leaving a subtle warmth in the air—but it wasn't the reason she'd said it. She'd sensed his thoughts were as preoccupied as her own had been and she wanted him to relax, just as she was determined to do so. She wanted him to know that she'd put their impassioned talk behind her and hoped that he could too.

'It is.' He pushed up out of his seat, his eyes raking over her, and the appreciation she spied lit her up inside.

She did love this dress. How the slinky fabric caught the light and gave the appearance of liquid gold. The slender shoestring straps and wrap style creating a low V neckline and allowing the floor-length skirt to part as she walked, revealing her leg from the thigh all the way down to her heels.

She felt sexy. She looked sexy. And that was the confidence she needed to get through the evening.

'You look—' he cleared his throat, stepped out from the table to greet her '—like you're missing a red carpet.'

Her smile faltered before she could stop it. She was too damned sensitive to his opinion, anyone else and she wouldn't care. 'Too much?'

'No.' The smallest of lines appeared between his brows, and his voice was gruff as he pocketed his hands. 'Not at all.'

'Good.' Her smile relaxed with her returning confidence. 'I have to say you look red-carpet worthy yourself.'

He wore dark trousers and a navy shirt unbuttoned at the collar, the fit emphasising his muscular build and trim waist, the colour setting off his tan and the blue of his eyes. He'd combed some product through his hair, taming the wild strands so that they were clear of his face. He'd shaved too, exposing his scar so completely and making something within her pulse. He wasn't hiding it from her, not any more.

She wet her suddenly dry lips and paused before him, pressing her palms into his chest before she could lose her nerve. His body contracted beneath her touch, his lips parting with obvious surprise as she lifted up on tiptoes to press a kiss to his cheek. It was how she would have greeted any man in her acquaintance, but the simple contact thrilled her to the core.

She paused—a second to appreciate his scent, another his warmth—and then she dropped back, moving away as his arm locked around her, keeping her close.

She looked up at him in question.

'You like playing with fire, don't you?'

Her own words came back to her, her make-up, her outfit, a confidence booster as she admitted, 'Only when it's fun.'

'Fun for who? You?'

'For the both of us.'

His eyes glittered, the pulse in his jaw twitched, and she pulled away before she could succumb to the urge burning through her very veins, because all she wanted to do was kiss him. Kiss him and forget everything.

One step free, two, and suddenly she was crushed up against hot, hard muscle, a frisson of excitement rushing south.

'Is this just some game to you, Catherine?'

'If it's a game where we both come away satisfied—' her voice was all breathy with lust '—I'm all for it.'

He growled low in his chest, the rumble filtering through to her. 'What do you want from me?'

'Right this second…you're a clever man, I'll let you work it out.'

His eyes darkened above her, his head drew closer, his voice gruffer still. 'What if I need you to spell it out?'

Her lips curved into a smile, power rushing her veins as she reached closer, the tips of her toes pressing into the ground, her palms smoothing over his shoulders and relishing the strength beneath, the hard muscle she so desperately wanted to explore…

She brushed her lips against his, a little flick of the tip of her tongue against his mouth, and her eyes connected with his. *What are you doing?* came the mental warning, but what left her lips was a simple, 'Enough?'

He lifted his hand, forking it through her hair. 'With you, I don't think it can ever be enough.'

And before she could overthink his words, he was kissing her, kissing her so deep and so thoroughly she was consumed by it. The carnal heat coursing through her as she savoured the taste of his mouth, the pressure of his lips, his tongue as it grazed against hers.

She moaned with the heady rush, her desperation, her frustration…it was everything and not enough at once. She raised her hands to his hair and tugged him closer, pressed her entirety against him. She could feel his heart pounding into her, or was it her heart pounding into him? She didn't know where he ended, and she began, and if they could just stay like this for longer, for ever…

A startled gasp filled the air and they froze, their heads snapping to the left, to a startled Dorothea, who looked about to flee.

'I'll come back!'

'No, no, it's fine.' His broken voice rasped along Catherine's spine and the world seemed to spin. Lack of oxygen through kissing was a real thing. Who knew!

She took a steadying breath, stepped away from him. She could feel her cheeks burning with it all—lustful heat, bashfulness and something that ran deeper…much, much deeper…and she wasn't about to examine it too closely. Not right now.

She smoothed her hands down her dress, making sure it was back in place and gave Dorothea an apologetic grimace. 'So sorry, Dorothea.'

'Don't you go apologising, that's the most exciting thing to happen on this island in for ever!'

Alaric snorted and Catherine's eyes shot to him—had

he really just snorted? She laughed, the sound giddy and happy and so very easy. He looked young again, less tense, the brightness to his eyes, the colour in his cheeks…the warmth deep inside her spread, her feelings with it.

Feelings she really needed to get a handle on. But how could she when she was barely accustomed to feeling this way. Not even with Luke.

This was new. Intense. And for all she'd assumed it was the old merging with the new, she wasn't so sure. Something about Alaric now got to her, dug beneath her skin, had her losing her trusty control…

'Let me help you with that…' She hurried forward to aid Dorothea and quit the panicked direction of her thoughts.

Alaric filled her glass with the red wine he'd been enjoying on her arrival.

Catherine set the side dishes down as Dorothea lifted the main dish from the tray and rested it in the middle of the table, opening up the parchment paper and scrunching it around the dish. Steam rose up, filling the air with the most delicious scent, and Catherine hummed her approval, her eyes closing as she truly appreciated it.

When she opened them again, she caught Alaric watching her, his eyes soft, his expression unguarded, and she saw the same confusing fear that she was starting to feel deep inside. This connection between them had the power to break them if they let it…

She gave him a tentative smile and he followed her lead; the two of them stood there, smiling. An all-knowing Dorothea between them.

'I'll leave you both to enjoy your meal. There are more vegetables in the kitchen should you want any.'

'I think we'll be okay,' he murmured, his eyes not leaving Catherine's. 'You get yourself home.'

'I'll clean up after you finish, and then—'

'No, I'll take care of it…' He turned to Dorothea 'You take the leftover veg and kleftiko to enjoy with Andreas. Have an early night.'

'Well, you don't have to tell me twice!' She grinned as she nodded to them both. *'Kalispera.'*

'Kalispera—and take a bottle from the cellar with you too.'

'Oh, you really are spoiling us! Something tells me I have you to thank, Miss Wilde.' She gave Catherine a wink that had her blushing all over again.

'Kalispera, Dorothea.'

She watched the woman go, the air thickening the further away she walked and the closer they came to being alone again. She looked back at Alaric to find him watching her, the look in his eye making her stomach spin.

'What?'

'I'm just wrestling with reality.'

'Wrestling with reality?' She took up her wine glass and sampled it. Rich, dry and satisfying. Good choice. Though nothing beat the appeal of the man opposite her, looking at her in a way that made her pulse race. 'That sounds quite serious.'

'Oh, it is.'

'Tell me, which bit are you struggling with the most?'

'That you're really here, the great Kitty Wilde—'

'Don't call me that.' It blurted out of her, surprising herself as much as him, and she added softly, 'Please.'

'Okay. As I was saying, it's hard to believe that you're really here, and that we're really doing this.'

'Eating lamb kleftiko and drinking a very expensive—' she squinted at the bottle and smiled '—red Bordeaux?'

He laughed softly as he shook his head. 'Never mind the food and the drink. Do you have any idea how famous you are? How many men would do anything to be in my position?'

She shifted in her seat. 'Don't say that.'

'Why?'

'Because… Because you're not any man, and it makes me uncomfortable.'

'Uncomfortable to own your fame?'

'No. Not really. I just… I'm me when I'm with you. There's no pretence, no act, just me.'

He leaned forward on his elbows. 'Well, just you, how about we eat this and enjoy one another's company?'

She nodded, pleasure sweeping through her as she felt a common ground form for the first time since she'd arrived.

Food was finished. Dorothea's kleftiko was divine as always. His dinner companion…well, she was something else. Always had been, always would be.

And Alaric wasn't naïve. Out of practice, yes. But not naïve.

He knew where things were heading. He also knew it was a bad, bad idea.

He hadn't been with a woman in over three years. The idea of breaking that celibacy with Catherine was insane, foolish, asking for trouble. How could he ever hope to go back to his life as it was after she left?

And yet, every time she looked at him, as a man, a man she desired in spite of his scars, he lost sight of the bad and remembered the good. The connection they had when they were younger, the connection so ready to surface now.

'There's a little left, do you want it?'

He shook his head. 'You?'

She shook her head.

'Another drink?'

'What are you offering?'

'What do you fancy?'

With each question their smiles grew. 'I have champagne, dessert wine, ouzo, a raki?'

She pulled a face. 'Isn't that the drink that strips your liver?'

He laughed. 'I wasn't suggesting more than a shot.'

She grinned and his breath caught. She really was beautiful and not what he expected. Not that he'd known what to expect. Her mother, he supposed. A woman so focused on her career that everything else—*everyone* else—blurred into the background. But she wasn't any of that, despite what he'd told her. He knew she wasn't.

He also knew that her pushing him to discuss the past, to face it and change his outlook for the future, stemmed from a good place. She cared.

And he loved that she cared. He loved it too much. It's that which told him to keep his guard in place. The guard that was swiftly crumbling with the lateness of the hour and the growing sparkle in her eye.

'How about champagne?'

'Sounds perfect.'

He stood and started gathering up the plates. She made to help and he took her hand, gave it a soft squeeze. 'I've got this. I don't want to risk you getting anything on that dress of yours.'

'What, this old thing?' She winked. 'Why don't you let me worry about that?'

He didn't even fight her on it, knowing full well that if she wanted to help she would, and the thought made him smile all the more.

They cleared the table and tidied the kitchen, making sure Dorothea didn't have much to do when she returned in the morning. It felt natural, *too* natural, to be doing such domesticated tasks beside her, but as they worked, she asked him about the origins of the house, and he stopped worrying about how it felt and concentrated on the details she wanted to know. The kind of farm it had once been, who had once lived here, how he'd discovered it…

But with every brush of her body against his, her perfume on the air, the sweet sound of her voice, it became harder and harder to resist pulling her to him.

'I take it you don't often clear up after dinner?'

He was reaching up into the cupboard for two champagne flutes when she asked, and he turned to look at her. 'Are you saying I don't look at home in my own kitchen?'

She pressed her lips together as her eyes danced. 'Something like that.'

'I'll have you know I do chip in on occasion, but I don't like to tread on Dorothea's toes. That woman has a scowl that'll send a grown man running.'

Her eyes continued to dance. 'I can believe it, only…'

He folded his arms. 'Only?'

She nipped her bottom lip, a tea towel in hand as she dried off the casserole dish he had just washed, and the comforting sight coupled with the fire in his veins made his heart pulse.

'Domestic duties carried out by a man…' Her eyes trailed over him. Hunger. Desire. It was all there in the flush to her skin as she stopped drying the dish and took him in. 'A man as well built and rugged as you, I don't know whether to laugh at the strangeness of it or declare it the sexiest sight I've ever seen.'

He was upon her in two strides. 'Let me help you with that.'

He tugged the dish from her, the towel too, dumping them on the side with a clatter. 'That's not help—'

'I wasn't talking about the dish.' He wrapped an arm around her and bit back a groan as she came willingly, pressing her body up against his heightened state. 'I'm talking about the doubts you raise over my masculinity.'

Her lips parted with a soft 'Oh…' that he swallowed with his kiss. A deep, thorough, knee-buckling kiss that had him spinning her into the countertop as she clung to his shoulders, her nails biting through his shirt.

Her frustrated whimpers resonated off the stone walls, his desperate groans too. She curved her leg around him, urging him closer and closer still, but it wasn't enough. He needed more. He needed her all.

She tore her mouth away, her breath coming in pants, his shoulders heaving in tune.

'Is this what you do when a woman emasculates you?'

'If it's you, yes.'

She stared up at him, her cheeks flushed, her eyes hooded, and it was the sexiest sight *he* had ever seen.

'Alaric?'

'Yes?'

'Take me to bed.'

The blood rushed his ears, his core, his ability to breathe lost as she offered him everything he could want. Everything he'd always wanted. 'But—'

She pressed a finger to his lips. 'No buts… I'm not asking for more after tonight. I'm asking to satisfy this need between us before it gets out of our control.'

Out of our control…

He already feared they were long past that point but he couldn't stop it. Not now.

And he didn't want to.

CHAPTER EIGHT

CATHERINE FOLLOWED HIM down the stairs, scarce able to believe this was happening.

The small voice at the back of her mind persisted with its warning. Be careful. That the implications for him, for her, for their futures that were worlds apart, were huge and so she'd made it clear—she wasn't asking for more, this was about one night.

But to be his first…after three long years…it wasn't like he'd had anyone else come here…

Could it really be as simple as walking away after?

Her heart fluttered up into her throat, nerves getting the better of her, and as Alaric pushed open the bedroom door, she tugged him back to her. Kissed him until her head was dizzy with it and she could no longer think, she could no longer worry.

'I've forgotten the champagne,' he said against her lips. 'You get yourself comfy and I'll go.'

She shook her head, pulling him into the room with her, needing his thought-obliterating presence, his warmth, to keep out the warning, the reservation. 'No, I don't need champagne. I just need you.'

And she did need him, more than she'd ever needed anyone, and it scared her as much as it reinforced her belief that this was meant to be.

'I like the way that sounds.' He lifted her up and she hooked her legs around his waist, their lips melding back together as though they'd never get enough. He backed her up against the bed, knelt on it as he lowered her down. 'Especially from you.'

And if he liked it, maybe he wouldn't object to her saying it more. Like every day for the rest of her stay and beyond. Could they continue this when her stay was over? Would it help him return to his family and the land of the living if she were to stay by his side for however long he needed? Could she do that? Would he want her to?

Her thoughts were as frenzied as the heat licking through her.

Stop thinking, she mentally berated herself, surrendering to his kiss, his touch, his body on hers. She kissed him harder, kissed him to mute her thoughts, kissed him to remind herself of what mattered right now…this.

He tore his mouth from hers, dragged kisses from her jaw to her ear and just beneath, where the sensitised pulse point made her whimper and writhe.

'This dress…it's killing me.' He caressed her through the fabric, his touch setting her skin alight. 'The way it looks against your skin, the way it feels…'

'It's a favourite.'

He murmured his agreement into the curve of her neck, his teeth nipping, his lips soft. He hooked his finger beneath one strap and teased it down.

'No bra too…'

Her insides quivered at the lustful heat in his voice, the thrill of what was to come.

'You really are killing me, Catherine.'

'If this is how dying feels—' she forked her fingers through his hair, watched him as he continued to unveil her '—I'd do it a thousand times over with you.'

It came out without thought, without reservation, and his eyes flicked to hers, passion blazing in their depths. She wondered if she'd said too much, overstepped an invisible line…panic pulsed through her, her fingers tightening in his hair.

'You and me both.' It was barely audible, a second's relief before the heat took over, warmth rushing through her core as he exposed one taut and needy peak to the cool air of the room.

She watched enraptured as he wet his bottom lip, the glimpse of tongue making her stomach clench, and he bowed his head, his breath sweeping over the sensitised nipple, his tongue following…

She gripped his shoulders, her nails clawing into his shirt as she arched into the caress, his name a moan on her lips. He cupped her breast, held her steady to his attention, his teeth grazing, his tongue flicking, his mouth sucking her in deep.

Pleasure surged fast and furious within her, her toes curling into the bed sheets as she grasped him like some form of anchor, fearing its intensity and revelling in it all the same. She pressed her head back into the pillow, clamped her eyes shut as she panted for air, cried out for more…

His hand fell to the tie at her waist, a bow the only thing holding her dress in place, and one sharp tug saw it undone.

'On second thoughts,' he murmured over her sensitised skin, 'this dress wouldn't be safe for the red carpet.'

'No?'

'No.' He rose up onto his knees, hemming her in with his thighs—it had never felt so good to be trapped. 'One wrong move and it's…'

He parted the fabric, uncovering her body to demonstrate his point, her small gold thong shimmering in the light as he hungrily took her all in.

'True.' Brazenly she lay there, goosebumps prickling over her skin, her nipples tightening further against the coolness of the room. 'But it does have its benefits for the after party…'

His eyes flashed to hers. 'This is the only after party I want to think about.'

She gave a soft laugh. 'Good. Now get back here.'

His grin was devilish as he dropped forward and she pressed her palms into his chest, preventing him from getting any closer. 'Not so fast.'

She reached for the buttons of his shirt, undid one and felt the tension in his body swell exponentially, saw his jaw tighten, his mouth too. There was a sudden hesitancy in his gaze, a battle between desire and something else.

She wet her lips. 'What is it?'

'I'm not—it's not…' His head dropped forward and his eyes squeezed shut. 'It's not pretty, Catherine.'

'Pretty?' she teased softly, stroking her hand beneath his chin to bring his head back up. 'And you accused me of emasculating you?'

He opened his eyes and she smiled up into his gaze. 'I want you, Alaric.'

She saw his throat bob and his eyes shimmer.

'I want all of you…' Slowly she unbuttoned another, and another, all the while holding his eye. 'I want every scar that makes you who you are now… I want you.'

His breath shuddered out of him, his eyes blazing into hers as he kissed her deeply. 'You have me.'

Her heart pulsed, her fingers unsteady as she stroked the shirt from his shoulders, down his back, savouring the heat of his bare skin, the strength rippling beneath her touch. He rose up when she couldn't reach any fur-

ther, tugging the rest of it away, and she couldn't breathe
for the sight of him. He was everything. He *made* 'pretty'
masculine. He was beautiful, sexy, magnificent, and *God*,
how she wanted him.

He came back to her, his hands planting into the mat-
tress either side of her, and she shook her head. 'Time to
even out the power dynamic.'

He frowned and she shoved him, forcing him onto his
back, and he laughed, the sound deep and husky and provoking the fire within.

'I should have known you'd want your way in the bedroom too.' He stroked at her bare thighs as she climbed
over him, pulling her arms free of her dress and tossing
it aside.

'Complaining?'

He stared up at her, his eyes so intense, so piercing.
'Not at all, princess.'

Princess. It didn't trigger a second's hesitation now.
She loved that he had a name for her, loved that this was
what he wanted too.

She lowered her hands to his bronzed chest, marvelling
at the sheer strength beneath her touch, the trail of dark
hair, the journey of scars that travelled down his side…

She leaned forward, her hair brushing against his skin.
'Do they hurt?'

His fingers flexed on her thighs. 'Not so much now,
they're mostly numb.'

'Do you mind if I touch them?'

His throat bobbed, his laugh tight. 'You can do anything
you like. I've told you I'm yours…'

For tonight, she silently reminded herself, pressing a
light kiss to his cheek, tracing the silvery line. 'You're one
hell of a specimen, Alaric, I'll give you that.'

Another tight laugh. 'I'm one scarred specimen.'

'So?' She met his gaze. 'They tell a story of your journey, your life…you shouldn't dismiss them, or hide them. Especially from me…'

She pressed a kiss to his collarbone, let her tongue caress the dip in this flesh—another scar, another piece of him. 'You are incredible.'

His nose flared with his breath, and his hands were so large as they lifted to hold her hips, but she wriggled free, dipping to take her desired tour of his body. She kissed every scar, caressed the silver lines with her tongue, her fingertips, showed him how beautiful he was, how strong, and sexy, and relished every groan he gave, every flex of his fingers, his body, as he succumbed to the pleasure she gave.

She reached the waistband to his trousers and rose, her fingers making light work of the button there, the zip too. She shimmied them away, his socks too, their shoes long gone in the journey from the kitchen to bedroom.

She stepped from the bed and his eyes followed her, her smile small. 'You lose yours and I'll lose mine.'

His eyes were dark, hungry, his smile carnal, and she didn't wait, she was too eager to please, too eager to watch his face change as she slid the flimsy fabric down her hips.

She straightened up and he shook his head. 'Catherine. You are…you really are going to be the death of me.'

'I hope not, because I really want this to last the whole night.'

His laugh was gruff.

'Never mind me.' She eyed his briefs. 'I'm waiting.'

He shucked them, the move so quick she squealed when he came at her, his hands on her waist as he pulled her back to the bed with him. He bowed his head to kiss her, her lashes fluttering closed as she wrapped her legs around his hips and positioned him just where she wanted him and—froze.

'Protection!' She bit her lip hard, pushing back the thought that swiftly came next, the memory, the pain… 'Do you have any?'

He cursed and dragged in a breath. 'Not here.'

She sagged beneath him.

'But somewhere?' she said with hope.

He rolled onto his back, his palm pressing into his forehead. 'I'm such a fool. I have some but they pre-date my move here.'

She wrapped her leg around him, rested her head on his shoulder as her fingers trailed the curves and planes of his torso, her heart and breaths still racing with her need for him.

'Are you on the pill?'

'No. It doesn't agree with me.'

She moved against him, her disobedient body unwilling to stop, though her heart and head told her they must. 'Go and check them anyway. They might still be good.'

'Or we could just…satisfy ourselves in other ways…' He stroked his hand down her side, cupped her breast as his thumb rolled over her nipple, and she bit back a whimper.

'We could, only—' she kissed him, brushing the words against his lips '—I want to explore so many avenues with you that it would be nice not to worry about restrictions.'

He laughed as he pulled away and she watched him go, a smile playing about her lips, her heart light and free as she refused to let anything spoil this night—not the past, not the future, nothing.

Alaric opened the bathroom cabinet and took out the packet he knew he had. After all, he'd only relocated it very recently to make room for Catherine in the master suite. He hadn't expected to be getting it out again. In fact, he'd almost thrown them away, but the act had felt too final.

Too final? He wanted to laugh as he scanned the packet for a date, struggling to read as his hand shook with the realisation that they were really doing this…and then what?

How could they possibly return to how things were come morning?

Would she expect more? Would he?

Didn't this change everything?

It's one night of passion, came the voice of reason, no more, no less. The future didn't come into it.

But what of Fred? Did one night of bliss make him a traitor to his guilt?

Though surely he would suffer more for having known her, and let her go.

His gut rolled with the emptiness of it, his heart too quick to follow, and he pushed it all from his mind, projecting her instead—Catherine, in his bed, naked and waiting.

He closed the cabinet and caught his reflection in the mirror, the flush to his skin making his scars more garish. Was she crazy? How could she want this? Him?

The contrast between them couldn't be more profound and yet…she *did* want him.

He felt it in every caress of her fingers, her lips, saw it in her eyes and heard it in her voice as she'd made him feel worshipped…*him.*

And shouldn't he be the one doing the worshipping when he had her in his bed?

He strode back into the master bedroom to find her just as he left her. Naked, smiling, wanton.

'I was about to come and look for you.'

'Like that?'

She pushed herself up onto one elbow and gave a nod.

'Now I wish you had…'

He threw the packet down on the bedside table and joined her, his hand reaching out to cup her hip, to stroke at her skin that was so impossibly soft beneath his touch.

How long had it been since he'd touched a woman? His fingers trembled with the truth—too many years to count.

'Miss me that much?'

She leaned into him, her eyes worshipping him all over again. 'Too much.'

She hooked her leg over him, forcing him onto his back as she planted her palms into his chest and let her hair tickle at his skin.

'How long has it been for you?'

He frowned. Was she in his mind? 'A while.'

'Am I the first since you've lived here?'

He chuckled quietly. 'Do you see me hiding any other women here?'

Her eyes sparkled with his tease. 'You want to take it slow?'

He scoffed as he fought the urge to roll her back under him and demonstrate his answer. 'You know that conversation about emasculating me…'

Now she smiled. 'I don't want to be too much for you.'

'Right, that does it.' He rolled her under him, relishing her squeal of delight as he covered her body with his. 'I'm taking the lead.'

He rolled his hips, her moan his reward. As was the surge of colour in her cheeks, her heavy-lidded gaze.

'I want you, Catherine. I don't need to go slow, I don't need your softness. I want this.'

'Then take me.'

He reached out for the packet and rose up, his eyes on hers as he sheathed himself and gritted his teeth against the rush within. Slowly he lowered himself over her, careful to keep his weight on his elbows as he kissed her, loving how she matched him move for move, her legs hooking around his hips, moving him against her.

'Are you sure, Catherine?' He had to ask. It would kill him to stop, but he would…

'I've never been more sure about anything. I want this. I want you, for however long I can have you.'

However long I can have you…

The words echoed through his mind as he took all that she was offering, all that made him feel so complete.

'Alaric!' She clung to his back, her eyes all vivid and blue.

'*You* are incredible.' He returned her compliment as he moved slowly, drawing out the sensation, controlling his need as he sought to build hers. 'You are beautiful… Caring… Kind.'

'Quit it, Alaric!' She clutched him tighter. 'You're filling my head with nonsense.'

'No.' He frowned, her reaction making him still. 'I'm filling it with the truth.'

She shook her head and squeezed her eyes shut.

'Look at me, Catherine.'

She refused and he stroked her hair back from her face.

'Look at me.' He cupped her face, held still until she opened her eyes, and when she did, he couldn't breathe. Her eyes were damp, wet with tears. His throat closed over, his voice hoarse as he assured her, 'You are all of those things and more, never believe otherwise.'

'More action, less words.' She tugged his mouth to hers, kissed him. 'I don't need the platitudes.'

'They're not—'

'Please, no more.'

What was this? His head told him to leave well alone, that whatever it was would only draw them closer together, but he couldn't. He wanted to understand. He *needed* to.

'Catherine, don't shut—'

She shoved him, forcing him onto his back as she tried to take control of the pace.

'Catherine?'

'Please, Alaric. I want this, I want you, no more, no less.'

'Talk to me.'

'No.' Her eyes pleaded with him. 'We're having sex. Fun. That doesn't need words.'

And yet she'd given him plenty. Made him feel desired, wanted, appreciated. Why wouldn't she let him do the same in return? Why did she look...*fearful*?

'What are you afraid of?'

It was his turn to ask the question.

'Nothing.' Though it caught in her throat and he held her hips steady, even as the demands of his body tried to override his heart and the need to hear the truth from her.

'Don't lie to me.'

'Please, Alaric, please.' She trembled in his hold. 'Let us have this.'

She fell forward, kissed him, her hands reaching for his and taking them above his head. He looked up into her eyes that were ablaze with so much and surrendered, giving himself over to her completely, letting her take her pleasure and deliver his own.

Tomorrow, they would walk away from this. They had to because the one thing he knew for sure—this couldn't happen again. He was drowning in her. Not steadily and slowly, not carefully or within his control, he was losing it.

He *was* lost. To her.

And that terrified him enough to keep his mouth shut and abide her demands, to let the thrill of what they were sharing in the now take over.

Because sex was finite.

It had an end.

And with it, this between them would cease to exist and life would be as it was. Safe. Steady. And wholly within his control.

No surprises. No fear. No guilt. No pain.

CHAPTER NINE

CATHERINE WOKE TO the smell of fresh coffee, the caress of the sea breeze across her naked skin and the sound of the waves rolling in the distance...bliss.

Her body ached in the most satisfying of ways and a smile was already on her lips as she untangled herself from the sheets and her lashes fluttered open. Sure enough, the glass door was ajar, a coffee pot was on the bedside table with two mugs, a jug of orange juice, glasses and glazed pastries. Oh, yum.

'Morning, sleepyhead.'

She rolled over to see Alaric stood at the foot of the bed, a towel slung around his hips, another hooked around his bare shoulders. His hair was damp, and his body still glistened from a very recent shower. If only she'd woken up a few minutes earlier, she thought, envying every small rivulet of water as it ran down his torso.

She took a second to catch her breath, another to try and moisten her very dry mouth. How could she want him so much already? They'd slept a few hours at most, the rest of the time they'd been hell-bent on sating this never-ending hunger.

'I was beginning to think I'd have to rouse you.' He lifted the towel from around his neck to dry his hair, an innocent enough move, save for the fact that she was left

watching his pecs and abs ripple, his arm muscles bulge…
Definitely yum!

She swallowed, lifted her eyes to his that were so
blue against his tan and the brightness of the room, and
stretched out, aware of how naked she was. His eyes raked
over her, projecting every salacious thought that mirrored
her own.

He still wanted her.

But they were in unknown territory now…the morning
after the most amazing night before.

Were they done? Or did the fact that she was still naked
with his eyes feasting over her mean that they could pur-
sue this a little longer because, seriously, if this was how
good it felt the morning after, how good would it feel after
a few days, a week, two…

She gave him a cat-like smile. 'And how, pray tell, were
you hoping to do that?'

His eyes flashed, his lopsided grin hot. 'That would
be telling.'

He rounded the bed to come up alongside her and
stopped short, some unknown emotion flickering across
his face as an invisible wall seemed to erect itself between
them.

She opened her mouth to suggest her own possibili-
ties fearing what was coming, but he got there first. 'We
should talk.'

She felt her lips pout and she really wasn't the pouty
kind. 'After coffee, yeah?' She pushed herself up to sitting.
'I'm no use to anyone without my morning hit.'

And she really wanted to live in the moment just a little longer…

He nodded, his smile small as he started to move away,
and she reached out, hooked her fingers in the towel around
his waist. 'I wasn't just referring to the caffeine hit…'

One sharp tug and he was on the bed with her, the towel in a heap on the floor, his naked body up against hers. And before she could declare herself triumphant, he was kissing her. She had known from the ease with which he'd landed beside her that he'd wanted it as much as her but to feel his mouth on hers sent her head spinning, her heart too.

'I knew I should have dressed before you woke up.' He brushed the words against her lips, his hands roaming over her as she raked her nails down his back.

'And spoil my fun?' She nipped his lip, playful punishment for the suggestion.

He hissed in a breath, taking up her hands, and threading his fingers through hers, he pinned them above her head. 'It's a good job I told Dorothea to take the day off, you're insatiable.'

'Funny, I was thinking the same about you.'

And then he was kissing her, so thoroughly that had there been any doubt remaining about what breakfast had entailed for him, it was obliterated now.

This was definitely her kind of wake-up call.

Almost an hour later, showered and dressed in a black bikini, she joined Alaric at the table outside her bedroom— or rather, *his* bedroom.

He'd made fresh coffee and whipped up some eggs, ham and slices of bread. The pastries had disappeared with their bedroom escapades and even the memory alone set off the heated flutters deep inside her.

'Wow, you really do know how to spoil a lady.'

He gave her the glimmer of a smile, his eyes not quite lifting to hers. 'If Dorothea found out I served just pastries for breakfast, she'd be beyond mad. Especially as she baked the bread fresh this morning and dropped it off on her way to the cove with Andreas.'

She smiled, her affection for the couple growing with

each passing day. 'Sounds like they have the perfect day planned.'

She only wished theirs could be just as perfect.

Pulling out the chair across from him, she sat and took up her coffee, using its familiar aroma to try and soothe her churning stomach. The elephant in the room was about to make itself known and she really didn't want it to spoil the day. Not when it had been so very perfect from the off.

She planted her elbows on the table and hid behind her cup, sneaking a peek at him beneath her lashes as he squinted out over the pool to the sea beyond. She sensed that his furrowed brow wasn't entirely down to the brightness of the sun and she didn't want to prompt him into revealing his thoughts.

He flicked her a quick look, and another. She lowered her cup to the table and touched a hand to her damp hair, suddenly self-conscious in her unmade state. For the first time she could remember, she'd skipped her morning hair and make-up routine. Not only had she been too eager to be back with him, but he'd succeeded in making her feel comfortable, beautiful, desired just the way she was, and she hadn't felt the need for her protective shield…though now she was reconsidering it as he sent her another look, his eyes narrowing.

'What is it?'

'You're not wearing any make-up.'

A blush crept into her cheeks and she tried for a nonchalant shrug. 'I thought I'd go without. You know, for a change.'

His eyes trailed over her, their depths warming with his smile. 'You don't need it.'

She gave a flustered laugh, filled with a contradictory mix of both relief and anxiety. 'You had me worried for a second.'

She was still worried…

'I mean it, Catherine, you're beautiful without all that.'

Emotion clogged up her throat, his kind words merging with those spoken during the night and making her wish this meant more, that it wasn't just a brief fling but a real, bona fide—

No, don't go there.

She picked up her fork. 'We should eat before these eggs go cold.'

'In this heat?' he murmured, knowing full well she was changing the subject.

'Humour me.'

He did but his eyes were still on her and she wet her lips, scooped up a healthy dollop of scrambled egg and popped it in her mouth. It was delicious—creamy and buttery, and *almost* the perfect distraction.

'This is tasty.' She covered her mouth as she complimented his culinary skills. Though to be fair she hadn't met a man yet who wasn't a pro when it came to scrambled, fried or omelette-style eggs. In nearly all pieces of romantic fiction, be it a book or a play or a movie, the man could always whip up a decent plate of eggs. The thought had a smile teasing at the corners of her mouth.

He eyed her suspiciously. 'What's so funny?'

'You don't want to know.'

Because she was pretty sure that if she told him what was really going through her mind, the unintended suggestion that they were living out their own romantic fairy tale right now, he'd baulk. Not that she wanted a relationship out of this. She *knew* she wouldn't get a relationship out of this. So why couldn't she let them tackle the elephant and be done with it?

Maybe because you're lying to yourself…?

He took up his coffee, sipped at it, his eyes not once releasing her from their spell. 'Try me.'

She shook her head. 'Men and eggs. It's a bit of cliché.'

'I'm a cliché?'

'Not you, per se.' She laughed at his mock wounded expression. 'But you and the cooking up of eggs—yup!'

She was pleased to see the flicker of a smile even though she knew she was about to ruin it. She couldn't eat another bite without getting the impending conversation over.

'So… I've had my coffee, we've had our fun, let's talk.'

He struggled over the mouthful of food he had just taken, and she cursed her timing. Maybe he wasn't about to destroy everything after all. Maybe if she'd just kept her mouth shut, he wouldn't have raised it at all.

'Last night was…' He leaned back in his seat, his frown deepening as he held her gaze.

'Fun?' she suggested with an easy smile—she was supposed to be an actor after all.

'That.'

'But?'

He continued to watch her, his mouth lifting to one side and creasing at the scar tissue there. She had the overwhelming urge to ask if he'd applied sunscreen. Not that he'd appreciate the mollycoddling any more than she had when he'd asked her the same.

He swallowed and looked out to sea, his fingers raking through his hair that had dried wild thanks to the rough attention of her fingers not so long ago.

'You can just come out and say it, Alaric. It was a one night only deal, it was our moment to indulge, and now we're back to…what are we exactly?'

A silent pause and then he looked at her. 'Friends?'

Her mouth parted, her body fit to burst with the overwhelming rush of warmth—Friends.

After all he'd said they couldn't be again…

Now her smile was genuine, because for all she wanted more, more of him, more of this, just more, at least he wasn't rejecting her friendship any more.

And that had to be a good thing.

A very good thing.

'Friends?' Catherine's eyes shone back at him in the late-morning sun, her smile breathtaking. 'Now there's a turn up for the books.'

Her voice was a teasing murmur and he had the over-whelming urge to take her hand and drag her back to bed. He wanted her and would go on wanting her long after she left his island. He knew it, just as well as he knew this thirst would never be quenched.

Clenching his jaw, he looked back to the ocean. Barely a ripple broke the crystal blue surface and he tried to in-stil the same sense of calm within.

'Wouldn't you say?'

And of course she would press him on it. She was the most confident, most tempting woman he had ever known.

'Yes, Catherine. I know what I said the other day. But I'm hardly the sort of man to share the last twelve hours in bed with you and declare you no one to me.'

'Lucky me.'

He gave a soft scoff. 'I'm not sure lucky is the word I would use.'

'Well, lucky for you, I'm the one using it.'

And God he was smiling, a laugh brewing as he took in her bright smile, her eyes that he'd drowned in over and over during the night…this morning too.

He'd been a fool to cross that line with her and think he could come back from it unchanged. An absolute fool.

But given his time again, would he go back and do it differently?

Hell, no. Which likely made him an even bigger fool.

He started to dig into his food, a way to keep his hands busy and her at a distance. Because he was just as hooked, just as in deep, even more so now he'd tasted her, felt that connection, felt how good they were together…how good it could be.

But they were friends, *just* friends, and he needed to get some distance between them again if he hoped to keep his heart safe and keep it that way.

CHAPTER TEN

As far as mornings-after went, Catherine deemed theirs as being rather pleasant overall. Civilised conversation, compliments exchanged, even some laughter along with an agreement that it had been fun but it wouldn't be repeated.

And the best bit—he'd declared them friends once more.

A bonus.

But five days later, she was forced to accept he'd only been saying what he thought she wanted to hear because Mr Elusive was back.

Each day he appeared less and less, in the gym, at the pool, for meals… He was ghosting her all over again and it was driving her to distraction. All the more so, because he'd *said* they were friends and she'd believed him.

She was annoyed but not so annoyed as to storm his study again. She didn't want to have to go to him. She shouldn't have to. And she refused to act needy for any man, particularly one that blew hot and cold and then ignored her so completely.

So she'd taken herself off to the trail for another run in the sun. Using the exertion and the oppressive heat to burn him out of her body and mind, not that it was working.

Thirty minutes in and she was *still* thinking about him.

Him and his smile. Him and his eyes. Him and his body and the amazing things he could do with it. More than that, she remembered the look on his face when he'd whispered all those sweet nothings to her and made love to her with— No, not made love…*had sex*.

Because making love…well, that was a different thing entirely, and she wasn't going there.

She swiped her sweat-banded wrist over her brow and turned the volume up on her earphones, using the music to drown out his voice and the images persisting in her head. She took in the beauty of her surroundings—the olive grove, the vibrant blue sea, the clear skies and the rocky path…

She was navigating a particularly uneven patch when the music cut out, replaced by her ring tone. She glanced at her watch. Kelsey. Her agent.

She slowed her pace and answered the call.

'Kelsey, what's up?'

'Are you…*exercising*? Please tell me you are, because with the way you're panting…'

She laughed and drew to a stop, hands on her hips as she sucked in a breath. 'I'm running and it's hot out here.'

'I make it four in the afternoon and you're running outdoors, in Greece, in the height of summer—are you crazy?!'

'A little.' She swiped her forehead once more, squinted against the sun as she watched a distant yacht on the water. 'What is it?'

'I've sent you an email about your press appearances prior to the launch.'

She frowned. 'And you needed to ring me because…'

'Because I need to make sure you look at it.'

'I always keep on top of my email, you know that.'

'True, but…well…'

'Spit it out, Kelsey, it's not like you to beat around the bush.'

'It's Luke.'

'What about him?'

'Well, he'll obviously be there.'

'Ye-e-es,' she drawled, her frown deepening. 'He is my co-star, so I kind of know that already.'

'I know, but—well, I—I just wanted to make sure you're going to be okay.'

'Of course I'm going to be okay, when am I not?'

'It's just with all the press reports lately, what with your mother's opinion being splashed about, coupled with—'

'Wait, back up a step. What exactly has my mother been saying?'

'You haven't seen?'

'No.'

'But it's all over social media.'

'Charlie deals with all that. I've muted my notifications.' Charlie was her PA and a great one at that. She only bothered her when she felt it strictly necessary. And anything her mother was or wasn't doing was of no interest to her.

'Right, of course she does.'

'Do I really need to know?'

'It's just your mother being your mother. She loves the attention and siding with Luke over the suggested affair brings her a *lot* of attention.'

'She's done *what*?'

She could sense Kelsey's grimace at her outburst, but it stung. And she shouldn't be surprised, she shouldn't be hurt, but she was all that and more. Her own bleeding mother!

She took a stabilising breath and another.

'Kitty?' came her agent's soft prompt.

'Luke and I are fine, Kelsey.' She softened her voice. 'It doesn't matter what my mother has said, everyone knows we don't get along and anyone that matters will take her words with a pinch of salt.'

It was the truth. The entire world knew of her estranged relationship with her parents, her mother in particular, and no one knew of the baby she'd lost. No one save for Flo and Luke, and that was the only news she couldn't bear to be made public.

'Good. That's good. It will certainly make things run smoother in front of the camera if you're both on speaking terms still.'

'We're good. We're more than good.' Luke had been incredible, trying to reassure her, trying to help her, not once blaming her for the miscarriage…but she blamed herself enough for the two of them. 'Was there anything else?'

'The red carpet launch LA—who are you taking?'

She frowned again. 'I think the plan is for Luke and I to go together?'

'Really? You want to provoke *that* discussion when the focus of the press should be on the movie and not the status of your on-off relationship.'

She thought of what Alaric had said on the very same subject. 'Any press is good press, right?'

'And what if he wants to attend with someone else?'

'Then I'll go alone.' She was frustrated now, and she knew it was coming through in her voice, her elevated heart rate not helping matters. Thoughts of Alaric helping even less.

'Why don't I ask around, see who—'

'Good God, Kelsey, I don't need a date. I'm quite capable of standing there alone.'

'But so soon after—'

'Leave it, Kelsey. Please.'

'Very well.'

'Is that everything?'

'Yes—oh, no, wait! How is the script coming along? Do you think you'll be in a position for me to start pitching it soon?'

'Hopefully.' That was the one thing going to plan this holiday. Her frustration over Alaric had given her the impetus to lose herself in the pages and the characters she'd been burning to write about for years.

'Excellent. I'll let you get back to your run, then. Just be careful in that heat, yeah? We don't need you suffering heatstroke, or worse, coming back all lobster-like and peeling…there's only so much make-up can do.'

She rolled her eyes. Heaven forbid she did something that stupid for aesthetics' sake. Never mind the cancer risks…

She could just imagine how Alaric would react if he'd overheard Kelsey…if he even came close enough to overhear a conversation again. God, he was frustrating. Caring so much in one moment and pulling a disappearing act the next.

'See ya, Kels.'

'Bye, sweetie.'

She shoved her phone back into the side pocket of her running shorts and took off at speed now. Her frustration over Alaric mounting with frustration over Hollywood and its obsession with perfection, with appearances. She wanted to scream into the wind, keep going until all she could hear was the pounding of her heart in her ears, the music and—

The ground shifted beneath her, a rock coming loose as a jarring pain shot through her ankle. 'Argh!'

She flung her hands out to soften her fall, but she was already tumbling, stone and dirt breaking the skin as she left the path and sunk into the prickly dried-out undergrowth.

Her music went dead, the squawk of the birds she'd disturbed and the trill of the insects the only answer to her cry as she squeezed her eyes shut and hissed through the pain.

Great. Just great!

Alaric stared at the screens in his study but his ability to concentrate was waning.

Waning? Who was he trying to kid…? It had been virtually non-existent since Catherine's arrival. All the more absent since their one night together… The memory alone was enough to send his body into overdrive, the ache in his chest all the more pronounced.

The ache of *guilt* he assured himself because he knew it couldn't be anything else, he wouldn't allow it to be anything else. And he was being a jerk—*again*—so he deserved all the guilt he could throw at himself.

But then he'd tried to be normal, to be a friend. He'd tried to go about his daily routine with her in sight, but every glimpse and his pulse would leap, his body would warm, and he'd smile that ridiculous impulsive smile…and he'd known he was in trouble. So much trouble.

Because he wasn't pretending to be comfortable around her, he *was* comfortable. She made him feel accepted in his own skin, his new skin, and she slotted in here.

She fitted into his life in the most perfect of ways, and the desire to keep her, to want her to stay, was getting harder to resist. She made him forget his guilt, she made him forget everything but the way she made him feel, and he knew that was wrong, so very wrong.

And so he'd avoided temptation altogether. In all likelihood she would detest him by the time this trip was over and then—

'Kyrios de Vere!' The door to his study burst open and

a flushed Dorothea appeared, her hands gesturing frantically. 'Come quick.'

He frowned, launching himself out of his seat and striding towards her. 'What is it?'

'It's Miss Wilde. She's had a fall, a nasty one.'

He cursed under his breath, his pulse spiking as he followed her out. 'Where is she?'

'Andreas is helping her back. He phoned ahead asking me to get you.'

'*Back?* Where's she been?'

'Running.'

He cursed again, felt the heat of the late-afternoon sun beat down on him as they emerged from the house and took a right, to the start of the trail, and… His chest contracted. There she was, hobbling, her arm hooked around Andreas' shoulders for support, her entire body covered in dirt, her running bra and shorts offering no protection at all. She was cut, grazed, her face, her knee, her ankle…

Another stifled curse and he was racing forward, the emotions he'd been working so hard to suppress rising with such force they were choking up his chest.

'What am I going to do with you?' He loomed over her and she glared at him, at least that's what he thought it was meant to be, but the small cut to her lip made it more of a pout and the hiss she gave told him the effort had cost her.

'I'm fine, thanks for asking.' She stared straight ahead. 'You can go back to your work.'

Andreas gave him a look and he stepped in. 'I'll take her.'

'You. Will. *Not*.' She hobbled back, her eyes glistening as she spoke, her rejection cutting deep, but he had to help her. He *had* to.

Closing the distance she'd created, he swept her up in his arms.

'Alaric!' She shoved against him. 'Put me down this second!'

'Quit it, princess.'

It was hurting her to speak. It was hurting him to see her in pain. Why did he feel like even this fall was his fault?

She harrumphed, folding her arms, her body tense in his hold, but at least she wasn't pushing him away now. He snuck a peek. She looked mutinous. Her eyes shooting darts in the direction of an innocent Dorothea as she hurried towards them.

'She's sprained her ankle, I think,' Andreas said to Dorothea. 'She'll need to get it raised and get some ice on it too.'

She nodded as she fell into step beside them, tutting away. 'I knew all this running out here was a bad thing.'

You and me both.

He gritted his teeth, his jaw pulsing with the effort not to say it as Andreas ran ahead to hold open the front door. He strode on in and headed for the stairs.

'I'll take her down to the bedroom. She'll need cleaning up. Can you bring the first aid kit, Dorothea? The ice pack and a glass of water too.' He looked down at her sweat- and dirt-stained face, feeling her pain like a crushing force within. 'Did you not even take a drink with you?'

She flicked him a look that quite accurately depicted the middle finger gesture and he bit back a relieved laugh. Feisty as ever.

'You can hate me all you like, but I'm not leaving you until I know you're okay.'

She mumbled something incoherent under her breath, but before he could ask, she started to tremble in his hold—shock. He held her tighter, wishing he could do more.

'Bring me a whisky too, Andreas.'

The man's brows hit the ceiling.

'It's not for me,' he explained, though he had a feeling he'd be wanting one too, very soon.

Andreas nodded and raced ahead as Dorothea branched off to the kitchen.

'This really isn't necessary,' Catherine grumbled through her teeth that were now chattering incessantly.

'I'll be the judge of that.'

'Dorothea and Andreas are more than capable of taking care of me.'

'You're my guest, you've got hurt on my watch. I'll be the one taking care of you.'

'So now I'm your guest.' She shook her head, grunted. 'You're the most confusing, contradictory man I've ever met!'

'And you're the most frustrating and stubborn woman, so I reckon we're even.'

She glared up at him. 'If you weren't carrying me down concrete steps right now, I'd… I'd…'

'What? Slap me?' He gave her an amused look that only riled her further. 'It's a good job I'm carrying you, then.'

Another emphatic harrumph and then she rested her head against his shoulder, and he forgot the reason she was in his arms, he forgot the reason he'd been hiding out, he forgot everything but the feel of her. The sense that she felt so right there, curled up against him, his arms around her, protecting her…

'I have it all,' Dorothea called down the stairs, her footsteps quick to follow as she hurried after them.

'And I have the whisky, two glasses too, just in case,' Andreas said, joining them.

'Thank you.' Alaric strode into the bedroom, making for the bed.

'You can't put me on there like this.' She started to wriggle against him. 'I'll ruin the sheets.'

He ignored her, placing her down as gently as he could. 'Dorothea, fetch a bowl with fresh water and ice please.'

'Of course.' She placed the items she'd brought down on the side table and left to get the rest.

'Do you want me to pour?' Andreas held up the whisky and glasses.

'No, it's fine. I can take it from here.'

He placed them on the side table. 'Is there anything else I can get?'

'Not right now. I'll call if we need anything.'

He nodded and looked back at Catherine, his face creased up with concern. 'You're in good hands, Miss Wilde.'

She gripped her arms around her middle and gave him a watery smile. 'Thank you, Andreas. For everything.'

Dorothea came bustling in with a bowl, cloths and a towel, placing them down on the foot of the bed. 'Right, let's get you cleaned up.'

Alaric touched a hand to hers. 'It's okay, I've got this.'

'Well, I'm not sure if…' She looked at Catherine and back at him, her hesitation obvious, and he gave her a smile.

'I'm quite capable, I promise.'

'Well, okay, if Miss Wilde is happy.'

Catherine didn't look happy, folded up like she was, knees bent, her head dropped forward, but as she looked up at Dorothea, she gave her a nod and managed another smile.

'Very well, call if you need anything else.'

'We will.' He watched her leave with Andreas, waiting for the door to close before looking back to Catherine and then the whisky. He uncorked the bottle and poured a small measure in both. 'Here, take a sip—it'll help with the shock.'

'I'm not—'

He stared her refusal down, shoving the drink into her hand and grasping her other to place both around the glass. 'You are. You're shaking.'

Dubiously, she eyed both him and the drink but took a disgruntled sip, wincing as the alcohol caught the cut in her lip.

'Is this you making up for the fact you've barely been near me since the other night?'

He reached over her and took up the spare pillows, careful not to knock her as he did so and planting them midway down the bed.

He took the glass from her hands. 'Lay back.'

She didn't move, just looked at him expectant. Waiting for the answer he wasn't going to give.

'Come on, Catherine, you need to get that ankle elevated and iced… Unless you want to find yourself immobile for even longer.'

Her lashes fluttered, the internal debate clear in her glistening blues but eventually, she lay back and gingerly lifted her leg into his awaiting hands. He looked at her ankle, the swelling already apparent near the bone, and fought to keep his expression blank.

'I'm just going to take your trainers off. Let me know if I hurt you.'

She scoffed and he flicked her a quick look. She wasn't scoffing about the potential pain from the sprain, she was scoffing about the pain he'd already inflicted.

'I'm sorry I've not—' carefully he unthreaded the lace on her trainer, loosening off the straps '—been around much.'

'Avoiding me, more like.'

He lifted the heel of her trainer, his other hand holding her calf steady and taking the weight. 'I guess.'

'You avoiding me warrants an *"I guess,"* not a denial, an extra apology.' She cursed.

He knew she was lashing out and why. She had good reason. He was the one in the wrong and she deserved an answer, an explanation. 'If I said I needed some distance between us, would it make you feel any better?'

She frowned. At least she'd stopped shivering but the way she was looking at him now was worse. Like she could see him for what he was—a fool, a man who knew she was too good for him, would always be too good for him, and yet cared for her anyway.

He focused on her foot instead, slowly easing the trainer away and lowering her leg to the pillows. He checked to make sure her ankle was higher than her heart and then removed her other trainer and sock. All the while he could feel her watching him, her curiosity mounting.

'You know, it's just a sprain. I can take it from here.'

'Not until I have you cleaned up. Your cuts need tending to.'

He took up the ice pack Dorothea had brought and curved it around her injury, trying not to wince when she did but feeling it all the same.

'Sorry,' he murmured when she gave a sharp gasp.

'*That's* not your fault.'

No, she was right there too.

'You can go now, Alaric, please.' Her eyes glistened with fresh tears—tears he knew she was refusing to let fall. 'I'm not some child who needs looking after. I can clean myself up.'

He wasn't leaving. If he had his way, free of the accident, free of the guilt, he'd never leave her. Ignoring her protests, he wrung the cloth in the bowl of clean water and brought it to the knee closest to him.

She hissed, her eyes watering all the more, her glare evident behind the tears. 'Please, Alaric, you're going to ruin the bedding too.'

'Do you think I care a damn about the bedding, Catherine?!' He shot her a fierce stare, knowing his inner torment was written in his face, in the thickness to his voice. 'Just lie still.'

He turned and picked up the whisky. 'Here, have some more. It'll help.'

She didn't move, her eyes mistrustful and tearing him apart.

'Please, Catherine, let me take care of you.'

She took a shaky breath, her lashes lowering as she reached out for the glass.

'Thank you.'

It came out so quiet and the tension between his shoulder blades eased. The relief in his heart so very evident.

He rinsed the cloth as she took a sip and gave another wince.

She touched a finger to the cut and cringed. 'I must look a sight.'

He looked at her, really looked, and he couldn't say what he truly thought. That even with a fat lip on the rise, bloody and wounded, she still looked beautiful. Beautiful and vulnerable, and it was a lethal mix to his defences.

He took her hand from her face, touched the cloth to her lip and tried to ignore the way it made him feel, the way she watched him beneath lashes that clung together with her tears and tried to understand him.

'It's a clean cut at least…' His voice was thick, raw, as raw as his heart felt. 'But I think you'll have a lump there for a few days.'

He reached for an ice cube from the tray Dorothea had

brought and wrapped it in a small cloth. 'Here, hold this over it.'

She didn't baulk, just placed her glass down and lay back into the pillows, her eyes to the ceiling as she held the wrapped ice to her lip, her other hand resting on her bare torso. Carefully, he tended to every cut, every graze, the tension in her entire body giving away her continued pain and discomfort.

By the time he'd finished, she looked ready to sleep, and as he brushed her hair back from her eyes, he gave her a small smile.

'I'll send for Dorothea and she can help you change. You look like you could do with some sleep.'

Her brows drew together, her blue eyes swirling with so many questions, so much emotion, he could feel her reaching inside him, silencing his voice, immobilising his body...

And then she blinked and looked away. 'Thank you for taking care of me.'

It was a whisper, so sad and defeated, and he wanted to reach for her, to say anything, do anything, to make it all better. But where did he even begin?

The problems were his, not hers.

'Just go, Alaric. Please.'

Fresh tears welled in the corners of her eyes and he fought the urge to wipe them away. He wanted to climb on the bed, pull her to him, whisper all the sweet nothings raging in his head, his heart, and hold her safe.

And it was that deep-rooted need that had him clearing up the debris and striding for the door. 'Call if you need anything. Dorothea will be straight down.'

'Not you. Got it.'

He could just make out the words said under her breath and forced himself to keep moving and not look back because he knew if he did he would cave. And he'd only end up confusing their relationship more, hurting her even more in the process.

And above all, he wanted to protect her, even if that meant protecting her from his messed-up self.

CHAPTER ELEVEN

CATHERINE LIFTED HER gaze from her laptop to see Dorothea crossing the poolside, straight for her. *Uh-oh, here we go.*

She lifted the brim of her straw hat and lowered the lid of her laptop to smile at the woman in the hope of softening whatever admonishment was coming and wondered what it was this time. She wasn't putting weight on her three-day-old injury and she was lathered in sunblock. She was being a good patient and she was getting some actual writing done. All was good with the world…well, almost.

'Your shoulder, Miss Wilde, it is in the sun!'

She looked to the left, to the right. Sure enough the sun had moved just enough to expose the tip of her shoulder, but she'd been so engrossed in her script she hadn't noticed.

'Oops, I'll just…' She shifted the laptop, made to rise, and Dorothea practically squeaked.

'You stay right there!'

The woman was already at her side, tilting the parasol to cover all of her once more.

'Maybe it is time you came inside?'

'I like it out here—the view is inspiring and it helps me to focus.' She'd been out there most of the day, the pool taunting her just a bit as she craved a decent swim, but three days into her injury, it was still too tender.

'Is there anything I can get for you?'

She gave Dorothea a smile. 'A new ankle?'

'Aah.' Dorothea's eyes softened, her smile full of sympathy. 'It'll be as good as new before you know it…so long as you continue to rest it properly.' The last she added in that matronly manner of hers and Catherine could feel her cheeks blaze.

Guilty as charged…

She'd been caught at least a dozen times already, trying to go about her day as normal, and each time she'd earned herself a stern ticking off from Dorothea or Andreas, even the distant glare from Alaric the one time he'd caught her trying some very early morning yoga. Very early because she'd hoped to avoid being caught. Yoga because there was nothing much else she could put her body through, and she was an exercise addict. She had to be. Her metabolism alone didn't keep her this trim.

'I'm trying, I just hate being so idle.'

'Me too, so I understand, but still, rest—*nai*?'

'Nai.'

'Now, lunch—what can I get you?'

'I'm fine. I'm still full from breakfast.'

She eyed her sceptically. 'Fruit and yogurt is not enough for the whole day.'

'I'll get something later if I'm hungry.'

'You said the same yesterday.'

'I wasn't hungry.'

'And the day before.'

She frowned up at her. 'I wasn't then either.'

Dorothea tutted under her breath. 'You'll waste away.'

Hardly. Though she kept the thought to herself. No exercise meant no calorie burn, which in turn meant weight gain. She'd already gained enough during her time on the island thanks to Dorothea's fabulous cooking and she couldn't risk any more. She had a red carpet movie premiere just around the corner and a dress that was made to fit like a glove. She absolutely could *not* put more weight on.

'I'm fine, honestly.'

Dorothea nodded but the severity in her expression didn't lift. 'You call if you need something bringing out. You're not to climb those stairs, understood?'

Her heart warmed in her chest as she stared up at the woman who treated her more like a caring mother than her own ever had and a genuine smile touched her lips, along with the surprising prick of tears.

Perhaps the emotional turmoil of the past year was catching up with her—*and perhaps you're more hurt by Alaric's avoidance of you than you care to admit?*

'Understood, Miss Wilde?'

She swallowed, refocusing on Dorothea. 'Perfectly… Thank you.'

'You're welcome.'

She watched her go, her mind awash with all that had happened since her arrival. She could see why Alaric chose to stay here. He wasn't as alone as she'd first feared, as alone as his sister and family believed him to be. Dorothea, Andreas, even Marsel, were more like family than staff. Aside from their respectful forms of address, they cared for him and vice versa.

They cared for her too. It was obvious in their warm brown eyes that lit up with their laughter, softened with their compassion and narrowed when they were cross with her for pushing her body too far too quickly. Yes, even when they were giving her a ticking off, she knew it came from a good place.

She shook her head and opened her laptop fully again, ready to get stuck into the adventures of her heroine, Maisy, once more. At least the script was going well. Having bed rest forced upon her meant there wasn't much else she could do to fill her time. And now she had a thorny plot issue to fix. How to get Maisy from the—

'Catherine! What the hell is wrong with you?'

Her eyes snapped up, the man striding towards her immediately dominating her vision and setting her pulse racing. Did he *have* to be so goddamn sexy *all* the time?

'Good afternoon to you too, Alaric.'

He shook his head, pausing at the foot of her sunbed, his hands fisted on his hips, his white tee straining across his chest…did he own T-shirts in any other colour because she'd yet to see him in one. Black would look good, maybe a soft grey…

'I'm kind of busy working so if you have something to say, just come out and say it and then we can both go back to our jobs.' She smiled sweetly. He was, after all, the one who was always too busy to spend any real time with her. The least she could do was return the favour.

'Dorothea says you're not eating properly.'

'Dorothea is worrying unnecessarily.'

He crossed his arms. 'So, you haven't been skipping lunch and surviving on fruit and yogurt all day.'

'No, I've eaten dinner too.'

'According to Dorothea you're only eating a fraction of what she serves up.'

Heat started to unfurl deep within her gut, and it wasn't the good kind. 'Alaric, you're not my moth—' She stalled. Her mother wouldn't care, her mother would be pleased that she was starving herself because she couldn't exercise it off. 'You're not the boss of me, you don't get to come out here and give me a ticking off.'

'I'm not giving you a ticking off.'

Her brows nudged the rim of her straw hat.

'Okay, I am. I'm just… I'm concerned, Catherine.'

'Well, don't be. Now if you don't mind…' Pointedly, she went back to her screen, though tuning him out was nowhere near as easy. Even his cologne reached her now, its rich woody scent teasing at the fire inside that was supposed to be all anger. Only it wasn't. And hell, that served to frustrate her more.

'Where would you like me to put it?'

Dorothea? She peered around him to see the woman returning with a tray of…

'Alaric!' She glared up at him. 'I said I was fine.'

'Tough, we're having a late lunch together.'

'We are not.'

'We *are*—' He broke off, looked away as he raked his fingers through his hair and took a breath before coming back to her, the effort to compose himself obvious. 'Sorry. Please, will you come and have some food with me?'

'Why?'

'Because I'd like to spend time with you.'

She laughed, the sound practically delirious. Did he really think she would cave that easily? That she would believe him even?

'Please, Catherine. I've been an arse, but I'm worried about you. I'm not going to force you to eat if you don't want to, but I would like to spend a little time together.'

'You would?' It sounded as dubious as she felt.

'Yes.'

'So, it's not because you want to make sure I eat something.'

'Can't it be both?'

She studied him intently, feeling her heart flutter in her chest as she saw how much he cared and remembered that he didn't, because he couldn't get away from her fast enough most days.

'I've missed your company.'

It was a raw confession, honest even to her dubious ears, and it cost him to admit it, but it cost her heart more. 'Okay.'

The beginnings of a smile flickered around his mouth, the sexy fullness to that lower lip, the dip in the middle of the top…if she closed her eyes, she'd remember how it felt to kiss them too. She'd also remember how he'd looked at her, with passion and something so much deeper blazing in those blue eyes, something that they hinted at right now.

'Thank you.' His smile widened and he turned to Dorothea. 'The table outside the bedroom is perfect. It's in the shade.'

She closed her laptop and set it down, swinging her legs over the edge of the bed. She shouldn't have agreed, she should have made him suffer like she had, but having him concerned for her made her feel…it made her feel too much.

She pushed herself up and limped forward.

'Oh, no, you don't.' He was by her side in an instant.

'I can walk! Granted, it's awkward but I can manage.'

'What's the point when I'm here to carry you?'

'Whoa, whoa, whoa…' She shook her head, waved him down. 'Help is one thing. Carrying me is—'

Too late, she was already up against his chest and it shouldn't feel good. It really, really shouldn't. But there was something about his strength surrounding her, the warmth of his body against hers…she gave an involuntary little shiver as she revelled in it.

'Are you—*cold*?' He eyed her incredulously.

'Don't be ridiculous.'

Her cheeks flamed and she pinned her hat in place as she hid behind its brim, her inability to act around him making them burn ever deeper. She was Kitty Wilde, an award-winning performer, but with Alaric she was Catherine. There was no facade, no act, just her…exposed, raw and utterly susceptible to him.

Maybe that was the problem.

She was herself…she couldn't hide.

No matter how much he pushed her away.

Alaric only had himself to blame. He was the one that had insisted on picking Catherine up, holding her to him, feeling the connection between them pulse and grow.

He'd been the one determined to step in as one look at Dorothea's face when she'd returned from the poolside to report the exact same news—Catherine isn't eating properly—had urged him to his feet, ready to do battle. Ready to throttle her mother too, but that was an age-old anger, an age-old fight he'd never been able to have outright.

But this, he could.

He glanced down to see her still tucked behind the brim of her straw hat and his frown deepened. Already she'd lost weight, and that wasn't healthy. You didn't lose weight that quickly unless you were sick or on some unsustainable diet. And it was most definitely the latter.

He lowered her onto a seat at the table. 'Are you comfortable? Do you want me to get another chair to raise your ankle?'

She shook her head without looking up. 'No, I'll be fine. It's been elevated plenty this morning.'

'When did you last ice it?'

'About an hour ago.'

'Would you like me to get—'

'Enough, Alaric!' Her eyes shot to his. 'Please sit down and stop fussing.'

He did as she bade, his frown unmoving though.

'So, this is what it takes to get some attention from you? A fall and a busted ankle?'

He set a plate before her and started dishing up the Greek salad Dorothea had prepared and gave her a smile full of forced tease. 'A bit extreme, wouldn't you say?'

'Don't flatter yourself. I certainly didn't do this on purpose.'

'No? I'm not so sure.' He continued with the teasing, desperate to lighten the mood and not get caught up in the look in her eye, the proximity of her bikini-clad body, the kimono she favoured doing nothing to conceal every inch of her appealing body.

'Funny, Alaric, very funny.'

He started slicing off a piece of fresh baked bread.

'No bread for me,' she rushed out.

'But it's still warm from the oven, you'll love it.'

'I'll love it too much, that's the problem.'

He shook his head at her. 'That makes no sense.'

He cut it anyway and placed it on a plate beside her salad. 'In case you change your mind.'

He served himself too, discreetly watching as she took a bite of salad and chewed it over, her eyes on the ocean. How did he broach it with her? It wasn't healthy not to eat, but at the same time, who was he to judge her, to criticise. She was right to say it wasn't his place and yet…

'Stop it.' Her eyes were still on the view.

'Stop what?'

'Stop looking at me like that.'

'I'm not looking at you like anything.'

'Right?' Now she turned to him, her brows drawn together. 'So, you're not judging me, then?'

'If you think I'm judging you, then it suggests you believe I have cause to.'

She shook her head, her lips twitching as she forked up more salad.

'I get that it's hard for you right now,' he tried softly, 'not being able to stick to your workout regime and—'

'What would you know of it?'

'I know you spend almost as many hours keeping active in some way as you do not.'

'And how would you know that when I hardly see you around?'

'I know, Catherine.'

'What?' Her laugh was harsh. 'Do you have cameras dotted about, keeping an eye on me? Is this actually a heavily guarded fortress and you use those computer screens of yours to watch the island's movements?'

'Stop trying to deflect.'

'I'm not.' She dropped her fork. 'Okay, I am. But I don't want to talk about my exercise and eating habits. What I want to talk about is you. I want to talk about Flo and the fact you're going to be an uncle. I want to talk about you coming back to the UK for a visit.'

His blood ran cold, her quick-fire change in focus making his stomach roll. 'We agreed not to talk about it.'

'We agreed not to talk about a lot of things, and I consider my diet very much out of bounds.'

'Your *diet* isn't sensible.'

Her cheeks flared, her lack of make-up making every flush far more evident, every expression far more pure and real, reaching under his skin, right to the very heart of him. He fisted his hand on the table, urging it all away.

'My *diet* is logical. If I'm not exercising, I'm cutting the calories I take in.'

'There's cutting what you consume and then there's not eating. You're inching towards the latter.'

'I'm eating now.'

'Only because I made you.'

'You *encouraged* me. You can't make me do anything I wouldn't do of my own accord.'

His chest eased a little. 'Good…but you can't deny that you love Dorothea's bread, and one slice isn't going to hurt you.'

'A moment on the lips, a lifetime on the hips,' she sing-songed.

'And now you sound like your mother.'

She paled in an instant.

'Hey.' He frowned. 'I was joking.'

'No, you weren't.'

'Well, can you blame me?' There was no use denying it—he'd been joking to an extent but what he'd said was true. 'She used to say it to you all the time. Family barbecues, weddings, birthday parties… If she even caught you looking at dessert, out it came.'

'Yeah, well, she was right to an extent.'

'Why was she right? Why do you have to worry about it so much?'

'Are you really asking me that when you know what I do for a living?'

'And what about body positivity? I thought that was all the rage now.'

'It's Hollywood, Alaric, it'll never change.'

'It will if the people within it change.'

She stared at him for a long moment and he started to think he was getting through to her, making a difference. 'Be that as it may, I still have to get into my designer dress for a movie premiere in a month's time. If I put on even the slightest bit of weight it won't fit.'

'So, get a new dress, you can afford it.'

'It's not that simple,' she choked out with a laugh. 'Do you know how in demand fashion designers are? We're booked in months in advance for the perfect outfit. It doesn't get thrown on last minute.'

He shrugged. 'Your fans, the press, they want to see you, the person in the dress. What does it matter what designer you're wearing, other than the fact you're putting money in their pockets by promoting their wares? Now there's an idea—you could go to an unknown for an outfit, elevate them to your level, rather than throwing money into the same few pockets.'

She tilted her head to the side. 'That's an idea I actually like, but still…even an unknown doesn't pull something off last minute.'

'Then you wear something off the hanger.'

Another choked laugh. 'Absolutely not.'

'Why?'

'Because it's not the done thing.'

'So what?'

'You really don't get it, do you?'

'Oh, I get it. But what it tells me is that all that talk about you not seeing me for this—' he ran the back of his fingers down his scarred cheek '—but who I am inside is bull.'

She frowned at him, her head shaking, her hand reaching out. 'That's totally different and you know it.'

'Do I, Catherine? Because if I listen to you right now, if I look at your actions over the last few days, the eating like a bird, testing your foot long before it's healed, your desperation to keep up appearances, it all becomes a lie. Ultimately, *you* care. Ultimately, it's all about how one looks.'

'In Hollywood, yes. But it's not me.'

'Right, Hollywood.' His laugh was harsh. 'And you and Hollywood are two separate entities.'

'Yes.' She shook her head. 'No. You're twisting my words.'

'You're beautiful, Catherine.'

'See!' She thrust a hand at him. 'Now you're just proving my point!'

'No, I'm not.'

'You are! Telling me I'm beautiful. It doesn't come easy. I work hard to keep myself looking like this. I deprive myself of the foods I like, I work out, I... I...'

She stopped as he shook his head. 'You're beautiful on the inside, Catherine.'

Her laugh was more a scoff. 'That old cliché.'

'Cliché?' He frowned at her, knowing full well he had her. 'But isn't that what you were trying to tell me the other day? That you, my family, they don't see me for my scars, they see who I am underneath?'

Her lips parted but no words emerged.

'Or did I misunderstand?'

'Of course you didn't,' she said softly, folding her hands in her lap. 'I meant everything I said.'

'Just like I meant everything I said in bed the other night, when I told you what I thought of you.'

She opened her mouth, closed it again, pursed it off to the side as she looked to the ocean once more, but he could sense the cogs were turning, that she was processing all he had said. That he had effectively used her own words against her. And it was risky to bring that night up again, the connection they'd shared coming to the surface, but this was more important than the protective wall around his heart.

'Okay. Okay. You win. I get what you're saying. My problem is that Hollywood is my home, not literally but in terms of my career it is.'

'And look what it did to your mother?'

She flicked him a look and he was surprised to see the hint of tears welling, her mother evoking such a deep reaction once more.

'You know how hard I've tried not to become her? That every day it's there as a mantra and still…' She shook her head. 'She creeps in, you know. But I wanted to be an actor. I wanted… I thought I could do it and avoid her mistakes…'

'You were always one for the stage. I don't think you would have been happy doing anything else.'

'Maybe.'

She looked so lost in her own world that he started to regret even pushing her as far as he had, but he wanted her to see it, needed her to see it. 'Honestly, Catherine. So what if you gain a few pounds? So what if you wear a dress off the hanger, or something from an unknown? You're still you. You're still the person who brings characters to life on the big screen, brings joy to people's lives—tears, sadness, happiness.'

The flicker of a smile crossed her lips. 'I'd like to be seen as more than that though, more than beauty over brains. I want to be the creator behind the scenes, I want to write the words that inspire such passion, I want to do more.'

He smiled in the face of her strength, her dream. 'And you will. I meant it when I said you put your mind to something, it happens.'

'I wish I could bottle you.'

He chuckled, feeling the tension in the air lift. 'I'm not sure I'd like that.'

'I would, then I could uncork you every time I doubted myself.'

She smiled at him, and for a second, time stood still, the world fell away. If only things were different, if only the accident hadn't happened, if only their worlds were compatible…

And then she lowered her gaze to the plate with the

slither of bread he had cut and took it up. 'It does look lovely.'

'You don't have to eat it,' he assured her. 'I just didn't want you to deprive yourself because you think it will in some way go against you.'

She laughed softly. 'It is just a piece of bread after all.'

'Hey, not just any bread. Dorothea will be down here with the rolling pin if she hears you say that.'

He offered her the small bowl of olive oil and balsamic vinegar to dip it in and watched as she scooped it to her mouth, her hum of appreciation making him want to groan too.

She chewed it over, catching a little drop from her chin with her finger and licking it clean. 'You know what this means though?'

He was so caught in the movement of her finger, her lips, it took a second for him to register what she had said.

'What's that?'

'You owe me a talk about home.'

Silently, he cursed. He'd walked straight into it, but…

'Lucky we have plenty of days left for that.'

'Is this you saying you're done hiding away?'

He gave her a tight smile. 'I don't really have a choice if I'm to make sure you rest that ankle properly and eat sensibly.'

'Ah…' She tore a piece of bread off and popped it into her mouth, her twinkling blues giving the impression of a gleeful child. 'So true.'

Tiny flutters erupted deep within his gut. 'I'm beginning to think you really did do this on purpose.'

'You'll never know, Alaric… I am an exceptional actor after all.'

He almost glanced at her ankle to double-check it was most definitely bruised and stopped himself. It was enough to still see the cut healing on her bottom lip…another part of her anatomy he really shouldn't look at but for a very different reason.

'Very funny, princess.'

CHAPTER TWELVE

CATHERINE SQUINTED OVER at Alaric sitting at the table outside her room, a book in hand, while she lounged under the parasol with her laptop. As promised, he'd spent nearly every waking hour within viewing distance, rarely getting close enough to provoke the persistent chemistry between them, but close enough to keep his eye on her.

And her, him.

She loved watching him unawares, free to look her fill without him knowing, free to take in the unguarded expression on his face. Over the past few days, she'd found herself doing it more and more, as though she was trying to imprint the memory in her brain so that when she left this place, she'd remember this moment and all the others.

And she hadn't given up hope yet of coaxing him off the island. Flo had messaged that morning to ask how it was going and she'd given her an honest answer—things were improving.

Because they were.

She hadn't told her that the reason was down to an injury she'd sustained, and it had forced him out of hiding. Flo didn't need to know that. And with her friend's pregnancy hormones she'd only go into over-protective mode and hop on a plane herself, a luxury she could readily afford, especially as she'd taken early maternity leave due to the concerns over her blood pressure. And she didn't want to be aggravating that either. So no, she told her everything was in hand and that she was slowly working her magic.

Magic which she really needed to be getting on with. She caught her lower lip in her teeth as she pondered her opening line…she didn't want to spoil the common ground they had found. A way to co-exist without him fleeing.

But she had less than a fortnight to change his mind.

'Out with it.'

She jumped at his low command, issued into the pages of his book.

'Beg your pardon.'

She felt her cheeks flush as he lifted his head, her breath catching as his piercing blue eyes met with hers, heating her from across the distance. 'I reckon you've been watching me for at least a chapter.'

'I have n—' His brows nudged up, a small smile playing about his lips, and she quit her denial, closing her laptop with aplomb. 'I fancy a swim.'

'You sure that's wise?'

'I won't know until I try.' She swung her feet to the ground and sat up. 'Could you help me to the pool, please?'

He watched her slip the kimono from her shoulders and she made sure to draw out the move as she spied the pulse working in his jaw. No, they definitely hadn't lost the spark. If anything, it had intensified with each passing day as they remained in one another's company and tried to fight it, to deny it.

'Of course.'

Closing the book, a thriller judging by the cover, he got to his feet and averted his gaze as he approached. She wondered if his heart was now racing in tune with hers, anticipation of their closing proximity making it hard to think straight.

She stood before he reached her, testing her weight on her ankle and finding it wasn't so painful if she was careful.

'It's not too—*oh*!' He'd wrapped an arm around her bare waist, taking her weight and making her insides thrum in one.

'You were saying?'

She wet her lips and looked up at him. If she was honest, she wasn't quite sure any more. His touch had done its usual task of clearing her head of all thought. And she should be used to it with him helping her everywhere and no longer avoiding her. But there was no getting used to the force of their attraction, or the way his eyes seemed to penetrate her very soul when he looked at her like he was now.

'I was saying…' She looked down and eased her foot forward, using him for support as they made their way to the pool edge. 'It's not too bad today.'

'Good.'

A breeze caught the brim of her hat, blowing it free, and her hand shot up, but he beat her to it, grabbing it and bringing his body around, his front facing hers as he caught both her and her hat and…*oh, my.*

She was pressed right up against his chest, his hand clutching the hat to her back, his other arm locked around her waist.

'Perhaps it's best we leave the hat here.' His voice was thick, low, and he made no attempt to move, no attempt to ease the closeness, to lift the moment.

She nodded, not wanting to risk anything else. Was he going to kiss her? He *looked* like he was going to kiss her…especially as his gaze fell to her mouth, the blue of his eyes drowned out by the lascivious dark and sending an excited jolt straight through her core. 'How's your lip?'

'It's—it's feeling much better,' she breathed, her tongue sweeping briefly across the said body part, easing its sudden dryness while teasing him too.

'Good…' It vibrated through him, his arms flexing around her.

'Alaric?'

He shook his head. 'Don't.'

A frown touched her brow. 'You don't know what I was going to say.'

'I can see it in your face.'

'And I can see it in yours.'

He shook his head. 'You're impossible.'

She gave the smallest of laughs, making her body vibrate against his. '*I'm* the impossible one.'

She could tell he was fighting a grin, could tell he was fighting the pull between them too, but he twisted to toss her hat onto the bed and tugged her towel over it to stop it blowing away. 'Come on, you said you wanted a dip.'

She wanted so many things in that moment and a dip definitely wasn't one of them.

It didn't matter if it was wise, or sensible, she wanted him. And the more time they spent together, the more the connection between them swelled and the more she felt his barriers fall.

She let him lower her to the edge of the pool and she did the rest, enjoying the cool water on her flushed skin as she looked up at him. 'You going to join me?'

'Are you going to behave?'

'Hardly.'

And then he laughed, the sound so glorious, so easy, so different to how he'd been when she'd first arrived, and hope bloomed warm inside her chest. Hope that she could convince him there was more to life than just his island, that he did deserve to live, really live…

She watched as he stripped his T-shirt and tossed it aside, dropping into the water beside her, his eyes finding hers both wary and warm. She reached for his hand and pulled him towards her, saying nothing as she closed the distance between them.

If she didn't try, she wouldn't get…

His eyes fell to her mouth and she did the same, her intent clear, hope soaring as he didn't pull away, hope soaring even more as she reached up, a hand sliding into his hair, her mouth sweeping against his…

'Catherine, this isn't a good idea.'

'It feels like a very good idea.' She dragged the words against his lips, felt his breath shudder through him, heard the groan deep within his chest, and then he was lifting her against him. Hard muscle against pliant flesh. He forked his hand through her hair, tugging her head back to deepen the kiss, his tongue delving and tangling with hers. It was explosive. Like a switch had gone off inside him, inside her…

The water sloshed around them as he backed her up to the wall of the pool, her legs wrapped around his hips, the heat within enough to contend with the sun blazing down.

He tore his mouth away, sucked in a breath as he pressed his forehead to hers, his hands deep within her hair. 'I've wanted to do that for days.'

'You *should* have done.'

He shook his head, his eyes searing hers. 'This can only get messy, Catherine. I don't want to hurt you. I don't.'

'Who's getting hurt? Not me? I'm not asking for a future. I'm not asking for more than my stay here. And I'd much rather spend it like this than constantly fighting it.'

She kissed him to add to her point, kissed him deeper to convince him, kissed him until he was kissing her back harder and more fiercely than she…then she tore her mouth away. 'Now tell me you want to fight this.'

'Hell, no, we're going to bed.'

What is the definition of insanity?

His mind pushed the question as they lay on the bed, naked. A white sheet drawn to the waist, his arm wrapped around her as she lay her head on his shoulder, her leg entwined with his.

The perfect moment.

Aside from the uneven beat to his heart as he considered the answer, knowing full well he was the very epitome of it.

Doing the same thing over and over again and expecting a different result…

In his case, succumbing to the chemistry between them again and not expecting the mark she left on him to grow.

Though maybe it wasn't insanity at all, maybe it was stupidity, because he knew where this would lead. He knew he was falling in deeper and deeper with her. He knew he'd have to fight harder to fend off the belief that this was possible, real, a relationship with a future.

'What are you thinking about?' She snuggled in closer, her head tilting up as her eyes searched out his.

He met her gaze with a smile that not even his worries could quash. 'I'm wondering how soon we can go again.'

'Liar.' She nudged him softly with her hip. 'Though I do approve of your answer.'

He chuckled, his fingers caressing her side as he looked back to the ceiling. He could quite happily lie there for the rest of the day, the week even—work, food, be damned.

'Can I ask you something?'

The loaded question pulled his body taut…so much for being content. 'Of course.'

'Why don't you paint any more?'

She shifted her head to eye the brightly coloured canvas above the bed. 'You're so talented.'

'Was. I *was* talented.'

She frowned at him. 'And you can't paint now?'

'I can't paint, I can't draw, I can't sketch.' He flexed his fingers on her hip, felt the constant tightness there. 'Not like I used to.'

She lowered her gaze to his hand, turned it over. Her fingers delicate as she traced the scar there. 'Have you tried recently?'

'No.' It came out gruff, partly with the pain she'd stirred up, and partly with the shiver her caress triggered.

'From where I'm lying, they still feel pretty talented to me.' She lifted his hand to her lips, kissed his palm softly. 'You should try again.'

He was about to refuse when she looked up at him. 'What does it matter if the work you produce has changed, it doesn't make it any less. You enjoyed it because it felt good for you to create, you enjoyed that time with just you and your canvas. The number of times I would visit when we were kids and you would be in a flurry of creativity, with that wild look in your eye. Almost like a mad professor.'

'A mad what?' He was laughing but this was news to him.

'You know, the nutty professor look—crazy hair, even crazier eyes?'

'Oh, cheers. Very attractive.'

She gave a dainty shrug, her smile small. 'I quite liked the look on you.'

He shook his head, pulled her in closer.

'You shouldn't stop creating just because your work is different now.'

'You'll have a hard time convincing the artist in me of that.'

'But it was therapy for you, creating back then. It would serve the same purpose now….and so what if it's different. Doesn't it make it special in its own way?'

He gave a soft scoff. 'To be reminded that I can no longer do something as well as I used to.'

She lowered her gaze to where her fingers played with the hairs on his chest. 'It's all subjective. There's no such thing as a perfect piece of art, just as there's no perfect book or movie or performance. Who cares if it's not as good in your eyes, if you come to get the same enjoyment out of creating it?'

He stared down at her, heard her words so perfect, so right. No perfect performance…he'd take his hat off to her now, throw her roses on the stage, because what she'd said made *perfect* sense. Sense he hadn't seen before. And he couldn't speak, only hold her closer as the emotion inside swelled.

Fear of not being good enough had stopped him from creating. Fear of the man he was now had stopped him leaving the island. Fear of being resented by his late friend's wife had stopped him from talking to her and dealing with his guilt…but now, with Catherine wrapped up in his arms, he didn't feel afraid any more, he felt capable of anything.

Ready to take out his sketchpad, ready to return home, ready to speak to Cherie…

Through her wholehearted acceptance of him, she'd crept beneath his barriers. Teaching him to embrace the man he was now, not fear it, or loathe it.

'Is this what you had in mind when you agreed to come here, to my island?'

'What?' She pushed up on his chest. 'Seducing you?'

'Luring me into your bed to fill my head with possibility.'

She laughed softly. 'The truth?'

He nodded, loving how her eyes sparkled down at him.

'I wanted to see you. Absolutely, I did. It's been so long...' Her lashes lowered, a second's avoidance as she seemed to withdraw into herself and then she looked at him again. 'I wanted to see how you were for myself and, of course, I wanted to convince you to come home once in a while. I also needed to escape my life...' She closed her eyes, her body trembling against him and exposing that pain again. Pain that revolved around Luke and it was like a knife twisting deep inside him.

'As for getting you into bed *per se*—' her eyes opened, locked with his, and her sudden smile almost had him forgetting the hurt that preceded it '—the second I saw you again I will admit to wanting all of the above.'

'You're totally serious, aren't you.' It was a statement, not a question. He was long past doubting her attraction.

'Err, yeah! All those feelings I had for you when we were kids, teens, imagine that and then being confronted by you now...your bad-boy vibe has a whole lot going for it.'

'My bad-boy vibe?' He choked on a laugh, grabbing her hand to press it to his scarred cheek and hold it there. '*This* gives me a bad-boy vibe?'

Her eyes shimmered into his. 'Hell, yeah.'

She eased her hand from beneath his, to trail it along the scar, her eyes alive with the heated direction of her thoughts, and he flipped her under him, so fast she cried out.

He started to roll back. 'Your ankle! I'm s—'

She cut him off with a kiss. 'My ankle is fine!'

And just like that he was perfecting insanity again.

CHAPTER THIRTEEN

A KNOCK AT the door woke Catherine in an instant and she shot upright, the bed sheet clutched to her chest, eyes wide.

"Alaric!' she whisper-shouted. 'Alaric!'

She shoved him and he grunted, wrapping his arms around her waist. 'What's the emergency?'

'There's someone at the door.'

He squinted up at her, raising his hand to ward off the light from the bedside lamp as she thrust it on. 'What time is it?'

'I've no idea. Late.' Very late, judging by the pitch-black outdoors and the very vocal sounds of the nightlife coming through the small gap they'd left in the sliding door.

The knock came again, followed by Dorothea's voice. 'Miss Wilde… Kyrios de Vere?'

She swallowed. Okay, so that cat was out of the bag… not that it had ever really been in considering her and Alaric had been inseparable for the past week, working together, eating together, sleeping together…ever since their silent understanding to enjoy this time while they could. Not that much sleeping had gone on which explained why they'd fallen asleep in the afternoon and the day had disappeared on them.

'I've brought food,' Dorothea called through the door. 'I thought you may be hungry?'

Alaric chuckled into her hip and she shoved him again.

'Well, she's not wrong.'

'It's not funny.'

'It is a little funny. And she's right, we could do with some food.'

She started to move off the bed—

'You can come in, Dorothea.'

And flung herself back, the sheets clutched to her chest again, as she threw him a mutinous glare.

He chuckled all the more, pushing himself up to sitting and settling back against the headboard, pulling her in closer as the door opened. A blushing Dorothea strode in, eyes averted, her tray out in front of her and loaded with a variety of food.

'I brought a selection as I wasn't sure what you would prefer.' She slid the tray onto the bedside table. 'Now what can I get you to drink?'

'Water would be lovely,' Catherine replied, surprised her voice sounded far more composed than she felt.

'And some…champagne?' Alaric looked at her for approval and she felt her cheeks burn further, her 'yes' more of a squeak as she thanked Dorothea.

'You're most welcome.' Off she went, happy to be on another errand, happier still to see them in bed together, Catherine was sure.

'I can't believe you did that.' She gave him another playful shove and he pulled her back against him, his grin heart-melting, his eyes alive with mischief, and then he kissed her. A long, deep kiss that had her limbs softening, a fresh wave of heat consuming her as her head emptied out.

'She knew anyway,' he murmured against her lips.

'So? We could have at least put some clothes on.'

'Are you kidding? That's not going to bother her. She's

just happy to see me acting like a normal, healthy man again.'

'You mean *virile*?' she teased, the sexual undercurrent building with ease.

He laughed. 'That too.'

She shook her head, her smile uncontainable. It was so easy to lose herself in him, in these days where the outside world couldn't intervene and everything felt so…perfect.

He leaned away to reach for a plate. 'You'll love these.'

She took in the neat pile of glistening vine-covered rolls he offered out to her. 'Ah, dolmades.'

His eyes widened in surprise.

'Hey, I am well-travelled, you know!'

'Clearly.'

She leaned forward, took one up and cupped her hand beneath as she bit into it and licked her lips to scoop up the remnants.

'Nice?'

She chewed it over, the taste explosion divine. Rice, dill, lemon, mint—yum!

She swallowed it down with a nod and a hum.

'Tell me how you're not the size of a house when you eat like this every day,' she teased, offering him a bite.

He laughed before taking it from her fingers with his mouth, chewing it over as his eyes danced. 'Like you, I train hard to balance it out.'

'That makes me feel better. It would suck if you were this trim and got to eat all you wanted without having to put in any effort.'

'Would it now?'

'Yup. Take it from a woman who knows the pain of exercise.'

He smiled at her. 'Ready for another?'

She nodded and he picked one up, pulling it away from her lips at the last second.

'But don't expect me to let you hop on the treadmill tomorrow—that ankle still has to heal.'

'Duh.' She stared into his eyes as she quickly pinched a bite. 'I'm not that stupid.'

His brows nudged upwards.

'I'm not!' She devoured the rest of it before adding, 'Or at least I was, but not now—not any more.'

'Because?'

'Because I'm beautiful on the inside.' She rolled her eyes and gave a laugh, but it caught in her throat. His eyes were on fire, stubborn, insistent, as he forced her to be serious.

'I mean it, Catherine.'

'I know you mean it.' She reassured him softly and he took up her hand, kissed it as his eyes lifted to hers.

'Just remember it…'

He held her eye as he pressed another kiss to her hand and she mentally added for him, *When we're no longer together.*

'Remember it?' he urged, the unsaid words hanging in the air between them, and she nodded.

'You know…' she whispered, her voice trapped in her chest as her heart beat wild with her feelings for him, feelings that were way out of her control, regardless of the untold pact that this would be over when she left. 'You could come visit and remind me as often as you liked…'

'Is this you trying to convince me to leave my island again?'

'Maybe…is it working?'

He shook his head but there was a smile in his eyes. 'You have shown me there's more to life than hiding out here, I'll concede that.'

She leaned back, surprise making her drop the sheet that was covering her modesty, and as his eyes dipped, their naughty gleam threatened to distract her.

'Behave!' She palmed his chest. 'Are you serious?'

He tugged his eyes from her nakedness, and it wasn't salacious heat burning into her now, it was his sincerity. 'Yes, you've shown me to accept the man I am now, to live and laugh again. You've given me hope that I can go home to my family, that I can contact Cherie and try to put it behind me, to move on in some way.'

'You don't deserve the guilt, Alaric.' Her voice was soft but no less vehement. 'You've suffered enough.'

'Perhaps.'

'Are you serious, or are you just humouring me?'

His smile lifted to one side. 'No, I'm not just humouring you. And yes, I'm serious. I'm not looking forward to it. I'm apprehensive about how Cherie will be, I'm apprehensive about how my family will receive me, hell, I'm apprehensive about being out in public at all, but...'

'Those you don't know don't matter, and those that do will love you all the more for coming back to them.'

His eyes softened, his smile too.

'And you're going to be an uncle, Alaric, that's exciting, special. Flo's been going out of her mind worrying about you.'

'I know.'

'But do you know her blood pressure is already through the roof, that she's been forced to take early maternity leave?'

He frowned. 'No. She never said...she...' He looked away, raked his hand through his hair with a curse. 'Why didn't she say anything?'

'I don't know. I guess because you've had so much going on it didn't seem fair. Or maybe she thought you'd see it as her way of guilt-tripping you into coming home again and didn't think that fair either.'

'I knew she'd been out of the office more, I just hadn't… I didn't…' He leaned forward, his knees coming up to rest his arms on them, his head hanging forward. He cursed again. 'I've been so wrapped up in my own world… How could I have been so selfish?'

'You weren't selfish.'

'No?' He rolled his head to look at her.

'No.' She placed a gentle hand on his back. 'You were suffering. And they understand why you left, granted they don't understand why you've stayed away, but when you explain, they'll get it. They'll just be happy to see you again.'

'I see my father regularly.'

'On a screen, Alaric, that's hardly seeing him. And even then, it's all business, isn't it?'

'What more would we talk about?'

She gave a soft scoff. 'Feelings! We all have them unless you're a robot and I *know* you're not. You care, you just like to pretend you don't.'

He said nothing and she stroked his back that was so tense beneath her touch. 'It's not too late, you know. The most important thing is that you're going to go back. They love you and they'll be ready to welcome you home, when you're ready to go there.'

She snuggled into him, forgetting all about the food as she lost herself in their conversation and the milestone they'd hit. 'It'll all work out, I just know it.'

He turned, pressed his lips to her hair. 'I like your optimism.'

'And I like you.'

It came out easily. Honest. And it hit home once more, just how much she liked him and just how much this had to be temporary because for all she denied being like her mother, her actions over the years had told a different story…her actions had told her just how selfish and messed up she was, and she would never expose Alaric to that side of her.

Never.

But what if she could do better? What if she could learn from the past and pave the way to a better future? One that allowed her to love, to be loved, to have it all?

But Alaric didn't know what she had done.

Alaric didn't know what had truly gone down with Luke.

Alaric didn't know just what a screw-up she was deep down and the idea of telling him, of cracking herself open and confessing…

And didn't that make her a nasty piece of work, when he was opening himself up to her, his insecurities, his worries, and still she hadn't told him the truth.

It crushed her inside, crushed her all the more as she accepted that she didn't just like him, she loved him. That she was *in* love with him, and she had to tell him the whole ugly truth. She owed him that at the very least.

She straightened up, drawing her knees to her chest, the sheet too. 'There's something I need to tell you, something that very few people know.'

His head snapped up. 'Are you okay?'

She couldn't answer.

'Are you sick?'

She shook her head. 'No. Not in the way you're thinking.'

He leaned forward, seeking to hold her eye, but she couldn't look at him. 'Flo knows and Luke… I haven't told anyone else.'

He reached out for her, but she leaned away. 'No. Just let

me… I need to get this off my chest, and if you hug me, I'll lose the ability to speak…' Her throat was already clamping closed, the well of emotion rising so sharply she couldn't draw a full breath.

He sat back against the headboard and she didn't need to look to know how wary his gaze had become. 'You know you can tell me anything, Catherine.'

She nodded. She did. But first, she needed to get it straight in her head. And she needed Dorothea to come and go again so that she could be sure there would be no interruptions because, once she started, it would all come spilling out, and then, who knew where they would be…

She was quiet for so long that he wondered if she would say anything at all and then Dorothea returned with the drinks and he realised she'd been waiting for them to be alone. Properly alone.

He poured a drink, one of each, and offered her them both.

She took the water while he favoured the champagne. Not that he felt ready to celebrate anything, it was more to ease his nerves that were fraught with whatever was coming.

'You understand my relationship with my mother better than most. My relationship with my father too. What there is of it.'

'Back then, yes. Not so much now.'

She nodded but said nothing more and he pressed, 'Do you see them much?'

'No. Not particularly. Mum never got over me hitting A-list status. Once she realised my growing fame didn't help her with the roles she was being offered, things turned nasty pretty quickly, and to be honest, I think she'd had enough of playing at family. They divorced soon after and Mum left to be with her latest toy boy and Dad…well, he fell into his own pit of despair and no matter what I did, what I said, he just…'

She gave the smallest of shrugs and his heart ached for her. There he was avoiding his own family who'd always been there for him, when she couldn't even hold the attention of hers.

'He just didn't care. Worse still, I look like her, so seeing me is just a constant reminder of his loss.'

A fire burned in Alaric's gut, his hands fisting as his dislike for the man took hold. He was her father, for Christ's sake, and instead of focusing on what he did have—the love of his daughter—he was so wrapped up in the callous wife he'd lost.

'Anyway, when Luke and I got together it was a whirlwind. It happens like that on set, you know. You're so wrapped up in the characters you're playing that the boundaries blur and before you know it, you're an item. And it's easier that way, dating on set. It's virtually impossible to find time to date outside of it, and we were happy, in our own way…'

She gave him a sad smile and looked away, her eyes lost to the outside world, her sadness, her pain, and his heart caught in his chest.

'I never wanted to become my mother, Alaric, I didn't. And so I found it easier not to get caught up in relationships in the first place, not to feel the pressure of dividing my attention between my work and my loved ones. I figured it would all come later, right? That I'd get to a point in my career where I was content and ready to settle down.'

'But then you met Luke?'

She gave a small nod.

'What happened?' he asked even though the question had goosebumps prickling over his skin. He didn't think he could bear it if she confessed her love for another man, her heartache even...

'I got pregnant.'

The blood drained from his face, shock assaulting him like a punch to the gut. 'You were...' He cleared his throat, tried again. 'You were *pregnant*?'

She shuddered as she took a breath, her eyes flitting to him so very briefly, but he couldn't miss the torment, the sadness, the pain.

'Yes. It wasn't planned. It was the last thing I expected—we expected.' Her voice cracked with emotion, her arms wrapped tight around her legs, the knuckles of the hand closest to him glowing white as she gripped her elbow. 'We were always careful, always used protection, but...but it failed.'

She started to rock, and he didn't dare move, not until he felt she was done.

'I took the morning-after pill—we had no choice. But it—it didn't work. A few weeks later I knew I had to take a test. I didn't feel any different, but I was late. Luke was beside himself, excited with it. He was talking of a future, full on, like it was all a done deal, and I...'

She cleared her throat, her voice so quiet when she spoke again. 'I was terrified. I wasn't ready. It wasn't the right time. I cared for Luke, I did, but a baby...' She shook her head, her body rocking all the more, and he could see the tears building, sense the effort it was taking for her to hold them back.

'What did you do?'

'Nothing. I did nothing.'

She turned to him now, her lower lip trembling, the tears in her eyes overflowing as they ran down her cheeks.

'I lost it. I didn't want it, and then it was gone, like it had never been.'

'Oh, Catherine…' He reached for her and she leaned away.

'Don't. I don't deserve sympathy. Don't you see, I was as bad as my mother in the end. I had a life growing inside me, I was a mother and I—I wished it away.'

'There's lots of reasons to lose a baby, but it never comes down to someone wishing it away, Catherine. You know that.'

She shook her head, stared at him. 'Do I?'

'Of course you do.'

'Luke said the same. He was so good to me, so sweet, but I didn't deserve his kindness… I didn't.'

'Of course you did, you were hurting and—'

'But he knew I wasn't ready. He knew I didn't want… I didn't want…' She couldn't finish and he couldn't stop himself reaching for her. He pulled her to him and this time she came, curling up against him as he rocked her, soothing every sob that wracked her body.

'It wasn't your fault.' He kissed her hair. 'It wasn't.'

'I couldn't marry him. I said yes because of the baby, because I thought it was the right thing to do. And when I lost the baby, I just… I couldn't go through with it."

'I'm sure Luke would have understood, Catherine. He would have been hurting, just as you are now.'

She sniffed, swiped her palm across her cheeks as she leant back to look up at him. 'I wasn't ready.'

He cupped her jaw, his thumb sweeping over her damp cheek. 'I know, princess.'

'But I—when I lost it, I broke down. I would have given anything to have that time again, to have nurtured it, treasured it. I wanted to be a mother. I wanted to wish away my career and have my baby back.'

Have her baby back *and* Luke? Was this more than just agony over a miscarriage? Was it agony over the only real relationship she'd ever had?

'I'm sure if you went to Luke and spoke to him, he would understand…' He forced himself to say, 'You could still have a future together?'

She frowned through the tears, her head shaking. 'I don't want Luke, I never *loved* Luke.'

His heart pulsed in his chest as her eyes widened into his, so much on show if he was willing to see it. 'What I felt for him is a fraction of what I feel for you, what I've always felt for you, Alaric.'

He clutched her tighter, pulled her up to his chest and sucked in a breath. 'You've got me, right now, you've got me.'

She shuddered against him. 'But don't you see, I'm just as bad as my mother.'

His laugh was tight, incredulous. 'I don't know how you can think that.'

'I wished away my own child.'

'You were blindsided by a pregnancy, that's very different to abandoning your own flesh and blood, Catherine.'

He continued to rock her, stroke her hair, kiss her head, wishing life could be different, that they could somehow merge the two worlds in which they lived to make them compatible.

'I'm ready now, Alaric. It's the reason this script is so important. It's not just about proving I'm more than just Kitty Wilde, the actor. I want my life back. I don't want to be a prisoner to twenty-four-seven filming schedules, PR appearances, interviews… I love film, I always want to be in film, but on my own terms and on the other side of the lens.'

'It sounds like you have it all planned out.'

He could feel the resolve building within her, the strength seeping into her limbs as she pushed up off his chest. 'I'm thirty now, it's time I took control of my life and made room for the people that I love.'

'Flo will certainly be happy to see more of you.'

'And you?' Excitement thrived behind the tears still glistening in her vivid blues. 'Could we see each other more?'

His chest contracted, his body icing over with the impossibility of it. 'I'm not… I know I've said I'll visit home, that I'll speak to Cherie too, but you…me and you—' he couldn't look at her as he finished '—we just don't work outside of this island.'

'You don't know that.' She reached out to touch her palm to his cheek, urging him back to her. 'I've never met anyone that makes me feel the way that you do, Alaric. It's always been there between us, but these past few weeks… it's changed everything. And I know you feel it too.' She lowered her hand to his heart. 'I *know* you do.'

'It doesn't matter what I feel, Catherine.'

He clutched her fingers, his intention to remove her touch, but he couldn't drag them away. He was lost in her gaze swimming with such passion, such confusion, and the contact, no matter what had driven him to stop it, felt unbreakable.

'Why?'

'You and I can't have a relationship.'

'And I repeat…' She sniffed, using the back of her free hand to swipe away more tears as she raised her chin to him. 'Why?'

He couldn't respond. His head was a mess of words, of sentences that didn't make sense, feelings that he couldn't identify, string together, make coherent.

'This feels different to me, this feels special,' she pressed.

'I haven't felt this way about anyone, and... I don't want to make another mistake. I don't want to be my mother. And you tell me that I'm not, so let me prove it, with you.'

'I'm not the man to prove it with, can't you see that? I don't belong in your world.'

'What world?'

'Show business. Hollywood. Being in the public eye. I can't do it, Catherine. Look at me. Can you imagine the tabloids, the cover stories that would appear?'

'Yes...' It came out as a whisper. 'And I wish I could protect you from it. I wish I could say it won't happen, but you and I both know it will. It doesn't mean we have to live in fear of it, that we should give them the power to keep us apart. I don't care what they say, I only—'

'You *should* care.'

'My mother would care, Alaric, and that's not me...or is this *you* proving you don't mean what you say?'

'Don't question my honesty, Catherine. I have never lied to you, and I have let you in. But I can't give you what you deserve.'

'And what is it you think I deserve?'

'The dreams you speak of...the award winning actor-cum-screenwriter. It doesn't matter that you'll be on the other side of the screen. If you go after your dream, you will still be on the red carpet, you will still be in the public eye, you will still be famous. As you deserve. But not with a broken man by your side.'

'You're not broken, Alaric.'

'I'm damaged goods to them.'

She might not find him so horrific, his family might not either. As the queen of appearances, she'd convinced him that he could return to his family and be seen once more, for who he was beyond the scars. And yes, he had the strength, the confidence, to accept who he was now.

But to stand alongside her in the very public eye, the difference so very marked. It would be the subject of every tabloid, the cover story of every gossip rag, the very epitome of Beauty and the Beast, and the press would go wild for it.

It didn't matter that she didn't see him like that, they would.

And to have his happiness splashed across the tabloids, rubbed in the face of Fred's family, Cherie, their child… It was one thing to return, but that…

'So, this really is it?' she said quietly. 'We have this time now and then it's over.'

'It's what has to happen.'

'Not if we don't want it to, not if you feel the same way I do.'

'How can I possibly know how you—'

'I *love* you, Alaric.'

His heart squeezed tight in his chest, warmth exploding out and dousing just as quick.

'I loved you in my teens, I love you all the more now. I know I'm not the best judge of it, not after how my parents were or how they treated me, but I know I don't want this to end, that I want to keep you as part of my life. I want to share the highs and the lows and be there by your side. And I have *never* felt like that about anyone.'

Be there, side by side…

His gut twisted, the pain in his chest like a physical burn, his confession riding his tongue—that he loved her, that he always had, that he always would.

But he couldn't tell her, he couldn't vocalise it and tear them both apart. In a month's time, a year, he would be a blip in her past and she'd move on with her newfound career goals and her dream for a family with someone that deserved her and wasn't so messed up.

'I'm not the right man for you.'

'And shouldn't I be the judge of that?'

He released her hand, threw his feet to the floor and gripped the edge of the bed as he hunched forward. 'Ten years ago, I would have said yes, I would have run with what's in my heart, but not now, Catherine. I'm barely happy in my own company. The idea of being surrounded by the masses on your arm, with you so perfect and me like this…and in the face of Fred's loved ones… I can't do it. I can't.'

'I'm not perfect, Alaric. You of all people know I'm not, and yet, you've shown me to love who I am.' He glanced back at her, unable to resist the lull of her words, their importance. 'To look in the mirror and like what I see, without the make-up. To let my hair dry however it may. To eat what it is I want to eat and not obsess about every calorie, every pound of weight. You've shown me that.'

Her voice shook with her sincerity, her cheeks flushed with the passion he'd instilled in her, and for the briefest of moments, he let it in, all of it. How much he loved her, how much it warmed him to know that he'd made a difference for her too. That she wouldn't leave this island the same person she was when she arrived. That she would be happier, more content, healthier.

'And those people, Fred's loved ones,' she whispered, her hand reaching out to rest on his shoulder. 'They will be happy to see you return to the land of the living, I promise you.'

He stared at her, quiet, contemplative.

'You said you were ready to face your guilt, to talk to Cherie, to move on…'

'Yes. I did. And I meant it.' He closed his eyes, his head filling with an anguished Cherie, their child, the graveside and the rain lashing down. He hung his head forward, shutting Catherine out, quashing the hope she was threatening to bring to life. 'But confronting the past and moving on is one thing, having a fairy-tale ending thrust in Cherie's face, in his family's face, is something else entirely.'

'You have a right to find happiness, Alaric, you have a right to—'

'Stop, Catherine, just stop!' The lull of her words, the picture-perfect future she was trying to paint, was crucifying him. 'I can't do it.'

'Can't or won't?'

He didn't answer. He couldn't. Heart pounding in his ears, he thrust up and strode for the bathroom. Hating himself as he did so, but knowing it was the right thing to do. He slammed the shower on, gripped the back of his head and pressed his forehead into the cold stone wall.

She deserved better, she *would* get better, when she was long gone from this place and the web of seduction he had unintentionally created. He got the beauty of the island, the beauty of escapism, and his presence in the midst of it *made* him the right guy for her.

But he wasn't.

And he couldn't fall into the trap of believing that he was because when it all fell apart, he would be the one unable to come back from it.

He'd be the one trying to claw back what he could of his confidence, of his life, with a heart torn in two.

CHAPTER FOURTEEN

SHE'D PUSHED HIM too far, and all because she'd been swept up in the realisation that she loved him. That she loved him and in three days she would be leaving, and this would be over…unless she could convince him otherwise.

She heard the sound of the shower turning on and fought the urge to follow him.

This wasn't part of the plan, her brain warned. Convincing him to return home to his family, yes, and he'd agreed to it. She could finally give Flo the news she'd been waiting for. Her friend would be ecstatic. *She* should be ecstatic too. Her script was almost done. Her escape had given her space to think, time to relax, time to…fall in love.

And that was the problem.

Falling in love hadn't been part of the plan but now that she felt it, truly felt what it was like to be *in* love with someone, she wasn't ready to walk away.

Not without a fight.

She pushed herself out of bed, taking the sheet with her, and froze. She could just make out the corner of a small book jutting out from beneath his pillow. A book she hadn't seen before. She frowned. What would he keep…?

Her eyes flitted to the bathroom and back again. Tentatively, she leaned over and pulled it out. There were no words, just a plain black cover with a pencil hooked into its spine.

She trailed her fingers over the soft leather. Was it a diary, a notebook, a…*sketchbook*?

Skin abuzz with nerves, with hope—she didn't want to invade his privacy but she had to know—she peeked inside and her stomach came alive. A thousand butterflies desperate to be free as she took in the artist-grade paper, the pencil marks…

Alaric was drawing again; there could be no other explanation for it being under his pillow, in the bed they now shared together.

She opened it fully, her eyes lost in page after page. Various shapes, shading techniques, lines, crosses, smudges… had he been testing himself?

The shapes began to morph into sketches that seemed to be abandoned halfway, of inanimate objects, a glass, a chair…she turned the page again and her hand flew to her mouth.

Oh my God. Was that…?

She dropped onto the bed. Her heart in her throat, her eyes misting over as she saw it for what it was—his first complete picture and it was of *her*.

So obviously her…

She was curled up in the bed sheets on her front, her hair spread out on the pillow, her lips softly parted, her eyes closed. The pencil scratches graduated from light to dark towards the middle, jagged lines, rough, almost wild, but the effect…it was beautiful, impassioned, filled with such feeling.

When had he…?

'You were asleep.'

She jumped, her fingers hovering over the page as her eyes shot to the bathroom doorway. She hadn't heard the shower turn off; she hadn't been aware of anything but the image.

Guilt bloomed in her cheeks, her heart rate wild as she tried to read his expression and failed. How long had he been stood there watching her, a towel around his waist, his body taut with tension?

'You sketched me?' It came out like a whisper.

'It was the only one I didn't bail on...the only one that...' He trailed off, his gaze falling to the drawing as his eyes narrowed. 'I hope you don't mind?'

'Mind?' She wanted to laugh and cry at once, her eyes going back to the breathtaking image. 'Are you crazy? It's incredible.'

She heard his footsteps approach, her heart kicking up in her chest.

'Not as incredible as the real thing.'

If her heart leapt any higher, she'd choke on the damn thing...

'Alaric...' Slowly, she turned to look up at him, wet her lips as she took in the fire now blazing in his blue depths. The question was on her lips again. How can he feel so much and still deny it, deny her? 'I'm not ready for this to be over between us.'

He reached out to cup her jaw, caress her cheek. 'We have three more days.'

'Three more days won't be enough.'

'Stay longer. Your script is going well, you can get it finished...' His fingers and his words were gently teasing her, coaxing her under his spell. 'We could even take a trip to the mainland. I can show you the sights I fell in love with, we can...'

But she was already shaking her head, she had to be real. 'I can't, I have press appearances scheduled, a red carpet

launch coming up and a new dress to source in all likelihood.'

'Of course,' he murmured, his other hand reaching out,
his fingers combing through her hair as he lowered his
mouth to hers. 'Reality beckons.'

'This *is* reality, Alaric. Right now.'

'This is too perfect, to be real.'

And she knew he meant it. She could see it in his gaze,
his belief that this only existed on his island, safe from
the world outside.

She opened her mouth and he trapped her denial with
his kiss. A kiss she let him take because it beat succumbing to the pain of leaving, of this being over.

Because this *was* real. This wasn't here today, gone tomorrow. She'd be feeling it long after she left the island…

Would he? Or would he truly draw a line under it and
move on like it hadn't happened?

She couldn't believe it.

She wouldn't.

Three days later, her cases loaded onto Marsel's boat and
only Dorothea and Andreas to wave her off, she was forced
to accept it had meant more to her than it had to him.

Alaric was as absent as he had been the day she'd arrived.

Looking away from the island as it shrunk in the distance, she rooted in her handbag for her phone. She wanted
to update Flo and…she frowned. There was a piece of
paper sticking out of her purse, a piece of paper she hadn't
put there.

She tugged it out, her fingers trembling as she recognised the artist-grade paper… She unfolded it and the entire world fell away save for the image in her hand. His
picture of her.

She gripped the handrail as her knees threatened to buckle, her eyes fixed on the sketch as her vision swam with unshed tears. He'd added a message to her sleeping form.

She dragged in a breath, looked up to the skies that were darkening to a menacing blue, the clouds blowing in thick and fast as she blinked back the tears to enable her to read…

You are you, Catherine.
Only you.
Beautiful inside and out.
Don't ever forget it.
Yours always,
Alaric x

She spun on the spot, gripping the handrail tighter as she stared back at the island, desperate for a glimpse of him. Was he there on the cliff edge, where she thought she'd spied him that first morning?

She leaned closer, her eyes watering against the sea spray and her hair whipping around her face.

'You be careful, Miss Wilde!' Marsel called out. 'The sea's getting choppy with the storm on the rise.'

Slowly, she leaned back in.

'Don't worry, we'll be on land before it's upon us,' he added, misreading her concern.

She gave him a weak smile, her eyes going back to the island, back to him as she willed him to wake up to the possibility of what they could have, if only he'd choose it.

Her. Happiness. And everything in between.

Alaric watched the boat disappear on the horizon, unmoving from his vantage point on the cliff. He hadn't been able to say goodbye, not without caving and promising her the world, promising her the impossible.

He wasn't sure how long he'd remained there for, only that the rain had started to lash with the wind, waking him from the stupor her absence had induced.

He turned away from the ocean that now rolled with the storm and headed back to the house. The scent of food greeted him as he walked in and his empty stomach made itself known. He hadn't eaten since last night, since his last meal with her…

'Well, it's about time you showed your face.' He looked up to see Dorothea in the kitchen doorway, wiping her hands on her apron. She wasn't smiling. 'Your dinner is ready. You can help yourself. Andreas and I are going to head home, unless there's something more you need.'

'No, that's fine. Thank you, Dorothea.'

He rubbed a hand over his rain-soaked face, forked it through his sodden hair. Weary to the bone, more tired and broken than he'd felt in so long. She stepped aside to let him enter the kitchen, but he could feel her eyes still on him as he took in the food on the centre island.

Souvlaki. His favourite. Only now it reminded him of Catherine and her first night on the island. Had it really only been four weeks ago?

'She loves you, Alaric,' came Dorothea's soft assurance. 'And you love her. It's as obvious as the love Andreas and I share.'

He heard her, but said nothing…he couldn't. His chest ached too much to speak, his gut writhed and his eyes pricked. And he didn't cry. He never cried, not even after… after…

'Why did you throw it all away?'

His head snapped around, his eyes spearing hers. But all he saw was his pain reflected back at him, his anguish.

Outside the storm rallied, thunder rattling the windows, rain pelting at the glass; it was nothing compared to the storm within.

'Come on, love.' Andreas appeared at his wife's side, his hand gentle on her shoulder. 'Leave the man be. We should get going before the storm gets any worse.'

She didn't even blink, her eyes on Alaric as she waited for the answer he just couldn't give. 'You should go... Andreas is right.'

She gave a small shake of her head, disappointment shining in her brown eyes as Andreas gave him a grim smile. 'We'll see you in the morning, Kyrios de Vere.'

He gave the faintest of nods and watched them leave, Dorothea's words churning him up inside. She was right, she was so very right. He'd thrown it all away, Catherine's love, and for what? Because he thought he didn't deserve it, that if Fred couldn't have it, he shouldn't. Christ, if Fred were here now, witnessing his pain, he'd kick his ass for being an idiot. He knew it just as well as he knew he was scared.

Scared of not being able to stack up, because he thought he wasn't worthy, and the world would see it, declare it...a real-life Beauty and the Beast.

But, so what?

What did it matter how the world saw them? Not when he had her love. And she had given it to him, over and over, and he'd what? Done exactly what Dorothea accused him of and thrown it all away.

Hadn't he spent his time convincing her that appearances didn't matter, hadn't she changed, learned from it, from him, and then he'd been a hypocrite. Not only throwing her love away, but his words of wisdom too. Because he was the one who'd let appearances get in the way of what truly mattered.

He hunched forward, his hands gripping his thighs. He felt sick, dizzy, the pain too intense to breathe. He needed to get to her, he needed to say he was sorry, but more than that, he needed to tell her that he loved her too.

He ran out into the storm, stared at the tumultuous heavens above and knew he was trapped. His island, his safe haven, was now his prison. He cursed the sky, let the rain beat down on him, punishing the fool in him.

But he was a fool no more. He knew what he had to do, and a plan was already forming. A plan that would prove he could do it, that he had it in him to not just leave the island but step straight into the limelight…for her.

'I'm coming for you, Catherine.'

And she would be worth every excruciating second under the lens because their love was worth it, and he'd rather face his fears by her side than live a life without her.

CHAPTER FIFTEEN

'HEY, KITTY, YOU READY?'

Luke reached across the back seat, took her hand in his and gave it a gentle squeeze.

She nodded, dragging her eyes from the street, the crowds, the flicker of camera flashes and the excited buzz…

'You sure? You've hardly said a word since we left the hotel.'

'I'm fine, honest.' She brushed down the skirt of her shimmering gold gown and remembered the last time she had worn it. The night she had seduced Alaric…or had he seduced her? A sad smile touched her lips.

She'd been right to think her designer dress wouldn't fit, Dorothea's delicious food and her injury had seen to that, but she looked healthy, and the forgiving cut to the wrap dress that Alaric had taken great pleasure in unravelling had been the perfect choice. Even if it did bring with it such poignant memories. From their first time together, to his insistence that she would look perfect in any dress because all the public would care about was seeing her, not the designer label, not the super-skinny frame, or the heavily made-up face, just her.

And she missed him. Missed him more than she'd ever known it possible to miss someone. It was as though she wasn't whole, that a part of her had been left behind with him, on his island. Not that he was there. No, she knew he'd gone back to the UK to visit his family, much to their pleasure, and Flo had been so very grateful to her. The emotion in her friend's voice as she'd told her of his visit to see Cherie and her daughter too, that he'd gained what he so desperately felt he needed, approval to live, some form of closure.

It had made Catherine cry when Flo had told her. Happy tears, bittersweet tears, as she acknowledged that he was free of the guilt, and still, he hadn't been able to come to her. And no matter what she did, she couldn't shift the lonely ache inside.

She gave a snort as she took in the crowds outside and recalled Alaric's words to her on the very same…

'For you, it must be worse. Surrounded by people day in, day out, and standing alone…'

Alone and yet surrounded.

'Are you really sure?' Luke pressed. 'I don't think I've ever heard you snort before a red carpet?'

'Sorry.' She tried for a laugh as she touched a hand to his thigh. 'Lost in my thoughts. Thanks for being my date.'

'Any time.'

She smiled and folded her hands in her lap. Luke had been her rock since her return from Greece. Every press event, every interview, when she lost her trail of thought or lacked the right enthusiasm, he filled the gap.

She couldn't stop herself getting swept away by the memories of the island, of Alaric and the picture he'd drawn, the message he'd written too. It had to mean more. It had to. She'd seen it in his eyes, countless times over—love.

But the more she thought on it, the more she doubted it

all. Had it really been there, or had she just projected her own feelings onto him?

It had been over a week, plenty of time for him to have seen Cherie, his family and reach out. Just a call, a message, anything...

The car came to a stop and she took an unsteady breath, unhooked her seat belt as Luke did the same.

'Time to get this show on the road.' His smile was full of encouragement as his door opened and he stepped out into the raised cheers of the crowd. The shouts for him to look this way as he reached back in to offer her his hand. She took it, stepping out beside him, and then it was her name being shouted along with his.

They smiled under the camera flashes, played their part as they were ushered to the barriers for autographs, handshakes, questions, photos...

'Kitty! Kitty! How does it feel to be back with your ex?'

Luke caught her eye as they exchanged a very slight head shake, a subtle roll of the eyes, their smiles never waning.

'Kitty! Luke! This way, what about a shot of the happy couple?'

'Miss Wilde, give us a smile!'

'Catherine!'

She stumbled in her heels. *Alaric?*

Luke caught her elbow, his brown eyes piercing hers. 'You sure you're okay?'

But she was already scanning the crowd. That voice, her name, it had to be him. But he wouldn't...not with all the press, the cameras, the public...

'Catherine!'

She craned her neck trying to see past the tight frontline, squinting against the camera flashes as she reached up on her tiptoes. She didn't care what she looked like, undignified, desperate…it was him, against all the odds, it was him, she just *knew* it.

'Miss Wilde, Mr Walker, we're ready to take you on through.' The procession organiser was there with security, ushering them on from a respectful distance, but she shook her head. She wasn't going anywhere.

'Catherine!'

She spun in the other direction and the crowd parted, realisation sweeping through the masses that something was amiss. Amiss for them, but not for her. And there he was. Straight down the middle, set back from the red rope barrier, his tall and broad frame dominating those around him, his tux cut to perfection, his face, those eyes, those lips…it really was him.

Her breath rushed from her lungs as she swept forward. 'Alaric!'

'Miss Wilde?' The organiser stepped in front of her as Luke cupped her elbow.

'Kitty? What's going on?'

'There's someone I need to go and see.'

He followed her line of sight before coming back to her. 'Is that him?'

She nodded. She'd told Luke everything, she'd had to after she'd stumbled over one too many interviews and he'd started to worry about her health, her state of mind, after all she'd been through. Some of it by his side…

'Will you be okay?'

She nodded, desperation sending her pulse racing. 'Please.'

His eyes narrowed as he took in the desperate flush to her cheeks, the pleading look in her eyes. 'Go. I've got this.'

'Thank you, Luke.' She rushed to give him a peck on the

cheek, a delight for the eager cameras, and then she was striding for the barrier.

'Miss Wilde, you can't...' Security tried to intercept her, but she wasn't stopping. Alaric was here, at her movie premiere, where there were cameras, there were journalists, the whole world was watching, and still, he was here.

Security stepped into the crowd, following her lead and creating a safe pathway, and as soon as she was free, she was racing towards him.

'Catherine.' It escaped him in a whisper that brought her up short, her eyes desperately searching his for confirmation of what this grand gesture was. 'You look... incredible.'

Warmth flooded her cheeks, her heart fluttering so wildly she thought it might escape. 'What, in this old thing?'

His smile lifted to one side, camera flashes flickering over him, over her, as the crowd shifted their focus from the red carpet, but he didn't seem to notice. Even as security scurried about keeping them at bay and their shouts built:

'Who's this?'

'Is this a new fella?'

'Can we get a name?'

'Wasn't he in that Avenger movie?'

She laughed at that one, tears choking up her throat.

'I'm sorry I let you go without saying goodbye.' He reached out, his hands gentle on her arms, their warmth permeating her skin, her body, her heart.

'Is that why you're here, to say goodbye?'

He laughed softly. 'No. I'm here to say I'm sorry that I let my fear get in the way of telling you how I felt. That even when I let you go, I should have told you still.'

'Told me what, Alaric?' Hope had turned her voice into a whisper.

'That I love you, Catherine. I love you so very much.'

She wet her lips, tears clouding up her vision. She was going to ruin her make-up, but she didn't care, he loved her. *Truly* loved her.

'Why didn't you?'

'Because regardless of my guilt, I still felt you deserved better, that I could never be pictured beside you and seen as equal. Not by the press, the public...'

'And you think I care about all that?'

'No. That's just it. I don't think you do. But I did.'

'And now?'

'Now I'm here, in front of all these cameras that I feared, in front of the world, telling you that I love you, and if you will have me, I'll spend my life making sure I'm worthy of you.'

She pressed a finger to his lips. 'Don't. Don't say that. You are worthy, you always were, because I love you, Alaric, and I always will.'

She combed her fingers through his hair, pulled him down to her lips and sealed her words with a kiss. The camera flashes and the noise from the crowd escalated with the wild fluttering within her heart, the heat of pleasure swirling through her limbs too, until a honk from a car had Alaric breaking away.

'I think we're causing a scene.'

'Wasn't that your intention?'

'Yes and no, but whoever the celeb is in that new car, they're not going to be impressed that the press are now circling us instead of the red carpet.'

'Then come with me?'

'Now?'

'Yes.'

He looked over her head, at the masses and smiled. 'Okay.'

She smiled with him. 'Even if it means getting your picture taken?'

'I think they already have plenty of those.'

'This one we're posing for…' She led him back to the carpet with the aid of the security team, and the procession organiser approached them, her carefully composed smile taking in their new arrival.

'Do we have space for one more?'

'Unlikely, I'm afraid.'

'It's okay,' Alaric said in her ear. 'I have Flo's ticket.'

'You haven't?' Her eyes shot to his. 'How long has she known? She was drilling me only yesterday about her outfit.'

He grimaced. 'Not long enough. I've pledged many hours of free babysitting in exchange.'

She laughed, so very happy that it almost felt like a dream.

'Kitty! Miss Wilde! Who's your friend? Do we get a name?'

She wrapped her arm around him as he did the same and they turned to face the flashes.

'This is Alaric de Vere…' An excited ripple ran through the crowd as recognition of his name spread and she looked up at him as he looked down at her. He didn't care that they knew who he was, that his scars now faced the camera and they'd capture them in their glare, he only cared for her and it was all in his eyes, his smile. 'The love of my life.'

He leaned closer to her. 'This is going to be the longest film in history, isn't it?'

'What makes you say that?'

'Because there are so many ways in which I want to

tell you I love you right now and nearly all of them require us to be alone.'

'Lucky for us I'm wearing the perfect after-party dress.'

He chuckled low in his throat, his mind doing the same journey back in time as her.

'Although…' she murmured, her smile for the crowd, her words for him '…what about a before party?'

He cocked a brow. 'Before?'

'I reckon there's time before the show begins and there's bound to be a quiet corner somewhere…'

His grin turned devilish. 'Are you serious?'

'More than…' She tugged him towards the cinema. 'It's time to live a little.'

'You don't have to tell me twice.'

She was pretty sure she'd told him plenty more times, but she wasn't about to argue the point.

He was here and their life together was truly just beginning.

EPILOGUE

Three years later

'ALARIC, DEAR, THE car is here!'

His mother called up the stairs just as Flo came bustling into the bedroom to help his wife, who was currently enacting some kind of jig in her form-fitting red dress.

'I knew I should have gone for something less…just less…'

Catherine flapped her hands about her, her nerves unusually on show, and he walked up to her, took her hands in his and smiled into her eyes. 'You look spectacular, and Flo has assured me she knows a trick to getting you zipped up.'

She eyed him sceptically as Flo bustled past him and crouched down behind her.

'I sure do, just…give…me…one…*tick*! And *voilà*!' Flo straightened up. 'You're in! This fabric is pure genius.'

'I don't know about genius,' Catherine murmured. 'I'm sure it didn't feel this tight two weeks ago.'

He laughed softly. 'May I remind you that you were only thirty weeks pregnant then? Our little girl has two more weeks on her now.'

She smiled up at him, her blue eyes wide and sparkling. 'True.'

'And the second one always shows more than the first,' Flo added, patting her own tummy that was currently concealing her third.

'You ready?' He smiled down at his radiant wife and gently squeezed her hands.

'I think so.' Her smile wavered and he lifted one of her hands to his lips, kissed it softly. 'You were like this with Max, remember, nine months of hormones and worrying, and out he popped, and you were Kitty Wilde the diva again.'

That earned him a scowl as she withdrew her hands from his and gave him a playful shove. 'Careful, dear husband, or you'll be sleeping in the nursery tonight.'

He chuckled, loving the fire that had crept into her gaze. 'I may need to. I have to be up at the crack of dawn to make sure everything's in place for the charity gala.'

Her smile filled with adoration. 'Have I told you how proud I am of you?'

He reached out and pulled her to him. 'Yes, but you can tell me again if you like. Though the charity venture was your idea.'

'No, my idea was that you joined a support group to talk about what happened, not to finance an entire charity to help others with similar experiences.'

'It was a natural development.'

'And it makes you feel good to know you're helping others. Every time you talk about it, your eyes do that thing.'

'That thing?'

'They sparkle.'

'Sparkle? Are you emasculating me again?'

'Absolutely not. It's *très* sexy…'

He chuckled, his chest rumbling against hers as he bowed his head to kiss her.

'Whoa, whoa, you two—come on! Mum's going to

make the driver a cup of tea if we keep him waiting any longer.'

Catherine gave him a quick peck. 'Flo has a point.'

She took his hand and led the way.

His mother was waiting for them at the bottom of the stairs, Max, their two-year-old son, in her arms and Alaric's father just behind. 'Thanks so much for watching the kids tonight.'

'You're very welcome. We could hardly let Flo miss out on her best friend's premiere. Not to mention her and David haven't had a night out in months.'

'Someone say my name?' His brother-in-law appeared in the hallway, bleary-eyed with his hair and tie askew.

'David!' Flo rushed up to him. 'Have you been asleep?!'

'Guilty as charged.' He grimaced as Flo grasped his tie and wriggled it back into position, attacking his hair next. 'Hey, two kids under three, another on the way, you've got to grab it while you can.'

Catherine laughed. 'You're really selling it.'

'It's a bit late for selling it, my love,' Alaric murmured, kissing Max on the forehead. 'This bun is well and truly cooked. Be good for Nanna and Grampy, okay?'

Max sucked his thumb in response as Nanna gave him a little bob. 'He's always good.'

'As for this one—' he placed his hand on the curve of Catherine's stomach '—not even born yet and she's off to a red carpet premiere.'

Catherine turned to look up at him. 'I'm not sure it's hormones after all, Alaric. This is *my* film, my script brought to life. What if people hate it? What if they don't get it?'

'Shh, my love, you will blow them all away. I promise.'

'You can't—'

He silenced her words with a kiss and earned them a disgusted *'Ew...'* from their two-year-old nephew, who came rushing in and did an about-turn, dashing back out again.

'And I think that's our cue to leave.' Alaric grinned, gesturing for the ladies to go ahead, his brother-in-law too, and then followed, giving his mum a peck to her cheek and his father a hand to the shoulder as he went. 'Thanks again for tonight.'

'You're welcome, son.' His father covered his hand.

'Good luck!' his mother added.

Luck. He didn't need luck. As he watched Catherine step into the car, her cheeks glowing, her stomach blooming with their daughter, he already felt like the luckiest man alive.

* * * * *

SLOW DANCE WITH THE BEST MAN

SOPHIE PEMBROKE

For Simon, after ten wonderful years of marriage.
Here's to many more. x

CHAPTER ONE

THREE DAYS AFTER CHRISTMAS, Eloise Miller stood on the ancient stone steps of Morwen Hall, her hands clasped over the buttons of her dove-grey wool coat, and waited for her childhood arch nemesis to arrive and all hell to break loose.

'I wonder if she'll wear the veil,' Laurel mused beside her. 'I mean, she sent me scampering all over the country looking for the absolute perfect lace confection, but I can't help thinking that Melissa really doesn't like it when people can't see her face.'

'Which explains those awful billboards for her latest film,' Eloise agreed, thinking of the monstrosities, tall as double decker buses, which featured little more than Melissa's flawless features, shiny blonde hair and slim, pale shoulders. Oh, and the name of the film, probably. But Eloise would bet money that no one who'd seen the posters could remember what the film was called.

Melissa had the sort of captivating beauty that made everything else fade into insignificance. Except the fact she was a perennial mean girl, of course.

'Do you think she's as…demanding on set as she has been over this wedding?' Laurel asked and, not for the first time, Eloise felt a burst of sympathy for her new friend. As Melissa's half-sister *and* wedding planner, Laurel had it far worse than Eloise. Not only did Laurel have to manage a whole five-day wedding celebration extravaganza for the rich and famous but, once this wedding was over, Eloise would never have to see Melissa again. Laurel would.

Mind you, having survived the teenage years, Eloise had been pretty sure that misery at Melissa's hands was over for her, especially once Melissa set sail for Hollywood and stardom. And once she'd actually found it, against all the odds, Eloise had been *certain* that she'd never have to get closer to Melissa Sommers than a movie poster ever again.

That was until Melissa revealed her engagement to A-list Hollywood actor, Riley Black, in *Star!* magazine, wearing a giant rock of a diamond on her left hand, and announced her intention to get married back home in England. And not just England—at Morwen Hall, the elite, luxury Gothic stately home turned hotel where she'd spent her teenage years working as a maid, and making Eloise's life miserable. Well, the last bit wasn't in the magazine, but it was all Eloise had been able to see when her boss had shown her the article.

'She can't possibly be as bad on set,' Eloise answered, shifting from one foot to the other to try and keep warm. She'd go back inside, but she knew the moment she turned her back would be the moment Melissa turned up, complete with her fiancé and his even more famous best man—Noah Cross. That was just the sort of luck she had. And, as the interim manager of Morwen Hall, it was her job to be there to greet their VIP guests. Even if they were planning on filling her hotel with *actors.* 'She's not that good an actress. They wouldn't keep casting her in all those blockbusters if she was as much of a pain to work with as she has been lately. Or as she was at Morwen Hall ten years ago, come to that.'

Laurel turned to look at her, curious. 'What was she

like? I never even met her until she was sixteen, after my dad, well…you know.'

Eloise did know. She suspected most of Britain—the world, even—knew the story of how Melissa Sommers had been brought up by her single mum, her dad visiting only when he could get away from his real family across town. Laurel's family.

'Organising this wedding has been the most time I've ever spent with her.' Laurel didn't add *thankfully* but Eloise could hear it in her voice.

'She was…' Cruel. Evil. Nightmarish. A total witch in a blonde wig. 'She liked to be the centre of attention,' Eloise said, conscious that Laurel *was* Melissa's sister, despite everything. She'd only met Laurel at the start of the wedding planning, six months ago, and most of their conversations so far had been wedding-related—with the occasional frustrated eye-roll and knowing glance when Melissa video-called in from LA with another hundred demands. But since Laurel had arrived at Morwen Hall the day before to set up for the wedding, Eloise had found it hard to believe that she and Melissa had even *one* parent in common, they were so different.

They had the same ambition, though. While Melissa had channelled hers into stardom, Laurel had taken a quieter route—setting up her own wedding planning company that was just starting to be featured in bridal magazines and websites. Of the two paths, Eloise felt strangely more envious of Laurel's than Melissa's. Eloise had never wanted to be a star, not really. But her own business… She shook her head. She had a good job at Morwen Hall. One she didn't plan to jeopardise by daydreaming.

'The centre of attention. I can believe that,' Laurel said with feeling. 'I guess maybe she feels she missed out on that, growing up. I mean, with our father staying with my mum instead of hers for so long.'

'Perhaps,' Eloise allowed. 'But I reckon she made up for it by stealing all my boyfriends.' She slapped her hand across her mouth as the words came out, but Laurel just laughed.

'*All* of them? How many did you have?'

'Two,' Eloise said mournfully. 'At different times, obviously. And, on both occasions, your sister managed to convince them that they'd be better off with someone else. Usually her.' It hadn't been too hard either. Growing up in the same town, going to the same school *and* working at the same hotel meant that Melissa had known all of Eloise's secrets. She'd known every embarrassing story to tell about her family, and which ones to pick for maximum effect.

And she'd had more than enough to choose from.

'Well, at least you won't have to worry about her doing that this time,' Laurel said.

'Well, no,' Eloise agreed. 'Since I don't have a boyfriend.' And hadn't had one for quite a while, actually, not that she was counting days. She'd rather wait and find the *right* one than try out any guy who came calling.

Not that she'd had any significant success since leaving school. In fact, the boyfriends Melissa had lured away might be considered the highlights of her dating career. Certainly a lot better than the one who'd left her for her mother. Or the guy at university who'd managed to screw her over both personally *and* professionally.

Maybe she just wasn't born to date. Heaven knew her mother had done enough dating for the both of them.

Laurel rolled her eyes. 'I meant I really think she's properly in love with Riley.'

Eloise found it hard to imagine Melissa loving *anybody* besides herself, but then maybe she'd changed. Organising weddings didn't tend to bring out the best in people. Maybe most of the time she was a total sweetheart.

Actually, no. That was even harder to imagine.

Still… 'I hope so,' Eloise said. 'I hope she's truly happy.'

Because the happier Melissa was, the better the chances of the wedding going off without a hitch, Melissa and Riley riding off into the sunset together and Eloise never having to see either of them again.

'Me too,' Laurel said. 'If only so I never have to organise another wedding for her. I mean, I know this is a huge coup for my new business and everything, but still…'

Eloise laughed, ignoring the pang of envy she felt at the excitement in Laurel's voice when she talked about her company. 'At least being the wedding planner means you got out of having to be maid of honour. I mean, have you seen those dresses she picked?'

Laurel pulled a face, probably feeling slightly queasy at the memory of the miles of icy blue-green satin and chiffon that had been sacrificed to make the bridesmaids and maid of honour dresses. 'Actually, it was never even suggested. I think Melissa was pretty set on having Cassidy Haven as maid of honour from the start. The celeb factor, you know.'

'You're probably right,' Eloise agreed. As far as she knew, Melissa and Cassidy's acquaintance went back to approximately one film, in which they had two scenes together. But, given Cassidy's rising star and box office gold reputation, that would be enough for Melissa.

A crunching noise echoed from the end of the driveway, getting closer. The sound of tyres on frozen ground, Eloise knew from experience. 'They're here,' she said, and Laurel raised her eyebrows with surprise.

'They are? Where?'

'Just coming around the bend.' At her words, the large

black four-by-four appeared from the tree cover and Eloise pasted on her smile. Time to start the show.

Laurel straightened her skirt and her shoulders, trying to pull herself up to her full height, Eloise supposed, although Eloise still had a full head and shoulders on her. She usually did with most people.

The four-by-four slowed to a halt in front of Morwen Hall and the driver stepped out to open the rear door. Eloise was vaguely aware of the passenger door opening too, but her gaze was firmly fixed on the blonde stepping out of the back seat, knees together, a picture of English elegance. Her light hair was fixed perfectly back from her beautiful face, her pale pink lipstick unsmudged. She hadn't even spilt any coffee on her snowy white jumper—cashmere, Eloise was sure—and white trousers.

Maybe celebrities really were another species. No human should look that good after an eleven-hour flight.

Eloise recognised Riley Black from the engagement photos and the occasional video call he joined them for during the wedding planning. He smiled up at them as he came around from the other side of the car to take his fiancée's arm. Laurel moved down a few steps to greet them and Eloise finally turned her attention to the fourth occupant of the car.

And promptly lost the ability to breathe.

Noah Cross had learned fairly early in his career how to tune out the meaningless chatter that came with the job but still pay just enough attention to assure whoever was talking that he was listening to them. The skill had served him well on movie sets across the world, in press junkets and at awards ceremonies.

Until he'd met Melissa Sommers.

The whole flight from LA he'd been trying to read a

new script his agent, Tessa, had sent him, to 'keep you too busy at this damn wedding to get into any trouble', as she'd put it. Normally, he'd have tossed the script in his suitcase, relaxed with a drink on the flight and looked forward to seducing a bridesmaid or two, just to keep in practice. But this script was from a writer he admired, one he'd dreamt of working with for too long now—Queenie Walters. Her films were renowned for being deep, thought-provoking, meaningful—and for winning every award going. Basically, the opposite of the sort of films he'd been making for the last seven years.

The sort of films that had led to Riley Black asking him to be his best man somewhere in the middle of nowhere, England, in minus temperatures in December.

Maybe it was time to start making a new sort of film.

So, back to the script.

It was good, that much he could tell, even from one cursory reading with Melissa chattering in his ear and Riley chiming in every few minutes or so. He could even tell it through the champagne he'd drunk to make the journey just a little more bearable.

He wanted to make this film. More than that, he wanted to *star* in this film.

He knew that the leading role wasn't the one his agent had suggested him for—that would be the light relief, the comic best friend. It was his own fault. He'd told Tessa he wanted to do something different, something other than action blockbusters and superhero movies. And she'd taken the not absurd mental leap and assumed he wanted comedy. She'd sent him a raft of terrible slapstick-without-humour typescripts to start with, until he'd asked for something a little…*better*.

Then she'd sent him *Eight Days After* and he'd known she understood at last.

Well, almost. She still saw him as the supporting actor.

He needed to convince her—and the director—that he was Best Actor material.

'And then she suggested that maybe I didn't need to have a veil at all!' Melissa crowed with laughter, regaling them all with yet another tale about her wedding planner, apparently oblivious to the fact that her fiancé had already heard it, the driver of the car didn't care and Noah was working very hard on not listening. 'Not have a veil! Can you imagine?'

'I heard that Rochelle Twist didn't have a veil at her wedding,' Noah said from the front seat, not looking up from his script.

'She didn't?' Melissa's eyes widened with alarm and Noah knew for certain that she would walk down the aisle without the veil on New Year's Eve. Well, unless she checked the Internet for photographic proof and realised that Noah was making it up to mess with her. As if he had any idea at all what A-list actresses wore on their wedding days.

It was still weird to think that he was up there on their invitation lists. The fact that Riley had asked him to be best man after just three films said a lot. Noah liked the guy well enough, but he wouldn't call him a best friend. They'd been out and got drunk a few times, played some poker. And Noah had spent one very long night listening to Riley weigh up the pros and cons of asking Melissa to marry him—the main pros apparently being 'it'd be great for my image' and 'she really wants to'. But that was about it. Did that qualify him for best man status? Apparently, in Melissa and Riley's eyes, it did.

Seven years ago, it wouldn't have done. Granted, seven years ago Melissa and Riley had probably been teenagers, but still. Back then, Noah had been a nobody, desperate for his big break but secretly afraid it was never going to come—the same as everyone else in town. He'd been living with his best friend Sally, sharing stories of awful auditions, commiserating over rejections with a bottle of cheap wine and trying to pretend that he wasn't crazy about her. Seven years ago, he'd been looking at a future of giving up, going home and admitting to his family that he'd failed, just like they'd said he would.

Then that fabled big break had come—the same day that everything else had been taken away from him.

Noah shook his head, trying to send the memories scattering. He didn't need them today—or any day, for that matter. Life was about the here and now, not the past.

And right now he was about to spend five days in some fancy hotel with a selection of the most beautiful women in the world. Surely he'd be able to find *some* way to pass the time.

The car turned off the main road onto a long sweeping driveway and past a pale sage-green sign with grey lettering, proclaiming the entrance to Morwen Hall. They were there.

Shoving the script back in his hand luggage, Noah peered out of the front windscreen, looking for the Hall itself. He hoped it was as nice as Melissa insisted it would be. He needed a break, a chance to unwind—preferably with company. It had been a long eighteen months making back to back films, plus the promotional efforts. Five days in the middle of nowhere didn't sound all that bad, really. Even if he did have to spend them with Melissa.

The car broke through the last of the trees surrounding the hotel and Morwen Hall loomed into view—all grey stone and huge windows, reflecting the weak winter sun. It looked like something out of a bad Gothic movie, with its turrets and arched windows, and Noah couldn't help but smile at the sight of it. Ostentatious, over the top and not quite the romantic vibe she thought she was going for. It suited Melissa perfectly.

'Isn't it gorgeous? It's *just* as I remember it,' Melissa squealed, and Noah recalled that Morwen Hall wasn't just a venue for her. She'd lived there, or worked there, or something of the sort when she was younger.

Noah looked at the building again and wondered what spending significant time in such a dramatic place would do to a person. Then he looked at Melissa again. *Question answered.*

'Look, honey, Laurel's come out to meet us,' Riley said and Melissa's face soured.

Noah looked to where Riley was pointing and saw two women standing on the steps outside the huge Gothic front door, a wooden creation with twisty ironworks over the top. He couldn't make out their features through the tinted glass, but presumably one of them was the hyper-efficient wedding planner, Laurel, who'd been sending Noah updates and asking him questions for the last six months.

He made a mental note to stay out of her way as much as possible for the next five days. Efficiency grew tiring quickly, he'd found.

The driver opened Melissa's door and the bride swept out. Noah opened his own door and followed, wishing he'd brought his sunglasses as he lost the protection of tinted glass and squinted into the winter sun, looking up at the Hall.

Yep, still just as Gothic.

But the women standing on the steps… The tinted glass definitely hadn't done them justice.

One was a petite brunette, all curves and smiles and bounce as she came down the steps to welcome Melissa with a hug. He hoped that was Laurel, who he'd vowed to avoid. Because the other…

The other stayed standing on the steps, her smile fixed and her hands clasped in front of her. She looked uncomfortable, as if she'd rather be anywhere else in the world. As if she was trying to fade into the background—something Noah wasn't used to seeing in the circles he hung out in these days.

She'd never manage it, though. She had to be nearly six foot in her sensible black heels, almost as tall as he was, and her pale features were topped with a cloud of blazing red hair, pinned tightly back to reveal the classical beauty of her features. He couldn't see the colour of her eyes from this distance, but he wanted to. He wanted to know if they were as striking as the rest of her.

Then she turned to look at him and he knew it didn't matter what colour they were—if this woman was looking at him, he'd never see anything else.

This woman would never disappear into the background *anywhere*.

And Noah hoped to be seeing an awful lot more of her over the next five days. Maybe he'd even get to find out what that beautiful hair looked like tumbling around her naked shoulders…

Shouldering his bag, he put on his most charming smile, hoped that the effect of the champagne had mostly passed and strode towards the imposing front door of Morwen Hall, and the equally imposing woman standing in front of it.

Maybe this wedding wouldn't be a complete disaster after all.

Noah Cross. Noah freaking Cross.

Okay, breathing was becoming an issue now. She really had to get hold of herself.

Eloise broke away from staring at the ridiculously handsome Noah Cross and sucked in a good lungful of crisp December air to replace all the oxygen that had been knocked out of her at the sight of him.

She was being ridiculous. *Of course* he was good-looking. He was a movie star. It was part of the deal. It definitely didn't mean anything important—that he was a nice person, or someone she wanted to spend time with. In fact, in her experience, it meant the exact opposite.

No. She was not her mother. She would not let her head be turned by the first attractive—*gorgeous*—man who looked her way. Hadn't she just decided that dating wasn't for her?

He probably wasn't even looking at her. He was probably looking at Morwen Hall. It was, after all, even more striking than her red hair, and considerably more beautiful.

That thought sobered her right up and knocked her back into business mode. She had a wedding to host, and an arch nemesis to deal with while she was doing it. She did *not* have time to get sidetracked ogling movie stars—especially given how many of them would be arriving later that afternoon.

Making sure her best fake smile was still in place, Eloise descended the front steps to join Melissa, Laurel and Riley on the driveway.

'Eloise!' Melissa cried, with what had to be phoney enthusiasm. 'It's just so *wonderful* to see you again, honey.' The 'honey' was new, Eloise noted, as Melissa leant forward to kiss the air a few inches away from Eloise's icy cheeks. Presumably something else she'd picked up in Hollywood, along with the fiancé.

'You've seen me on video calls for the last six months, Melissa,' Eloise said, still smiling so hard her cheeks ached.

'Oh, but that's not the same thing *at all.*' Melissa stretched a slender white arm around Laurel and Eloise's shoulders. 'Isn't this just *perfect?* My *oldest* friend and my favourite *half*-sister, working together to give me the wedding of my dreams.'

'It sure is perfect, honey,' Riley agreed, his southern accent far more pronounced than in his films.

Of course she'd think it's perfect, Eloise thought. *She's got the two people she wants to make miserable most in the world waiting on her hand and foot as the culmination of six months of demanding the impossible from them. It's her every dream come true.*

Apparently Hollywood stardom wasn't enough for some people. They had to come back and crush the little people they left behind too.

She glanced to her left and caught Laurel's eye, wondering if the wedding planner was having the exact same thoughts. Even if she was, neither of them would say anything, not with their careers riding on this. That was probably what Melissa was banking on. That, or she honestly thought they were grateful to her for condescending to use their services for her wedding.

Actually, knowing Melissa, it was probably the latter.

Eloise bit her tongue all the same, reminding herself of what really mattered: her promotion. If she pulled off this wedding, Mr Richards, who owned Morwen Hall, had promised her that she'd be made permanent manager in the New Year. Not to mention the huge boost the hotel would get from the exposure. That was a good thing. A good, secure job with a hotel that was doing well. That was a sensible career goal.

All she had to do was make it through to January the first without telling Melissa what she really thought of her, or giving her any reason to complain about Eloise's professionalism. How hard could that be?

Oh, yeah. Very.

But Eloise was determined to do it all the same.

'This is quite some place, Melissa. I can absolutely see why you chose it. It's perfect for you!' Noah Cross's voice was weirdly familiar from those times she'd sat in cinemas watching him beat up bad guys and seduce beautiful women on screen. It was just plain odd to hear him apply those dulcet tones to Morwen Hall. 'Moody, well built… and I guess it has one hell of a history.'

His upbeat tone made the comment sound complimentary but, as he met her eyes, Eloise realised he knew *exactly* what he was saying. The humour in his gaze only grew as Melissa frowned—not enough to cause lines, though—and said, 'Well, yes. It is quite special.'

It was a shame Noah Cross was an actor, Eloise thought. Otherwise, she had a feeling he might be exactly her sort of person.

'Why don't you all step inside?' she said, deflecting Noah's observations. 'It's freezing out here and I'd love to show you all around the old place, tell you a bit about its history.'

Noah sprung up the steps beside her, even as Melissa said, 'Of course, I already know everything there is to know about Morwen Hall.'

Eloise's smile became a little more fixed. 'I think you'll find we've changed a *few* things since you were last here, Melissa.' *Eight years ago.*

'Well, I for one can't wait to learn all about this place.' Noah slapped his hand against the heavy wood of the front door and the ironwork rang out an echo. 'And whether or not there are any vampires hiding in there waiting to suck my blood.' He flashed a smile that Eloise couldn't help but return.

'No vampires,' she promised. At least, as long as you didn't count Melissa. 'But I can't promise you might not see the odd ghost.'

Noah raised his eyebrows. 'I don't believe in ghosts.'

'That's good.' Eloise grinned back at him. 'Better just hope they don't believe in film stars either.'

Noah laughed, warm and dark and deep, and Eloise tore her gaze away from him. She didn't need to notice the way he tipped his head back when he laughed, or the long line of his neck, or his designer stubble. It was all totally irrelevant to her, and her job.

But she stole another look before heading back inside all the same.

CHAPTER TWO

THE INSIDE OF Morwen Hall was rather more what Noah had been expecting than the weirdly Gothic exterior. With its calming pale green walls and dove-grey trim, the luxurious but comfortable velvet and leather sofas in the main lobby and the deep pile rugs laid over the original stone floor, it was hard to believe Eloise's stories of ghosts. Inside, Morwen Hall could be any luxury five-star hotel anywhere in the world. Still, Noah couldn't shake the feeling that there might be more to this house, under the surface, than its owners wanted anyone to see.

And more to its manager too. Noah found his gaze fixed on Eloise as she shrugged off her pale grey coat, revealing a demure charcoal skirt suit beneath that went perfectly with the sensible black heels. He supposed that with such arresting hair and eyes brightly coloured clothing was just overkill.

Still, he couldn't help but imagine what she'd look like in the sort of dresses the actresses he knew wore on the red carpet. Something that showed off her figure instead of hiding it. Noah was a connoisseur of women's figures, and Eloise's definitely looked like one he'd like to explore further.

'Melissa, Riley, would you like me to show you to your suite?' Eloise asked. Noah supposed it was only polite to deal with the bride and groom first. Besides, it would mean she had more time for him afterwards—and more time for him to talk her into having a drink together later.

Melissa frowned ever so slightly, a tiny line appearing between her eyebrows. 'Actually, I need to speak with my wedding planner.' She slipped a hand through the crook of Laurel's arm and led her off to the side. 'Why don't you get our best man settled first?'

Noah hefted his carry-on bag over his shoulder. He hadn't seen his suitcase since the airport so he assumed it was being dealt with somewhere, and would magically appear in his room when he needed it. He loved hotels. They were almost as good as film sets for having your every need seen to before you even knew what you needed.

'You'll turn into one of those puffed up idiots who don't know the value of a hard day's work.'

His dad's voice in his head made Noah scowl, as it always did, but he shook the expression away before Eloise turned to face him and replaced it with his habitual charming smile.

'Right. Okay.' Eloise surveyed him with something akin to displeasure on her face, which gave Noah slight pause. Usually, women were *delighted* to score some alone time with him. And, from the way Eloise had stared at him on arrival, he'd naively assumed that she'd be the same.

Apparently, he was missing something here.

'If you'll just follow me, Mr Cross?' Eloise said, every inch the professional, as she headed for the elevators at the back of the lobby. They had a Gothic-style metalwork design painted on the doors, which amused Noah. As an attempt to make them fit in with the rest of the surroundings of Morwen Hall, he supposed it was as good a try as any.

'Guess these didn't come with the building, huh?' he

asked as she pressed the button to call one. 'The elevators, I mean. Sorry. They're "lifts" here, right?'

'That's right,' Eloise said with a nod. 'And no. They didn't have lifts when Morwen Hall was built.'

From her tone, Noah suspected she was already writing him off as a dumb American movie star. Well, she wouldn't be the first—hadn't his own father done the same? And there had been plenty more since—journalists, interviewers, all sorts. It was always fun to prove them wrong.

'Gothic revival, right? So, nineteenth-century? I'd guess…1850?'

If she was surprised Eloise didn't show it. '1848, actually. At least that was when work started.'

'Sounds like you know a lot about the place. Have you worked here long?'

The elevator pinged and the doors opened. Eloise motioned for him to enter first, which he did, then she stepped in behind him, pressing the button for the top floor.

'Since I was sixteen,' she said as the doors swished shut.

Of course. She was Melissa's oldest friend. She, and the Hall, were presumably the reason they were having the wedding in England in December in the first place. 'And that's when you met Melissa, right. Nice of her to want to come back here for the wedding, I guess.'

'It's just lovely,' Eloise said, her tone flat.

Noah was beginning to suspect that 'oldest friends' might not be the most accurate of descriptions for Eloise and Melissa's relationship.

'She must have a lot of fond memories of working here,' he pressed.

'I'm sure she does.' Eloise didn't place any extra emphasis on the word 'she', but somehow Noah heard it. From what he knew about Melissa, he wasn't overly surprised. Oh, she was sweetness and light to directors, producers and other stars, but he'd seen her berate one of the catering assistants for not having *exactly* the right kind of chia seed for her salad. He knew that sort of person—who could be anything you wanted if you mattered, and hell on wheels if you didn't. Hollywood was full of them.

He prided himself on trying not to ever become one of them. Whatever his father thought.

He'd learned how to be a star and still be gracious from watching Sally. It was one of the many lessons his best friend had taught him. After she got a recurring role in a weekly drama, she'd still been, well, Sally. Lovely and sweet and kind and patient with everyone from her co-stars to the guy on the street begging for enough quarters to buy a coffee. Sally had been the most genuine person he'd known in a city full of actors.

Just remembering that much pricked at his heart and Noah knew it was time to change the subject.

'Enough about Melissa,' he said as the elevator reached its destination and the doors parted again. 'So you've worked here, what, eight years?' He'd guess ten, based on Melissa's age, but everyone liked a little flattery, right?

'Ten, actually,' Eloise corrected him, and he hid a smile. He still had it.

'Must have seen a lot of changes here.' That was a given too, right? Everything changed. Whether you wanted it to or not.

'Yep. Melissa left, for one.' Eloise shut her eyes briefly. 'Sorry. I shouldn't have said that.'

'Yes, you should,' Noah insisted. Not least because it was the first real thing she'd said since they'd met and for some reason—perhaps because he'd been remembering Sally—Noah wanted her to be real. Maybe it was just that he had enough fakes in his professional life already—not that it usually bothered him. People who were putting on an act, being who they thought you wanted them to be, never wanted you to look too deep or get too close, so they never looked too deep or too close in return. And that suited Noah perfectly.

Too deep and too close led to the sort of pain he wasn't willing to feel again.

But Eloise… Maybe it would do him good to see some reality again. As long as *he* wasn't the one getting real.

'So… Oldest friend?' he asked as she led him along a wide corridor, carpeted in deep, dark green pile. They really did go all out with the luxury at this place. Not that Noah was complaining. He'd worked hard for years to earn this sort of luxury. He deserved it. And he would ignore any and all voices inside his head that said otherwise. Even if they did sound like Dad.

What was it about this place that was dredging up all those old insecurities he thought he'd left behind seven years ago? He bit back a laugh. Hadn't Eloise warned him he might find ghosts here?

'We've known each other pretty much all our lives.' Eloise sighed. 'Born in the same hospital, went to the same playgroup, same schools, then had the same part-time jobs as chambermaids here at Morwen Hall.'

'So you basically lived the same lives until Melissa set out to conquer Hollywood?' Interesting. He'd expect Eloise to show a little more envy, in that case, but mostly she just seemed…inconvenienced by Melissa's arrival.

'Not *exactly* the same lives,' Eloise said. 'But yes, there were similarities, I suppose.'

'And you never fancied Hollywood?' With Eloise's striking looks, he was pretty sure she'd have found some work at least. But Eloise laughed.

'No, not for me.'

'How come?'

She paused outside door number three-one-nine and flashed him a smile. 'Too many actors. Now, let me show you your room.'

He was *almost* sure she was joking, Noah decided, as Eloise gave him the nickel and dime tour of his suite. For all that Morwen Hall was unlike any building he'd ever been in from the outside, he'd expected the rooms to be fairly standard. 'Luxury hotel' didn't have so many different meanings, in his experience.

The main room of the suite confirmed his guess—there were a couple of creamy sofas, a coffee table laden with magazines and local information, a large window with a round table and two wooden chairs in front of it, a TV, fridge, desk, the usual. But then Eloise led him through to the bedroom.

'Huh.' Noah stared at the giant four-poster bed in the middle of the bedroom, decked out with heavy forest-green drapes and blankets over crisp white sheets. The wall behind the bed had been left bare, exposing the original stone of the house, but with tapestries hung either side of the four-poster for warmth. A pile of cushions and pillows in varying shades of green and different textures sat by the wooden headboard, ready to sink into.

'Do you like it?' Eloise asked and, for the first time, Noah heard a hint of uncertainty in her voice. 'With Melissa and Riley out in the Gatehouse suite, this is the best room in the hotel.'

'It looks it,' Noah said, eyeing the bed appreciatively. He had some awesome ideas for that bed.

He turned his attention back to Eloise, wondering if she might be willing to help him out with some of them. Given the way she was backing away, probably not.

'Well, if you're all settled…'

'What are you doing this evening?' Sometimes you

just had to take your chances, Noah had learnt. And right then he needed a distraction from all the thoughts of the past that had been plaguing him since he'd arrived—since he'd started reading that script, he realised. *That* was it. It wasn't about ghosts, just a story that hit too close to home.

Still, a night with Eloise would probably cure that too.

'Melissa and Riley have planned a welcome drinks party in the Saloon for all their guests,' Eloise said promptly. 'If you head down to reception for seven—'

'You'll be there?' Noah gave her his warmest smile, feeling she might be missing the point slightly.

'In my capacity as Hotel Manager? Absolutely.'

Definitely missing the point. Was she just shy, starstruck or honestly indifferent to him? Noah couldn't tell. A perverse part of him almost hoped it was the last option. It had been too long since a woman had offered him a real challenge.

'In that case, I'm looking forward to it,' Noah said. Perhaps he'd fit a nap in before seven. That would get him back on his game.

But first he had to finish reading the script before his agent called to ask what he thought.

Work before fun, whatever the press wrote about him.

'Great,' Eloise said, sounding as if she was dreading every second. 'I'll see you then.'

As the door shut behind her, Noah made himself a promise. Before Melissa and Riley said 'I do' he'd get Eloise the Hotel Manager to warm up to him—or even warm him up.

No one ever said that Noah Cross wasn't up for a challenge.

Eloise shut Noah's door behind her and felt every muscle in her body relax for the first time since she'd spotted him outside the hotel. The last thing she needed this week was a distraction—let alone a stupid girlish crush.

Sucking in a deep breath, Eloise made a resolution before striding down the corridor back towards the lifts: under no circumstances would she allow a ridiculous attraction—to a *film star* of all people—to derail any of the plans for Melissa and Riley's wedding.

All she needed to do, she reminded herself as she waited for the lift, was to make it to January the first. Then her lovely, normal, sensible and stable life would return and she could forget all about Melissa Sommers until her inevitable divorce and remarriage. No, even then, surely Melissa wouldn't return to the scene of the crime, so to speak. It had to be bad form to hold a second wedding at the same venue as the first.

If this wedding went well, it could be the last time she had to see Melissa Sommers—ever. If that wasn't motivation to not mess it up, nothing was.

Downstairs in the lobby, Melissa was still berating Laurel about something or other. Eloise got close enough to hear the words 'wedding favours' and 'an embarrassment' and backed off to loiter at the reception desk until they were finished. Anything wedding-related that wasn't actually part of the venue was, unfortunately for Laurel, Laurel's problem. And, as much as she liked Melissa's half-sister, Eloise had enough problems of her own at Morwen Hall without borrowing other people's.

After a few minutes where Eloise pretended to check the reservations system on the computer, Laurel approached, her smile fixed and tight. 'I'm afraid I'm going to have to abandon you for a few hours. Melissa needs me to pop up to London.'

'Wedding favours?'

Laurel nodded. 'Apparently the ones we decided on three months ago are now passé and embarrassing.'

'Of course.' Eloise sighed. There was no way to tell whether Melissa was seriously unhappy with the favours or just trying to make Laurel's life difficult. Either way, Laurel would need to fix it. 'So, what's the plan?'

'Apparently she's made some calls and there are now one hundred and fifty alternative favours—something to do with artisan chocolates and mini personalised perfumes, I think—waiting at some boutique in central London. So I'm off to pick them up.'

'A wedding planner's work is never done.'

'Especially not with this wedding.' Laurel gave her a tired smile. 'Anyway, I'm going to hitch a lift with the next car arriving from the airport and get it to drop me off on its way to pick up the next set of guests—there should just about be time, as long as the traffic's not too awful.'

'How will you get back?' Eloise asked because she probably shouldn't grab hold of Laurel's leg and beg her not to leave her alone with these awful people.

'The last car heading back from the airport will have to swing past and pick me up.' Laurel sighed. 'And I'll just have to pray that the guest inside isn't some absurdly high maintenance celeb that objects to travelling with the help—or taking a significant detour.'

Eloise laughed. 'I cannot *imagine* where you might have got the idea that Melissa would be friends with that sort of person.'

'I know, right?' Laurel smiled again, a real grin this time. Then her expression turned more serious. 'Will you be okay here without me? Really? I know there's still masses to do...'

Eloise waved away her concerns with a flap of her hand. Laurel panicking all over London wouldn't help either of them, or get this wedding going. 'I'll be fine. Everything's set up for the welcome drinks, and Chef's already in the kitchen working on the canapés and such, so I'm free to supervise the check-ins. Once I've shown Melissa and Riley to the Bridal Suite, anyway. I hope they like it.'

'How could they not? It's gorgeous.' Laurel tugged the strap of her messenger bag higher up on her shoulder. 'Right, I'd better go. Good luck!'

'You too. May all your favours be cutting edge and perfect.'

'That's the hope!' Laurel waved as she shoved the heavy front door open with her shoulder, and then Eloise was alone with Melissa and Riley. Exactly the scenario she'd been hoping to avoid.

With a bright smile, Eloise turned to walk towards the bride and groom, who were indulging in a nauseating public display of affection in her lobby. Because this week wasn't awkward enough already.

'If you two are ready, I'd love to show you both to our Bridal Suite. I think you'll agree it's something a bit special.'

Melissa pulled away from Riley, who kept his hand low on her hip. 'I can't wait to see it! You've converted the old gatehouse, Laurel said?'

She sounded enthusiastic enough, which gave Eloise hope. Maybe Melissa *had* grown up at last and all the tensions of the last six months were just the usual stresses of being a bride, plus the added stress of doing it all in the limelight. It seemed unlikely but Eloise lived in hope.

'That's right,' she said, leading them out of the hotel's front door and down the steps to the driveway. 'It's just a short walk from the Hall proper, but we find that our happy couples enjoy the privacy.'

Riley's mouth twitched into a grin at that. 'I bet they do. I know I plan to!'

Melissa dodged his hands as he grabbed for her waist again. For a moment she looked so girlish and young that they could all have been sixteen again. Except, Eloise reminded herself, if they were, she definitely wouldn't have been invited to hang out with them.

'Not until after the wedding, you don't!' Melissa squealed as she danced across the driveway in her ridiculously expensive leather boots and impractical bright white coat. Her blonde hair shone in the winter sunlight, her pale skin flawless as she smiled.

It was, Eloise decided, a good job she wasn't the jealous type.

'Can you believe it?' Riley asked, falling into step with Eloise. 'She's making me wait until after the wedding. I have the most beautiful fiancée in the world and I'm not even allowed to touch her.'

'Oh, like you haven't touched me plenty before,' Melissa said with a flirtatious laugh. 'I seem to remember you could barely do anything else for the first month or two…'

Eloise picked up the pace just a bit, relieved when the Gatehouse came into view around the edge of the trees.

'Not for the last forty-eight hours!' Riley protested. 'It's cruel and unusual torture; that's what it is. Eloise agrees, don't you?'

Eloise pretty much thought it was none of her business, and she'd rather keep it that way, but the client was the client.

'I think that seeing the Bridal Suite might tempt her resolve,' she said diplomatically.

'That's why he won't be staying in it until the wedding night.' Melissa's tone was triumphant, and the small smile on her face as she looked at Eloise made it clear that she knew exactly what she was doing. 'Oh, didn't Laurel tell you that Riley would need a separate room until Saturday?'

Eloise bit the inside of her cheek in a desperate attempt to keep a hold on her temper. Melissa knew perfectly well that she hadn't—probably because she'd never mentioned it to Laurel in the first place. In fact, Eloise suspected that she'd just come up with it at that moment and was now using the idea to play Eloise and Laurel off each other. That would be just the sort of thing she would do.

Well. Eloise might have fallen for it when she was sixteen. But she wasn't sixteen any longer.

'Actually, she did suggest it might be a possibility so I've got a very special room put aside for Riley in the hotel, just in case he needed it.'

Riley looked impressed. Melissa looked murderous. Eloise smiled serenely and moved past them both to unlock the door to the Gatehouse.

'Now, how about we take a look at where you'll be spending your first night as man and wife?' she said. Then she could get onto building an extra hotel suite for Riley. There had to be a solution somewhere. She just hadn't thought of it yet.

Even Melissa had to be impressed by the Gatehouse Suite, and Riley's eyes were huge as Eloise gave them the tour. Morwen Hall was a luxury hotel from top to bottom but the Gatehouse kicked that luxury up a notch further. The stone building had been completely renovated—walls had been knocked through to turn what had been a small family home into a spacious suite for two. Downstairs was laid out as an open-plan living area, with a small kitchen counter running along one side. It wasn't a functioning kitchen—that wasn't what guests needed here. Instead, it had a small fridge filled with champagne and another stuffed with high-end chocolates, caviar and other delicious treats. A top of the range coffee machine with quality china fulfilled guests' caffeine needs, and an extensive menu was available twenty-four hours from direct dial to the front desk.

Downstairs was, Eloise thought proudly, impressive. But upstairs blew it away.

The four-poster bed that dominated the room was larger even than the one that had rendered Noah speechless. The bed linens were snowy white Egyptian cotton, with luxurious touches in jewel-coloured satin and silk accessories. The large bay window—complete with cushioned window seat—looked out over the river, and the en suite bathroom featured both an ultra-modern shower for two and an old-fashioned roll top bath.

'It's gorgeous,' Melissa admitted eventually. Then, apparently unable to resist criticising *something,* she added, 'And I'm sure I'll be fine, all the way out here.'

It's two minutes from the hotel. Less if you don't stop to grope your fiancé.

'Well, I'll make sure you have my room number,' Riley said, wrapping an arm around Melissa's waist and giving the four-poster a good, long look. 'Just in case you need me to come down here and…save you.'

Rolling her eyes, Melissa pushed him away. 'You and Eloise should go and find your room. I'm going to take advantage of that lovely bath.'

'Right,' Eloise said, thinking fast. 'Your room. Just follow me!'

As they left Melissa to her bath, Eloise spotted the first of the guests' cars pulling up the driveway. She was out of time, and all chaos was likely to break loose soon. And Riley still needed a room, even if she doubted he'd actually end up sleeping in it at all.

Mentally, she ran through the rooming list for the wedding in her head. After Noah's, the next best room in the hotel had been earmarked for Riley's brother, Dan. He wasn't bringing a guest, so at least that would only be one person to rehouse. Plus his flight was the last one in, so that gave her more time to try and fix things. And if the worst came to the worst and she couldn't magic another room from a no-show, or persuade Melissa to let Riley back into the Gatehouse, at least Dan and Riley might not be *too* horrified about having to share…

It was the best she could do for now. Decision made, Eloise covered the distance between the Gatehouse and Morwen Hall with large strides, leaving Riley trying to keep up. She'd show him to his room then get back down to supervise check-in. Laurel would be back to help—and provide much-needed moral support—before the welcome drinks.

And then all Eloise had to do was resist the considerable charms of Noah Cross for the evening.

How hard could that be?

Then she remembered Noah's smile, and realised that there was a very real possibility that she might be doomed.

CHAPTER THREE

IN THE END, the nap had to wait.

Noah placed the script reverently on the bed in front of him and reached for his phone without ever looking away from the cover sheet. He didn't want to break the magic spell the writing had cast over him before he spoke to his agent. He wanted to live in this feeling—in the brilliance and excitement of a perfect story. The way he felt he knew every one of the characters inside out as if he *was* the characters.

This film—this was the one he'd been waiting for.

He couldn't remember being this excited about a part since… Well, since he'd first moved to LA with Sally.

Swallowing hard at the memory, he pushed it aside and punched the right combination on the screen to call Tessa, his agent.

'I want this part,' he said, the moment she picked up.

'Noah?' She sounded sleepy. Noah did a quick mental calculation of the time difference and winced. Then he decided that, since she was awake now anyway, he might as well continue.

'*Eight Days After*,' he said. 'I want the part. The lead. None of this supporting actor stuff. I want the main attraction.'

'Really?' Tessa was awake now, if the pep in her voice was anything to go by. 'You think you're right for Marcus?'

'Definitely,' Noah replied, ignoring the surprise in her voice. 'Trust me. They want me in that role. I will knock it out of the park.' There was a pause on the other line, and Noah's confidence took a slight dip. But not for long. He hadn't got where he was by letting criticism knock him back. 'What? What did they say about me? You might as well just tell me—you know I'll hear it eventually anyway.' That was how Hollywood gossip worked. Confidences were never kept, and secrets always got out. You just had to front it out and live with whatever people had to say about you, Noah had found. He just didn't let the gibes and the comments get past his defences any more. They didn't hurt if he didn't let himself feel them.

'Stefan, the director…he's worried you might not have the, well, depth for the part.'

'For Marcus?'

'For the best friend part.'

Noah blinked. 'The best friend *has* no depth. He's basically there to lighten the mood so that no one slits their wrists in the movie theatres.' If Stefan didn't believe he could even pull off *that* part, Noah had a harder path to climb than even he'd anticipated.

'Still. This is a very different movie to the sort you've been in before.'

'Lately,' Noah countered.

'Since you became an actor anyone has heard of,' Tessa shot back, and Noah winced. Had it really been that long since he'd made a film that *mattered?* He knew that it had. He'd not taken on a part with substance since he'd got his big break in a summer blockbuster.

So why now? Why this one?

Noah shook his head. It didn't matter why. It only mattered that he get it. One way or another.

'What will it take to convince him?' he asked.

'That you can play the best friend?'

'No.'

Tessa sighed. 'Look, Noah, I think they've already got someone in the frame for Marcus—and no, before you ask, I don't know who. They're being cagey, though, so that probably means someone big.'

'Someone they're not sure of, or they'd be telling everyone.'

'Maybe. Why does this matter so much to you?' Tessa asked. 'I mean, you've been perfectly happy for years playing the big budget hero, the action guy or whatever.'

'You mean as a more looks than talent kind of actor,' Noah translated. He'd heard the talk as well as she had.

'You said it, not me. But yeah. So what's changed?'

Noah sank back against the pillows on the four-poster bed, trying to find the right words. 'It's…it's this script. I mean, I knew I was ready for a change. It's been seven years since…' Since he'd taken a part that made him look too deep, search too far to find the character. Since he'd done anything more than drift through his roles without having to think too much about the emotions behind them. Since he'd risked feeling at all.

'Since what happened to Sally.' Tessa was one of the few people who knew that story. One of the many reasons Noah had stuck with her as his agent even after he had agencies banging on his door wanting to sign him.

'Yeah. But it's more than that. There's something about this script, Tess.' Something that made his heart race, made him want to reach for something more, something better, something deeper, for the first time in a long time. 'The way it talks about the human condition, about loss, and connection and love…'

'I know,' Tessa said quietly. 'That was why I was surprised you want to do it. They're usually exactly the things you try to avoid.'

That was the problem with having the same agent for almost a decade. They got to know you—and your weaknesses—too well.

'Yeah, well, maybe it's time for a change.' In career terms, if not personally.

'Okay, be honest. Is this about that interview last month?'

'You know I don't let those things get to me.' Even if they *had* said that his films were getting more brainless by the season.

'That one would get to anyone. There's no shame in wanting to make better movies, Noah.'

'Exactly!' Better movies. That was the goal. And totally achievable without opening himself up to all the things he'd built walls against years before. 'So you'll get me the part?'

'I'll get you a video call with the director,' Tessa corrected. 'That's the most I can do. Then it's up to you. But you're really going to have to blow them away.' The warning was clear in her voice. They didn't want him for the part. If he wanted it…he'd have to show them they couldn't do it right without him.

'I will.'

'I mean it. This part needs real feeling and—'

'You don't think I can do it,' Noah realised. 'And here I thought agents were supposed to be an actor's biggest cheerleader.'

'I can dig out the skirt and pom-poms if you like.' Tessa

sighed again. 'Look, I know you *used* to be able to do it. That's why I signed you.'

'And I thought it was for my pretty face.'

'That too,' she admitted. 'But mostly it was your talent. The way you connected with an audience. But these days… Noah, you don't even connect with the women you sleep with. Be honest. Do you really think you can do this? Look deeper inside yourself and find all that good stuff I haven't seen in years?'

Could he? Noah wasn't sure. 'Honestly, I'm not even sure those parts are still there.'

'Well, if you want this role, you better hope they are.'

'You'll get me the video call?'

'I'll get you the call,' Tessa promised. 'The rest is up to you. But Noah…'

'What?'

'Your acting ability wasn't Stefan's only concern,' Tessa said.

'It should be the only thing that matters,' Noah shot back. 'So what? What else?'

'He doesn't…how did he put it?' Tessa took a breath and started again. 'Stefan wants the film to be the focus, the thing everyone is talking about. Not your love life.'

'I don't have a love life,' Noah pointed out.

He hadn't been in love since Sally died. How could he be?

'You have women. Lots of women, whether you love them or not.'

'I don't.' Why did he have to say it? Tessa already knew. But somehow it felt important to be clear. As if he'd be betraying Sally if he let there be any doubt.

And he already had enough guilt to deal with, knowing he hadn't lived up to being the best friend that she needed.

'You go out with a lot of women and you're seen doing

it. People take photos. The photos show up in magazines, on the Internet, and people talk about them.' Tessa's words were clipped, her tone impatient. 'You know this, Noah, and you know the effect it has. Don't be obtuse.'

'The effect it has? The way it drives up ticket sales, you mean?' Because being seen, getting out there, that was as much a part of his job as showing up and playing a part. In some ways it felt like just another part he was playing: Noah Cross, Film Star.

'Not this time,' Tessa said. 'This isn't the sort of film you're used to, Noah. Stefan wants people talking about the meaning, the theme, the soul of the film. Not who you're sleeping with tonight.'

'So you're saying, take the part and give up sex?' Because if that was the case… No, he still wanted the part.

'I'm saying, try a little discretion for once. Okay?'

Discretion. That he could do. 'Fine.'

For a moment, Noah had an image of bright red hair and sparkling eyes. Eloise. With her arresting beauty, she was anything but discreet. Anyone would remember seeing him with her.

Apparently, this wedding had just got a whole lot less fun.

'I'll be discreet,' he promised. 'I'll be so discreet you won't even know I'm here.'

Tessa snorted. 'I'll believe it when I see it.'

By late afternoon, Eloise felt as if her feet might fall off. She'd known the high heels were a mistake. Normally she wore low wedges or boots, but today she'd felt the need for something a little smarter. They weren't even all that high—certainly lower and more sensible than Melissa's expensive spike-heeled boots—but apparently running around Morwen Hall in them all day had beaten her feet into submission. She was ready to retire to the tiny bedrooms they kept for staff members working big events and soak her feet in the not quite full-size bath for an hour or two. Preferably while eating chocolate and sipping red wine.

But, instead, she still had a few more guests to welcome and show to their rooms—including the brother of the groom, who still didn't know his room had been taken over by Riley himself. In all the chaos, Eloise still hadn't found a solution to that either. Unless he wanted her room, and she'd just have to sleep behind the reception desk. She certainly couldn't risk going home, not while Melissa was on the premises. As much as Eloise trusted her deputy manager, she wouldn't leave *anyone* to deal with Melissa alone.

Wearily, Eloise stepped back behind the reception desk and, once she was sure no one could see, slipped her feet from her shoes and let the cool stone floor soothe her feet through her tights. *That* was better.

For a moment, she honestly believed she might get a small break in the craziness of the day to get herself together before the nightmare of the welcome drinks that evening.

Until Melissa's scream cut through the air.

Eloise let her eyes flutter closed just for a moment as she steeled herself for whatever was about to happen. When she opened them again, Melissa was bustling across the lobby, a towel wrapped around her hair, wearing a coat and boots over black silky leggings and a matching top that Melissa obviously classed as loungewear, and probably cost more than Eloise earned in a month.

'Is something the matter, Melissa?' Eloise asked in her calmest, everything-will-be-fine voice. Inside, she just prayed that whatever the problem was, it wasn't the Gatehouse. If Melissa had a problem with the Bridal Suite they really were in trouble.

'It's Cassidy!' Melissa shrieked. 'She just called from Aspen! She's broken her leg on the slopes!'

'Cassidy,' Eloise repeated, her mind running through the guest list again in the hope that this might mean she had a spare room after all... 'Wait, your maid of honour Cassidy?'

'*Yes!*' Eloise winced as the pitch of Melissa's voice reached parts only dogs could hear.

Okay, that was a problem. But Eloise was sure one of Melissa's other celebrity bridesmaids would be willing to step up to the job. And in the meantime... 'Does that mean she and her family won't be attending the wedding after all?'

And I can give their room to Riley's brother?

Melissa gave her one of those were-you-born-this-stupid looks that Eloise had learned to hate during their childhood. '*Of course* they're coming. Well, not Cassidy—apparently she can't fly. But Dillon—her husband—will still be here. He says he's bringing an "old friend" actually.' The way she said it, Eloise could actually hear the air quotes around the words. She tried not to pull a face, but clearly she was never going to understand celebrity marriages. Who brought their mistress to a friend's wedding when their wife was laid up in hospital?

A melodic chiming noise filled the lobby and Melissa shoved one perfectly manicured hand into her coat pocket and pulled out her phone.

'Kerry? Thank God you called back. Did you hear about Cassidy? Well, what do I do? When are you getting here, anyway? Tomorrow! I need a new maid of honour before tomorrow!'

Kerry, Eloise recalled from many contract negotiations

and emails, was Melissa's agent. Why she was the first port of call in a maid of honour crisis, Eloise wasn't sure. But she suspected it was another one of those things she didn't understand about Hollywood.

'Someone who knew me back when? You think we should play up the "local girl made good" angle?' Melissa asked, not bothering to lower her voice at all. 'Isn't it enough that I came back to this dump in the first place?' She rolled her eyes. 'Fine, fine. If that's what you think will sell. Yeah, I'll ask her. Okay. Bye.'

Dump? Had Melissa really just called Morwen Hall a *dump?* It might not have been the peak of luxury ten years ago, but these days it was *spectacular*.

She was so annoyed she was still grinding her teeth in annoyance when Melissa turned back to the reception desk and said, 'Right, change of plan. You're my new maid of honour.'

Eloise blinked. 'What?'

'You.' Melissa pointed at Eloise, jabbing a nail against her breastbone. 'You're going to put on the very expensive pretty dress I've already paid for and walk down the aisle in front of me. You're going to smile for the cameras. You're going to say wonderful things about me, and tell the reporter covering this wedding how close we were growing up, and how Hollywood hasn't changed me at all. *Okay?*'

'Why?' Eloise asked, baffled. Then, as she stared down Melissa's frown, she figured it out. 'This is because of all those articles lately, isn't it? The ones calling you a diva who's forgotten where you came from.'

Melissa sniffed. 'I don't read that sort of trashy magazine.'

'Isn't it the same one that's covering your wedding?' Melissa didn't answer that one. 'So, let me guess. Your agent thinks that if you have an old friend as part of the wedding party it'll show how down-to-earth you still are, with your million-dollar wedding at a five-star hotel.'

'Something like that.'

'Yeah, I'm not doing it.' Not a chance. It was bad enough that she had to put Morwen Hall at the disposal of an ungrateful Melissa and her celebrity mates. The last thing Eloise wanted was to have to be part of this whole debacle. 'Why don't you ask Laurel? She *is* your half-sister.'

Melissa pulled a face. 'No way. Besides, she wouldn't fit in the dress. Have you seen that girl's cleavage?' Eloise had, and was rather envious of it, actually, but she didn't think that would dissuade Melissa.

'The chances are *I* won't fit in the dress either,' Eloise pointed out instead. She knew she was on the skinny side of slender, because that was just how her body and metabolism worked—especially when she was rushing around Morwen Hall all day, every day. But Hollywood celebs were a different category of thin, weren't they? And Eloise *definitely* wasn't that.

'Oh, you will,' Melissa assured her. 'Cassidy had to put weight *on* for her last part, if you can believe it. Something about fat girls being funnier.' Well, that sounded like a film Eloise would go out of her way to avoid. 'So we'll do the dress fitting first thing in the morning then.'

'Wait! I didn't say I'd do it!' But Melissa was already walking away, her panic about her friend apparently forgotten now the role had been filled. 'I already have a job at this wedding, remember? I'm in charge of the venue!'

'Then you'd better find someone to take over for you. You'll be fine,' Melissa called back over her shoulder as she headed back towards the Gatehouse. 'Just do everything I say.'

'Yeah, because that always worked out so well when we were kids,' Eloise grumbled as the front door swung shut. That was how she'd walked in on her mother kissing the first proper, grown-up boyfriend Eloise had ever had, a week before she'd left for university. Because Melissa had sent her down into the prop room at the theatre to retrieve something or other she obviously didn't really need. Afterwards, Melissa had claimed that she couldn't *possibly* have known that they were down there, but really, wasn't it all for Eloise's own good anyway? She'd practically done her a favour...especially since everyone had been talking about them for weeks behind Eloise's back. Melissa had truly believed that she'd done the right thing sending her down there to find out the truth for herself.

And maybe she had. She'd certainly cemented Eloise's decision to never trust another actor. If only she'd also warned her about business students.

Maid of honour for Melissa Sommers. How on earth had this happened? And the worst part was—

'Sounds like we'll be spending even more time together.' Noah's voice was warm, deep and far too close to her ear.

Eloise sighed. That. That was the worst thing. Because the maid of honour was *expected* to pair up with the best man, and that would not make her resolution to stay away from Noah Cross any easier at all.

She turned and found him standing directly behind her, close enough that if she'd stepped back a centimetre or two she'd have been in his arms. Suddenly she was glad he'd alerted her to his presence with his words.

She shifted further away and tried to look like a professional, instead of a teenager with a crush. Looking up at him, she felt the strange heat flush over her skin again at his gorgeousness. Then she focused, and realised he was frowning.

'Apparently so,' she agreed. 'But I'm sure I'll be far too busy with all the wedding arrangements—'

'Oh, I doubt it,' Noah interrupted, but he still didn't sound entirely happy about the idea, which surprised her. Perhaps she'd misread his flirting earlier. Maybe he really was like that with everyone and, now the reality of having to spend time with her had set in, he was less keen on the idea. 'Melissa has quite the packed schedule for the wedding party, you know. She's right—you're going to have to find someone to take over most of your job here.'

Eloise sighed. She *did* know. She'd helped Laurel plan it, after all.

And, now she thought about it, every last bit of the schedule involved the maid of honour and the best man being together.

Noah smiled, a hint of the charm he'd exhibited earlier showing through despite the frown, and Eloise's heart beat twice in one moment as she accepted the inevitable.

She was doomed.

She had the most ridiculous crush on a man who clearly found her a minor inconvenience.

And—even worse—the whole world was going to be watching, laughing at her pretending that she could live in this world of celebrities, mocking her for thinking she could ever be pretty enough, funny enough...just *enough* for Noah Cross.

Eloise felt the blood drain from her head as she gripped the edge of the reception desk to try and conquer the dizziness that overcame her at the idea.

Ten years on and Melissa Sommers had just delivered her into hell all over again.

Perfect.

CHAPTER FOUR

'You look like you need a drink.' In Noah's experience, that was a good line with stressed out women. But in this case it wasn't a line—well, it wasn't *just* a line. Eloise looked as if she might keel over at any moment. Her already pale skin had faded to the same white as the expensive sheets on his four-poster bed and her bright eyes were huge in her face. Most women he knew would have loved to have been tagged to play maid of honour for Melissa Sommers, and few of them would have objected to spending more time with him as best man either.

But Eloise, he was learning quickly, wasn't quite like all the other women he knew.

Maybe he couldn't indulge in the sort of fun he'd planned with her—not if he wanted that part, and he did. But they were going to be spending a lot of time together, it seemed. The least he could do was help her out, and get to know her a bit.

If not in *quite* the way he'd like…

'I'm fine.' Eloise's voice was faint and not at all believable.

'Sure you are.' Noah didn't bother hiding his sarcasm as he took her elbow. 'Look, at least come and sit down for a few minutes.'

'With you?' Eloise's gaze shot to his face, then she shook

her head and looked away again. 'I'm working. I can't sit down and I definitely can't drink.'

'Yeah, well, you look like death—no offence. So you kind of need to do something if you don't want to scare the guests.'

Eloise scowled at him, a little colour finally coming back into her cheeks. 'If I'm so terrifying, why aren't I scaring you away?'

'I don't scare easily,' Noah said. 'Haven't you seen all my horror movies?'

'No,' Eloise said, but he was pretty sure she was lying. Maybe she *was* a closet star-struck fan. Except in that case he'd kind of expect her to be nicer to him. 'Look, I'm fine. I just need a moment alone.' She stepped away, towards the other side of the lobby. Noah followed, pausing at her side as she fiddled with the latch on the glass doors that led out to some sort of terrace. 'You don't need to watch me, you know.'

'You're nice to watch,' Noah said with a shrug. Looking was still okay, right? Looking was discreet. He hoped. 'It's not exactly a hardship.'

'I meant… I just need to get some air.'

'Fine by me,' Noah agreed. Then he followed her out onto the terrace, ignoring her heavy sigh.

'What is it with you?' Eloise snapped as he shut the door behind them.

'Me? Nothing at all. You, on the other hand, looked like you were about to pass out, all because some blonde asked you to wear a pretty dress. I mean, I know it's probably stupidly expensive, but still. Formalwear doesn't usually cause fainting fits, in my experience.'

'Yeah, well, clearly you've never experienced formalwear around Melissa Sommers before.' She stalked to the edge of the terrace, leaning on the stone wall as she stared out over the river beyond. Noah gave her a moment then rested his arms beside hers, enjoying the view.

Despite the bitter cold, the air felt fresh on his face, waking him up after a long night of travelling. He felt… alive, somehow, in this place. More alert, more open to the world around him.

Or maybe that was the anticipation of his video call with Stefan, the director of *Eight Days After*. It was strange, but it felt as if that script and this place had become intertwined in his mind, as if being at Morwen Hall would help him become the actor he needed to be to do the part justice.

'Why are you following me around?' Eloise asked eventually, after long moments.

'Honestly? I'm not sure.' Noah shook his head, trying to make sense of it himself. 'There's something about you. The moment I saw you this morning, I wanted…' He broke off.

'I've seen the photos and read the reports,' Eloise said drily. 'I know what your sort wants when it comes to women.' Of course she did. Because, apparently, he wasn't at all discreet about that. He wondered what people would make of the truth—that most of those women on his arm were there to be seen, the same way he was. Often, that was as far as things went.

Noah gave a self-deprecating laugh. 'Reports of my promiscuity may be greatly exaggerated. Besides…that wasn't what I was thinking.'

Colour flooded Eloise's cheeks, the pink clashing with the vibrant flame red of her hair. 'Of course not. I didn't mean… I wasn't assuming that you wanted to…'

Time to put her out of her misery. 'Not because you're not attractive. You're gorgeous.' Her cheeks turned a deeper pink at the compliment. 'And don't get me wrong. I'm totally planning on flirting with you some more later.'

If he didn't at least flirt, the world's media would think he was sick or something, and that publicity could be even worse. Maybe.

'You mean you're not now?' If she thought this was flirting, he could have totally snowed her if he had the chance. He sighed at the idea of the lost opportunity.

'Right now, I'm just making sure you're okay. And wondering what the deal is with you and Melissa.'

'*That's* why you're following me around? Because you're nosy?'

'Not *nosy* exactly.' Men weren't nosy, were they? Curious, perhaps. Nosy was for old ladies and people on the neighbourhood watch. 'I just…you intrigue me. And I can't explain why. Except that maybe it has to do with this movie I might be making… Anyway, that doesn't matter. What matters is, I'm interested. I find myself wanting to know more about you, which is unusual for me, I assure you. But, since I do… I'm a good listener, really. If you wanted to talk about why the idea of being Melissa's maid of honour makes you want to throw up or pass out, I'll listen.'

'You mean you'll stand there until I tell you, whether I want to share or not.'

'Basically, yes.'

'Great.' Eloise sighed, then turned to rest her back against the stone wall of the terrace, staring back at him with those big blue-green eyes. 'Fine. You want the whole sob story? I don't know what Melissa Sommers is like on set but when she was a teenager she was a bully, a cheat and she made my life a misery. In fact, part of me wonders if the only reason she's holding her wedding at Morwen Hall—and the only reason she asked her half-sister to be her wedding planner, come to that—is so that she can lord her success over all the little people she left behind. And I know I sound bitter and jealous, but I'm not—really,

I'm not. I wouldn't be Melissa for all the tea in China. But that doesn't mean I'm not allowed to hate her a little bit.'

'I never said it did,' Noah replied, bemused. Where had Eloise been hiding all that anger and all that rage all morning? Ever since he'd arrived, she'd been professional, courteous, distant, and never even the slightest bit inappropriate. He'd been starting to think he might never get under that pale skin. But now it seemed that Eloise had limits—just like everyone else—and Melissa had just passed them.

What had she called Melissa? A bully and a cheat. 'Well, I guess I can see why you don't want to be her maid of honour.'

Eloise gave a watery chuckle and hid her face with her hands. 'It's going to be horrendous.'

'Oh, it won't be that bad.' Noah slung an arm around her slim shoulders for moral support and she stiffened instantly. If she'd felt anything like the tingles that ran up his arm at the contact, he didn't blame her.

That wasn't like it was with all the other women he'd dated either. It seemed nothing about Eloise was usual.

'You'll wear the dress, pose for some photos, give a couple of short interviews, dance with me...'

Eloise groaned. If he didn't have such a healthy ego, Noah might be starting to take some offence around now.

'You don't like dancing?' he asked.

'I don't like any of it.' Eloise lifted her face and he could see the edge of fear in her eyes. She wasn't exaggerating. Something about the maid of honour job really had her off-balance. 'I hate being the centre of attention.'

'I'm pretty sure that's going to be Melissa, however expensive your frock.'

Eloise shook her head. 'You don't get it. I hate people looking at me. I hate anyone noticing me, noticing what I do.' Which explained her prickly reaction to his attentions, at least. 'You can't understand—your entire life is basically about shouting, "Hey, look at me!" and seeing how many people you can get to turn around.'

'My whole career, a decade of work, reduced to a schoolyard attention grab.' Noah gave an overly dramatic sigh, hoping it might lighten the mood. 'The saddest part is, you're right. But now I've seen the error of my ways, I'll go and become a hotel manager instead.'

'I didn't use to be a hotel manager,' Eloise said, ignoring his attempt at humour. 'I was a chambermaid for years, then worked my way up. My whole career at this hotel has been about fading into the background, not being noticed by the rich and famous who come to stay here. Putting on a show, a spectacle, but not drawing attention to myself. The whole point is that every stay is supposed to go so seamlessly that no one ever notices I'm here, working away in the background.'

Noah couldn't help it; he let out a bark of a laugh. 'The background? Honey, you couldn't fade into the background if you tried.'

Eloise pulled a face. 'I know, I know, the hair stands out.'

'It's not the hair,' Noah said, although that was part of it. 'It's you. Your beauty. That would stand out anywhere.' At least, it did to him. Although, maybe that was just because he knew now that he couldn't have her.

He pulled back, away from Eloise, and strode over towards the doors to the hotel again. It unnerved him, just a little, how easy it was to listen to Eloise talk. How natural his replies felt. How, without even thinking about it, he let in some real feeling between the jokes.

She was looking at him curiously now and he knew he needed to end this moment. People always wanted a secret in return for their own. And he had no intention of giving up any of his.

'You think I'm beautiful?' she asked, her eyes wide and vulnerable, and Noah swore silently in his head.

Because she meant it. He could tell that much straight away. This wasn't the usual coyness of a Hollywood actress, or the 'I'm a model but still don't believe I'm pretty' type of false insecurity. She was honestly surprised.

'I can't be the only person to tell you that,' he said, searching for a way out. Because that lack of self-awareness, that would be his undoing. He'd only known one other person so artlessly unaware of her own beauty.

Sally.

And he really wasn't thinking about her any more this weekend. It had been seven years, for goodness' sake.

'No, but you're the first movie star to say it,' Eloise said, and the moment was broken. Because he'd never been a movie star to Sally. He'd just been her best friend.

But to Eloise he was Noah Cross, the brand—and that was all he needed to be. She didn't need to see any deeper, and he didn't need to worry about having to let her in too far. He just had to keep his eye on the prize—his name in that little golden envelope when they announced the coveted award for Best Actor, once *Fight Days After* came out.

And all he had to do to achieve that was not sleep with Eloise, and knock his audition out of the park.

At least one of those should be no trouble at all. He just wished he could be entirely sure which one.

Eloise let herself back into the hotel, her dizziness faded but replaced by a strange confusion after the unexpected interlude with Noah on the terrace. At least he'd retreated up to his room to let her recover her wits in peace. She couldn't cope with any more of that intense conversation and gaze right now.

What had all that been about? She'd expected to get hit on by sex-crazed or drunk actors looking for a fling at the wedding—it happened often enough while working at the hotel, however much she tried to fade into the background. The rich and famous, in her experience, seemed to expect to be able to seduce anyone they wanted. And actors were the worst—they were all about the quick, meaningless fling. Which was still better than the times they pretended it was something more, that they'd fallen for her charms at first sight and couldn't live without her in their beds.

She knew better than to believe them. Her mother had been the queen of that game, and look how that had ended up.

No, she knew actors, knew the entitled clientele of Morwen Hall, and she knew how they behaved.

Noah Cross was not living up to the stereotype and it bothered her.

Of course there were probably *some* actors and actresses who managed to stay happily married and faithful, or who were looking for long-term love. She'd just never met any of them. Or seen them in the celebrity magazines in the staffroom. And she'd *never* expect Noah Cross, famed ladies' man, to be one of them.

In fairness, she had no evidence that he was. He'd admitted he was flirting with her—even if he didn't seem inclined to take it any further.

Either way, he hadn't gone about it the way she'd expected. She'd expected the flattery, the lusty looks, the charm. She hadn't expected him to ask questions about her history with Melissa, or to show such concern for her well-being.

Actually, he'd seemed pretty surprised by that too, so maybe this was a new thing for him.

The main doors opened again and Laurel burst through, followed closely by a guy who looked a lot like Riley.

Very closely.

Eloise narrowed her eyes as the man rested a hand on Laurel's waist, and Laurel jumped with surprise. There was definitely something weird going on here.

Pushing thoughts of Noah's weirdness out of her head, Eloise covered the lobby in long strides, ready to decipher Laurel's weirdness instead.

'Hey. You're back!'

Laurel's smile seemed a little forced. 'I am.'

'And you brought company.' Eloise's gaze flicked up to the man with his hand on Laurel. He really did look an awful lot like Riley. Which probably meant...

'Eloise, this is Dan. Riley's brother.' Of course. But that didn't explain his and Laurel's closeness. 'Dan, this is Eloise. She's the manager of Morwen Hall.'

'Pleased to meet you,' Dan said, placing the shopping bag he was carrying on the ground and holding out his hand.

'Acting Manager,' Eloise corrected automatically, as she took it and shook. The title wasn't hers yet—and wouldn't be unless this wedding went off without a hitch.

'Not for long,' Laurel said, and this time her smile seemed real. 'So, what's been happening here?'

'Cassidy, the maid of honour, has taken a fall while skiing and broken her leg, so her husband is bringing his mistress to the wedding instead.'

Also, I seem to have an odd connection with the best man that makes me want to tear his clothes off, even though he's the sort of man I despise, and he seems more interested in getting to know me.

Maybe she'd save that information for later, when she and Laurel were able to grab a moment alone. She needed to talk to *someone* about it.

Laurel's mouth fell into an open O shape, her eyes almost as wide. 'So Melissa doesn't have a maid of honour?'

Eloise winced. 'Not exactly. She's making me do it.'

She hadn't thought Laurel's eyes could get any wider but her response to this information proved her wrong. 'You poor, poor thing.'

At least she didn't have to worry about Melissa's half-sister being offended she hadn't been chosen. That was something, Eloise supposed. 'Yeah. I'm thrilled, as you can imagine. And it means I'll have to call in my deputy to cover for me at the hotel this week. He will *not* be thrilled. I can probably keep on top of the wedding events at least, so he only has to deal with the guests.' She sighed. 'What about you? How did the favours go?'

And what's the deal with you and your future half-brother-in-law?

'Fine, they're all sorted.' Laurel waved her hand towards the large glossy shopping bag that Dan had picked up again. 'Then I got Dan's car to pick me up on the way back.'

'That was…convenient.' Eloise stared rather pointedly at where Dan's hand was *still* resting on Laurel's waist, and the petite wedding planner blushed.

'Um, yes. Actually, I meant to tell you… Dan and I…'

'So I see,' Eloise said when Laurel appeared at a loss for how to finish that statement.

'We had sort of been keeping it under wraps,' Dan said, pulling Laurel closer to his side. Laurel stiffened for a moment then relaxed against him, her cheeks a little pink. 'What with the wedding and everything. Didn't want to steal Melissa's thunder, you know? But now the secret's out anyway…'

'This is brilliant!' Eloise burst out, the answer to at least one of her problems coming to her in a flash. Laurel looked a little startled at Eloise's sudden enthusiasm, at least until she explained. 'Melissa has insisted on Riley staying in a separate room until the wedding night, so I had to give him Dan's—sorry, Dan.' She gave Riley's brother a quick smile. 'But if you two are together, then that's fine because you'll be sharing anyway!'

'Sharing…right.' Laurel's smile had frozen into that sort of rictus again.

Eloise frowned. 'As long as that's okay…?'

'Of course!' Laurel said, too brightly. 'I mean, why wouldn't we?'

'Exactly,' Dan said, not looking quite as certain as Eloise might have expected either. 'Why wouldn't we?'

They were looking at each other now, not Eloise, staring into each other's eyes. Eloise definitely got the feeling she was intruding on a moment.

Quizzing Laurel on exactly *when* she'd found the time to go falling for Riley's brother would have to wait until she could get her alone. For now, she'd just chalk it up to fate and cross one more thing off her epic to-do list. At least now she could get on with the next thing on that list—the welcome drinks.

'Well, I'm glad that's all sorted,' she said, clapping her hands together in the hope it might bring Laurel and Dan back to the present.

It didn't. Eloise gave up.

'See you both later, then,' she said, and headed upstairs to her room to change into something more suitable for a maid of honour to wear while resisting flirting with the best man.

CHAPTER FIVE

'THAT IS A very boring dress,' Noah said as he handed Eloise a flute of champagne. He'd been watching her since he'd arrived at the bar for the welcome drinks, and she hadn't welcomed a single drink yet. She had to be desperate for one. He knew he was.

He'd intended to stay away from Eloise this evening, despite his promise of a flirtation earlier. Tessa had sent him a pointed text message saying she hoped he was behaving himself, as she had a call booked in with Stefan about the audition. Clearly she was serious about this, and so he would be too.

But then he'd spent an hour making small talk with the other wedding guests and, by the end of it, he was desperate for a conversation with somebody who had never even wanted to be in a film. Which, at Melissa's wedding, basically left Eloise.

When had this sort of event grown so meaningless? All industry chatter and gossip, and nothing of any substance. Unlike Eloise's boring black shift dress which, in his opinion, had far too much substance. It could have done with a little bit of sheer fabric somewhere, or even just a little less weight. It hung over her body like a sack. Eloise's body, Noah had decided from watching her move around the room, needed the sort of fabric that flowed, that moved with her, showing off her long, lean lines and gentle curves.

From the way Eloise was scowling at him, he guessed she disagreed. Oh, well. He was getting used to it.

'I didn't realise we'd reached the stage in our acquaintance where you felt comfortable insulting my fashion sense.'

'I like to skip ahead to the good parts. Why waste time on the small talk?' He flashed her his most charming smile and she just rolled her eyes.

Eloise Miller was going to be a challenge to win over—especially if he wasn't allowed to seduce her. Fortunately, Noah loved challenges.

'Well, you'll get to see me in the hideous concoction Melissa has chosen for the bridesmaids soon enough,' she assured him, then raised the champagne flute to her lips to take a sip. 'Hopefully, that will be an interesting enough dress to keep you satisfied.'

Noah had a feeling that whatever dress Melissa had picked, it wouldn't be anywhere near enough to satisfy him. Even standing beside Eloise, just watching her cool, pale skin and her blazing hair, he felt too warm, as if he might get burnt if he touched her. But that didn't stop his whole body aching to reach out anyway. What was it about this woman? She wasn't even trying—and he'd had enough women try with him to know—and yet she kept pulling him into her orbit, keeping him tethered there until it was physically hard to pull away.

The room was filled with beautiful women, yet the only one he could see was Eloise.

And that was going to be a problem. Because he really couldn't sleep with her. He was being discreet—and that definitely meant no public fling with the maid of honour.

'I'm sure the bridesmaids' dresses will be lovely,' he

lied, trying not to imagine Eloise in something slippery, something low-cut, something that just fell off her skin as he pushed it aside…

'No, you're not,' Eloise cut into his thoughts. 'You know as well as I do that Melissa will have chosen something designed to make *her* look even more beautiful. Which, given the A-list beauty status of the rest of her bridesmaids, means that we'll all be wearing sackcloth and ashes, or whatever the modern wedding equivalent is. In this case, something in blue-green satin and chiffon, I believe.'

'You'd look good in anything,' Noah replied without thinking, and she looked at him with wide eyes.

'Thank you,' she said, sounding surprised. 'But I'd reserve judgement until you've seen the dress, if I were you. Melissa is not above using her powers of fashion for evil.'

They stood side by side, observing the room, and Noah wondered if she was supposed to be working, doing something, instead of standing here with him. Then he wondered if, actually, he was meant to be doing something, in his capacity as best man. Then he decided he didn't care. He was exactly where he wanted to be.

'Did you know about those two?' Eloise nodded across the room to where the little wedding planner and Riley's brother were talking with the parents of the groom. As they chatted, Dan reached out and rested his hand at the small of Laurel's back and she leant against him, apparently finding strength and support in his nearness.

For a moment Noah couldn't help but think that looked nice, having that sort of connection. And then he remembered the price and shook the thought away.

'No. They're together?' *That* hadn't come up in any of the emails and schedules Laurel had been sending over for months.

'Apparently.' Eloise's gaze didn't move from the group

across the room, but Noah couldn't be sure if she was watching Laurel and Dan or taking in Melissa's mother's thunderous face. It looked as if someone else hadn't known about the relationship either. He wondered if the bride knew yet… That could be interesting, when she arrived. Melissa believed in making an entrance, and that required being fashionably late. 'I don't know if it's serious. I mean…it's not like Melissa and Riley, is it? Another showbiz marriage destined to fail.'

'Not all marriages end in divorce,' Noah said mildly. 'Only, like, half. Maybe three-quarters, in Hollywood.'

The look Eloise gave him was scathing. 'That's a rousing argument for the institution of marriage.'

He shrugged. 'It's not really my thing.'

'Yeah, I get that.' She tilted her head a little to the side as she considered him. Noah tried not to shift from one foot to the other, giving away his discomfort. Usually, he was used to being scrutinised from the other side of a camera or a screen. Up close and personal, it felt a little invasive. As if Eloise was looking deeper than he wanted her to know existed. 'So, how did Riley rope you into being best man, then? You guys must be pretty close, I guess.'

'Not really,' Noah admitted, glad the focus had shifted away from him and onto Melissa and Riley for a while. Their wedding was a much safer topic. 'I mean, we've made a few movies together, done the press junkets. But that's about it.'

'Huh.' She was looking again. Studying him.

'What?' Noah shifted his weight from one foot to the other and swapped his empty champagne flute for a full one as a waiter passed.

'I just figured…the way they both talked about you when we were doing the planning—especially Riley—I figured you were a bigger part of their lives.'

'Riley said that? I mean, he made it sound that way?' He'd always assumed that Melissa had insisted on Riley asking him, purely for the celebrity cachet that came with having Noah Cross as best man. But maybe he'd been wrong. After all, as his agent had pointed out, he wasn't always the best at connecting with people on a deeper level. Even his friends.

'Yeah. He did.'

'I… I don't usually like to get too close to people I work with,' Noah said, wondering why he felt as if he needed to make excuses to this woman. It was her eyes, he decided. The way they seemed to look right into his soul—assuming he still had one after a decade in Hollywood. He was pretty sure some of the women he'd dated would claim otherwise.

'Or anyone else,' Eloise suggested.

Noah tried to ignore her remark but, seeing as it came so soon after Tessa's comments on the phone, he couldn't help himself from asking, 'What makes you say that?'

'I've seen the photos,' Eloise said with a shrug. 'All those pictures of you with a different woman every week. Not exactly the hallmark of a guy who gets up close and personal. At least, not in the non-physical sense.'

She sounded too casual as she said it, too desperate for him to believe she didn't care what he did with women. And, on less than twelve hours' acquaintance, why would she?

But she did. Noah was almost certain of it.

And he couldn't do a single thing about it.

'There's nothing wrong with having a little fun,' he said lightly, watching her face carefully to read her response. 'As long as everyone involved knows that's exactly what it is.'

'Just fun. Casual. Meaningless. Shallow.' She met his

gaze with her own fierce blue-green eyes. How was it she seemed to see right inside him, yet he couldn't read her at all? He prided himself on his ability to decipher people— to read enough to understand them without ever needing to get too close. But Eloise was a mystery.

Noah hated mysteries.

'That's right.' He moved a little closer, slowly, so as not to spook her. Just enough that the sleeve of his jacket brushed against her bare arm.

She flinched.

He was right. She cared, for some reason. His inability to even contemplate monogamy bothered her, and he could not begin to understand why.

But he intended to find out. If he understood her, maybe he'd stop being so obsessed with her—stop feeling the need to be near her, to question her, to deepen their acquaintance. Because deep and meaningful was the last thing he wanted, with any woman. Whatever Tessa said.

Eloise's tongue flicked over her lips as she raised her eyes to his then looked away again.

Perhaps he was making this too complicated. Maybe Eloise's problem had nothing to do with deeper motivations at all.

Perhaps she just wanted him the same way he wanted her.

And if that was the case he had an even bigger problem.

He had to be sure.

'A fling is always good for making a wedding a little more entertaining, don't you find?' he asked, and watched her cheeks turn pink.

Gotcha.

She wanted him. And he *really* wanted her.

Okay, so he couldn't have her. But that didn't mean he couldn't play a little. Just to keep in practice.

He could find out exactly what issues she had that stopped her from even contemplating a bit of fun. He might even get her to lighten up a bit.

It would be his good deed for the day or something.

Even Tessa would have to approve of that. Right?

He was flirting with her.

Noah Cross, Hollywood heart-throb and womaniser extraordinaire, was flirting with her.

She hadn't been sure earlier, couldn't quite tell if his easy charm was just something he pulled out for all the ladies. Sure, it felt personal and attentive and tingly—no, not tingly. She didn't do tingly. Anyway. She hadn't been one hundred per cent certain that his flirtatiousness had anything to do with *her* exactly. He could have been like that with every woman he met for all she knew. In fact, he probably was.

But this, now; this was personal. Focused. He was staring deep into her eyes, as if he hoped to find the meaning of life there—or at least a way into her underwear.

Well. Noah Cross was going to be sorely disappointed.

'I've never had a fling at a wedding,' she said, purposefully omitting the 'before' from the end of the sentence. 'Before' implied she was thinking about doing it this time, and she wasn't.

Oh, all right, she was. Any straight woman with a pulse would at least *think* about it if Noah Cross propositioned her, she was sure. But thinking was as far as Eloise was willing to go.

'Don't you think you should give it a try? Just once?' Noah leaned in a little closer. 'How else will you know if you like it or not?'

Eloise pulled back, fixing him with her sternest manager stare. This would all be so much easier if her whole body didn't hum at the very sight of him. 'And who, exactly, are you suggesting I have this fling with?'

Noah attempted a self-effacing look, which—kudos to his skill as an actor—almost looked realistic. 'Well, there is always that old tradition about the maid of honour and the best man. But really, the whole room is full of attractive men—or women, if that's your thing. All of them famous and at least half of them single—or acting as if they are, anyway.'

'I don't date actors,' she said, the response as automatic and instinctive as saying yes to a cup of tea. 'And I definitely don't have meaningless flings with them.' That wasn't who she was. She'd worked hard to shake off the assumptions people in this town had made about her, based on her family and her upbringing. She wasn't about to abandon her reputation now for one night with a movie star, just because he made her body respond in ways she'd forgotten it could.

Except he'd only offered himself as one possibility, hadn't he? Clearly he wasn't overly invested in this flirtation. It was all probably just a game to him. To get the repressed hotel manager to cut loose and go wild.

Well, not her. Not a chance.

'Never?' Noah raised his eyebrows. 'Wow. What did we poor, defenceless actors ever do to you?'

'Not to me. I told you. I don't date actors.' It was *technically* true—Derek hadn't been an actor when she'd started dating him. He'd been a director. But then the leading man had fallen sick and he'd taken on the role—starring opposite Eloise's mother. And from there it had been an old, familiar story.

She didn't want to get into what so many actors had done to her mother. Or, more to the point, what her mother had done to them—and, by extension, what she'd done to Eloise and her father. Derek, the boyfriend her mother had stolen from her, had only been one in a long list of leading men she'd seduced then cast aside. If Eloise had needed proof that actors were all the same, she could pull out the box of old programmes her mother had kept from her amateur dramatics days and put together a list of names that made her point for her. And that was just in her home town. How much worse must Hollywood be? She didn't want to find out.

And Noah didn't need to know her sordid history. Especially since she absolutely was not going to sleep with him. No matter how much she wanted to.

A waiter passed and Eloise grabbed another glass of champagne. Melissa was paying for it, and it was her fault that Eloise had found herself in this position in the first place.

'So, you've never dated an actor but you hate us all indiscriminately anyway. Interesting.' Noah leant back against the bar behind him. 'Care to tell me why you cling onto this prejudice so tenaciously? Especially since we've established that any fling at this wedding won't be happening between us?'

He wasn't the sort to give up—Eloise knew that after only a day in his company. If she had to guess, she'd say that Noah was the sort of guy who liked to understand something well enough for his own purposes and then move on. He was only interested in the surface knowledge, enough to fake a part, she supposed.

Well, surface she could do. She just didn't want to get down to the deep, painful memories that lay underneath it.

Of course, she was pretty sure Noah didn't want to either. If she actually broke down and gave him her sob story, he'd run in the other direction. That was something to keep in reserve, in case she needed it.

'You're all the same,' she said with a shrug. 'You fall in love for the length of time it takes to get a movie made, or to star in a play. Then, once it's all over, you're onto the next leading lady or love interest. Half your relationships are film promo, as far as I can tell.'

Noah raised his eyebrows. 'Wow. You really do have a chip on your shoulder about this.'

'Tell me I'm wrong,' Eloise challenged. 'You said yourself you were just looking for a fling.'

'There's nothing wrong with a fling, as long as both parties know what they're getting into,' Noah said mildly.

'Which is what, exactly?' Of course he'd think that. It was the perfect justification for never having to have a real relationship. 'A meaningless encounter with someone you never really get to know?'

'What's so wrong with that?' Noah asked with a shrug. 'Maybe we're not supposed to know the innermost depths of *everyone* we meet.'

'Perhaps not. But…don't you want that connection?' Eloise had to admit she did. Which might be the reason she didn't date so much. She hadn't met many guys over the past few years she wanted to get to know that well. But that sounded a bit too much like conceding the point, so she didn't say it.

'Real and deep doesn't mean for ever, Eloise.' There was a harshness to Noah's voice she hadn't heard before. 'The most real and important relationship of my life lasted barely twenty-four hours.'

She blinked. That was definitely new. 'That must have been…intense.' She couldn't imagine it. From his tone she could tell that, whatever the relationship was, it had mattered—and mattered deeply. She couldn't imagine how it must have felt to have that and then have it taken away again. What had happened? She wanted to ask but, before she could find a way to phrase the question, Noah spoke again.

'It was.' He flashed her a smile that was so at odds with the conversation Eloise wondered for a moment if she'd missed the joke. 'Enough for one lifetime, anyway. Which is why I prefer things my way these days—fun, light and easy.'

'And never getting in too deep,' Eloise said, frowning.

'That way you don't drown,' Noah joked. 'I know when I'm out of my depth.'

She wanted to ask more, wanted to try and understand his attitude. Not to understand Noah himself, exactly, she realised, but to try and get some perspective on her mother. Was this how she'd felt? Or had she just been incapable of real love, as Eloise had always believed?

Maybe Noah was too. In which case, it was just as well she had no intention of getting any closer to him. A fling might be his sort of thing, but it wasn't hers. It never had been.

And she was firmly ignoring the small voice at the back of her head whispering, *How will you know if you never try it?* Especially as it sounded exactly like Noah Cross.

'So, who was she?' Eloise asked, but Noah wasn't listening any more. And, as she followed his gaze to the doorway, Eloise forgot what she'd been asking about.

Melissa stood in the entrance, arms wide, wearing a stunning forest-green gown that left her shoulders and a great deal of cleavage bare, before nipping in at her waist and following every curve down to her knees, where it flared out again.

'Now *that* is not a boring dress,' Noah murmured. 'Of course, it would look better on you.'

'Liar.' Melissa looked as if she'd been born to wear that dress, and the smile on her face said she knew it.

'It's true.' Noah pressed up behind her as the crowd gathered around the bride. 'You have the height to pull it off—your legs would look endless. And that colour… made for a redhead.'

'Maybe.' But she'd never have the confidence to wear it. Not in a million years.

'Of course, you'd have to wear your hair down,' Noah added, touching the hundreds of pins that kept her hair firmly out of her way when she was working. 'Which would be an added bonus.'

Clearly the guy had a thing for redheads. Which was funny because she'd never seen him with any on the red carpet.

'I thought we'd established that we weren't going to be having any sort of fling,' she said drily. 'I'm pretty sure that means you can stop with the compliments now.'

Noah shrugged. 'I figured we could be friends instead. Friends compliment each other.'

Did they? Eloise wasn't sure she'd know. But that might just be because Melissa had always been her baseline for friendship.

'Friends?'

'Yeah,' he said. 'Friends. Think you can manage it?'

'I'll give it a try,' she replied drily. Friends with another Hollywood star. Hopefully this one would go better than her friendship with Melissa.

'Everyone! My fiancé and I are just so delighted to welcome you all here to celebrate our wedding.' Melissa beamed around the room and Riley stepped out of her shadow, looking awkward in a dinner jacket, and gave a little wave. 'I hope you all have just the best time—' She cut off abruptly, her smile replaced by a sudden scowl.

Eloise tried to figure out what had changed, and followed Melissa's gaze to…oh, dear.

Dan had his arm around Laurel and, from where Eloise stood, she could see him staring up at Melissa, a challenge in his eyes.

'What the *hell* is going on here?' Melissa asked, her hands on her hips.

'Guess we weren't the only ones who didn't know about Laurel and Dan,' Noah murmured as Eloise headed into the fray to smooth over the situation.

Playtime was over.

Noah sighed, putting the script to one side again, and wished that the curtains of the four-poster bed didn't feel as if they were closing in. He had shut them to try and give himself a cosy cocoon in which to read through the script for *Eight Days After* again, looking for those deeper resonances he knew he'd need to hit to get the part. But instead he just felt trapped.

Maybe Tessa was right. Maybe this wasn't the part for him. He was a good actor, he knew that. But this role… maybe it cut a little too close to home.

He thought back over his conversation with Eloise. Now there was a woman who believed in deep and meaningful. He almost wished he could just get her to explain it to him, so he could fake it well enough to get the part without ever actually having to feel it himself. If there was a woman in the world who could do it, Noah would place money on it being Eloise. There was something about her eyes, her expressions. The way everything she felt or thought was telegraphed out to her audience in her face. He could almost see the thoughts floating across her eyes, like subtitles on a foreign movie.

She didn't think much of him—that was certain. Which was a shame, given his body's automatic reaction whenever she was near—but also probably just as well, under the circumstances.

No, it was just as well they'd established the 'no fling' ground rules. Not only was he not in the market for it right now, but she was clearly out for love, marriage, the whole shebang. And he most definitely wasn't. Noah wasn't the sort of guy who'd let a girl carry those sorts of hopes into bed with her, even if it was the only way to get her there. It wasn't fair and it wasn't worth it. He was always very clear about what he was willing to offer.

And he'd only ever offered more once. Only to have it all taken away twenty-four hours later.

Suddenly restless, Noah pushed the curtains aside and jumped off the bed, heading for the minibar.

He shouldn't have mentioned Sally to Eloise. Oh, he might not have said her name, might not have gone into detail, but Eloise was the sort of woman who asked questions. She'd want to know more and, given how much time they were likely to be spending together over the next few days, she'd try her hardest to find out. Noah foresaw a lot of time spent sidestepping questions in his future. Good job he'd had all that fancy media training. Avoiding Eloise's questions would be as hard as any interview he'd ever sat.

He supposed he'd started it. He'd wanted to play, wanted to pick at her secrets and truths. It was only fair she got to do the same in return.

Noah poured a healthy measure of whisky into one of the glass tumblers on top of the well-stocked refrigerator, then bypassed the sofa to head back to the bed, leaving the curtains open this time. He took a sip, savouring the burn of the alcohol in his throat. This was what he needed to focus on—the here and now, the current moment. Not a woman seven years dead, or the future he had lost that day.

Eloise might think that all actors were only in it for the

cheap thrill, the quick, meaningless satisfaction. But she was wrong. He'd wanted more once—and he'd had it too.

Just not for very long.

He'd spent his whole teenage years in love with one woman. And when she finally realised she might feel the same…he'd let her down, just when she'd needed him most.

He knew how it felt to have his heart ripped from his chest, and he wasn't about to go seeking that again.

He took another gulp of whisky. He didn't need the memories tonight. He needed to focus on the script and how to fake those deeper emotions he'd locked away inside the day Sally died. Because he had no intention of ever feeling them again.

CHAPTER SIX

IT HADN'T TAKEN much to convince Melissa that making a scene about her half-sister and brother-in-law-to-be getting together at her own wedding wasn't the best PR plan she'd ever had, especially with the reporter covering the wedding watching. Melissa had looked stormy for a moment, then reverted to the sweetness and light actress the rest of the room—those who didn't actually know her very well—were expecting. It was almost disconcerting to see the shift, Eloise thought.

Still, she hadn't felt confident leaving Melissa alone with Laurel until the crowd of guests had mostly departed to their beds. Noah had called it quits some time earlier, whispering a goodnight in her ear as he left.

Eloise had spent more of the night remembering the feel of his lips so close to her than she would ever admit to him. By the time morning rolled around, she hadn't had nearly as much sleep as she'd hoped to get.

Yawning, she stretched and reached for her smartphone, sitting on her bedside table. They had another big day ahead of them—especially with the Frost Fair that afternoon. Melissa had wanted something wintry, magical and British for her guests to enjoy as a pre-wedding event. Eloise and Laurel had come up with the idea of a traditional Frost Fair, like they used to hold on the frozen River

Thames back in the seventeenth and eighteenth centuries. If nothing else, it would provide quite a spectacle, Eloise was sure.

Of course, first she had to get through a dress fitting with Melissa.

Pressing the screen on her phone, Eloise called Laurel to check on her plans for the day, and quickly checked in with her deputy about anything that might come up while she was being fitted for her maid of honour dress. Laurel, Eloise couldn't help but note, sounded far grumpier than Eloise would if she'd spent the night with a guy as gorgeous as Dan. She hoped that Melissa's reaction the night before hadn't caused problems between the two of them. Laurel deserved a nice guy.

Eventually, she couldn't put it off any longer. Showered and dressed in a knitted navy dress and knee boots, Eloise headed down to the conference room they'd put aside for the final dress fittings that morning. Melissa was already there, holding court over the two other bridesmaids while a harried-looking woman unpacked pins and measuring tapes and dress bags.

'And here's the replacement maid of honour,' Melissa said, looking up as Eloise entered the room. 'I hope you didn't eat too many of the canapés last night, Eloise, or you'll never fit into the dress!' The bridesmaids both laughed, and Eloise bit her tongue to keep from responding. Apparently Melissa had already forgotten her comments about Cassidy, the previous maid of honour, putting on weight for a part. She'd probably remember in time to make another joke at Eloise's expense, once she had the dress on.

She really hadn't missed Melissa at all in the past decade, Eloise thought.

'We were just talking about how Laurel and Dan tried to steal my thunder last night,' Melissa went on.

'And failed,' one of the bridesmaids, who Eloise faintly recognised from her most recent cinema trip, said. Was she Iona? Eloise wasn't sure. After a while, all those Hollywood blondes started to look the same to her.

'Of course they did!' said the other bridesmaid, who Eloise was almost certain was called Caitlin. 'As if anyone cared about anything except how fabulous Mel looked in that dress last night.'

They all turned to Eloise, apparently waiting for her agreement. 'It was a very beautiful dress,' she said, hoping that was good enough. From what she'd overheard, plenty of people had an opinion on the groom's brother and bride's sister getting together. Some were even giving odds on their relationship outlasting Melissa and Riley's.

'And so is yours!' Melissa clapped her hands together as the seamstress pulled the first bridesmaid's dress from its bag. 'Not as gorgeous as mine, of course, but still. What do you think?'

Eloise stared at the icy blue-green concoction of chiffon and silk. The colour wasn't one she'd ever choose to wear but it was very appropriate for a winter wedding, she supposed. If they insisted on having photos taken outside, her skin colour might actually match the dress. That would be nice.

'It's lovely,' she lied, as she got a good look at the laces at the back of the corset top. Corsets were for people with curves, weren't they? And she didn't have nearly as many of those as Melissa, or the bridesmaids. Eloise had height, long legs and a slender body, none of which, she imagined, were going to be shown off to their best advantage by this dress.

Which shouldn't bother her at all. This was effectively

a job, and she wore boring grey suits to work every day and never worried about whether they complemented her complexion. Why should she care now?

Because you'll be standing next to Noah Cross.

She wished she could pretend that she just wanted to look good in the world's media when the photos came out but, given that she was starring in this wedding alongside people who'd made the top ten in the world's most beautiful people list, there wasn't a hope of that to start with.

No, what she was really thinking about were Noah's words the night before. 'That is a very boring dress.' Even though they'd established there would be no romance between them, a small part of her couldn't help but wish the dress Melissa had picked might have wowed him, just a little.

She sighed. He'd just have to deal with a non-boring but faintly hideous dress, she supposed.

Stepping behind the screen they'd set up, Eloise slipped into the dress and pulled the corset top up over her non-existent curves.

'Let me tighten that for you,' the seamstress said, coming up behind her and yanking on the laces. Eloise winced as all the air flew out of her body. Apparently someone was determined for her to have curves, even if breathing had to be sacrificed.

Once she was suitably tightened and tied, Eloise stepped out into the main room, where the other two bridesmaids were already in their dresses. Apparently actresses didn't have the same privacy issues as normal people. On each of them, the icy blue looked stunning against their blonde hair, and their delicate curves, quite possibly emphasised by breast implants, were highlighted to perfection. Looking at them, Eloise was surer than ever that Melissa's comment about Laurel's cleavage not fitting in the dress was just another excuse not to make her half-sister maid of honour.

'Well, don't you look…?' Melissa trailed off and gave her a patronisingly encouraging smile. 'I told you the dress would fit, didn't I? Corsets are marvellously forgiving.'

'I'll just need to let down the hem a little…' The seamstress fussed around her with the measuring tape.

Eloise wanted nothing more than to strip the dress off right there, no matter who was watching, and get back to hiding in her professional grey suit.

But then she heard Noah's voice from the door to her left. 'Wow.'

Fixing a smile onto her face, she turned to look at him, hoping against hope that he was a good enough actor to make her feel slightly less like an ugly stepsister in a pantomime.

'You look… Wow.' Noah's gaze ran the length of her body before it met her own, and Eloise swallowed as she realised he wasn't acting. Or if he was he was a lot better at it than his films suggested.

'Noah Cross lost for words,' Melissa said, her light tone sounding forced. 'I never thought I'd see the day.'

Noah broke away from staring at her, and Eloise tried to take a deep breath to recover from the intensity of his gaze. Then she remembered the corset and settled for a few shallow ones instead.

'Melissa, I don't think you know how to pick a boring dress.' He said it like a compliment and, from the way Melissa's cheeks turned pink, it might have been the nicest thing he'd ever said to her. But Eloise felt a small glow inside her, knowing that he was making a private joke, just for her, and that Melissa would never get it.

'I'm glad you approve,' she said, apparently placated. 'Now, are you ready to teach your pupil her steps?'

'Steps?' Eloise asked as Melissa and Noah both turned to look at her. She didn't like the sound of that at all.

'For the first dance at the reception,' Melissa explained. 'Obviously, it'll just be Riley and me on the dance floor to start with, but then we've planned for the best man and maid of honour to join us, followed by Iona and Caitlin and their partners. Didn't Laurel mention it?'

'It didn't come up,' Eloise said, her voice faint. She'd been far more concerned with the details of the catering and the rooms than what was actually going to happen at the wedding reception itself. Speeches and dances and so on were Laurel's department, not hers.

At least, they had been.

'It's not a complicated dance,' Noah said, obviously trying to be reassuring. But he didn't get it. It wasn't the steps that bothered her. It wasn't even being in Noah's arms and having to restrain herself from kissing him, hard though that might be. No, it was all the eyes that would be on her as she stepped out onto the dance floor that made her hands shake and her knees wobble. It was being the centre of attention. That was what caused that big ball of anxiety in her chest to double in size.

'Just try your best,' Melissa said, her voice dripping false sympathy. 'Everyone will know you're not a professional, so they won't be expecting much.'

'Well, that's okay then,' Eloise ground out between her clenched teeth.

'Why don't we go practise somewhere else?' Noah suggested, looking between them. 'Far away.'

'Good idea,' Eloise said, stepping back behind the screen to get out of the ridiculous dress in a hurry.

'Oh, I think it would be much better to do it here,' Melissa said as Eloise tugged on the corset strings. 'After all, Eloise might need someone to show her how it's really done. And really, Eloise, I think you'd better keep the dress on. You want to know how it feels to dance in costume, don't you?'

Eloise gave up the unequal fight with the corset strings. Apparently it was time to dance.

Noah stood awkwardly in the middle of the room, waiting for Eloise to join him. She'd stepped back out from behind the screen at Melissa's request, her face red and mutinous.

'Shoes!' Melissa jumped up and dashed across the room, a blur of blonde as she reached into one of four boxes laid out on the table under the window. 'What size are you, Eloise?'

'A seven,' she said, still not looking at Noah, or Melissa, or anywhere that wasn't the floor.

Somehow, Noah got the distinct impression that Eloise wasn't looking forward to dancing with him.

'Cassidy is a six, but I'm sure you'll be able to squeeze into them, won't you?' Melissa smiled sweetly as she handed over the shoes, and Noah prepared to dive in and separate them if Eloise finally lost the last scraps of her composure.

She didn't. Instead, she looked at the shoes in her hand and pulled a face.

'They have ribbons.'

'I know! Aren't they beautiful?' Melissa squealed. Noah hadn't really sensed 'beautiful' from Eloise's tone. 'Go on, put them on. You'll want to practice the dance in them.'

'I don't want to practice the dance at all,' Eloise muttered as she bent to put on the shoes, but Melissa ignored her.

It took some effort, even Noah could see that, but eventually the shoes were on, ribbons tied, and Eloise was proclaimed ready to dance.

'Now, it's a nice simple waltz, really,' Melissa said. 'I'll tell you what, I'll demonstrate with Noah so you can see what Riley and I will be doing. Then you can step in and give it a go.'

Melissa moved into his arms before Noah could agree to the plan, and Iona started up the music. The familiar theme tune from Melissa's biggest movie so far rang out through the room and, over her shoulder, Noah saw Eloise roll her eyes. He smirked at her and she returned the smile, her cheeks finally back to their normal colour.

'Noah! You missed your cue.' Melissa stamped one dainty foot on the floor and Iona started the music once again. 'It's just as well we're rehearsing today. Obviously you haven't been practising on your own.'

'Every morning for twenty minutes, just like you asked, Mel. I swear,' Noah lied shamelessly. It was a waltz. He'd learned how to waltz for his sister's wedding when he was eight. If he could do it then he could do it now.

This time, he hit his cue perfectly, sweeping Melissa around the floor easily. But his attention wasn't on his dance partner. It was on Eloise, watching from the sidelines. Her cheeks might no longer be bright red with embarrassment, but with every bar of the music she grew stiller and smaller somehow, fading away in that ice-blue dress.

That dress. When he'd walked in and seen it, it had blown him away. For all that he'd been spending the last twenty-four hours staring at Eloise, he'd not had a chance to see her in anything that accentuated her figure so well. Even the colour, which he wouldn't have picked for her, added a strange otherworldliness coupled with her blazing hair. She looked like some mythical princess of ice and fire—and utterly unlike the woman who draped herself in shapeless suits and boring black dresses.

But now, as he whirled around the room with Melissa in his arms, she seemed to be retreating back into herself.

She'd said she liked to fade into the background, and he hadn't thought it possible. Until he saw her in action.

She'd made herself nothing, and he wanted to drag her out into the light again. Wanted to show her off, to see her beauty reflected around her. Wanted to show *her* how beautiful she was.

But, more than that, he wanted to protect her from Melissa and whatever plans she had that involved making Eloise's life miserable.

Was this what not sleeping with a woman did to him? He couldn't have her in his bed, so instead he started finding other reasons to be near her? They'd agreed to be friends, but this felt like something…different. Something that could be a whole lot more troublesome.

Tessa would probably rather he just slept with her and got it over with.

But Stefan the director might not. And until that part was in the bag… Eloise was still off limits. And maybe even after that, if what Tessa said was true. Noah could be staring down a long period of acting-enforced celibacy.

Unless… Tessa had only said to be discreet. He hadn't thought that could be possible with Eloise, with the world watching them at Melissa's wedding. But they were *supposed* to be spending time together. Nobody could talk about that. And seeing her fade into the background, realising how much she truly didn't want to be watched… If there was anyone he could have a discreet fling with, despite his celebrity, it would be Eloise.

If he could convince her. Which was by no means a sure thing, given her feelings about actors.

The music came to an end at last, and Melissa hugged him close before stepping away again. 'Right! Eloise's turn.' She turned to her maid of honour, smiling in a way that Noah could only describe as predatory.

She was waiting for Eloise to fail, he realised. If it hadn't been for the world's media watching, Melissa might even have waited until the day to tell Eloise about the dance and let her humiliate herself in front of everyone. But, since she wouldn't risk her perfect wedding that way, this was obviously the next best thing.

No wonder Eloise looked as if she'd rather be anywhere but there.

He moved towards her, reaching out a hand to pull her into his arms.

'I apologise in advance for treading on your feet,' she said, and he smiled.

'You'll be fine. I'm hardly a professional dancer either, you realise? I'm best known for smashing through walls and beating people up.'

'That's true.' She looked rather pleased about that fact, strangely.

'So you *do* know my films.' He grinned, more pleased by the fact that she was looking a little more relaxed at last than by the acknowledgement of his fame.

Eloise rolled her eyes. 'Yes, fine. Everybody knows Noah Cross. You're on, like, every billboard and every bus.'

'Not *all* of them.'

'Most, then. All those big budget blockbusters you're always starring in.' She frowned. 'But you didn't always do those, did you? Didn't I read somewhere that you used to be on the stage?'

This time, Noah *was* surprised. 'Yes, actually. Not many people remember my touring actor days now, though. I did a three-year stint as a stage actor, touring in a company that took Shakespeare all over the States.'

'Huh.' She tilted her head to look at him. 'I suppose I could buy you as Hamlet.'

'Not Romeo?' He waggled his eyebrows in a suggestive manner, and Eloise laughed as the music started up again.

Melissa's voice rang out around the room. 'And dance!'

Of course, he hadn't had time to actually talk Eloise through the steps, since they'd been busy discussing him, but she seemed to have picked up the basics from watching Melissa anyway. 'You're a quick study,' he said as they spun.

'My mum made me take dance lessons when I was younger,' Eloise admitted, still looking down at her feet. 'I did ballet, tap, modern, lyrical and even a couple of terms of ballroom. Apparently I haven't quite forgotten everything.'

'Then why were you nervous?' Noah asked. She'd been terrified at the prospect of dancing; he'd seen it in her face. But why, if she already knew she could do it?

'It's not the dancing,' Eloise admitted. But, before she could tell him exactly what the problem was, Melissa was striding across the floor towards them.

'You're doing it wrong,' the bride said, grabbing Eloise's arm and yanking her away from Noah.

'I thought she had it, actually,' Noah objected, but Melissa had already taken up her ballroom position.

'No. I'll show you again,' she said to Eloise with exaggerated patience.

Noah raised his arms and met Eloise's gaze over Melissa's shoulder. She raised her eyes to the heavens, and he smiled.

Maybe he'd tread on Melissa's toes while they danced. That might persuade her to give up on the lessons.

Or at least put Eloise back in his arms, which couldn't be a bad thing.

CHAPTER SEVEN

MELISSA DRILLED THEM in their dance for far longer than Eloise thought was strictly necessary—she wasn't *that* bad, she was sure. Eventually, though, Melissa had to let Eloise go, once she pointed out that if she didn't there would be no one to check that everything was ready for the Frost Fair.

Noah took the opportunity to escape too, which Eloise was grateful for. It had felt too good, dancing in his arms. And the connection between them—even if it was born entirely out of mocking Melissa—seemed a little too easy. She wasn't an idiot; she knew Noah was just playing with her. What she didn't understand was why he was still bothering. She'd made her position on the subject of having flings with actors painfully clear the night before.

Maybe that was it—the challenge. She could see Noah as the kind of guy who grew tired of always getting everything he wanted handed to him on a plate. Some people were happy to carry on that way, enjoying the ease that sort of life gave them. But Noah… She got the impression he liked to work for things a little more. Hadn't he said something last night about a new role in a film, something more challenging? Yes, that had to be it. She was a different sort of challenge; that was all. The moment she gave in, all the fun would be gone for him.

She had to remember that.

Dressed again in her navy work dress and chocolate leather boots, Eloise hurried down to the riverbank, her coat wrapped warmly around her. The preparations for the afternoon's Frost Fair were well underway—which was just as well, as Laurel would be bringing the guests down from the hotel within the hour.

Wooden stalls were laid out all along the riverbank, a temporary street of tempting offerings to eat, drink or enjoy. The river that ran beside the hotel rarely froze and, even if it had, it would have been a health and safety impossibility to hold the fair actually *on* the ice, like people would have done at the Frost Fairs of old. But, with the rustic stalls, the lute music drifting through the icy air as the musicians warmed up and the smell of the hog roast cooking, it *almost* felt authentic.

Authentic enough for Hollywood, anyway, Eloise figured.

Pulling out her clipboard, she did the rounds, checking in with every stallholder, every caterer, every entertainer, from jugglers to ice carvers. Everything was looking good until she reached the small stage set up at the far end of the fair, ready for the acting troupe Laurel had hired to entertain the masses with excerpts from Shakespeare's plays.

'How's it going?' she asked a dour-looking man unloading period costumes and props onto a rack.

Hang on. No, he wasn't unloading. He was taking the costumes off the rack and putting them back into the suitcase.

'Not great,' he said, reaching for another doublet. 'The troupe minibus gave up the ghost halfway down the M4. The guy they sent out to fix it said it's dead as a doornail. I'd come on ahead with the costumes and props, but I'm only the stage manager-slash-accompanist. You want period sound effects or music? I'm your man.' He shook his head. 'Not a lot of use without the actors, though. Figured I might as well pack up again.'

'Wait. Don't… Stop packing up. Please. Just stop it.' The man held up his hands and stepped back as Eloise reached for her phone.

'Your call, love, but I don't see what good they'll do you.'

'I just need to make a phone call…' Turning away, Eloise stabbed at her phone until it rang Laurel, holding it tight to her ear and praying that the wedding planner would have an idea.

Click. 'You have reached the voicemail of Laurel Sommers, wedding planner.'

Of course, to be any help at all she'd have to actually pick up the phone. Eloise hung up and tried again.

After she got put through to voicemail for the fifth time, Eloise gave up.

'Okay, look, we'll sort this out,' she said, turning back to the man with the props. Except now he wasn't alone.

'Alas, poor Yorick!' Noah held a skull at arm's length as he quoted the line from *Hamlet*, looking utterly in his element.

Hadn't he said he'd been a Shakespearean actor once? Maybe he could be again…

Spotting her, Noah put down the skull and walked towards her. Eloise pasted on her brightest, most winning smile and hoped he still wanted to keep playing their little game. Because she needed a big favour.

The Frost Fair, Noah had to admit, was quite the set-up. It looked like something from some high fantasy epic movie, rather than a historical. Stallholders were wandering around in that pseudo-period costume that seemed to work for peasants of all eras, mostly in shades of brown and green with the odd berry-red hat for a spot of colour. The river rushed past beside the stalls, flowing over rocks and under bare trees. The spot must be beautiful in the summer, he realised. No wonder Melissa had wanted to come back here.

When he came across the stage, he couldn't resist—especially when he saw the box of props waiting there, just asking to be used. It might be a cliché, but in his experience it was a rare actor who could resist a bit of *Hamlet*.

Then he saw Eloise, lowering her phone from her ear, her red hair the brightest thing in the whole fair. Even her sensible brown knee boots and knitted navy dress made him want to reach out and touch her.

And when she smiled…his heart contracted in his chest.

Then his eyes narrowed. That was not the smile of a woman planning a seduction. That was the smile of a woman who wanted something. Well, he wasn't above giving—as long as he got something in return.

In all honesty, if it was Eloise asking, he'd probably do it for free. Just to see some more of that smile.

'What do you need?' he asked as she approached.

Her smile faltered for a moment, then came back stronger than ever. 'The troupe of actors we'd hired to perform today can't make it. Their minibus broke down about a hundred miles away.'

'That's a shame.' Noah was pretty sure he could guess now what she wanted, but he was going to make her ask, all the same. Given how incapable of saying no to her he felt right now, it was only fair.

'I don't suppose you're feeling in the mood to reprise some of your more famous Shakespearian roles, are you?'

'Fancying some Romeo at last, huh?'

'Or Hamlet, or Benedick, or Puck… I'm not fussed, as

long as there's someone up on that stage performing when our guests arrive.'

'Aren't I one of those guests?'

Eloise shook her head. 'You're the best man. That means pitching in and fixing whatever goes wrong with the wedding.'

'I suppose it does,' Noah said slowly, an idea forming in his mind. 'And I guess as maid of honour you have to do the same, right?'

Her eyes widened. 'Well, in principle…but you're the actor here. This really seems like a job for you.'

'Ah, but it would be so much better with two, wouldn't it?' Noah said. 'Monologues are so boring. But a good bit of dialogue…that'll get people watching. So, how's *your* Shakespeare?'

'Rusty. Very, very rusty. I mean, I used to help my mum learn her lines, and she did a few of Shakespeare's, but that was years ago. As was my A-level English Lit course, for that matter.'

'Your mum?' Noah frowned. 'She was an actress?' Did *that* explain Eloise's strange prejudice against actors? Had one messed her mother around? Or was her dad an actor?

For someone he knew so little about, he felt strangely invested in her past. And in her immediate future, come to that.

'Of a sort. Look, it doesn't matter now. The point is, I don't know the lines. Any lines. For any play.'

'You don't need to,' Noah told her, pushing aside his questions about her parents for a time when Eloise was less stressed. So, some time next year, probably. The woman had been stress incarnate since he'd met her. Strange—that wasn't something he'd ever found attractive before. 'We'll do readings rather than acting out the scenes. It'll work fine and you don't need to worry about remembering anything.'

Eloise frowned. 'I suppose. But…'

Now they were getting to it. 'So, what's the real reason you don't want to do it? Worried I'll show you up? Trust me, I wouldn't. It's a long time since I've done Shakespeare too.'

She pulled a face. 'That's not it. Well, yes, partly, I suppose. You're an actual actor. I'm someone who's just read the plays a few times.'

'I'm an actor who mostly beats people up in films these days,' he reminded her. 'But, actually, I'm looking to get into some different roles, so maybe a change of pace will be good for me. And I think fooling around on stage with me will be good for you too. We can just do the comedies, if you like. It'll be fun.'

'Fun? Standing up there with the famous and the beautiful watching me make a fool of myself? *Not* my idea of a good time.'

'That's what you're worried about? Them?' Noah shook his head. He knew from personal experience that nobody attending this wedding thought too much about anyone except themselves. 'I really wouldn't.'

'Easy for you to say. I don't…' She swallowed and met his gaze. 'I told you. I really don't like being the centre of attention.'

So that was it. 'That's why you didn't want to do the dance either,' he said, remembering how she'd shrunk away, almost disappearing into the wall, when she'd been watching him and Melissa dance that morning. 'And why you wear such boring clothes.'

'Leave my clothes out of it,' she grumbled. 'Not everyone has to be a peacock like Melissa.'

'Or a show-off like me,' he finished for her. 'But it

doesn't matter. That's the joy of acting. *You're* not the centre of attention at all—your character is. You can be someone else for a while. It's fantastically freeing.'

'Really?' Eloise didn't look entirely convinced.

'Sure. Why do you think so many actors are screwed up as human beings? It's not the job that does it. It's the reason they choose the job in the first place. Who else would pick a career that lets them escape from themselves?'

'I suppose,' Eloise allowed. 'But that doesn't change the fact that it *would* be me up there on the stage. Making a fool of myself.'

'I won't let you do that.' He reached out a hand to take hers. 'Come on. It'll be fun. I promise.' It would be, he was certain. And fun was definitely something Eloise needed more of in her life.

She sucked in a deep breath, so deep he could see her chest move. 'Okay,' she said at last. 'Let's do this.'

If women in Shakespeare's time really wore dresses as uncomfortable as the one Noah picked out for her, suddenly Eloise understood why they always looked so miserable in paintings. She'd almost rather be wearing the hideous bridesmaid's dress. Almost.

'Perfect,' Noah said as she stepped out from the Portaloo she'd used as a changing room. Apparently stardom wasn't all it was cracked up to be.

'I feel like an idiot.'

'But you look like a star,' Noah promised.

Eloise glanced down at the corseted bodice, the intricate lacing and embroidery and the full skirt. The deep winter green of the fabric suited her, she knew, and the golden stitching added something special to the dress. But it wasn't until she met Noah's gaze and saw the warmth and approval in his eyes that she truly believed she looked okay.

More than okay, if the way Noah's gaze travelled her body was anything to go by. She almost wished there was a full-length mirror around so she could see for herself.

But she knew that the prettiest costume couldn't hide her from the reality of what she was about to do.

Why had she agreed to this? How had she let him convince her? He hadn't even really had to try—he'd just smiled at her and told her it would be fun, and she'd fallen for it.

This was why she needed to stay away from Noah Cross. Something that would be a lot easier if they weren't both in the wedding party from hell.

'Are you ready?' Noah asked as they stood at the side of the stage.

'No.'

Noah smiled, and handed her the first reading they'd decided on—one of her favourite exchanges between Beatrice and Benedick from *Much Ado About Nothing*.

'You can do this,' he whispered. Then he took her hand and led her out onto the stage.

It had been so many years since she'd done this, Eloise had thought she must have forgotten how. But as she stood there, script in shaking hand, it all came flooding back. The tiny local theatre in her home town, just a few miles away from where she stood now. The scruffy red velvet seats in the audience. The way the wood of the stage smelt. The heavy curtains that rose and fell on their shows.

Eloise, twelve years old, standing in the chorus line of their latest musical, watching her mother fall in love with her leading man, rehearsal after rehearsal. And her father in the wings, humiliated again. And knowing, even then, that this affair wouldn't last either. That everyone would talk—in whispers, if her dad was around, and openly if he wasn't—and predict when they might make it official.

Whether this time Letitia would leave, find a man who could be equal to her instead of staying with her boring, grey old husband.

And every time she would threaten to walk out, there'd be scenes—on stage and off. And every time, as the last night ended, Eloise would know it would all be over soon. That her mother would never really leave, never really chase the perfect happiness and true love she claimed she wanted.

Because if she was happy, where would the drama be? Letitia lived for the drama, not the love.

She'd even chosen drama over her own daughter when she'd seduced Derek away from her. Eloise was under no illusions about what mattered most to her mother—or to actors in general.

Noah gave her a look and she took a breath, smiled and began the act. She'd taken all the drama classes, played her parts in the society beside her parents, so she knew what she was doing.

But she would never be an actress. Not when she'd already seen how much happiness it could destroy.

It was easy to lose herself in the lines, the humour, the characters. Noah had been right about that, at least. Up there on the stage, she could almost believe she was another person and that made it a lot easier.

They hadn't planned a full performance, as such, so there was no start time and no audience waiting patiently for them to start. Instead, they began the scene as the guests started to mill around the Frost Fair, and waited to be discovered. By the time Eloise looked out from the stage after the third scene she and Noah had chosen, she was amazed to find that they had drawn quite a crowd.

As they applauded, Noah took the script from her and gave her the next one. Eloise frowned as she looked at the highlighted passage. This wasn't one she'd agreed to. They'd said comedies only, and *Romeo and Juliet* was most certainly *not* a comedy.

'Ready?' Noah whispered and, before she could answer, said his opening line.

It was the scene at the masked ball, Eloise realised as she responded. That short, incredibly flirtatious and sexy scene where they dance and talk and...

'Then move not while my prayer's effect I take.'

She barely had a moment to register Noah's words before his hands were at her waist, tugging her close. He kissed her lightly, just a brief press of his lips against hers. But it was enough. Enough to send sparks through her whole body, to leave her aching and desperate for more.

Wait. He'd just said something. Which meant she had another line.

Somewhere, from the recesses of her memory and an abiding love for the movie version, she found it.

'Then have my lips the sin that they have took.'

Noah grinned, still holding her against him.

'Sin from my lips?' he said. *'O trespass sweetly urged. Give me my sin again.'*

Again? Eloise's eyes widened but he just kept smiling at her—before dipping her deeply over his arm and lowering his lips to hers.

There was nothing brief about this kiss. Nothing perfunctory. And nothing about it felt like an act.

Her hands tightened on the fabric of Noah's doublet as he deepened the kiss, teasing her mouth open and driving her wild. Her whole body reacted to the sensation of his lips on hers, tightening and tensing with the need to take things further. If they hadn't been in public...

A whoop went up from the crowd and reality came crashing in on her. They weren't just in public. She was on a stage, in front of the Hollywood elite, some of her staff and probably her teenage nemesis. Making out with a famous actor like some girl with a crush.

She tried to pull away but, since Noah was the only thing holding her up, she didn't get too far. Fortunately, he seemed to sense the change of mood and slowly raised her back to a standing position, only ending the kiss at the last possible moment.

The audience cheered, clapping and whistling, and Eloise knew her face had to be the same colour as her hair.

'Okay?' Noah whispered, too soft to be heard over the crowd.

But Eloise couldn't answer. The only words she could find were Juliet's.

'*You kiss by the book,*' she declared, and the crowd laughed.

She was glad someone found it funny. Because, as far as Eloise was concerned, that kiss meant only one thing.

She was in big trouble.

'*You kiss by the book.*'

Eloise sounded suitably stunned, but the way she projected the line into the crowd left Noah uncertain. Was she still acting? Or had the kiss affected her the same way it had him?

Because he definitely hadn't been acting.

Oh, the first kiss, sure. That had just been a joke, almost. He'd slipped the short *Romeo and Juliet* exchange in while Eloise had been getting changed, partly because it was one of his favourites and partly because it gave him an excuse to kiss her. He'd purposefully kept that first kiss light and relaxed, giving her the freedom to pull back any time she liked, even if it *was* only an act.

But from the moment his lips had met hers he'd known

that wouldn't be enough. The electricity between them, the way her touch sparked through his body, heating him to boiling point even in the freezing English air...that *couldn't* all be pretend, could it? And then, of course, he'd had to know for sure.

So he'd kissed her. Properly.

And his whole world had tilted.

The audience were applauding again, and Noah realised he'd almost forgotten they were there. He hadn't been playing to the crowd for once, or thinking about how his moves would look on the big screen. The only thing that had been on his mind was the woman in his arms.

Never mind Tessa and her admonitions to behave. Never mind his reputation. Even the role of Marcus hadn't mattered for the long moments where he'd held Eloise.

He blinked and the spell was broken, and the real world surged back in.

Her final line spoken, Eloise tried to make a dash for the edge of the makeshift stage but he grabbed her hand to keep her with him, his mind churning. When she glared at him, he explained softly, 'We have to take a bow.'

Her glare didn't lessen, but she gave a sharp nod and took her place beside him. Hand in hand, they bowed to the assembled audience, who whooped and cheered even louder.

'What were they serving at those drinks stands?' Noah asked. Because he was good, he knew that, and Eloise had been fabulous, but this level of enthusiasm still seemed a little over the top. Unless they'd seen the truth behind the kiss—but he doubted that too. This crowd wouldn't know truth if it kissed them.

'Spiced apple cider.' Eloise didn't look at him as she answered, smiling out at the crowd as they took their second bow.

'Alcoholic.'

'Apparently very.'

'Encore!' someone in the crowd yelled but Eloise shook her head and, before Noah could stop her, she was across the stage and descending the steps, ready to disappear back into the mass of people filling the Frost Fair. Suddenly Noah was alone on the stage, wondering if her reaction to the kiss meant she was more or less likely to let him do it again.

Because one thing he was very sure of. He wanted to kiss Eloise Miller in a way he hadn't wanted to kiss anyone for years.

In fact, he wanted to do a lot more than kiss her. Discreetly, of course. But that kiss had proved that Eloise was worth taking the risk.

And, after the way she'd responded to him, she was going to have to come up with a better excuse than *I don't date actors* to convince him that she didn't want exactly the same thing.

CHAPTER EIGHT

ELOISE REFUSED TO dwell on the memory of Noah's kiss, instead throwing herself into traipsing around the Frost Fair to make sure that everything was going perfectly. Then, when the stallholders started looking irritated at her interference and Laurel assured her that she had everything in hand, Eloise stormed off back to the hotel to get out of her ridiculous costume and into something more appropriate for Melissa's hen night.

By the time the bride, bridesmaids and other favoured female guests were gathered for games, pink drinks and the wearing of feather boas in the main bar that evening, Eloise could still feel the memory of Noah's lips against hers.

How was she supposed to think about anything else after a kiss like that? She'd barely managed to focus on her job long enough to check everything was in place for the hen night. And choosing a dress… Well, what did one wear after wearing Juliet's best frock all afternoon? Eloise's wardrobe certainly had nothing so fancy. In the end, she'd settled on another navy dress—one of four in her wardrobe. This one, at least, was made of more slippery material than her thick, knitted work one, and it skimmed over her body in a way that suggested that she might actually have some curves under the fabric. Somewhere.

Just in case Noah felt the sudden need to reprise their roles of Romeo and Juliet, she told herself. After all, if it was *Juliet* kissing Noah rather than Eloise, that couldn't be so bad, right?

No. That was crazy. And that was *exactly* the sort of thinking that had seen her mother fall into affair after affair with her leading men.

Eloise had sworn her whole life that she wouldn't make the same mistakes. That she wouldn't get caught up in the spectacle of a love affair and miss the reality underneath. She'd rather a boring, predictable romance to the high drama of the ones her mother had enjoyed anyway. And she wouldn't let movie star good looks and charm sway her from that.

No matter how incredible his kisses were.

They'd said friends. That was what she had to stick to. That was what she needed to get her through this nightmare of a wedding—a friend.

'Of course, Eloise had *loads* of practice at being on stage, didn't you?' Melissa waved her champagne flute across the table in Eloise's direction as she spoke, and Eloise scrambled to try and catch up on the conversation she'd been ignoring in favour of reliving Noah's kiss.

'Sorry?'

Melissa rolled her eyes. 'The girls were just talking about your performance at the Frost Fair this afternoon.'

'You were fantastic!' one of the guests Eloise had met only briefly, and didn't recognise from the movies at all, said. She had a feeling the woman was the wife of a director or something similar. 'You really brought the whole Frost Fair to life.'

Eloise looked down at her hands to try and hide her blush.

'And I was saying how you'd had lots of practice on the

stage,' Melissa went on. 'Totally different to the movies, of course. But all those years taking part in those local plays with your mum was obviously good for something, wasn't it?'

Melissa's gaze met hers as she spoke, and Eloise felt the threat in her words as she mentioned her mother. A chill ran through her at the calculating look in Melissa's eyes. The unspoken message was clear: upstage the bride again, and everyone would get to hear about Eloise's mother's antics.

Everything Eloise had spent the last ten years living down would be public knowledge all over again.

'Perhaps it's time for the first game?' Eloise stood and clapped her hands together, deflecting the conversation away from herself.

Melissa, mollified for the time being, beamed as her guests threw themselves into games that thrust her back into the centre of attention. Eloise, meanwhile, found herself watching from the sidelines, noting every other instance of Melissa manipulating the evening to keep herself on top. Like the way the bridesmaids were all just slightly less beautiful and famous than she was. Or how guests with little to give in a professional sense were kept on the outskirts of the gathering, while much attention was given to those in power—directors, actresses with more Hollywood pull. The tiered system Melissa had in place was obvious, now she knew what she was looking for.

Clearly Melissa had managed to keep her reputation for sweetness intact in the film industry, the same way she always had when working at Morwen Hall. But Eloise was sure there must be people in Hollywood who had experienced the other side of Melissa too—as she had all those years ago.

She couldn't help but wonder what would happen if one

of those people suddenly became more famous and powerful than Melissa.

'Time for Balloon Question Time!' Laurel, official hen party planner, clapped her hands and distracted the group from laughing at the male body parts they'd all been making out of modelling clay for the previous game. Eloise, having observed their efforts, was glad of the change of pace.

'Now, this game has a bit of a twist,' Laurel said, looking at Eloise with an apology in her eyes as she spoke. 'We have twenty questions in these twenty balloons in the net. The pink balloons hold questions for the bride. The purple balloons have questions for the bridesmaids and maid of honour to answer.'

Eloise groaned, hoping the sound was covered by the excited chatter of the other hens and the music playing in the bar. Just what she needed—more attention.

'So, ladies, line up and prepare to pop balloons! Bride, bridesmaids and maid of honour, come on down!' Melissa, Iona and Caitlin followed Laurel's instructions and took their seats on the barstools lined up on the platform by the bar. Eloise followed more slowly.

'Want to give me a heads up?' she whispered to Laurel as she passed.

'Sorry, no can do. I didn't set the questions. Melissa did.' Laurel patted her on the arm. 'On the plus side, if you refuse to answer any of them, you get to drink a shot.'

More alcohol. That would help.

The first few balloons went well. Each guest took a turn popping one, then reading out the question inside, directing it at the bride or attendants depending on its colour. Melissa answered questions about her first boyfriend—where she shot a warning look at Eloise before lying through her teeth—and the role she'd most like to play on film,

Marie Antoinette, which Eloise could totally see. Caitlin answered the question about her biggest regret, and Iona one about her favourite memory of Melissa.

And then, with the next purple balloon, it was Eloise's turn.

'Well, this seems very appropriate today,' Laurel said, grinning. Eloise felt something inside her relax. Laurel obviously felt that this was a safe question. How bad could it be? 'Eloise, tell us—in detail—about your best ever kiss.'

The room burst into laughter—all except Melissa, who sat stony-faced beside her. She must have written the questions before the Frost Fair, Eloise realised. Laurel had been setting up the games while the festivities were still going on, so she must have had the questions beforehand. There was no way Melissa wanted to draw attention back to Eloise and Noah's kiss.

'I think we all *saw* the answer to that this afternoon!' Caitlin said, and took another sip from her bright pink cocktail. 'So, tell us! How did it feel?'

Melissa snorted—which led Eloise to assume she'd had one too many cocktails. 'As if we don't all already know that? Noah Cross must have dated almost every woman in this room.'

'I went to an awards ceremony with him,' Iona said. 'But he never kissed *me* like that.'

'Or me,' someone else piped up.

'He didn't kiss me at all,' another woman added. Eloise frowned. She might think that Noah's playboy reputation was a lie, except anyone who kissed like he did had clearly been practising a *lot*.

'It was just a kiss,' Eloise said, realising that the hens were still waiting for an answer. 'It wasn't even a real one. We were acting.'

'Looked pretty real to me,' Caitlin said.

'That is sort of the idea, Cait,' Melissa snapped. 'Although I appreciate you might not have reached that lesson in your drama training yet.'

There was a moment of stunned silence, and Melissa obviously realised she'd stepped out of her perfect friend character. She turned to Eloise and beamed. 'It did look very real though, I suppose. But then, that shouldn't be such a surprise, should it? It must be in the genes.'

Iona frowned. 'In the jeans? They were in period costume.'

'Genes with a G,' Melissa said sharply. 'Eloise's mother was an actress too, you see, locally, anyway. And she was absolutely famous for her ability to make all her leading men fall in love with her. Wasn't she?'

Eloise froze, the shame and humiliation cresting over her like a wave, just at the reminder. Melissa knew every single story that had ever been told about Eloise's mother. Her own mother had been the one spreading the rumours, most of the time.

She tried to tell herself that it didn't matter—that these people, flown in for the week for a wedding, would be out of her life in just a few days. They didn't care about her, didn't care about her past. They had no importance in her life.

But knowing that didn't make any difference. The humiliation she'd endured at the hands of her mother's behaviour for so many years hadn't faded, even now. She wouldn't ever shake those painful memories, she knew. The whispers, the whole town talking about her, casting sympathetic—or worse, mocking—glances at her father. Everyone she knew expecting her to turn out the exact same way.

'She sounds like quite the lady,' Caitlin said, eyeing Eloise with more interest than she'd ever shown previously. 'Did she ever try to make it professionally?'

'She used to be a dancer in London, didn't she, Eloise?' Melissa asked lightly. 'You know the sort.'

'Sure.' Iona laughed. 'Well, everyone has to start somewhere.'

'And those without the talent stay there,' Caitlin finished, sending a ripple of amusement through the crowd.

'It was sad, really,' Melissa said. 'She must have been quite beautiful once, I suppose. But you know how older women get sometimes, when they're worried about being left on the shelf, or can't find satisfaction in their marriage. They start running after everything that moves, no matter how ridiculous they look. She even went after your own boyfriend once, didn't she, Eloise? And got him too, as I recall.' She shook her head. 'Poor woman; she clearly had issues.' As if that false sympathy, tacked on the end, somehow made up for the fact that she was trashing Eloise's mother's name—and Eloise's reputation at the same time.

'Does Noah know about your family tendency to seduce co-stars?' Melissa turned her most innocent smile and wide eyes on Eloise.

Eloise couldn't take it any more. 'Melissa, could I please have a word with you outside?' she ground out between clenched teeth.

'But darling! We're all having so much fun here!'

'I just remembered something about the arrangements for the…ah…photo shoot tomorrow. I'd hate for anything to go wrong.'

Melissa rolled her eyes and slid off her barstool. 'Oh, fine. Honestly, finding capable people these days… You guys all carry on having fun! I'll be right back.'

Eloise stalked out of the bar into the empty corridor, breathing deeply in the hope that she'd be able to talk to

Melissa rationally and calmly. Like a grown-up. Like she'd never managed to do with her before.

'So, what's the problem?' Melissa asked, all trace of her affected friendliness gone.

'I'd rather you didn't bring my mother into conversations, please,' Eloise said as calmly as possible. 'My family history has no bearing on this wedding, and I'm sure your friends don't care about who my mother slept with over a decade ago.'

'I'm sure they don't either,' Melissa said, her tone sharp. 'Your mother was a slut and a disgrace, but who cares about that now, right? But if *you're* sleeping with Noah Cross, you can bet everyone in Hollywood will care about that. It'll be the biggest story of my wedding—and that is unacceptable.'

'I'm not…I'm not sleeping with Noah. I only just met the guy,' Eloise said, taken aback.

'So? What difference does that make?' Melissa asked. 'He's a huge name, he's gorgeous, he's loaded and he's interested. Of course you're going to sleep with him. You'd be an idiot not to. But *not* at my wedding, okay?'

Melissa turned and strode back into the bar, her perfect smile in place on her perfect face. Eloise stared after her, stunned.

'But…But I'm not sleeping with Noah Cross,' she said again, to the empty hallway.

'And isn't that a crying shame?' Noah said from behind her.

Noah hadn't meant to gatecrash the hen night. It was just that he felt about ten years too old for the stag do. Not in actual age, he supposed, but in maturity. And, given that he regularly expected to be the least mature guy at the table, that was saying something.

Riley might be getting married, but he still seemed like a kid to Noah. It was as if the whole wedding was a game, another act. That at the end of the day he could take his ring off and go back to being just Riley again—no harm, no foul.

Marriage meant somewhat more to Noah. That was why he had no intention of ever entertaining the institution.

Still, even knowing that not everyone in Hollywood shared his opinion on the importance of marriage, he hadn't expected the stag do to feel so…shallow. Meaningless.

Irrationally, he blamed Eloise. She was the opposite of shallow. She'd given him false expectations for the rest of the world.

He hadn't even been looking for Eloise, particularly. He'd been looking for a drink—a proper one, not a cup from the keg Riley had insisted on, as a homage to frat movies past. But when he'd heard Eloise's voice…he had to admit that maybe it had been her he'd been looking for all along.

Melissa spat out something hateful about Eloise's mother, and Eloise responded with a denial. Noah moved in closer, in time to hear Melissa rate all the things about him that mattered in her world, none of which were anything he'd want to feature in his obituary.

Then she left, and Eloise was alone in the hallway.

'I'm not sleeping with Noah Cross,' she said.

Noah stepped out of the shadows. 'And isn't that a crying shame?'

Eloise spun round, her eyes wide. 'What are you doing here?'

'Just looking for a drink.' Was it the lights, or was that something akin to lust that he saw in her eyes? 'And you.'

'Why?'

He didn't have an answer. It should have been easy—*I want you. I desire you.* He'd been sure that was all this was, this strange attraction between them. A game, a flirtation. A friendship with edge, that was all. At least until the kiss they'd shared at the Frost Fair.

Now…now he had no idea what this was, or why the need to be with her was thrumming through his body like a second heartbeat.

But it was. And he did need her. Right now.

Discretion be damned.

Noah moved forward, closing the distance between them in just a couple of steps. Eloise licked her lips, just a quick brush of her pink tongue against her lower lip, but it was enough to drive Noah wild. Enough for him to imagine those lips on his own again. To imagine them on his skin, covering his body, while his own mouth touched every single inch of her…

No, he had no idea what this was between them. But he knew he was done fighting it.

He wrapped his arms around her waist, just as he had on the stage that afternoon. But this time there were no costumes, no parts. No Romeo, no Juliet. Just Noah and Eloise.

She stared up at him, her lips parted, her pupils so large they almost eclipsed the blue-green of her beautiful eyes. She wanted this as badly as he did; he could see it.

But the most frightening thing was, he wasn't sure that a kiss would be enough. Or one night. Or several nights.

He wanted her body, sure, but what scared him was how much *more* he wanted. What was it about Eloise that made him want to look deeper? To know more, to understand?

Deeper was off the table—and had been since Sally.

But if it hadn't been…he had a feeling that Eloise was

a woman he could have shown every inch of his soul, and come to know hers in return.

He shook his head, just an inch or so, just enough to dismiss the thoughts. He'd known the woman a couple of days. That wasn't what this was about, for either of them.

All he needed to concentrate on was kissing her again.

He didn't say anything—words were unnecessary now. As he stared into Eloise's eyes he knew she understood everything he wasn't saying. He tilted his head, lowering his lips to hers, and she rose up on her toes to meet him, pressing her body against his. He could feel every inch of her pressed against him, warm and soft and wanting where they touched, and he couldn't help but deepen the kiss. It took everything he had not to sweep her up against the nearest wall and make love to her, without a thought for who might see or what they'd think. Or what might get back to Stefan, the director, who needed to believe that Noah could control his baser instincts.

Usually, he could, Noah was sure. He remembered having control, willpower, restraint once. Before he'd met Eloise.

He'd never felt this before—this desperate, unthinking desire. He'd dated the world's most beautiful women and he'd had true love, yet none of them had ever inspired this sort of passion down deep inside of him.

Noah didn't want to think too much about what that meant. He just wanted to enjoy it.

But then Eloise pulled away.

Noah let his hands fall from her waist as she stepped back, staring up at him, her mouth half open as if she wanted to talk but couldn't quite get the words out. After a moment of wordless staring, she swallowed and said, 'Not here. Please, not here.'

'Right. Of course.' This was a bad idea. This was every-thing he'd sworn he wouldn't do this week. 'I should go.'

But then Eloise met his gaze and shook her head before she turned away, stalking up the hallway towards the stairs.

He watched her go, his whole body at war with his mind. His feet ached to follow her, his arms to reach out and grab her. But his mind told him to stop this now, before it grew too much. Too dangerous.

Never mind that it could jeopardise the first movie role he'd been excited about in seven years. As much as he wanted it right now, the film seemed like the least impor-tant thing in his world.

There was a reason he didn't normally feel this way about women—he didn't let himself. But Eloise had pierced through every defence he'd ever built in less than forty-eight hours. How much more damage could she do with another day?

His eyes fell shut as he willed his body to leave it be.

But this time his body won out.

It took seconds to catch her up, halfway up the stairs to the third floor, but she didn't acknowledge his presence at all. Which at least meant she wasn't sending him away. In silence, they made their way up the stairs, down darkened hallways, to a room at the far corner of the hotel.

Eloise's hands shook as she reached for her key, and he leaned over to take it from her without thinking. She rested against the door, her back to the wood as she looked up at him, her eyes vulnerable now. Wary.

'I said I wouldn't do this,' she whispered. So had he. But some things couldn't be denied.

'Because you don't want to?' he asked softly. 'Or be-cause Melissa told you not to?'

'Because I'm not normally this person.'

'Do you want to be?'

If she said no, he'd walk away. The frustration might kill him but he'd do it. But he didn't think she would. He'd seen something deeper in her—something more than she'd admit to. She might try and hide herself in those dark and dull dresses, might pin her beautiful hair back so it didn't blaze so brightly, but she couldn't hide who she really was for ever.

And Noah had a feeling that the real Eloise Miller would be spectacular.

How could he not want to see her in all her glory?

'If you ask me to go,' he said, his voice hoarse, 'I'll go.'

She bit her lip, then reached out to take the key from him again.

'Don't go,' she whispered, and Noah's whole soul sang.

CHAPTER NINE

WHAT WAS SHE DOING? What on *earth* was she doing?

Well, Eloise thought as Noah kissed her deeply, pressing her up against the wood of her bedroom door, whatever she was doing felt *fantastic*.

But then reality caught up with her.

'Nobody knows,' she managed to get out between kisses.

Noah tilted his head back from hers and she missed his lips the instant they were gone. 'What?' he asked, sounding hazy with lust.

Good. She shouldn't be the only one losing her mind over this strange attraction between them.

'Nobody knows,' she repeated. 'This is our secret, okay?'

He nodded. 'Fine. Great. Anything. Just open the door.'

The man had a point, Eloise conceded as she turned within the circle of his arms and struggled to open the door with shaking hands. If they didn't get to a bed soon it was very possible they'd both be naked in the corridor within five minutes. Maybe less.

Finally, the door gave way and they tumbled into Eloise's room. It wasn't anywhere near as grand as Noah's, but she didn't imagine he cared very much right then. She definitely didn't.

As she fell onto the bed, Noah's body covering hers, Eloise's last coherent thought before giving in to pleasure was, *As long as it's a secret, no one can get hurt*.

Later, much later, Noah drew lazy patterns on her skin with his clever fingers, and Eloise couldn't even find the energy to care that she was naked beside one of the world's official top ten most beautiful men, and he was staring at her. Her. Boring, embarrassed and blushing Eloise Miller, with her too bright hair and her too tall and straight body.

'You're really good at that,' she managed eventually, the first words either of them had spoken since they'd fallen apart in each other's arms after what seemed like hours of pleasure. In reality... Eloise squinted at the clock. How had it only been forty-five minutes since she'd been telling Melissa she wasn't sleeping with Noah Cross? 'Practice, I suppose.'

'Maybe I was just very, very motivated.' Noah pressed a kiss to her bare shoulder, then carried on up her neck. Eloise squirmed until he captured her lips and she let herself sink into the kiss.

It was secret. He'd promised. It was just them, just one night.

She could let herself have this, and enjoy it. Just this once.

Noah raised himself up on one elbow so he was looking down at her. Eloise wondered where he'd found the energy. Blinking and breathing were taking all of hers.

'What Melissa was saying before...' Noah trailed off, and Eloise would have groaned if she had the strength. The last thing she wanted to talk about while in bed with Noah Cross was Melissa. 'About your mother...' Noah began again, and she realised she was wrong.

The absolute last thing she *ever* wanted to talk about was her mother.

'It doesn't matter,' she said quickly, hoping she could end the conversation before it really got started. 'It was a long time ago.'

'It seemed to matter to you earlier. I mean, you promised Melissa you wouldn't sleep with me because of it.'

'And look how well that turned out.'

Noah's smile took on a hint of smugness. 'Chemistry like ours…you can't promise that away. Trust me, I tried.'

'You tried?' If the last couple of days had been Noah trying *not* to sleep with her, he sucked at it.

'Not very hard,' he admitted. 'But you're not the only one who needs to keep this a secret. There's this director… Anyway, it doesn't matter. Let's just say it's not in my best interests to have this be public knowledge either.'

That was good, Eloise thought. If they both needed it to stay secret, they'd both be more motivated to keep it that way. And that meant there was a chance she might survive this week after all.

'So why did you risk it?' she asked, frowning. She wasn't the sort of woman men took risks over. That was definitely her mother, or Melissa. Not her.

'Because I couldn't not,' Noah said, smiling. 'I know my limits when it comes to resisting beautiful women.'

'You've experienced this a lot?' Eloise didn't like that idea. For her, this was a completely new feeling. The idea that Noah had this with every woman he met… It wasn't that she thought she was anything special, exactly. But if she only got one night with him, she at least wanted it to be one he'd remember.

'Never,' Noah swore, his gaze fixed on hers, truth in his eyes. 'Not like this.'

'Me neither,' Eloise whispered. And, worst of all, she

was very afraid she might never feel it again. She'd gone twenty-six years without ever feeling anything close, so it didn't seem likely that the kind of intense passion she had with Noah was waiting for her around every corner.

'I don't do this,' Noah admitted, and Eloise raised her eyebrows. He obviously sensed her scepticism because he went on, 'Not the sex. Yes, I've slept with women. Probably less than you think, but that's not the point. I mean…' He sucked in a deep breath. 'Normally, this is easy. Casual. I don't feel the need to ask questions, to get to know a woman's personal history. But with you…it's different. *You're* different.'

Something in Eloise's chest tightened. Part of her wanted to be pleased, to be proud to be something more than the usual casual encounter that Noah indulged in. But another, larger part of her heart was curling up in the corner of her ribcage, wishing he'd move on and stop noticing her.

Because, whatever he said, she knew the truth. He might not feel it now, but Noah Cross didn't do deep and meaningful. Maybe he wanted to hear all about her childhood woes, but would he give her anything in return? She doubted it.

But still she found herself saying, 'What do you want to know?'

'She was an actress, right? Your mother?' Eloise nodded. 'So, is she the reason you don't date actors?'

'I don't date actors because I've known too many of them,' Eloise said with a sigh. 'And most of them were sleeping with my mum.'

Noah winced. 'Ah.'

'Yeah.' She turned onto her side so they were face to face in the darkness, what little light there was coming through the window glinting in his beautiful eyes. 'She was a big fish in a small pond, I guess. She'd been on the West End stage before she had me. She was pregnant when she met my dad.'

'He's not your biological father?'

Eloise shook her head. 'No. But he was the one who was there for me, every moment. Every step of the way.'

'So, what happened? They got married?'

'They did. And they moved out here, back to the town where my dad had grown up. His family were all gone but…he loved this place, and he wanted Mum to love it too. But she didn't.'

Eloise sucked in a deep breath, preparing herself for the rest of the story. Living it had been horrendous, but surely just telling it couldn't be that bad.

She'd never had to tell it before. Everyone else around here just knew.

'The one thing she did like was the Theatre Society. Our town has a small community theatre. A proper stage, raked seats—the whole thing. So, after I was born, Mum joined the Theatre Society. And because she had the experience on the London stage, well, she became the main attraction pretty quickly, I think. As long as I remember, she had every starring role in every play or show they did there. And if she didn't…well, she'd threaten to walk out until they changed their minds. They couldn't afford to upset her, you see. She was their star.'

'I've known actresses like that,' Noah said drily. 'And actors too. They're not fun to work with.'

'No. I can't imagine Mum was, for most of the people in the society. But her leading men…' This was the hardest part. 'Every production, it was the same story. They'd cast the best-looking guy against her, and every time Mum would make him fall for her. Whether she fell for them too, I don't know. She always claimed to be desperately in love with them—at least until the show was over. Then she'd drop them and come back to Dad, until the next show. But by then…she'd destroyed those men's lives. Their marriages were in tatters, their reputations ruined. Some had left their families, lost their friends, sometimes even their jobs, for Mum. And she just forgot them the minute the curtain came down.'

'How many times did she do this?' Noah asked, his voice soft.

'Too many. I don't know. Maybe six, or seven? It didn't start until I was about ten, I don't think—or, if it did, she was more discreet about it. But by the time I was a teenager, everyone knew what she was. What she did. And every guy swore she wouldn't get him—but she always did. If she wanted a man, she had him. And every time my dad was left humiliated.'

'But he always took her back. Why?'

'He loved her.' It was as simple and as awful as that. 'And she loved him too, I think. In her way. She always came home in the end, full of apologies and talk about how things would be different. And they were, for a time. It just never lasted.'

Eloise had always known, from watching her parents, that love was as much a trap as a blessing. That she had to be careful who she fell in love with—because that would be the rest of her life, right there. She could leave, or he could, but it wouldn't change the fact that she loved him, and she'd carry that with her every day.

Was it any wonder she'd never let herself feel that deeply before?

And she wasn't going to start with Noah Cross.

'And Melissa held your parents' behaviour over you?' Noah guessed.

'For years. She made sure everyone knew—and told

everyone who'd listen that I was just like my mother. So no girls would be friends with me in case I stole their boyfriends, and no guys would risk being seen with me in case people made fun of them. I didn't even have a proper boyfriend until just before I went away to university. There were a couple of guys at school…but Melissa stole them away pretty fast. Then Derek…'

'Derek?' Noah prodded when she trailed off, and Eloise sighed. This was the most humiliating bit.

'The summer before I left for uni, I was in a play at the Theatre Society. I'd been in loads before, but always in the chorus or helping backstage. This was my first real role. And Derek…he was the director. Older than me—he was twenty-five, I think, to my eighteen. But he took a shine to me. He was my first real everything, I suppose.'

Noah shifted closer, something Eloise hadn't thought was possible until she felt his arms holding her tighter. 'What happened?'

'Mum had the lead role, of course. But her leading man broke his leg a couple of weeks into rehearsals. Derek stepped in…'

Noah winced. 'And your mother?'

'Did what she always did.' Eloise shrugged. 'I don't know why I thought it would be any different, just because he was my boyfriend instead of someone else's husband.'

'How did you find out?'

'Melissa, of course. She sent me down to the prop room to fetch something when she knew they were there together.' Eloise swallowed at the memory, her throat suddenly tight. If she thought about it too long, she became eighteen again—in the grip of infatuation, sexual awakening and too many hormones, and seeing all her dreams and illusions shattered in one instant, as she saw her mother half naked against the prop table, and Derek kissing her.

Noah cursed. 'What did you do?'

'I shut the door, walked away and pretended I'd never been there. I finished with Derek, of course, who didn't seem all that disappointed. And then I ran away to university.' She'd been searching for freedom, the ability to be herself, without the baggage of her family history. But all she'd found was that she was the same shy, scared and gullible little girl in a different town.

'And after college you moved back here?' Noah sounded surprised. 'You even came and worked at the same hotel. Why?'

'It was my home,' Eloise said firmly. 'I couldn't let them take that from me. When I first took the chamber-maid job here at sixteen, I guess I was just looking for some freedom. But when I came back...it was a safe place. My place.'

'I guess I can understand that,' Noah said, but his tone said he couldn't.

She sighed. 'Also...university wasn't the fresh new life I was hoping for. Turns out I was the same naive and gull-ible Eloise there too.'

She'd thrown herself into her business studies and, in her final year, a relationship with another student. Every-thing seemed perfect—they'd talked about setting up an events business together, about heading out into the real world and making it big. Everything she'd dreamed of seemed close to coming true—running her own business, living her own life, making a success of things at last. Until he'd run off with her best ideas and the only friend she'd made at university, leaving all her classmates talk-ing about it.

Really, was it any wonder she avoided love these days?

'Do you want to tell me?' Noah asked, and Eloise shook her head.

'Let's just say, at least the guy who screwed me over personally *and* professionally at uni wasn't an actor.'

Noah didn't press for the whole sordid story, which she appreciated. She'd shared enough of her past disasters for one night.

Instead, he kissed her shoulder and asked, 'Where are your parents now?'

'My dad died while I was at university. My mum… she's still in town. Her memory is going, though. Early onset dementia, the doctors said. She can't even remember everything she did back then. These days she's just a harmless old lady, I suppose. And the town… Well, they haven't forgotten, I don't suppose. But there are newer and better scandals to talk about most of the time.'

'Until Melissa came back and brought it all up again.'

'Yeah.'

Noah sighed. 'Well, I guess that explains a lot about your attitude to actors.'

With a laugh, Eloise lay back, breaking the intense connection between them. She felt lighter, somehow, for telling him everything.

'Of course, you're still hugely biased against us.' Noah followed her, his body pressing against hers as he kissed her again. 'Not all actors are the same, you know.'

'Maybe not,' Eloise allowed. 'But a lot of them are. Look at you—a different girl on your arm in every photo.'

'That's different.'

'How?'

'That's…it's not me,' Noah said. 'It's the Noah Cross the press and the public want to see.'

'So it's all an act. But do the women you take out know that?'

'Always.' Noah's eyes were serious above her. 'I'm always upfront. It's one night, or several, but it's never serious. They know the deal. I never fall for them, never tell them I love them, never give them any expectations.'

'So you try never to hurt anyone.' But was he protecting them or himself? Eloise couldn't be sure. 'Isn't that kind of lonely?'

'Sometimes.'

'So why do it?'

Noah didn't answer. Instead, he rolled over to lie beside her again.

'What about your family?' Eloise asked instead. 'You've heard all about mine. Tell me about yours. Are they proud of you?'

Noah barked out a harsh laugh. 'Not exactly. My dad's opinion of actors is about as good as yours. He thinks we're all entitled, self-obsessed, narcissistic idiots. Not that he'd put it in those words.'

'Why?' Eloise asked. 'I mean, why does he think that? And what about your mother?'

'I grew up in standard middle America. My family were God-fearing, humble and happy to stay at exactly the same level they'd always been. Working a factory job, drinking beer on a Friday night and never looking for anything different.'

'But you weren't,' Eloise guessed.

'No. My best friend and I...we always talked about getting out of town, escaping to LA and seeking fame and fortune.' Noah gave a half smile at the memory. 'I always thought it was a bit of a pipe dream—until the day she said, "Let's go".'

'And you went.'

'Yeah. I did.' He smiled at her. 'And the rest is history.' Leaning in, he pressed kisses over her shoulder, obviously hoping to distract her. But Eloise had more questions.

'Why did you want to know about my mother?' she

asked. 'And don't say it's because I'm different. Everybody is different. If you want to know me… I need to know. Why?'

Noah shifted beside her, lying flat on his back as he stared at the ceiling. Eloise turned onto her side and he wrapped an arm around her shoulders, pulling her close, almost absently, it seemed. Was he always like this with a woman after sex? He said the conversation was new, but what about the closeness? Eloise knew she'd never have the courage to ask.

'I can't completely explain it,' Noah said eventually. 'But I'll try.'

'Good enough.' Resting her cheek against his chest, Eloise felt his heartbeat thrumming through her body, in time with her own, and listened.

'When I first saw you… I wanted you, I'll admit that. You're gorgeous, Eloise, whether you know it or not. And there was something about you. I wanted to be close to you. I thought…' He gave a little laugh, low and meek. 'I thought you might be an easy conquest to make the wedding a little more fun.'

'Which I was.' Eloise shrank back at the realisation, but he held her close against him.

'No. No, you were anything but.'

'We're naked in my bed, Noah. I think I've been conquered.' And how easy she'd been for him to claim.

'I think… I think you might have done the conquering,' Noah said after a moment, and Eloise stilled in his arms. 'My agent told me I had to behave this week, if I wanted this director to take me seriously for a big role. No flings. And I tried, I really did. I knew you weren't like the other women I see. You didn't know the rules yet. You saw…more of me. Deeper. And when I kissed you this afternoon…'

When he didn't continue, Eloise said, 'What? What happened then?'

Noah hauled her up his body so she was staring into his eyes, every inch of her pressed up against him.

'When I kissed you, I knew none of it mattered. I couldn't help myself. I knew I had to be with you.'

CHAPTER TEN

HE'D GONE TOO FAR. Noah knew that the moment the words left his mouth. And if he hadn't known the shock in Eloise's eyes would have told him.

'For tonight, I mean,' he said, backtracking fast. 'I couldn't leave Morwen Hall without one night with you.'

'And now you've had it.' Eloise pulled away, and he resisted the urge to tug her close again. He wasn't staying—this wasn't love, wasn't for ever. They both knew that, whatever the crazy attraction between them would have them believe.

'So, what's next for you?' Eloise asked, putting a few inches of blanket between them as she propped her head up on one hand to look at him. 'After you leave Morwen Hall, I mean.'

What was next? He had no idea. He couldn't think beyond this bed, beyond this moment. Beyond her.

'What's this film where the director needs you to be celibate?' she went on, and Noah breathed a sigh of relief. That was safe. They could talk about the film, about his career. That had to be less perilous than the spiral of feelings sleeping with Eloise had opened up inside him. Or the connection her confessions about her parents had started to foster between them. 'More beating people up and saving the world?'

He huffed out a laugh. 'No, actually. It's more of a relationships movie. About a guy trying to move on after his wife's death. It starts eight days after she dies, and follows him through to eight years later.'

'Sounds deep and meaningful,' Eloise said. 'Both things I thought you tried to avoid.'

'In my personal life? Sure. Professionally…it could be a good move.' Except that wasn't why he was doing it; Noah could admit that to himself, even if he couldn't admit it to her. He needed something more in his life. More than the superficial and the meaningless.

He just wanted to do it on his own terms. That way, at least, he could protect himself from the dangers of feeling too much.

The problem was, when he was with Eloise he could feel himself wanting more. Suddenly everything he'd always relied on—a fleeting connection, the ability to walk away unchanged—wasn't enough. And the other way lay madness—he knew that from experience.

'You really want this part, don't you?' Eloise asked, and when he turned to her she was watching him too closely.

'How did you know that?' he asked, staring back. He hadn't said how much it mattered to him, hadn't even hinted at anything beyond a professional reason for wanting the role. But Eloise had known all the same.

'I pay attention,' she said. 'So, what is it about this film? Why do you want this part so much?'

'The script is…astonishing. It's the kind of film that wins awards.' But that wasn't all and Eloise seemed to realise that. She stayed silent, waiting for him to say more. 'It spoke to me, I guess. I just knew I had to make this film.'

'The same way you knew you had to have me?' Eloise shook her head, red hair tumbling over her bare shoulders. He remembered pulling the pins out of it one by one and watching it fall loose. The sight of her undone had taken his breath away. It still did. 'This is quite your week for strange, compelling feelings.'

'It is. I blame you.'

She laughed. 'Why? For acting out Shakespeare with you and putting you in touch with your inner Romeo?'

'Because ever since I saw you I've wanted something more than I have.' He inched closer, resting one hand on her waist. 'You know, I spoke to my agent about this part and she told me that if I wanted it I'd need to start looking deeper, start accessing the feelings I've locked away for years.'

'As well as swearing off sex?' Eloise shook her head. 'She's tough. But…maybe she's right.'

'Maybe she is. But that doesn't change the fact that I don't know how. It's been years. But when I met you… I knew you were the sort of person who felt deeply. Who saw deeper, who found meaning.'

'So you thought I could help you get the part?' She frowned. 'I'm really not sure how that would work.'

'That's not it,' Noah said, at a loss for how to explain it. 'I tried staying away from you, but every time I saw you it seemed more impossible. I tried keeping my distance anyway, tried keeping it just physical. But the moment we kissed…there was more of me in that kiss than in the last ten movies I made.'

'I felt it,' Eloise murmured. 'So why not finish what you started? Look deeper. Feel more. Be the guy you need to be to get that part. I'll listen.'

'I showed you mine; you show me yours?'

'Basically. Isn't that part of what looking deeper means? Dealing with your past? You've heard all my childhood traumas. What are yours? It has to be more than disapproving parents, right?'

Noah's jaw tightened as the memories flooded over him, so intense even after all these years that he worried he might be swept away by them. It felt wrong even thinking about Sally now, here, in bed with Eloise. But he had to admit she was the first woman he'd slept with that he'd ever considered talking to about what had happened.

Could he do it? Should he?

He'd be leaving in a few days. Whatever this connection was between him and Eloise, it would be over the moment he left Morwen Hall. He didn't worry about Eloise spilling all to the Internet, or trying to make money by selling her story. He might have only known her a couple of days but he knew she wasn't that person. Especially now she'd told him about her mother.

Eloise was safe. And if he wanted the part, maybe this was what it would take.

'There was a woman,' he started, then stalled.

'Isn't there always?' Eloise asked sadly. She moved out of his arms and, for a moment, he thought she was going to get out of the cosy, safe cocoon they'd made in her bed. Then she settled against the headboard, still naked, and tugged his arm until he curled up against her side. She settled her arms around him and waited for him to continue.

Noah kissed the top of her breast and rested his head on her shoulder. When was the last time he'd been so *close* to a person, when they weren't actively having sex? Had he ever been? If he had, he couldn't remember it. Not even with Sally…

He was supposed to be telling Eloise all about Sally.

'She was my best friend,' he said eventually.

'The one you moved to LA with?'

'Yes. She was…she was my family, more than my real family ever were. They didn't understand me or the life I wanted to lead. Sally did.'

'She sounds great.' Noah listened for any hint of jealousy or envy in Eloise's voice, but it wasn't there.

'She was. We got a flat together to start with, but then she met this guy. She'd won a part on a TV show, and he was one of the other actors. She was crazy about him. But he wasn't a good guy. I couldn't put my finger on exactly what it was about him, but I knew he was wrong for Sally.'

'What happened?' Eloise asked. 'And when did you realise you were in love with her?'

Noah sighed. It said something about his levels of emotional understanding that, even seven years later, Eloise knew after five minutes what it had taken Noah years of friendship to realise.

'I think I was always in love with her. Right from the day we met, back at grade school.' She'd walked straight up to him, stuck out her hand and said, 'I'm Sally. You're my new best friend.' And that was all it took. 'But I guess when we hit high school, I realised it for real.'

'And you didn't do anything about it?' Eloise asked, surprise clear in her voice.

'I wasn't Noah Cross, Film Star then, remember. I was nothing. And Sally…she was all I had. The only person in town who understood me—who I was, what I wanted, what mattered to me. I couldn't risk losing that.' The idea of her walking away because she didn't feel the same way had been far too terrifying for him to take the chance.

'So what changed? I mean, I assume something did.'

'Yeah. She moved out of our flat and into his house, and I realised I'd missed my chance.' He'd waited too long and he'd lost her. It had felt like the end of the world—until he'd learned what real loss meant. 'But I figured she was happy, so I should be happy for her. But then she showed up one day with a black eye and I knew I had to get her out of there.'

Eloise stayed silent but her arms tightened ever so slightly around him. He put his hand over hers and squeezed. Even after all this time, the horror he'd felt as he'd seen the bruises marring Sally's perfect skin could still make him feel sick to his stomach.

'I took her home and we talked. She told me it had been going on for months. I couldn't believe I hadn't noticed. I still can't.' He dipped his head, hiding his eyes from hers. She didn't need to see the shame in them. The guilt. He'd been so busy thinking about himself—about how he felt, what he'd lost, his own emotional turmoil—that he'd missed what was right in front of him and let the woman he loved get hurt. 'She agreed to leave him. And then...'

'You told her how you felt,' Eloise guessed when he didn't continue.

'Yeah.' The feelings were all coming back now, whether he wanted them or not. Those deep, hidden feelings that he'd locked up for so long, because he knew what came next. Knew he couldn't have all that hope and that happiness without the pain that followed. 'Sally...she told me she thought she might feel the same, or that she could one day. We kissed and, just for that brief moment, everything was perfect.' He stopped, just wanting one more moment of that peace, without the fear that snapped at its heels. They lay together in the quiet of the room, listening to the sounds of the hen and stag parties still going on downstairs, and for a moment Noah believed that could be the end of the story.

But then Eloise broke the silence. 'I almost don't want to ask what happened next. But I think I have to.'

With a sigh, Noah pulled away, out of her embrace. Sitting up on the edge of the bed, he stayed facing away from her as he spoke, every word cutting through him as it formed on his lips. 'We agreed to take it slow. We'd already waited so long, and we had our whole future together to figure it all out. The next day, she went back to his house to pack up her stuff while I was out at a call-back audition. I asked her to wait until I could go too, but she wanted to get it done. He was supposed to be at work but…

'I got the part—my first big movie role. I raced home to tell Sally, but when I got there the flat was empty. And then the police called.'

There was a rustle of sheets and then Eloise's body was pressed up against his from behind, her warmth flooding through him as she pressed kisses against his shoulders. But those kisses couldn't erase the guilt he carried every day. He should have been there—not just that day, but every day before that. He should have been looking outwards, not inwards. He should have been there for her.

But he wasn't.

'He'd beaten her. So hard she'd blacked out, they think. And when she fell…her head cracked open on the corner of the table. She died in moments.'

'Oh, Noah, I'm so sorry.' Eloise spoke against his skin, holding him tight to her. 'So, so sorry.'

They were just words, Noah knew. They couldn't fix anything. Couldn't heal the searing pain that had cut through him that day and never fully gone away. His scar tissue might not show on the outside, but it was still there and he felt it pull most days.

But the thing about scar tissue was that it healed thick and hard, and painless. He might feel the tug around it, like healthy skin, but the dead area—his ability to love, to feel those deeper emotions—they didn't hurt at all.

They couldn't.

So he didn't look inwards, not any more. He looked outwards—to easy, casual relationships, to films that focused more on explosions than feelings. And he pushed the guilt and the sorrow down beneath that scar tissue and pretended they weren't there.

Until he'd met Eloise, and read a script that could change his career. And now all those emotions he'd sworn not to feel again were bubbling up, filling him, and he knew he had to beat them back down before they destroyed him.

He couldn't waste emotion on himself. If he had to feel, it would be as a character—safe in another person's fictional life, where the emotions couldn't hurt him. If he felt that pain at all, let it be for the part, for his career. Because Noah Cross didn't deserve to feel any of those things—love, loss, hope—ever again.

'I know I can't say anything,' Eloise whispered, close to his ear. 'I know I can't fix it. But I'm sorry. And whatever you need right now—distance, alcohol, whatever. Just say. I can give it.'

There was only one way to forget, Noah had found, and that was to drown out the memories. Alcohol helped, so did work. But the best thing was sitting naked in bed beside him.

He turned, sweeping her into his arms in one fast movement. 'You,' he murmured against the skin of her neck. 'Let me have you again. Let me forget.'

Eloise nodded, and he bore her down to the bed again, determined to block out the emotions once more.

He'd use them, if he had to. But not as himself. He'd save it all for the part.

He could give Eloise his body, even his memories, but that was all.

Everything else, he'd already given up.

CHAPTER ELEVEN

ELOISE WOKE EARLY, after nowhere near enough sleep to deal with the day ahead. Beside her, Noah slumbered on, one arm wrapped loosely around her waist. She twisted onto her side to look at him, his face peaceful in repose.

In the early morning light, still grey and cold as the sun just started to peep over the horizon, it was hard to imagine all the secrets and wounds they'd shared the night before. After his confession, Noah had made love to her like a man possessed. A man driving out his demons, she supposed.

Did he blame himself for Sally's death? She suspected so, even if he knew intellectually it wasn't his fault. Guilt and grief had a funny way of twisting things in a person's mind.

She felt a tug, somewhere in her middle. A compulsion to try and fix him, to help him feel again. Not just to get some movie role, but because he needed it. She'd thought Noah was just another self-centred, narcissistic actor—like her mother. But that wasn't it. He honestly didn't believe that letting people in and feeling something for them could end well. Which, given his experiences, she could sort of understand. She even agreed with him a lot of the time.

But to *always* feel that way… That was a very lonely way to live. Far lonelier even than hers.

She shook her head and prepared to inch out of his arms without waking him.

'Where are you going?' he asked, tightening his hold on her without opening his eyes.

'I thought you were asleep.'

'I was acting.' His eyes opened and he blinked lazily. 'You okay?'

'Sure. Why wouldn't I be?'

'Last night was…intense.'

That was one word for it. Eloise had never experienced anything like it—not the exchange of confidences, or the sex. Everything seemed to be on a higher level with Noah, seemed to strip another layer of her defences away.

'It was,' she admitted. 'I feel…naked, I guess.'

Noah smirked. 'You kind of are.' Hauling her closer, he angled himself above her again, but there was something different in his passion in the morning light. A desperation she hadn't seen in his eyes before.

'I'm not going to tell anyone, you know,' she said before he could kiss her.

'I know.' His mouth tightened a little and she stretched up to kiss it lightly.

'I want to keep this a secret too, remember.' The last thing she needed was Melissa finding out her latest scandalous story.

Noah frowned. 'Why is that again? Usually I have to stop women shouting from the rooftops after they've slept with me.'

'Really?' Eloise raised her eyebrows and he smiled, the emotions of the night before clearly fading again as he returned to his usual laughing self.

'Well, stop them going to the papers and telling all, anyway. So, why don't you want anyone to know? Is it Melissa?'

'Partly,' Eloise said. How could she put it in a way that wouldn't offend him? 'But it's more than that. I don't want to be another one of your women, with everyone talking about me—and pitying me once you walk away. We both know you're leaving at the end of the week. We have a built-in time limit.'

'I suppose,' Noah said slowly. 'I'm not sure I like being your dirty little secret, though.'

She laughed. 'Who said anything about dirty?'

'I was here last night, remember?' He waggled his eyebrows at her.

'Besides, you're the one who said you wanted a private fling,' Eloise reminded him. 'No strings, no catches—and no gossip.'

'So I'm getting exactly what I want from the situation,' Noah said. 'But what about you?'

'I'm doing okay,' she said, but it was already too late. Noah slid down her body, covering her with kisses and, just for a moment, Eloise let herself imagine having this, having him for longer than a week.

But that way madness lay.

'So, other than *magnificent* sex,' Noah said between kisses, 'what's in it for you?'

Eloise considered, but it was hard to think with his mouth against her skin. 'I like how I feel when I'm with you. Who I am when I'm with you.'

'Yeah?' Noah stilled, resting his head against her hip.

'Yeah.' How could she explain it without adding to his ego? 'I couldn't have done anything like performing on the stage at the Frost Fair without you there, telling me it would be fun. Maybe a few more days with you will give me the confidence I need to move on in my life. Get out of my rut.' Maybe chase the dreams she'd long given up on—her own business, getting away from this place, finding her own success. Maybe even finding a man she could love, who would stay, and want her for who she was. She didn't mention that part, though. Not as Noah began kissing her stomach again.

She wasn't thinking about any man but him for the time being.

By the time Eloise emerged from the pleasurable haze Noah had put her in, the sun was fully up and she was in danger of running late.

'Maybe tonight we can do this in my room,' Noah said as he kissed her goodbye at the door. 'Try out the four-poster.'

Eloise grinned. 'Maybe. Now go! We need to be downstairs for the wedding party photo shoot and interviews in half an hour.' She pushed him out of the door and he headed off down the corridor, whistling. 'And remember…'

'Nobody knows,' he said, turning and walking backwards. Then he blew her a kiss and she shook her head.

Maybe trusting Noah with a secret relationship was expecting too much from him. As much as he said he wanted it kept between them too, to help convince that director, she wasn't sure he was actually capable of being discreet. But the thought of being in his bed tonight…that was too good to give up. She'd just have to hope he could *act* discreet, just for a few days.

Then he'd be gone. But Eloise wasn't thinking about that.

Instead, as she headed towards her bathroom, she thought that if only she'd known this was going to happen from the start, the bedroom crisis she'd faced on arrival day could have been solved an awful lot more easily.

Thirty minutes later, Eloise hurried from the lift into the lobby. Most of the wedding guests were already milling around, ready to go out on the local tours Laurel had arranged for them while the wedding party were busy with the photographer and the journalist from the celebrity magazine covering the wedding.

'You look nice,' Laurel said as she approached, clipboard in hand, from the reception desk. 'Kind of…glowy.'

'Thanks.' Eloise tried not to blush.

She might have spent just a little more time than normal on her hair and make-up that morning, and put a bit more effort into her choice of suit—a deep charcoal skirt and jacket with a silky cream blouse and high heels. Even though the magazine people would be providing outfits for the photo shoot, and doing her hair and make-up, Eloise had felt like making the effort.

After all, trying to match up to the kind of good looks parading around Morwen Hall at the moment was a full-time job. Nothing to do with the gorgeous guy who'd just spent the night in her bed. Probably.

Oh, who was she trying to kid? She wanted to look nice for her *boyfriend*. That was what Melissa and the other girls would have chanted, back when they were pre-teens at school. But Noah wasn't her boyfriend. And he wasn't sticking around. Two more days and it would all be over, so there was to be absolutely no falling for the guy.

He'd just stay her own delicious little secret.

Well, not so little, actually.

'Are you okay?' Laurel asked, her eyebrows drawn together in concern. 'You're turning red.'

'Fine. Just fine.' Eloise willed her skin colour to return to normal.

'Well, good. Because Dan and I are off to supervise the coach tours, so you're on your own with Bridezilla today.' Across the lobby, Eloise saw Dan watching, waiting for Laurel, as if he couldn't keep his eyes off her. Obviously a man besotted. Good. Whatever concerns she'd had when she'd first seen them together must just have been nerves—coming out as a couple could do that, she supposed.

Something else she and Noah wouldn't have to worry about. Nobody would ever know about them.

'You're not staying for the photo shoot?' Eloise asked.

Laurel shook her head. 'One of the advantages of not actually being part of the wedding party. We are surplus to requirements this morning. Plus we'll probably have a lot more fun on the tours.'

'I bet.' The lift pinged behind her and Eloise turned to watch it open, even as she spoke. 'Wish I was coming with you.'

The lift doors opened and Noah stepped out, his dark hair perfectly messy above those dark chocolate-brown eyes, his stubble just the right length for scraping over her skin and his shirt collar open under his jacket, showing hints of the collarbone she'd kissed her way along the night before…

'Are you sure?' Laurel asked, watching her. 'Seems to me you might have your own fun right here.'

'I don't know what you're talking about,' Eloise said, and went to go and see her not-boyfriend.

'Ready for your close-up?' Noah asked as Eloise approached across the lobby.

She certainly looked ready. She'd left her hair down and it tumbled in waves over her shoulders, blazing red against the dark grey of her jacket and the creamy shirt that matched her skin. He wanted to touch it, to touch her. To reach out and kiss her, to show every other person in the hotel that she was his, even if only for a few days.

But he couldn't. Because he'd promised her they'd be a

secret, and because one more fling might ruin his chances at getting the film role of the decade.

He knew the reasons. But it still felt like a stupid idea. Anyone who looked at them would know they'd been together, he was sure. At the very least, anyone who'd been paying any attention to Eloise would know she'd been up to something last night. Her whole body screamed relaxed satisfaction, and the smile she gave him told him everything he wanted to know—that they'd be doing it again. And soon.

Thank God. The self-imposed time limit was already weighing heavily on him. In only a few days he'd be gone. That was not a lot of time to make the most of his connection with Eloise Miller.

He didn't let himself consider the possibility of it carrying on beyond New Year's Day. Eloise's life was here, and his was everywhere else. She wanted for ever love, the deep and lasting kind, the sort she could rely on. He wanted anything but that. And, to be fair, she'd not given him any signs that she wanted anything more from their fling. Yes, their connection had been immediate and their chemistry explosive. But just because they'd shared secrets and feelings didn't mean they had to share a life.

Maybe he was destined to only ever have meaningful relationships that lasted a day or two. And maybe that wasn't the worst thing in the world.

At least this time, when it was over, it would be his choice and everyone involved would still be breathing. He'd take that as a win.

'I can't believe they actually want to take photos of me,' Eloise said, standing just an inch or so too close. She wanted to keep this a secret but she didn't even know what she had to hide, Noah realised. Understandably. Eloise wasn't the sort of woman who would have done this before.

'You're the maid of honour,' he pointed out, shifting his weight from one foot to the other to create the illusion of distance between them. 'Kind of important to the wedding party.'

Eloise rolled her eyes. 'I'm the understudy. And I'm only doing it because Melissa's PR person thought it would look good.'

'And you do look very, very good this morning,' Noah murmured, too softly for anyone else to hear.

Eloise's cheeks flushed the same pink as her skin did after making love. Just the sight of it made Noah want to drag her back off to bed for the rest of the day, photo shoot be damned.

He wasn't quite egotistical enough to believe that the way Eloise was coming out of her shell—performing at the Frost Fair, dressing like she didn't hate everything about her body—was entirely down to sleeping with him. But her words from earlier that morning had stayed with him all through his shower and getting dressed. She liked who she was when she was with him. Not what other people thought of her because she was on his arm, not what being seen with him could do for her career because, if anything, it might damage it, if Melissa really kicked up a fuss.

Just who she was with him.

Noah wasn't sure he'd ever had that sort of an effect on someone before. It was intoxicating.

As the coaches finally left, Eloise led him down the corridor towards the rooms they were using for the photo shoot and interviews, but as they passed a small, empty office, Noah's willpower ran out. Again.

Tugging her into the office after him, he shut the door and placed his back against it, effectively stopping anyone from interrupting. And her from leaving.

'Noah…' she said as he pulled her into his arms, but

any real complaint in her voice was drowned out by the smile spreading over her face.

'What is it about keeping things secret that somehow makes it even sexier?' He kissed his way up her neck and was rewarded with a low moan.

'We've got to go,' Eloise said.

But Noah countered with, 'Just two minutes,' and she gave in rapidly.

Ten minutes later, they finally made it to the photo shoot.

'You're both late,' Melissa said, eyeing them suspiciously.

'My fault,' Noah said cheerfully as he headed towards a clothing rail hung with suits and shirts. 'I overslept after the stag do, so poor Eloise had to come and wake me up.'

Melissa didn't look convinced but, since Eloise had already slunk away to the other side of the room where Caitlin and Iona were both choosing cocktail dresses from a second rail, she at least didn't push the matter.

Noah tried to pay attention to the questions he was being asked by the stylist, and the clothes options in front of him, but it was almost impossible to keep his gaze from Eloise. He found it fascinating, watching her go through the rigmarole of a styling session and photo shoot for the first time. She looked constantly wide-eyed and bewildered and he wanted to be over there, talking her through it, reminding her that being the centre of attention wasn't the worst thing in the world.

But then the real centre of attention—the bride—would glare at him and he'd hear Eloise's voice in his head again, saying, *Nobody knows*, and make a concerted effort to look away.

Even if he didn't last long.

'We're taking shots of all the members of the wedding

party in formal dress, to go alongside the photos from the actual wedding tomorrow,' the photographer explained as she positioned Noah where she wanted him, against the backdrop of the main fireplace in the reception area. 'Melissa didn't want there to be any chance of the actual wedding outfits getting out before the big day—understandable, given the amount of money she's being paid for the exclusive—so we just went with some traditional formalwear in complementary colours.'

'Sounds great,' Noah said absently, wondering what Eloise was wearing right now. And how quickly he could get her alone to take it off her.

'If you could just look at me…?' the photographer asked, and Noah brought himself back to the present with considerable effort.

This was part of the job; he knew that. And he needed to give it his full attention.

Once the photos were taken he was whisked off for his interview, where he was asked questions about his friendship with the bride and groom, how he liked Morwen Hall, his latest film, the usual. He smiled, said the right things and kept his guard up just in case the interviewer—a journalist called Sara that he'd worked with a few times before—slipped in anything controversial. She didn't and, overall, Noah decided it might have been the most straightforward interview he'd ever had. Apparently not being the main attraction had its advantages, sometimes.

As he stood to leave, he saw Eloise standing nervously beside the door to the smaller coffee bar area they were using for the interviews.

'Want me to stay?' he asked softly. Eloise shook her head, but Noah was sure that had more to do with her determination to keep things between them a secret than because she wanted to do the interview alone.

Maybe he'd just hang around nearby. Just in case.

Pouring himself another cup of coffee from the machine set up on the bar, Noah waved goodbye to Sara and took his cup just around the corner, to a high-backed wing chair looking out over the riverfront. Far enough away that no one was likely to notice he was there, but close enough that he'd be able to hear if Eloise got into trouble. Sure, the questions lobbed at him had been soft balls, but Eloise wasn't used to this sort of thing.

For a while, things seemed to go well. He couldn't always make out all the words but Eloise's voice stayed low and even, with a hint of laughter from time to time. She was good, Noah decided, listening intently. Calm and composed, but with enough pauses to show that she was thinking about her answers.

But then, just when Noah had decided they must be wrapping up, Sara threw in one more question.

'I've heard stories that you and Melissa weren't really all that close growing up. That her asking you to step in as maid of honour had more to do with PR than friendship. Do you have anything you'd like to say on that?'

Silence. Placing his coffee cup on the table, Noah peered around the back of his chair, enough to see the alarm on Eloise's face. His body tensed at the sight, desire to save her rising up in him. Without thinking, he got to his feet and crossed to where they were sitting.

'Almost done?' he asked. 'Only I promised Melissa I'd run her maid of honour through her paces again before tomorrow. We have to dance, you see.' He took Eloise's hand and pulled her to her feet. She stumbled and he caught her against his chest, holding her for just a moment too long.

Sara looked between them as Eloise stepped back, not looking at him.

'So, you two must have grown very close, preparing

for the wedding together,' she said. 'Anything to all those old sayings about the best man and the maid of honour…?'

Eloise's cheeks flamed red and Noah cursed silently. He should have known better than to get involved, but he just couldn't sit there and watch Eloise struggle.

'I'm sorry,' she said, stepping backwards and almost tripping over the chair. 'I need to go…check the arrangements for the rehearsal dinner.'

And then she was gone, racing out of the bar before either of them could object.

'But I thought you were supposed to be dancing?' Sara asked knowingly.

'So did I,' replied Noah.

CHAPTER TWELVE

THE RESTAURANT WAS blissfully empty when Eloise arrived. The rehearsal dinner wasn't for another few hours, but already the decorations were up, the tables laid and the menus displayed against the festive floral decorations.

Sinking into her assigned seat, Eloise rested her elbows on the crisp white table linen and placed her chin in her hands.

Well.

That had been a disaster.

As much as she'd like to blame Noah for everything, she knew that a large part of the fault lay with her. It was her cheeks that bloomed bright red at the mention of a relationship between her and Noah. Why couldn't she control her body? Of course, if she could she might never have slept with him in the first place.

And, whatever trouble that was likely to get her into now, she couldn't quite bring herself to regret it.

'Hey,' Laurel called as she walked through the entrance to the restaurant, crossing to where Eloise was slumped at the table. 'Everything ready here? We just got back. Everyone's gone to get changed for the rehearsal dinner. Which I'm guessing you will be doing too…?' She left it hanging, as if she wasn't entirely sure Eloise didn't plan on attending in her suit.

'Yeah.' Eloise glanced at her watch. 'Oh, yes, I'd better get moving. Did the tours go okay? Nice romantic day out with Dan?'

'Yes, thank you,' Laurel said simply. 'What about you? How were the interviews?'

'All fine,' Eloise lied.

'And how is the very gorgeous Noah?' Laurel raised her eyebrows expectantly.

Eloise groaned. 'Don't ask.'

'So there *is* something going on with you two! I knew the gossip was wrong.'

'Gossip?' Eloise jerked her head up. 'What gossip? What are they saying?'

'Nothing bad, I promise.' Laurel pulled out the chair next to Eloise and sat down. 'Nobody's laughing or anything. In fact, everyone seems to think that you're keeping Noah at arm's length. I take it that's not entirely the case?'

'It's a secret,' Eloise blurted out. 'I don't want anyone to know.'

'Well, so far, they don't. In fact, from what I heard, people are pretty amazed. They've seen him hanging around, chasing after you—apparently that's not his usual modus operandi.'

Eloise sat back in her chair and stared at her friend. 'Really? How do you mean?'

Laurel shrugged. 'Seems he usually lets people come to him. He's the chase-ee not the chaser, if you see what I mean.'

Eloise bit her lip, unsure how to feel about this news. Did that mean she meant more than the usual women he dated? After the things he'd said the night before, she'd almost started to hope that she did. Even if this was just a momentary fling, it was nice to know it wasn't meaningless.

But then, was she just fooling herself about that too? They'd been naked in bed at the time. And Eloise knew better than to trust a guy when sex was on the cards. Was it just her poor, inexperienced heart hoping for more?

And, if so, what more was she hoping for? What *more* could there be, really, when he was leaving the day after tomorrow? When no one would ever know what had happened except for him and her.

Well, and Laurel. But she didn't count.

Their whole relationship was a moment out of time. A fantasy.

And maybe the real reason she hadn't been mad at Noah for almost giving them away to the interviewer was that, deep down, she wanted it to be real, in a way it couldn't be if no one knew. Yes, she didn't want to be another of his women, cast aside when he was done with her—that was why keeping this secret was so important.

But if she mattered to him…

No. He'd made it very clear that he couldn't feel that way, couldn't let those deeper feelings in and out, not after Sally. Letting herself believe, even for a moment, that he might care more for her than their short-term fling would allow was dangerous…but exhilarating. Like opening up to him the night before had been—emotionally and physically. And like all the other steps into the spotlight she'd been taking since Noah had arrived.

But letting herself fall in love with Noah Cross was a step too far.

'Are you okay?' Laurel asked and when Eloise looked up she saw her friend was frowning at her. 'You look… scared.'

'I'll be fine.' Eloise pasted on a smile for Laurel's benefit. 'I need to go get ready for tonight.'

And decide how close to the spotlight she was willing to go. Before she got burnt.

Noah went straight from coffee to whisky, once Sara had packed up and departed to get ready for the rehearsal dinner. He'd stayed in the bar near the lobby so he could keep an eye out for Eloise, but there was no sign of her—even when the coaches returned and all the rest of the guests traipsed in.

Unfortunately, in the chaos of people, he also failed to see Melissa approaching.

'Right,' she said, standing beside his chair as the crowd thinned out. 'Time for you and me to have a talk.'

Noah winced and tried to get to his feet, but apparently the whisky was already working because he felt his head start to spin, then Melissa's hand was on his shoulder, pushing him back down into his seat.

'So. Tell me about Eloise,' Melissa said, taking the seat opposite him. 'Or, more specifically, *you* and Eloise.'

There was no sign of the sweetness-and-light Melissa Sommers who'd been playing to the camera and the media all morning. This Melissa was all business and looked about ready to rip his head off—and Noah was pretty sure it wasn't out of concern for her friend getting hurt.

'There's nothing to tell,' he said with a shrug. The lie came out easily; he was an actor, after all. But, even as he said it, Noah realised he didn't *want* to lie. He wanted to tell the whole world that he was…what? Sleeping with Eloise? *Dating* her, even?

No, he realised. What he really wanted to do was tell the world that Eloise was *his*.

Except she wasn't. At least, not more than temporarily. They hadn't discussed exclusivity because they hadn't had to. Their whole love affair was set to run out in forty-eight hours or less. When would either of them have time to cheat?

If he had more time, he thought he could probably talk Eloise into being open about their relationship—into telling the world, if necessary. She was warming to the spotlight, at least, and getting over her fear of being the centre of attention. And if it was a proper relationship rather than a casual fling, then Stefan, the director, couldn't possibly object—Noah's romantic life would grow boring to the world's media the moment he stayed with one person for more than a week. But time was the one thing he didn't have.

And didn't *want*, he reminded himself. Half of the thrill of his fling with Eloise was knowing they had to make the most of every moment. If he had for ever stretching out in front of him to spend with one woman, he'd be running for the hills. That was just who he was.

Even if that woman was Eloise.

Yes, they'd shared some secrets, and the intimacy had been nice. New, unfamiliar but…comforting, somehow. He'd felt lighter, better, in her arms.

He'd gone deeper with her than with any woman since Sally. But deep was one thing—falling the whole way was something else altogether.

'I saw the two of you this morning,' Melissa said, her eyes narrow with suspicion. 'If you expect me to believe—'

His phone rang, loud and shrill, on the table, cutting her off. 'I do,' Noah said, picking it up. 'Now, if you'll excuse me? It's my agent.'

Even Melissa had to respect the importance of an agent's phone call. She sat, sulking, in her chair while he got up and paced across the lobby and through the front doors out onto the steps.

'Tessa? What's the news?' The winter air was bitter

and Noah huddled against the side of Morwen Hall to stay out of the wind. He figured this weather was still warmer than the chill Melissa was emitting in his direction today.

'Not your love life, for once. Not a hint of an inappropriate sexual encounter anywhere on social media today. I'm impressed.'

'I can show restraint when it matters,' Noah lied. 'Did you get me the video audition?'

'Yes, I got you your call,' Tessa said. 'But they want to talk early this afternoon—evening for you, I guess. You're free, right?'

'Right now, yes,' Noah said. 'But it's the rehearsal dinner for this wedding in an hour or so—'

'Then you'll have to be late,' Tessa interrupted. 'If you really want this part, this is your one chance to convince him.'

Noah took a breath. This was his career at stake. 'What do I need to do?'

'You need to sell it, more than ever before. You need to show them that you get this guy, inside out.' Tessa paused, and Noah knew she was wondering whether he was really capable of it. Ouch. 'Should we talk it through now? Get some ideas going? I've been making some notes…'

'No,' Noah said firmly. 'I've got this. I know this character. I do.'

'So, convince me.' When he didn't answer, she sighed. 'Noah. If you can't sell it to me you're sure as hell not going to sell it to these guys. Then we'll both be on their blacklist for wasting their time.'

'Fine. He's…he's grieving.'

'I think we got that from the dead wife.'

'Yeah, but he's not just grieving for her. He's not just lost a woman he loved. He's lost all hope that he can ever have that again. He's scared—so damn scared to take any more risks with his heart, now he knows how much it can hurt. How it can destroy you, take you right back to the bone and leave you to rebuild everything. And when you do…you're not the same. You can't be. You're a mass of scar tissue that can't feel anything any more, and you're *happy* about it. Because at least it hurts less that way.'

Tessa was silent on the other end of the phone. Noah grasped for the stone balustrade lining the steps down from Morwen Hall, desperate for something to keep him balanced. Grounded.

Because he hadn't been describing a character, he realised. He'd been talking about himself, the same way he'd talked to Eloise in bed the night before. The way he *never* talked.

'Where did that come from?' Tessa asked after a minute. 'Noah, I've never… Are you okay?'

'I'm fine,' he managed. Then he laughed. 'Let's just say I've found a new muse.'

'Are actors allowed muses?'

'This one is.' Except he wasn't, not really. Eloise wasn't his. She was just a temporary distraction.

'Well, whoever she is, hang onto her. Sounds like she's just what you need. As long as you're not sleeping with her,' Tessa said crisply. 'Now, go. Get ready for that call. You've got thirty minutes.'

Time enough to get ready for the rehearsal dinner, so that when he was done with his call he could head straight down there and find Eloise. Not because she was his muse, or because she might be mad at him, or even because she was so sexy he couldn't go another few hours without her again.

Just because he wanted to see her. And because they didn't have much time left.

But Noah intended to make the most of every second.

* * *

Eloise smoothed down her cocktail dress as the lift doors opened at the restaurant floor. The dress the stylist had chosen—a beautiful silver and black-edged halter-neck—had looked so good in the photo shoot that she'd asked if she could keep it to wear to the rehearsal dinner that evening. Yes, it was a little more showy than she'd usually wear, but she couldn't wait to see Noah's face when he saw her in it.

If nothing else, it was *definitely* not a boring dress.

She might not be as beautiful as Melissa, in her pale pink gown that showed off every curve and slender line of that famous body, and she knew she couldn't live up to the beauties Noah usually had on his arm. But, in this dress, Eloise felt beautiful in herself. And that was enough for her.

The restaurant floor was already buzzing by the time Eloise arrived. Whereas a more normal wedding might just have a rehearsal dinner for the wedding party and family members, Melissa and Riley had wanted a wedding extravaganza and that was what Laurel and Eloise had given them. For the rehearsal dinner—ignoring the fact they hadn't actually *had* a rehearsal of the wedding itself because Melissa said she'd played a bride on screen often enough to know what to do—they were holding another drinks reception in the bar area, then a special dinner for all the guests in the restaurant. The wedding party, along with Melissa and Riley's families, would then retire to a private room, where they could do the usual speeches and gift presentations.

'Now *that* is a dress.' Noah's voice, warm and appreciative, behind her, was already so familiar that Eloise smiled even as she turned to face him.

'Somehow, I had a feeling you might like this one.'

'I do.' He raked his gaze up and down her body and for once Eloise didn't even blush. He'd seen more, after all. 'It looks fantastic on you.'

'But let me guess.' Eloise leant closer to keep her words private. 'It would look better off.'

Noah met her gaze and smiled, and Eloise knew there was a promise in that smile. 'That goes without saying.'

'You're in a good mood,' Eloise said, taking in his sparkling eyes.

'I just gave the best audition of my life, over video chat.'

'For the part? *Eight Days After*?'

'That's the one.' Noah grinned again, as if he couldn't quite bring himself to stop. 'If they don't give me the part after that, then they never would have. I gave it everything and was pretty darned good too.'

Eloise wondered what it must be like to live with that sort of self-confidence, even if only in a professional sphere. 'You found a way to go deeper, then?'

'Yes.' His expression dropped into something more serious, but so compelling Eloise couldn't have looked away if she'd wanted to. 'You. You helped me talk about Sally, helped me examine what *I* felt back then, so I could transfer it to the character. I'd been putting off dealing with that for a long time.'

'I'm not sure one conversation counts as dealing with it,' Eloise warned. Grief was a tricky thing—especially when it had been blocked and ignored as long as Noah's had.

'But it's a start,' he said. 'And I have you to thank for it. However can I repay you?' His lips curved up into a smile again, but this one felt more intimate. More seductive.

'I have some ideas…' she said.

Noah leant in, just a little more, and in a flash Eloise remembered where they were—in the middle of the bar, surrounded by celebrities and at least one photographer.

She pulled back, and spotted Melissa watching them from across the room. She didn't look happy.

'Time to mingle.' Eloise gave him an apologetic smile. 'But I'll see you later?'

'Most definitely.' She felt Noah's eyes on her as she walked away and she knew, deep down, he was definitely imagining her naked. And she loved knowing that.

She spent the drinks reception chatting with the other guests, many of whom she'd failed to speak to at all before then—a side effect of being so caught up with Noah, she supposed. Since many of them just expected her to nod and smile politely as she listened to them regale her with their best stories of celebrity life, she had plenty of time left for daydreaming about the night ahead, once she and Noah were alone again.

Tonight, there would be no secrets between them. No emotional outpourings and confessions.

Just them, and one perfect night before the wedding from hell.

She couldn't wait.

Eventually, it was time for the party to move through to the restaurant for the dinner. Eloise groaned inside when she spotted the menu, and remembered that Melissa had wanted a seven-course tasting menu, with matching wines. Add in the speeches and the gifts for the groomsmen and bridesmaids and it would be hours before she could escape with Noah.

Then she saw him, sitting beside her place at the table, and realised there was no way she was going to make it that long.

'You switched the place settings,' she whispered as she slid into her seat. 'Melissa will be mad.'

'It's worth it,' Noah replied. 'I'm not taking the chance

of another groomsman seducing you away from me while you're wearing that dress.'

'You get very territorial over your flings, don't you?'

'Not usually.' Noah frowned just a little, then glanced around to make sure no one was listening. Leaning in, he murmured, 'Look, I reckon I can make it through maybe two of these taster courses before I have to have you again. So, when I leave, wait a couple of minutes and follow me, okay?'

Heat flared through Eloise's body. Just knowing he wanted her as much as she needed him was an incredible aphrodisiac. Still, the more sensible part of her brain was screaming that this was a stupid idea. It was the rehearsal dinner! They would definitely be missed, and Melissa would be furious if she realised where they'd gone…

She should say no. She *had* to say no.

'Okay,' she whispered, and Noah smiled.

A storage cupboard wasn't exactly high on Noah's list of Most Seductive Spots, but right now he'd take what he could get. Sitting next to Eloise in that dress and not touching her—not even a hand on her back or a kiss on her cheek—had been physically painful.

And okay, fine. It wasn't the dress that was causing the problem.

It was her.

In lots of ways, it was just as well that in two days' time there'd be thousands of miles between them. Any less and he'd be tempted to hurry back and have her again, regardless of the rules.

He just hoped five thousand miles would be enough.

Time passed excruciatingly slowly as he waited to hear Eloise's footsteps in the corridor outside. Surely it had to have been three minutes since he'd left the table? He'd chosen the cupboard for its proximity to the restaurant, and the fact he could see out the crack of the open door to watch for Eloise. Any further away and he'd run the risk of her not finding him. And that was not an option.

But right now he had to think about something else. Imagining Eloise was driving him insane, and if he didn't slow down that dress she looked so incredible in wouldn't survive its first encounter with his hands.

Think about the film. The audition. Noah smiled in the darkness. The director had pretty much offered him the role on the spot, he'd been so impressed. Noah had managed to channel all those emotions he'd been repressing into the part, just as he'd planned. And, yes, it had stung—but it wasn't quite so painful when it was a character feeling those things instead of himself. He could do it, he knew now. He'd do the part justice; he'd win that award—and he could move on and leave all the awful pain and emotion behind him when he did.

Stefan had reiterated Tessa's point about how important it would be to keep his personal life low-key, so the focus would be on the film not the stars, and Noah had agreed readily. Whatever he had with Eloise would be over soon enough and afterwards…he didn't think he'd be hurrying into anything else for a while. He could take a break.

He'd dropped Tessa an email to let her know how it went, then hurried straight down to the rehearsal dinner to tell Eloise, to celebrate with her.

And what a celebration he had planned…

Apparently it was impossible to think about anything but her.

Finally, the restaurant door swung open and Eloise stepped out, her cheeks flushed with more than just wine, he was sure. She'd sat so tense beside him at dinner, he was certain she'd been resisting her urges almost as hard as he had.

It was hard to imagine that when he'd first met her he'd thought her reserved and stand-offish. Maybe with others. But with him she was a free spirit, giving everything she got and more.

He waited until Eloise was about to walk past the cupboard, then reached out a hand and dragged her inside. She squeaked with surprise, but then her hands were slipping under his jacket and up his back so he didn't think she was too traumatised.

'That was excruciating,' she murmured against his neck, as he lifted her to rest against a conveniently located pile of boxes.

'You're telling me.' He nudged her knees open with his hips and stepped between them, pressing up against her body. 'I almost didn't make it past the first course.'

'I noticed.' Her hands moved round to the front and unbuttoned the top few buttons of his shirt, and she leant in to kiss along his collarbone. 'I thought you were going to drag me out of there ten minutes ago. Or maybe just take me on the table, in front of everyone.'

'Not very secret, that.' He slid his hands up her bare thighs.

'No, not very secret.'

For a moment he held his breath, waiting for her to say something more. To say it didn't have to be a secret. To say that she wanted the whole world to know about them. That she didn't care what Melissa or anyone else said about them. That she trusted him not to let them mock her in the press.

But she didn't. And she shouldn't. Because that wasn't the deal they had. It wasn't even what he wanted really, logically.

This was a fling. That was what she'd asked for, what he'd promised.

So that was what he had to give her.

Even if he was starting to feel as if he wanted more.

As if he wanted everything.

'I've never had sex in a cupboard before,' she murmured against his ear, and Noah dragged himself back to focus on what he *could* have. Eloise, here and now, wanting him. 'You're providing me with all sorts of new experiences this week.'

'I'm a full service secret fling,' Noah said, untying the back of her halter-neck and lowering the zip to reveal her bare breasts. 'No bra?'

'Seemed like a waste of time.' Eloise gasped as he dipped his head to kiss her.

'Agreed,' he said when he came up for air. 'Now, let's see what else you're not wearing under this—'

A flash of light cut him off as the cupboard door he was leaning against opened, sending him tumbling into the hallway, pulling Eloise with him. He blinked at another flash and saw Melissa, Sara the journalist and her photographer standing over them.

And suddenly nothing was secret any more.

CHAPTER THIRTEEN

ELOISE YANKED HER dress back up, trying to make herself respectable again, even though the sinking feeling inside told her it was already far too late.

Scrambling to his feet, Noah pushed her behind him, giving her the cover she needed to fix her dress. But his shirt was still open, exposing exactly what they'd been doing.

Not that anyone could be in any doubt after that display.

What had she been thinking? She'd *known* this was a terrible idea from the start. But then Noah would say something to convince her and there she'd be, half naked in a cupboard.

Or outside a cupboard. With her teenage nemesis arching her eyebrows and the world's media taking photos.

'Well, really,' Melissa said too loudly, her words echoing off the walls. 'Some people just don't know how to behave at a respectable wedding, do they?'

Eloise wanted to ask her to keep it down before anyone else heard and came out to investigate, but that was probably why Melissa was doing it in the first place, she realised. She hadn't managed to keep Eloise and Noah apart, so she'd decided to go the other way. If they were intent on stealing the limelight at her wedding, she was going to ruin them.

Abject humiliation. Melissa wouldn't settle for anything less than making sure Eloise's whole world knew who she was and what she'd done—the same way she had when they were teenagers and the guy Melissa had a crush on asked Eloise out instead. Soon, the whole school knew every story about Eloise's mother and believed that she was just the same and the guy never spoke to her again.

The only difference was that this time Melissa had made sure the actual whole world would know, through the power of the media and the Internet.

Never mind the humiliation Eloise's mother's antics had brought her over the years, this was a million times worse. And the most awful part was that she'd done it all herself. There was no one to blame except her own suddenly overactive libido…and the secret part of her heart that hoped to be something more than a fling to someone like Noah Cross.

She'd had ideas of her own importance, her own entitlement to the spotlight—and now she'd been burned.

'Melissa, come on,' Noah said, laughing lightly as he tried to reach for the photographer's camera. She stepped back out of his reach and Eloise knew that no one in their right mind would give those photos up. Noah Cross, caught in the act? That had to be worth a fortune.

And nobody would care if her reputation was shredded in the process.

She had to get out of there. She had to get a million miles away from this spotlight, right now.

'I have to go.'

Holding her dress in place, she pushed past Noah and the others and ran towards the lifts. She could hear him behind her, calling her name, making excuses, but she couldn't turn back, couldn't listen.

This wasn't her world, even if Noah and Melissa's celebrity lives had infiltrated Morwen Hall. Soon they'd be gone and she could get back to quietly living down her mother's reputation. To her responsible, boring, staid and lonely existence.

It had to be better than the shame and humiliation burning through her right now.

Noah watched Eloise run away and had to force himself not to chase after her. She didn't want this—she'd made that clear from the start.

This was his fault. She'd wanted secret and in his desperation he'd ruined that.

And now he had to fix it.

'So, Noah. Any quote to go with our pictures?' Sara asked, holding out her phone and showing it was recording. Another part of his life on the record.

He'd wanted to tell the world about him and Eloise. But not like this.

Stefan. The part. He'd promised he wouldn't do this, promised he'd keep things low-key. And this was pretty much the opposite. The role he'd thought he had nailed—this could ruin everything. Send him back to playing brainless action figures for another seven years. Unless he could convince people that things with him and Eloise were serious, something more than a fling. Maybe then he'd get a second chance from Stefan...

The idea was intoxicating. He could play at love with Eloise, enjoy what they had for a little longer, until it came to its natural conclusion when no one cared and the world wasn't watching. He could still have everything he wanted if Eloise went along with it, if he lied... He could turn this round, still be the good guy maybe.

But first he had to get a handle on himself, on all the emotions rushing through him at the speed of light. As if, after spending so many years not feeling them, now he'd let them in they were making up for lost time. Embarrassment, fear, anger, lust—they all surged through him, swirling around into a toxic mix that left him close to losing it.

No. He wasn't that man. He'd never been the celebrity yelling at reporters or causing a scene. He wouldn't start now—not least because it would only make things worse for Eloise, and he couldn't do that to her.

Cold realisation flooded through him. The only thing he could really do now was protect Eloise. Even if it meant giving up on the part he wanted so much. Because he couldn't promise her for ever, couldn't ask her to act out a sham relationship. Couldn't break her heart a few months down the line when she realised that what she saw really was all he had to give—there was nothing deeper.

He couldn't hurt her any more than he had to. And the only way through this with minimum casualties was to lessen the impact of what had happened.

Which meant pretending it was nothing at all.

He couldn't do it—couldn't pretend what he and Eloise had was nothing. It might not be everything but it was *something*. He couldn't deny Eloise that way, not after everything she'd done for him.

Except he was doing this *for* her. So he had to.

Maybe he couldn't. But Noah Cross, celebrity, notorious womaniser and charmer could.

It took only a second to switch on the character—the one he'd been playing since the day Sally died. It was so familiar that, until this week, he might even have said it was the real him.

But it wasn't. He knew that now. He'd found the person he was underneath all that scar tissue. He just wasn't sure if he'd ever let him out again, except for when he was in character.

'What is there to say?' he said with a shrug and a crooked smile. 'You know how it is at weddings. All that romance in the air. A fling always makes it a little more entertaining, right?' He cringed inside as he remembered saying the same thing to Eloise at the welcome drinks. Could that really have only been two days ago?

'So, it's nothing serious is what you're saying,' Sara pressed.

Noah forced himself to laugh, to sound as light-hearted and as uncaring as he *should* be about the situation, trying not to think what Stefan would think. 'Sara, I'd think you—and the rest of the world—know me a little better than that by now.'

'So, just business as usual for Noah Cross then,' Sara said. 'Another wedding, another woman.'

'Basically.' This felt so wrong. Even though he was only telling the truth, saying what he and Eloise had agreed should be the case, he could tell by the creeping sense of shame filling him that something had changed.

Eloise wasn't just a fling. Wasn't just another woman.

Except she had to be. And he needed to rebuild his walls to keep her behind them before he left.

Especially if he wanted to save her from a mauling in the media and Melissa's wrath.

'She's nothing to me,' he lied, 'and I'm nothing to her. Just a spot of fun. Now, if you'll excuse me...' He started to move towards the elevators, hoping to catch up with Eloise, but Melissa grabbed his arm and dragged him around the other way.

'Absolutely! We've got a rehearsal dinner to finish, remember, best man?'

'Right.' Noah smiled weakly and went back to work.

Eloise would have to wait.

* * *

Another night with no sleep, Eloise thought as the sun peeked over the horizon the next morning, hazy behind the grey winter clouds. And this time for far less satisfaction than the night before.

She hadn't had the courage to go back to the rehearsal dinner, although she suspected Noah had. She'd heard him banging on her door around midnight, asking her to let him in, but she'd ignored him. Maybe he'd thought she was asleep, or angry, or out. She didn't care. Eventually he'd grown tired and left her in peace.

Not that it had been very peaceful.

She'd stripped off that wretched dress and curled up in her warmest, softest pyjamas, make-up removed and hair brushed out. She'd cocooned herself in her duvet and tried to forget, tried to sleep. But every time she closed her eyes all she could see was that camera flash and Melissa's arched eyebrows.

How could she have been so stupid? How could she have put herself in a position to let Melissa humiliate her all over again? Melissa always had to be the queen bee, had to have the highest profile. It was her wedding. Of course she was going to obsess about it being all about her. And, yes, she had Riley—hot up-and-coming star. But in Melissa's world Noah was a bigger catch, one who'd eluded capture by every woman in Hollywood. Of *course* she was going to freak out about Eloise—sad, quiet little Eloise—sleeping with him. At her *own* wedding.

She was an idiot. All she'd needed to do was keep the lid on her libido until the wedding was over. How hard would that have been?

Eloise sighed. Impossible, apparently.

Eventually, she'd given up on sleep and logged onto the Internet on her tablet, refreshing Sara's magazine pages until the exclusive she'd known was coming flashed up on the screen at last.

There she was. Eyes wide from the camera flash, her hand wrapped over her chest covering her nudity. Noah lay underneath her on the floor, then in later photos stood in front of her, looking mussed but gorgeous. Charmingly contrite having been caught, his shirt open a little too far, his hair ruffled beyond the usual fashionable mess. He could have stepped out of an advert for aftershave, not been caught falling out of a cupboard moments before having sex.

Whereas she… There was no doubt what she'd been doing. She looked exactly the type of girl Melissa had always told people she was.

Why could men get away with that sort of behaviour and women couldn't?

Bracing herself, Eloise scanned down through all the photos to the text underneath.

Since half of Hollywood has decamped to England for the wedding of Melissa Sommers and Riley Black, we can report exclusively from Morwen Hall on all the wedding high jinks! Starting with this gem from the rehearsal dinner—best man Noah Cross has found some entertainment to make the week even more fun than Melissa and Riley planned: seducing the maid of honour!

It went on to detail who she was, how she knew Melissa and why she'd stepped in at the last minute.

Then it got to what really mattered.

So could this be true love for eternal bachelor Noah? Apparently not.

He said, 'She's nothing to me, and I'm nothing to her. You know how it is at weddings... A fling always makes it a little more entertaining.'

Looks like we'll have to wait a little longer to see Noah walk down the aisle himself!

Eloise threw her tablet down onto the covers and wished she'd never looked.

Of course he'd said that. He'd never suggested anything else—in fact he'd said practically the same thing to her at the welcome drinks. She'd known what she was getting into. Like he'd told her the night before—he never gave his women false expectations, never fell for them, and never ever told them he loved them.

He played fair. It was only her heart that had cheated.

She'd been so sure that she could play the same game he did, that it wasn't the same as her mother's games if no one mentioned love. But, in the end, she'd ended up exactly where all her mother's men had: alone, heartbroken, her reputation in tatters and everyone talking about her. It was exactly the way she'd felt after she'd found her mother sleeping with her boyfriend, or the day she'd realised that her university boyfriend had been using her all along—stupid, naive, gullible and humiliated.

She was just where she'd always promised herself she'd never be again. And all thanks to Noah Cross.

Because she'd let herself believe, just for a moment, that what they had could be something more than either of them had promised each other. That it could be for real—not a secret, not a fling, not anything to hide or be ashamed of.

And that moment was all that it took for her to fall head over heels in love with Noah.

Closing her eyes, Eloise fell back against the bed and

swore softly. Turned out she really was every bit as stupid and naive as Melissa had always told her she was.

Noah awoke feeling worse than any hangover had ever left him and he hadn't drunk more than a glass of wine the night before. He'd stuck the rehearsal dinner out until the bitter end, flinching when Melissa told the guests that Eloise had gone to bed with a headache. By midday they'd all know exactly why she'd gone to bed, he knew, but at least the lie had preserved her peace and dignity for a few more hours.

He'd tried to speak with her after the dinner but there'd been no answer at her door. He hoped she'd been sleeping, but knew it was far more likely she'd been avoiding him. Well, she couldn't do that for ever.

Forcing himself out of bed, Noah dressed quickly and headed straight for Eloise's room. He needed to speak to her before anyone else did. Hopefully before she saw the photos on the Internet, for that matter—although, since he'd already had a furious voicemail from Tessa, ranting about him throwing away his chances that morning, that was probably a long shot.

'Eloise?' He didn't want to shout—he knew that attracting more attention to them could only make everything worse—but when she didn't answer his third knock he had to raise his voice. 'Let me in, Eloise.'

There was a shuffling noise inside, then she yanked the door open, looking furious under her rumpled red hair. She was wearing what had to be the most unflattering pair of pyjamas in history and Noah realised that it didn't even matter. She had bags under her eyes as if she hadn't slept, and mascara on her cheeks, and her pyjamas had pictures of grumpy cats on them, and he still wanted her.

Eloise, however, did not look like she was having the same problem.

'What are you doing?' she whisper-shouted at him. 'Do you want even more people showing up to take photos of me half dressed?'

Noah decided not to point out that the cat pyjamas covered considerably more of her body than last night's dress. 'Can I come in?'

Eloise scanned the hallway and, finding it empty, stood aside, still glaring at him.

'Look, we both have a wedding to get ready for in four hours,' she said, shutting the door behind him. 'So, whatever you have to say, make it quick.'

She folded her arms over her chest and stared at him, and all of Noah's intended words fled. He'd planned to talk about how they could minimise the fallout from last night, how to deal with Melissa today…but instead he found himself saying, 'I'm sorry. About last night. I know that was the last thing you wanted.'

'I'm not sure many people want to be caught half naked in a cupboard, Noah.'

'You'd be surprised.' If it meant getting their photo taken with him, Noah had found that some women were willing to do anything. But Eloise wasn't one of them.

She shot him a disgusted look. 'Of course. I'm sure your many admirers would be grateful for the chance.'

'That's not what I meant.'

'I don't care.' She rubbed one eye with her fist and he realised again how exhausted she looked. Had she slept at all? 'Look, I've already seen the photos online, read all the quotes. So kind of you to point out that I was equally indifferent to you, by the way, since, after all, I mean nothing to you.'

Noah winced. 'I'm sorry, okay? I was trying to downplay it all for your sake! You're the one who didn't want to be another woman cast aside and presumably heart-broken when I left them. *You* wanted to keep it a secret. And, since that was off the table...I figured that this was the next best thing.' He'd given up his chance at the movie role of a lifetime to try and protect her, and this was the way she thanked him?

Eloise stared at him so long he started to worry he'd grown an extra head while he'd slept. 'Did you honestly believe that telling them I was just a meaningless fling would *help*?'

'You're the one who insisted that nobody know!' Couldn't she see he'd done the best he could in a bad situation? 'We both agreed this wasn't anything serious. Just a fling to kill a few days, right? Get the chemistry out of our system. That's what we *agreed*.' They'd had a deal and he'd stuck to it. He'd *protected* her—at his own expense! So why was he the bad guy?

And why was Eloise staring at him so sadly, her eyes huge and wet and her cheeks pale?

'You're a fool if you still believe that,' she said softly.

Noah's whole world tilted, for the second time since he'd met Eloise. What was it about her that kept him permanently off balance? 'What?'

He could see her throat move as she swallowed, as if she was preparing herself for something hard. Something she didn't want to do.

'I know what we agreed, what we said. I was there too.' She met his gaze head-on and he felt it down to his core, past all those carefully built defences he'd put back up. As if they didn't exist for her at all. 'But I want more. And I think you do too. Being with you...it's so different to any-thing I've ever had before.'

'Well, yeah,' he said awkwardly. 'I mean, it would be.

My world, the way I live…it's a new experience for you, I get that. You've been hiding out in this hotel for so long…'

Eloise shook her head violently. 'That's not what I'm talking about and you know it. I don't care that you're a movie star. I don't care that you're famous or rich or in demand or even that you're leaving tomorrow. I care that you spoke to me like you trusted me…that you listened to me when I told you my secrets. I care that you made me see it was okay to come out of my shell, to try new things, to let people see the real me. I care that when you touched me…my whole world lit up.'

'That's just sex.' The defence was automatic. Sex he knew. Sex was safe. The other stuff… Any of that he still had left he needed to save for his next movie role—if he got one that was worth anything at all after this. 'And the talking… I told you. I wanted to get this part and they needed me to act deep.'

'Are you honestly trying to tell me that everything between us happened because you wanted to win some role in a film?' She raised her eyebrows as she stared at him, and he knew it was crazy. Knew that what had happened between them transcended not just his career but his life so far.

And that was why it scared the hell out of him. He'd had something close to this once—and he'd lost it the moment he'd admitted to it.

He wasn't taking the chance of feeling that pain again.

'You know us actors,' he said, shrugging as casually as he could. 'We'll do anything for a shot at an award.' Not that he had a hope of that now—but Eloise didn't need to know that. If she realised what he'd given up trying to protect her she might read something more into it than there was.

Her mouth actually dropped open. A director would

tell her she was overacting, but Noah knew better. Eloise didn't act. She was who she was, and it was glorious.

But he knew something else too. She didn't believe she was worth it, and he could use that now. Because looking deeper was one thing. Falling in love was another altogether—it would take him all the way into his soul and out the other side and it could burn him up on the journey. If he wanted to hold onto Eloise, that was what he knew it would take—everything.

And he didn't have it in him any more.

'You know, the saddest thing is, you might really believe that,' Eloise said, her voice soft. 'You might actually believe that you're just an actor and it's all just a role. But you're wrong. I saw the real you, I know it. And I think we could have been happy. I don't know how it would have worked, or what would have happened next, but we'd have been happy. And it doesn't matter now because you won't even try. You won't let yourself feel anything as real and as deep as love. Even if it could give you everything that's been missing for the last seven years.'

'You're wrong,' he said but, even as the words came out, he knew he was lying.

He could have been happy.

But how long for?

'I'll see you at the wedding,' he said. And then he turned and walked out on love. For good.

CHAPTER FOURTEEN

'TOLD YOU SHE wouldn't wear the veil.' Laurel sidled up to Eloise as they stood outside the ceremony room, waiting for the signal to start the procession. Caitlin and Iona were fussing with Melissa's train while the bride checked her reflection one last time and straightened the tiara on her—veil-less—head.

'You were right,' Eloise said, viewing the proceedings with a strange detachment. As if she were watching the action on a cinema screen, not really part of it at all.

Quite a lot of the last few days seemed like that now, actually.

'You okay?' Laurel asked, lowering her clipboard and looking up at her, concern in her eyes. 'I heard… Well, there's been a lot of talk this morning.'

'I'm sure there has,' Eloise replied serenely. Of course there would be. Everyone staying at Morwen Hall would have woken up to the comedy gold that was her falling out of a cupboard half naked with Noah Cross.

But at least they didn't know the worst of her humiliation. Noah was right about that—he'd defended her from the mortification of everyone in the world knowing that she'd fallen in love with Noah and been rejected. They were the only two people in the world who knew exactly what had happened between them that week.

In a way, their fling was still a secret. Others might speculate but they'd never know the truth of it.

That mind-set was the only thing that had got her through Melissa's snide comments and the half jokes and sniggers from the other bridesmaids as they'd got ready together that morning. The make-up artist Melissa had hired had tutted and despaired aloud at the bags under Eloise's eyes, but some serious application of concealer and other potions from her magic bag of tricks seemed to have hidden them well enough. The icy blue-green dress had been laced tight enough to give her some semblance of curves and her red hair curled and pinned up on the back of her head, leaving her neck bare.

Eloise couldn't help but feel as if she'd been prepared for an execution.

'You seem very…calm,' Laurel said. 'Serene, even.'

Eloise gave her a small smile and raised one shoulder in a half shrug. 'What else is there to do?'

'I suppose.'

She'd realised after Noah left, after she'd wailed and sobbed and thrown things at the door he'd left through, that this was it. The lowest she could go. The whole world knew everything about her that she'd wanted to keep secret, and they probably all thought the worst. Either she was a fame-hungry slut seducing Noah in a cupboard, or a crazed fan lusting after him and thinking herself in love, when he was just using her for a bit of light relief.

But the thing was, neither of those were true. They were all an act—every theory, every story.

And, underneath them all, she was still Eloise Miller. Still in love with Noah Cross. Not the film star, but the man.

And no amount of humiliation could hurt as much as knowing that after today she might never see him again.

But he'd given her something, at least. She knew now what she needed to do next. He'd been right about one thing, somewhere in the middle of all his lies. She'd been hiding away at Morwen Hall for too long—too scared to go after her own dreams, to risk stepping into the spotlight and fighting for what she really wanted.

She'd fought for Noah. She might not have won him but she'd taken the risk and told him the truth—that she loved him. That was a big step.

And as soon as this wedding was over she would take another one. She'd hand in her notice at Morwen Hall and step out of hiding at last. It was time to go after all those other dreams she'd been too scared to chase—her own company, a career she could feel passionately about. Her own life, somewhere else.

She had a lot of planning to do, Eloise knew. But if she took nothing else away from her encounter with Noah Cross, she would have this: she wasn't afraid of the spotlight any more.

How could she be? After all, it couldn't ever get worse than this. And that thought was strangely liberating.

The string quartet at the front of the ceremony room started a new piece and Melissa gave a little squeal. 'It's time!'

'Good luck,' Laurel whispered as they lined up in their assigned order. 'I'm going to head in and watch from the front.'

Eloise nodded to show that she'd heard her, but otherwise kept her focus on the task at hand. All she had to do was get through the rest of the day, and then she could fall apart and start again. Just another ten hours until the clock ticked past midnight and they entered a whole new year.

A fresh start. Just what she needed.

The doors opened and Eloise took her first careful, measured step, her bouquet held up at just the right height, right foot first, as instructed.

They'd opted to hold the ceremony in the old ball-room—one of the few rooms inside the hotel that retained some of the original Gothic charm. The high, peaked windows let in the winter light through thick glass, glinting off the displays of bright white flowers on every sill. The chairs the hotel staff had laid out in neat rows were now filled with the rich and famous, and at the end of the long aisle stood the celebrant, flanked by Riley, the groom, and Noah. The best man. The only man for her.

And the one man she was certain she could never have.

Eloise concentrated on her breathing as she made her way steadily down the long aisle, ignoring the whispers and muffled laughs around her. Then she heard the gasps and 'ah's as she reached the halfway point and knew that Melissa had made her entrance too. Nobody cared about Noah Cross's fling any more. Melissa was the main attraction—just as she should be, and just as she'd wanted.

Eloise was more than happy to give up *this* spotlight to her.

As she approached the celebrant, Noah turned at last and she focused on not losing control as she saw his face. He didn't look like his life had just been ripped apart— probably because it hadn't.

Was it really all just an act for him? All that they'd shared, could it really have only been a means to an end? She didn't want to believe it, but maybe she should. He was an actor. He was everything she'd always suspected he would be. Even all he'd shared about Sally—maybe it was just a sob story designed to get her into bed.

Except she'd already been in bed.

And except that it had felt real.

Eloise might not be very well acquainted with love, but

now she'd felt its effects, a small part of her couldn't give up the hope that maybe he felt it too.

Noah looked right at her and Eloise dropped her gaze. She couldn't let him see how badly he'd hurt her. Despite everything, she still had her pride.

But then something made her glance up again to study his face, just for a moment—and she *knew*.

Noah Cross was a brilliant actor. But even he couldn't out-act love.

The only problem was, love didn't make a blind bit of difference if he wouldn't let himself feel it. He probably didn't even know himself.

Which meant that Eloise was no better off than she'd been when he'd left her bereft that morning. In fact, she might be worse.

Because now she knew that *both* of them were going to lose what might have been the most important thing in their lives.

The ceremony was excruciating. Not just watching Melissa and Riley pledge undying love, when everyone in the room knew it probably wouldn't last five years. In fact, when he'd arrived there had been someone at the back of the room giving odds.

Noah hadn't placed a bet. He didn't bet on love these days.

No, the worst part had been the way Eloise wouldn't meet his eyes—except for the one brief moment when she'd frowned at him, as if seeing something she didn't expect. He'd wanted to ask her what she thought she'd seen, what depth she thought he'd sunk to now. But the room was full of eyes and, besides, even if they hadn't been in the middle of a wedding, he'd given up that right when he'd walked out on her that morning.

'Dearly beloved, we are gathered here today...' The celebrant droned on, using the movie script version of the wedding ceremony that Noah suspected they'd paid extra for. This wasn't a marriage, wasn't a declaration of love. It was the ultimate act—a chance for Melissa and Riley to show the rest of the world what they didn't have, not realising how much more some couples *did* have. True love. A connection that couldn't be broken by failing box office receipts. A partner they could rely on. Someone to grow old and grey with, not plan plastic surgery with.

Someone who saw into their soul, and loved them anyway.

He bit the inside of his cheek to force himself to stop thinking about it, as he handed the rings over to Riley. What did it matter to him how shallow this whole day was? It wasn't as if he was searching for anything deeper. He wasn't even willing to get as far as a third date, let alone the altar. He had no moral high ground here.

Suddenly, the room erupted into applause and Noah realised he'd missed the 'I do's and everything that went with them. Moments later, they were all parading back out of the ballroom, ready to have photographs taken to immortalise this very special day in print and online, while the rest of the guests got to eat canapés.

He wanted to go and stand by Eloise, to tell her jokes until she looked less...absent. She looked as if she'd mentally checked out of the whole day already. Not that he could blame her. He'd heard enough of the talk that morning—and, as expected, it was all about her. No one expected anything else from him, he supposed.

No, even if she didn't just slap him the moment he got close, he couldn't do anything to make this day any harder for her. It just felt wrong, watching her try to fade into the background, to disappear at the celebrity wedding of the year. She belonged in the spotlight, whatever she be-lieved. She was so vibrant, so bright, so real. That was what the world should be looking at, not the superficial and the showy.

The world should be looking at Eloise the way he was. As if she was the most important person on the planet. She deserved no less.

He wanted the world to see what real love looked like. Not fake Hollywood romance like Melissa and Riley's. Not him and whichever woman he took out that night. Real love—the sort that had shone out of Eloise like a holy truth that morning, when she'd told him she loved him.

The world should see that. And they should see it re-turned. They should see the truth of his feelings—the way his soul felt lighter when she smiled at him, the way his life lit up when she was beside him, the way he could tell her anything, could admit anything and still be loved…

The way he loved her.

He loved her.

His skin felt tight, his blood too hot, as if the words might explode out of him at any moment, right there in the middle of the wedding photos.

He was so crazily in love with Eloise Miller it might have actually driven him mad. And the thought of leaving without her ever knowing that…

He knew he should. She deserved better—someone with less scar tissue, fewer war wounds from love. And, whatever he felt, he didn't know if he could do it. Didn't know if he could take that risk and give everything, fall that deep and risk drowning in love.

But suddenly he knew he had to try.

In all the activity of the wedding day it was easy enough for Eloise to avoid spending any quality time with Noah—

especially since Laurel had kindly switched around the place settings so that she didn't have to sit next to him at the top table. But, despite managing to keep her distance, she spent the whole day dreading what was still to come.

The moment she had to get out on the dance floor with Noah.

Had the wedding been anyone's except Melissa's she'd have begged for mercy from the bride, or come up with some excuse. But Eloise refused to let Melissa know just how much she didn't want to be out there, dancing with Noah.

How was she supposed to concentrate on the steps when his arms were around her? How could she stand all those people staring at her, watching them together, thinking they already knew all their secrets?

But, one way or another, she'd have to get through it. Then tomorrow he'd be on a plane, flying away from her, and it would all be over.

She bit the inside of her cheek to stop the tears. That was supposed to be a comforting thought.

Eventually, she'd pushed her food around her plate so many times that everyone else had finished eating. She managed to excuse herself during the speeches, to go and check that the ballroom was ready for the evening reception, so she didn't have to hear Noah wax lyrical about the sort of love he didn't believe he was capable of. That might have driven her over the edge.

'Nearly there,' Laurel said as she led the guests—laughing and more than a little tipsy—through to the ballroom a short time later. 'Just get through the dancing and it's all over. I'll deal with the rest from there. Okay?'

Eloise nodded. 'Thanks.'

Laurel's response was a fierce hug. 'We can't let them break us. Whatever they do. We're stronger than that.'

'I know,' Eloise said. She just wished she believed it in her heart as well as in her head.

Before she had time to think of escaping, the Master of Ceremonies was announcing the first dance and Melissa and Riley took to the floor. Eloise watched them spin elegantly around the room and waited for Noah to approach, steeling herself for his touch again.

'May I have this dance?' She spun to find him standing behind her, his hand outstretched, and gave a sharp nod as she took it. All business—that was the key. This was part of her job…that was all.

Except…

Noah pulled her into his arms as he led her onto the dance floor and she focused on a point over his left shoulder just so she didn't have to look into his eyes and see what was missing there. See again how wrong she'd been to think this could be anything more than a fling.

'Eloise,' he murmured, and she felt his voice all the way through her body. 'Look at me. Please.'

She didn't want to. But she couldn't resist the need in his voice. Setting her jaw, she turned her head, just enough to meet his gaze—and promptly stumbled over her own feet at what she saw there.

Noah caught her, kept them moving, but Eloise wasn't concentrating on the dance any longer.

She was watching his eyes, and feeling the depth of the emotion radiating from them.

'You were right,' he said, as the dance continued. 'I've been wanting to tell you all day, almost since the moment I saw you walking down the aisle towards me, and I realised. I don't want to be safe—not if it means I can't have you. I want more. I want love, and I'm willing to take the risk to get it.'

They were the words she'd been waiting for, but Eloise

couldn't trust them, not yet. 'You say the right thing for a living, Noah. Why should I believe you this time over all the things you said this morning?'

'Because I was an idiot. Because…because I was so scared of losing you I couldn't let myself close enough in the first place. But I realised something today. Losing you might destroy me, but no more than letting you go without even giving this a try would. I should have known last night, when I lied to that reporter about what you meant to me. I wanted to tell a different lie, you know. To tell her that it was serious, that we were together—because that would have got me the role I wanted so badly. I told you, I promised the director no flings. But if I'd told them this was a real relationship, I might have got away with it.'

'But you didn't,' Eloise said, confused. Why hadn't he? He wanted that part desperately; she knew that. So why not take the easy way out? 'Why not?'

'Because I was trying to protect you, crazy as that sounds. So I gave up the part for you—and I ended up hurting you even more. I'm so sorry, Eloise.' He pulled her closer, so close that his lips could touch hers if she just moved an inch. But she stayed motionless, wanting to hear every last word he had to say. 'But I promise you, this isn't an act. It's not a part I'm playing, I swear. It's just me, putting my heart on the line for what I hope is the last time. And I'll take that risk every single day if I have to, if it means you'll keep on loving me as much as I love you.'

The music had stopped, she realised belatedly. They weren't dancing any more; they were just standing in the centre of the dance floor, so wrapped up in each other she couldn't see anything else. But she knew what was happening.

Everyone was watching them. The guests, Melissa, Laurel, Sara the journalist and her photographer…everyone.

And, whatever happened next, it would be recorded for posterity on the Internet, she was sure.

And she didn't care. Not one bit.

Because Noah was letting his walls down at last, and she was there to walk right in.

She smiled and his whole body sagged with relief as he gathered her close and kissed her, long and hard and deep.

'This is it, though,' she said, the moment they broke apart. 'You can't shut me out again, once you've let me in.'

'I know. I won't. I won't let you down again.' He kissed her again, swift and soft. 'But… I can't change who I am either. People will be watching us; you know that.'

'Noah, they're watching right now.' She laughed. 'Melissa is going to be furious.'

'I don't care about Melissa. Or any of them. I only care about you.'

'And I'll be fine.' She smiled up at him, certainty running through her veins. 'I wouldn't risk it for anyone else. But for you…I'll stand in any spotlight you want, as long as you're at my side.'

Because this was for ever. She'd known it from the moment they'd first spent the night together, even if she hadn't let herself admit it until later. And, even if it wasn't, it would still be worth it.

Because this wasn't Hollywood. This was real love.

And Eloise was going to get her happy ever after, after all.

Noah grabbed Eloise close and kissed her again, trying to put all his love, his relief and his truth into that one kiss. This was right. This was the way things were meant to be, the story he was meant to be a part of.

And thank heavens Eloise was willing to let him.

Eventually, he broke the kiss, keeping Eloise tight in his arms. Around him, the guests had broken into applause, with the odd whoop and cheer, and for once Noah thought he might be the one to blush. But when he looked down at Eloise, her cheeks were their usual pale, creamy white above her perfect smile.

'We should probably take a bow,' she said, amusement in her voice. 'I mean, that was quite a show we just put on there.'

He was pretty sure she was joking, but he pulled away to stand at her side all the same, taking her hand in his and swinging them up as he led them in a bow. Laughter went up around the room, and when he stood straight again he could see Melissa glaring at them. He blew her a kiss. That should annoy her.

'So, Noah, am I right in thinking you might like to amend your statement from last night?' Sara asked, her phone recording as before, and her photographer already taking shots of him and Eloise.

'Yes,' he said. 'I most certainly would.'

Then, turning to stare into Eloise's loving eyes, he said the truest line of his career.

'This isn't a fling. It's for ever.'

Eloise smiled. 'And for ever starts now.'

EPILOGUE

'Noah! Noah!'

The reporter yelled across the press area, and Noah pasted on a smile as he turned to answer her questions. The smile became more genuine when he realised it was Sara, the reporter who'd broken the story about him and Eloise.

'Are you pleased with the reception *Eight Days After* has had at the festival?'

Was he pleased? No, he was ecstatic. The film had made its debut at the fringe film festival that afternoon, and already it was the only thing anyone there was talking about.

Of course, if it hadn't been so popular, maybe he'd have been able to escape the interviewers a little earlier and get back to Eloise…

Eloise. Just the thought of her made him smile. Thankfully, Stefan had seen how important she was to him, and realised that having Eloise at his side meant that Noah would be calm, centred and everything he needed to be to give his all to the film.

'I'm thrilled,' he said honestly. 'I think it's an important film, a fantastic script, and it has a real message of hope for viewers. I'm glad that those people who've seen it seem to agree.'

'And that's not the only thing they agree on,' Sara said, looking down at her notepad. 'Consensus across the board is that it's your best performance to date—and that you're going to sweep the board with this one come award season.'

'I can't speak for that,' Noah said modestly, while hoping against hope that she was right. 'I'm just glad I managed to pull it off.'

'And why is that, do you think?' Sara's lips twitched up into a knowing smile. 'Could it be that true love might have inspired you to greatness?'

Noah laughed. 'Inspired me to greatness? I don't know about that. But I do know that I'm late to meet my girlfriend. Today's a big day for her too, you see. So, if you'll excuse me…'

He was already halfway across the room before Sara responded. After all, Eloise was waiting for him. Eighteen months ago he'd sworn that he'd never let her down again. And he intended to keep that promise for the rest of his life.

Eloise checked the set-up one last time, then glanced at her watch. Where was Noah? He'd promised he'd be there on time.

'I'm sorry!' She heard his voice before she saw him, pushing his way past circus performers and a waitress carrying a tray of specially designed festival cocktails. 'I'm here!'

'Just as well,' Eloise said with a smile, as she stepped into Noah's arms for a brief kiss. 'From what I hear, you're the star of the festival.'

'Not me, the film.' Noah stepped back and looked around the outside space she'd commandeered for the opening night party. 'And that's only until they see this place. Wow! This is quite the show you're putting on, honey.'

Eloise shrugged. 'The festival committee said they

wanted a spectacle, so that's what I'm giving them.' A garden party complete with entertainment, music, the best canapés on the West Coast, magical lighting and some of the special touches that Eloise's company—Spectacle Events—had become famous for, over the last year and a half.

And what a year and a half it had been. While Noah had thrown himself into his role in *Eight Days After,* she'd focused on pursuing the dreams she'd let fall by the way-side for so long. It was as if having found her way into the spotlight, and with Noah at her side, she suddenly knew she could achieve anything.

The best part, she'd found, was the evenings they spent together at Noah's LA home—her home now too—talking through their day, preparing a meal and eating it together, or just kissing until they fell into bed.

Which wasn't to say there hadn't been difficult moments too—times when one of them was working too many hours, or when Noah retreated back into himself after an emotional day's filming. But the difference, Eloise had realised, was that now she had the confidence to call him out…and he had the faith and trust in her to let her.

Tonight was the culmination of eighteen months of love, laughter and hard work—for both of them. Spectacle Events had started small, with just Eloise and her clipboard organising baby showers and birthday parties, but it had grown as word got around. She wasn't naive enough any more to believe that some of that word of mouth didn't have something to do with her being Noah Cross's girl-friend—but she also knew she wouldn't have landed the jobs she had, or been able to expand into real offices with an actual staff, if she wasn't good at what she did.

She was proud of herself—and even prouder of Noah. She'd watched the film the night before, with Stefan the director and the rest of the cast, rapt as Noah nailed every emotion, every moment of pain or guilt his character felt. She'd squeezed his hand tight at the most emotional parts, and known that he'd be offered any part he wanted after this performance.

'I couldn't have done it without you,' he'd murmured as the credits rolled.

And now, tonight, it was her turn to shine. To show Hollywood what she was capable of.

And she was nervous as anything.

'I'm so glad you're here,' she said, reaching out to take Noah's hand again.

'I wouldn't be anywhere else.' Noah tugged her close, back into his arms. 'Especially as I have something I need to ask you. Before the world and his wife descend on this shindig of yours.'

'Oh? What's that?' Eloise asked, glancing away towards the entrance. Was that the first group of reporters and guests arriving?

When she looked back, Noah was down on one knee, and her eyes widened.

'Eloise Miller…' Noah started.

'Is he proposing?' The shout came from the entrance, where one of the waiters was trying to hold back a couple of reporters.

'He was trying to!' Noah yelled back. 'Think you could give us a minute here?'

Eloise shook her head. 'You know they won't. A photo of you down on one knee might be more valuable than the one of us falling out of a cupboard.'

'The world is always watching, huh?'

'Seems like it.'

Noah reached into his pocket and pulled out the most beautiful ring Eloise had ever seen—a large emerald-cut diamond on a platinum band. 'How about you and I really give them something to talk about?'

He pushed the ring onto her finger and Eloise felt a moment of perfect calm settle over her, even in the middle of organising the biggest event of her career, and with the world's media watching.

This. This was exactly where she was meant to be and who she was born to be—and to be with.

She tugged Noah to his feet and wrapped a hand round the back of his head as she pulled him down to kiss her.

'Honey,' she said as they broke the kiss, both breathing heavily. 'They're going to be talking about Noah and Eloise Cross for centuries.'

Noah grinned at her use of his name. 'Oh, yeah? And why's that?'

'Because true love is the best story in the world,' Eloise said, and kissed him again.

* * * * *

WHEN DA SILVA BREAKS THE RULES

ABBY GREEN

PROLOGUE

CESAR DA SILVA hated to admit that coming here had had any effect on him, but his gut was heavy and tight as he stood on the path near the grave. He asked himself again why he'd even come and reflexively his fingers closed around the small velvet pouch with its heavy weight in his hand. He'd almost forgotten about it.

He smiled cynically. Who would have thought that at the age of thirty-seven he'd be obeying urges and compulsions? Usually he was the king of logic and reason.

People drifted away from the open grave a short distance across the hilly green space. Ornate mini-mausoleum-style headstones dotted the cemetery in the hills of Athens, its grass no doubt kept generously watered in the Greek heat.

Finally there were only two men left by the grave. Both tall, of similar height, with dark hair. One had slightly darker and shorter hair than the other. They were broad, as Cesar was, with powerful builds.

It was no wonder they were all similar. He was their half-brother. And they had no idea he even existed. He saw one put his hand on the shoulder of the other. They were Rafaele Falcone and Alexio Christakos. They all shared the same mother, but had different fathers.

Cesar waited for icy rage to surge upwards upon seeing this evidence of the family he'd always been denied, but instead he felt a kind of aching emptiness. They came towards him then, talking in quiet voices. Cesar caught his youngest half-brother's words on the slight breeze—something like, *'Couldn't even clean up for the funeral...?'*

Falcone replied indistinctly, with a quirk to his mouth, and Christakos riposted, smiling too.

The emptiness receded and anger rose up within Cesar. But it was a different kind of anger. These men were joking, joshing, just feet away from their mother's grave. And since when did Cesar feel protective of the woman who had taught him from the age of three that he could depend on no one?

Galvanised by that very unwelcome revelation, Cesar moved forward and Falcone looked up, words dying on his lips, smile fading. Falcone's gaze was enquiring at first and then, as Cesar drilled holes into him with his stare, it became something else. Cold.

With a quick flick of a glance to the younger man by his half-brother's side, Cesar noted that they'd also all inherited varying shades of their beautiful but treacherous mother's green eyes.

'May we help you?' Falcone asked coolly.

Cesar glanced over them both again and then at the open grave in the distance. He asked, with a derisive curl to his lip, 'Are there any more of us?'

Falcone looked at Christakos, who was frowning, and said, *'Us?* What are you talking about?'

Cesar pushed down the spreading blackness within him and said with ominous quiet, 'You don't remember, do you?'

But he could see from the dawning shock that his half-brother did, and Cesar didn't like the way something inside him tightened at that recognition. Those light green eyes widened imperceptibly. He paled.

Cesar's voice was rough in the still, quiet air. 'She brought you to my home—you must have been nearly three, and I was almost seven. She wanted to take me with her then, but I wouldn't leave. Not after she'd abandoned me.'

In a slightly hoarse voice Falcone asked, 'Who *are* you?'

Cesar smiled, but it didn't meet his eyes. 'I'm your older brother—*half-brother*. My name is Cesar Da Silva. I came today to pay my respects to the woman who gave me life…not that she deserved it. I was curious to see if any more would crawl out of the woodwork, but it looks like it's just us.'

Christakos erupted. 'What the *hell*—?'

Cesar cast him a cold glance. Somewhere deep down he felt a twinge of conscience for imparting the news like this, on this day. But then he recalled the long, aching years of dark loneliness, knowing that these two men had *not* been abandoned, and crushed it ruthlessly.

Falcone still looked slightly shell-shocked. He gestured to his half-brother. 'This is Alexio Christakos…our younger brother.'

Cesar knew exactly who he was—who they both were. He'd always known. Because his grandparents had made sure he'd known every single little thing about them. He bit out, 'Three brothers by three fathers…and yet she didn't abandon either of *you* to the wolves.'

He stepped forward then, and Alexio stepped forward too. The two men stood almost nose to nose, Cesar topping his youngest brother in height only by an inch.

He gritted out, 'I didn't come here to fight you, brother. I have no issue with either of you.' *Liar*, a small voice chided.

Alexio's mouth thinned, 'Only with our dead mother, *if* what you say is true.'

Cesar smiled, but it was bitter. 'Oh, it's true all right—more's the pity.' He stepped around Alexio then, before either man could see the rise of an emotion he couldn't name, and walked to the open grave.

He took the velvet pouch out of his pocket and dropped it down into the dark space, where it fell onto the coffin with a hollow thud. In the pouch was a very old silver medallion featuring the patron saint of bullfighters: San Pedro Regalado.

Even now the bitter memory was vivid. His mother was in a black suit, hair drawn back, Her features as exquisitely beautiful as any he'd ever seen. Eyes raw from crying. She'd taken the medallion from where it hung around her neck on a piece of worn rope and had put it around his neck. She had tucked it under his shirt and said, *'He will protect you, Cesar. Because I can't at the moment. Don't ever take it off. And I promise I will come back for you soon.'*

But she hadn't come back. Not for a long time. And when she finally had it had been too late. Something had withered and died inside him. *Hope.*

Cesar had taken off the medallion the night he'd let that hope die. He'd been six years old. He'd known then that nothing could protect him except himself. She deserved to have the medallion back now—he'd had no need of it for a long time.

Eventually Cesar turned and walked back to where his half-brothers were still standing, faces inscrutable. He might have smiled, if he'd been able, to recognise this familiar trait. An ache gripped him in the region of his chest where he knew his heart should be. But as he knew well, and as he'd been told numerous times by angry lovers, he had no heart.

After a taut silence Cesar knew he had nothing to say to these men. These strangers. He didn't even feel envy any more. He felt empty.

He turned and got into the back of his car and curtly instructed his driver to go. It was done. He'd said goodbye to his mother, which was more than she'd ever deserved, and if there was one tiny piece of his soul that hadn't shrivelled up by now then maybe it could be saved.

CHAPTER ONE

Castillo Da Silva, near Salamanca

CESAR WAS HOT, sweaty, grimy and thoroughly disgruntled. All he wanted was a cold shower and a stiff drink. A punishing ride around his vast estate on his favourite stallion had failed to put a dent in the dark cloud that had clung to him since his return that afternoon from his half-brother Alexio's wedding in Paris. Those scenes of chirpy happiness still grated on his soul.

It also irritated him intensely that he'd given in to the rogue compulsion to go.

As he neared the stables his black mood increased on seeing the evidence of a serious breach of his privacy. A film was due to start shooting on his estate after the weekend, for the next four weeks. If that wasn't bad enough, the stars, director and producers were all staying *in* the *castillo*.

He wasn't unaware of his complicated relationship to his home. It was both prison and sanctuary. But one thing was sure: Cesar hated his privacy being invaded like this.

Huge equipment trucks lined his driveway. People were wandering about holding clipboards, speaking into walkie talkies. A massive marquee had been set up, where locals from the nearby town were being decked out as extras in nineteenth-century garb.

All that was missing was a circus tent with flags flying and a clown outside saying, *Roll up! Roll up!*

One of his biggest stable yards had been cleared out so that they could use it as the unit base. The unit base, as a film assistant had explained earnestly to Cesar, was where the actors got ready every day and where the crew would eat. As if he cared!

But he'd feigned interest for the benefit of his friend Juan Cortez, who was the Lord Mayor of Villaporto, the local town, and the reason why Cesar had given this idea even half a second's consideration. They'd been friends since the age of ten, when they'd both had to admit defeat during a fist fight or remain fighting till dawn and lose all their teeth. And they would have—both were stubborn enough.

As his friend had pointed out, 'Nearly everyone has been employed in some capacity—accommodation, catering, locations, the art department. Even my mother is involved in making clothes for the extras and putting up some of the crew. I haven't seen her so excited in years.'

Cesar couldn't fail to acknowledge the morale and economic boost the film had already brought to the locale. He was known in the press for his ruthless dealings with people and businesses—one journalist had likened his methods to those of the cold, dead-eyed shark before it ate you whole. But Cesar wasn't completely heartless—especially if it involved his own local community.

More than one person caught a glimpse of his glowering features and looked away hurriedly, but Cesar was oblivious, already figuring out how he could rearrange his schedule to make sure he was away for as much of the next four weeks as possible.

To his relief, his own private stable yard, which was strictly off-limits to the crew, was empty when he returned. He wasn't in the mood to deal with anyone—not even a groom. After unsaddling his horse and hosing him down, Cesar led him back to his stall and made sure he was secure, patting his still quivering flesh after their exertion.

It was only when he was turning to leave again that Cesar spotted a movement out of the corner of his eye and turned to look.

And stopped breathing, and thinking.

In the other corner of the quiet stable stood a woman. Cesar felt slightly dizzy for a moment and wondered if he was seeing an apparition.

She was wearing a white corset that cinched in her waist to almost impossible proportions while provocatively pushing up the abundant swells of her breasts. Long wavy golden hair was pulled back from an ethereally beautiful face and left to tumble down her back. Very feminine hips curved out from that tiny waist and a long, voluminous skirt almost touched the ground.

She was stunning…exquisite. She was Venus incarnate. She couldn't be real. Nothing so perfect existed in reality.

Almost without realising that he was moving, Cesar closed the distance between them. She didn't move. Just stared at him, looking as transfixed as he felt. Imbuing the moment with an even headier other-worldly feeling.

Her eyes were huge and blue…piercing. She was tiny, and it seemed to call to some deep, primal part of him. Evoking an alien urge to protect.

Her face was small and heart-shaped, but with an inherent strength that elevated it out of the merely beautiful to the extraordinary. High cheekbones. Elegant straight nose. A full, lush mouth made for sin and sinners. Skin like alabaster.

There was a beauty spot close to the edge of her upper lip. She exuded an earthy and very feminine sexual allure. She couldn't be real. Yet every single ounce of his masculinity was humming and throbbing in reaction to her luminosity.

As if to check that he wasn't losing it completely, Cesar reached out a hand, noting with almost dispassionate surprise that it trembled slightly. He cupped his hand near her cheek and jaw, without actually touching her, almost afraid that she might disappear if he did…

And then he touched her…and she didn't disappear. She was *real*. Warm. Skin as soft as silk.

A movement made his eyes drop and he saw her chest moving up and down rapidly with her breaths.

'*Dios,*' he said faintly, almost to himself, 'you are real.'

Her mouth opened. Cesar saw small, even white teeth. Her tongue-tip pink. She said, 'I…' and then stopped.

Just that one tiny word had been uttered in a husky voice, making Cesar's whole body tighten with a need that was unprecedented.

Sliding his fingers further around her jaw to the back of her neck, silky hair tickling his hand, Cesar tugged her into him and after a minute hesitation she came, stumbling ever so slightly. All he knew, once he felt the barest whisper of a touch of her body to his, was that he couldn't hold back now even if a thousand men tried to stop him.

He lowered his head and his mouth touched hers, and all that sweet, soft voluptuousness pierced him right to the centre of his being, and threw him into the pit of a fire of lust so strong it obliterated everything he knew, or thought he knew.

Cesar felt her hands clutching at him, grabbing his shirt. Any resistance vanished when her mouth opened under his, and his arms tightened around her as his hungry tongue thrust into that hot, moist cavern.

However sweet that first initial taste had been, it turned to pure sin. Decadent and rich. Her tongue was sharp and smooth, teasing. Stoking his levels of arousal so that every bit of blood seemed to be rushing to the centre of his body, making that shaft of flesh lengthen and stiffen painfully.

Moving his hands to her waist, encircling it, Cesar almost groaned aloud when he felt his fingers meet. That evidence of her intense femininity pushed his body over the edge, made it betray him as if he were an over-sexed teenager.

He could feel her chest, struggling with constricted breath, moving up and down rapidly. Blood surging anew, Cesar lifted a hand and dragged it up between their bodies, itching to touch that smooth pale skin.

When he came into contact with the swell of one breast his body pulsed with a need that shocked him. He broke the contact of their mouths for a moment, resting his forehead against hers, overwhelmed at the strength of his desire.

'Please…'

Her voice sounded even huskier…needy. The way he felt. He needed this woman *now*. Needed to free himself and lift up her skirts and plunge right into the centre of that taut, smooth body. To feel her legs wrap around him.

On some very dim and distant level Cesar was aware that he had become animalistic. Reduced to the cravings and needs of a base animal in an effort to achieve a kind of satisfaction he'd never anticipated before.

But that still couldn't stop him. Not after that husky *please* had filled the space between them.

Branding her mouth with his again, the kiss was open-mouthed and carnal. Electrifying.

In the act of lifting up her skirts, almost desperate now, Cesar jerked and flinched when a flash of light seemed to illuminate the world for a second. Like the crack of a whip. Shattering the heady moment.

Lifting his head from where their mouths were welded together, Cesar could only see two huge pools of blue, ringed by long black lashes. That plump mouth was pink. He could feel her chest moving against his.

Then there was another flash, and a rapid jarring, clicking sound. He flinched again. Some vague notion of reality and sanity returned from a long distance. He turned his head, but it was the hardest thing to do—to look away from that face. Those eyes.

He saw a man standing at the entrance of the stables holding a camera up to his face. It was the equivalent of having a bucket of cold water thrown over him. Suddenly reality was back.

Cesar straightened up. Instinctively he pushed the woman behind him as he snarled at the man who was backing away, still shooting, 'Get out of here. *Now.*' One of Cesar's grooms appeared near the door and he rapped out at him, 'Get Security now—and get that man's camera.'

But the photographer had disappeared, and even though Cesar's groom darted away after him Cesar had the sinking feeling it would be too late. He'd reacted too late himself.

Becoming aware of rapid harsh breathing behind him, Cesar turned around.

And almost fell into the pit again when he saw those huge blue eyes staring up at him and that body which made him ache.

But reality had intruded. This woman was no apparition or ghost. She was flesh and blood, and he had just lost his legendary control spectacularly. *Dios*, had he gone mad?

Accusingly, Cesar asked, 'Who the hell *are* you?'

Lexie Anderson was barely aware of the sharp accusation in the deep, deliciously accented voice. She couldn't seem to get enough breath into her challenged lungs to speak. All she could ask herself was: *what the hell had just happened?*

She remembered wandering away from the camera tests

while they set up the lights and finding these quiet stables. She loved horses, so she had come in to investigate.

Then the peace had been shattered when this man had appeared in the courtyard on a huge black stallion. He'd swung down off the horse's back and from that moment on everything had got a little hazy.

Lexie had been mesmerised by his powerful physique and the play of muscles under his close-fitting polo top and jodhpurs as he'd tended to the horse. And that had been before she'd seen his face properly. When he'd heard her and turned around.

He was stunning. Beautiful. But with a masculine edge that made 'beautiful' sound too…pretty. He was hard. Edgy. Dark. Messy dark blond hair. A sensually sculpted mouth surrounded by stubble shadowing a very masculine jaw.

But it was his eyes that rendered Lexie a bit stupid and mute even now, as he waited for her reply. They were green—unusual and stark against dark olive skin. Not hazel, or golden, or light green. Something between all three. Unnerving. Mesmerising.

And he smelled of *man*. Sweat and musk and heat. Along with something tangy. Woodsy.

Lexie shook her head, as if that might make all this disappear. Maybe she was having some bizarre dream. Because she knew that what had just happened was unprecedented. She did not react to complete strangers by letting them kiss her, or by feeling as if she'd die if they didn't *keep* kissing her.

She remembered his big hands around her waist, then reaching under her skirts to pull them up, and how she'd burned between her legs for him to touch her there.

Now was most definitely *not* the time to be assimilating that cataclysmic information.

'I'm…' She stopped, her tongue feeling heavy in her

mouth. She tried again. 'I'm Lexie Anderson. I'm with the film.'

Lexie's face burned when she realised exactly how she was dressed, and how this man's eyes had widened when he'd seen her. Belatedly self-conscious, she went to cross her arms but realised the corset only made things worse—especially when those green eyes dropped to her heaving flesh again.

Feeling trapped now—literally backed into a corner—and not liking it, Lexie forced her legs to move, wobbly as they were, and stepped cautiously around him.

He turned to face her. Eyes cool, unreadable. Hands clenched into fists by his sides. 'You're Lexie Anderson... the lead actress?'

She nodded.

He looked at her, his eyes no longer unreadable now. Angry. 'And how did you get in here?'

She blinked, not understanding for a moment. 'I didn't see any sign or a gate...I just saw the horses—'

'It's off-limits here. You should leave—now.'

Anger gripped Lexie. She'd just behaved in a way that was completely out of character. The last thing she needed was to feel the lash of *his* censure. Stiffly, she replied, 'I didn't realise this was off-limits. If you can tell me how to get back to the unit base, I'll happily leave.'

His voice was harsh, curt. 'Turn left. It's at the end of the lane and to your right.'

Seething inwardly now, because she had been over-come by the first rush of physical desire she'd ever felt, and it had been for some anonymous person who worked at the castle and not even someone she *knew* or who was particularly charming, Lexie stalked off, tense as a board.

Then she heard the man curse and he commanded, 'Wait. Stop.'

Lexie stopped, breathing hard, and turned reluctantly again, rigid with tension.

He walked towards her, his movements powerfully agile, and she stepped back. His eyes flashed but she just tipped up her chin. What was wrong with her judgement? There wasn't anything remotely forgiving or alluring about this man. He was all hard edges and brooding energy.

He looked grim. 'That was a paparazzo. He got our picture.'

She'd forgotten. Her brain was refusing to work properly. Lexie could feel her blood draining south. The man must have feared she was about to faint or something, because he took her arm and none too gently drew her over to a haystack by the entrance, where he all but pushed her down onto it.

She ripped her arm free and glared up at him, hating the betraying quiver in her belly at his touch. 'There's no need to manhandle me. I'm perfectly fine.'

As if to confirm her worst suspicions, the young groom came running back, his face red.

'Well?' barked the man.

Lexie felt like standing up and telling him to go and take out his aggression on someone his own size, but she was disgusted to feel that her legs might not hold her up.

'Señor Da Silva…'

The groom spoke quickly after that, in incomprehensible Spanish, but Lexie was now gaping at the tall, angry man who was answering equally gutturally and quickly, making the groom turn puce and rush off again.

Lexie was too shocked to care for the groom's welfare any more. He turned back to her and she said faintly, 'You're Cesar Da Silva…?'

'Yes.'

He didn't seem to be too thrilled she'd made the connection. She'd thought he was a worker! Lexie hadn't recognised him as the owner of this entire estate because he was famously reclusive. Also, she'd never expected *the* Cesar Da Silva to be so young and gorgeous.

She had to will down her mortification when she thought of how she'd been all but crawling all over him like a hungry little kitten only minutes before. Begging. *'Please.'*

Oh, God.

She stood up. She had to get out of here. This was not her. She'd been invaded by some kind of body-snatcher.

'Where do you think you're going?'

Lexie looked at him. Anger flashed up again—at him and herself. She put her hands on her hips. 'You just told me to leave, didn't you? So I'm leaving.'

She moved around him again, towards the entrance, relieved that her legs were working.

'Wait.'

Lexie stopped and sighed heavily, turned around. She arched a brow, hiding how damn intimidating she thought he was. 'What now?'

He couldn't have looked more stern. 'That photographer got away. My groom saw him get into a car before any of the security guards could be alerted. I would imagine that right about now he's emailing pictures of us to any number of agencies around the world.'

Lexie felt sick. She felt even sicker to think that she was potentially going to be splashed across the tabloids *again*. And with Cesar Da Silva, one of the most reclusive billionaires in the world. It would be a sensation and it was the last thing she needed—*more* intense media interest.

She bit her lip. 'This isn't good.'

'No,' Da Silva agreed, 'it's not. I have no desire to become the centre of some grubby little tabloid sensation.'

Lexie glared at him, incensed. 'Well, neither do I.' She pointed a finger at him. 'And *you* kissed *me*.'

'You didn't stop me,' he shot back. 'And what were you doing in here anyway?'

Lexie burned. No, she hadn't stopped him. Anything but. She'd been caught up in a dreamlike state of…hot insanity.

'I told you.' Her voice was stiff, with the full ramifications of what had happened sinking in. 'I saw the stables, I wanted to see the horses… We're doing camera tests with Make-up and Wardrobe, and while they were setting up the lighting…'

She tensed as realisation hit.

'The camera tests! I have to go back—they'll be looking for me.'

Lexie went to rush off, but her arm was caught by a big hand. She turned and gritted her jaw. Those green eyes were like burning gems in his spectacular face. His hand on her arm was hot.

'This isn't over—'

Just then a PA rushed into the yard, breathless. 'Lexie, *there* you are. We've been looking all over for you. They're ready to shoot again.'

Lexie pulled free of Cesar Da Silva's grip. She could see his irritation at the interruption but she was glad, needing to get away from his disturbing presence and so she could try to assimilate what had just happened.

Lexie tore her gaze from his and hurried after the officious PA, who was speaking into the walkie-talkie microphone that came out of her sleeve near her wrist. Lexie heard her saying, 'Found her…coming now…one minute…'

Her head was reeling. She felt as if in the space of just that last…fifteen minutes?…her entire world had been altered in some very fundamental way.

She'd let that man…who had been a complete stranger… walk up to her and kiss her. Without a second's hesita-

tion. And not just kiss her...*devour* her. And she'd kissed
him back.

She could still feel that dizzying, rushing sweep of desire like a wave through her body. Impossible to ignore or
deny. Immediate. All-consuming.

It was crazy, but she'd felt protected by his much larger
bulk when he'd put her behind him as soon as he'd seen the
paparazzo. Lexie wasn't used to feeling tiny, or in need of
protection, even though she *was* physically small at five
foot two. She'd been standing up for herself for so long
now that she wasn't usually taken unawares in a situation
like that. It sent a shiver of unease through her.

The photographer.

She felt sick again. Memories of lurid headlines and pictures rose up. Before she could dwell on it though, they'd
entered the yard where the camera tests were taking place
and everyone snapped to attention as soon as she appeared.

The cameraman beckoned her over. 'Right, Lexie, we
need you over here on your mark, please.'

Cesar paced back and forth in his office, behind his desk.
If it were at all possible his black mood had just become
even blacker. Like a living, seething thing crackling around
him. He had a file open on his desk and there were clippings and pictures strewn across it.

It was a file on Lexie Anderson. And it was not pretty.

One of the film assistants had furnished Cesar's office
with files on everyone involved in the film. As much for
security purposes as for a little general knowledge about
the cast and crew. He hadn't even looked at them before
now, because he hadn't been interested.

The files generally just held people's CVs. Except for
Lexie's file. Her file was fat, not only with her CV, covering work which consisted mainly of TV and some indie
movies before she'd shot to stardom via some vacuous-

looking action movies, but also with numerous clippings from papers and magazines.

There were pictures of her, scantily clad, for a lads' magazine some years previously. One image showed her posing as some sort of half-dressed cheerleader, in nothing but thigh-high socks, knickers and a cardigan, teasingly open just enough to show off the voluptuous swells of her breasts and the sensual curve of her tiny waist. Her hair was down and tumbling sexily over her shoulders.

It was exactly the kind of image that Cesar found a complete turn-off, but right now he was having to battle with his own body to stop it responding as helplessly as if he were an over-sexed teenager all over again.

Cesar cursed and picked up the picture, throwing it aside. It fluttered to the floor. She was an actress. That was what she did.

But much worse than that were the more recent pictures and headlines: *Luscious Lexie—Homewrecker!* The tabloids had indulged in a feeding frenzy because she had been involved with a married actor who had subsequently left his heartbroken wife and children. He and Lexie weren't together now, though. According to the salacious copy, once he'd left his wife, heartless Lexie hadn't been interested any more.

Cesar knew that he couldn't have cared less what any lead actress got up to in her spare time, or with whom. But he'd kissed this woman in a moment of extreme madness only a short time before.

The imprint of that petite lush body against his was still branded into his memory. No woman had *ever* got him so hot that he'd lost control like that. He'd been moments away from backing her into a wall and thrusting up into her slick body if they hadn't been interrupted by the paparazzo when they had.

Cesar cursed. And then his phone rang. He answered it abruptly.

His solicitor's voice came down the line, 'Cesar, I've got some news you're not going to like.'

If his solicitor could have seen Cesar's expression right then he probably would have put the phone down and run. But he couldn't, so he went on, oblivious.

'You were photographed at Alexio Christakos's wedding this morning in Paris.'

'So?' Cesar offered curtly, his mind still full of lurid images of Lexie Anderson and her effect on his body.

His solicitor in Madrid sighed heavily. 'Well, it would appear that some very industrious reporter decided to do a quick search, to see if there was any connection between you and Christakos. They came up with the fact that the recently deceased Esperanza Christakos was briefly married to one Joaquin Da Silva, years before she became a renowned model.'

For a second Cesar saw only blackness. He sat down. 'How did they find this?'

'It's not a secret who your mother was, Cesar,' his solicitor pointed out carefully. 'It's just never been discovered before...the connection...'

Cesar knew this. His mother had left so long ago that no one had ever seemed to have the inclination to go digging. He came from the Da Silva dynasty and that was all people cared out.

Until now.

Cesar managed to give an instruction to his solicitor to monitor the media attention closely and put his phone down.

The press would have a field day. He was the estranged half-brother of two of the most renowned entrepreneurs in the world. It would be open season on prying into their lives. For speculating on why nobody had ever spotted the connection before now. And so on, and so on.

He was well aware that this was hardly big news—people discovered half-siblings all the time. What he wasn't prepared for was the prospect of ignominious media intrusion into an area of his life that had always been shut away. Not acknowledged.

The only time the reality of his brothers had been acknowledged, it had been used to taunt him. To drive home the fact that he was not the chosen one. That he could trust no one. Ever. As much as he hated to admit it, the scar was still deep. He only had to think back to earlier that day to remember how it had felt to be so black and bitter next to their happiness and ease with the world. A world that had taught them they could trust. That mothers didn't leave you behind.

Cesar cursed the maudlin direction of his thinking. Cursed himself again for having gone to Christakos's wedding.

With this film on his estate his privacy was already being well and truly eroded. Now this.

And then another picture of Lexie caught Cesar's eye and a headache started to throb behind his right temple. He feared that the reclusive life he'd lived for so long was about to slip out of his grasp unless he could do some serious damage limitation.

CHAPTER TWO

'MISS ANDERSON? MR Da Silva would like to see you in his office, if you could spare a few minutes?'

Lexie knew it wasn't really a question. It was an order, and she chafed at the autocracy, already imagining his dark, forbidding expression. He'd been a complete stranger to her less than a couple of hours ago, known only by his reputation and name, yet now his saturnine image was branded like a searing tattoo on her brain. *His taste…*

Hiding her reaction, Lexie just shrugged her shoulders lightly and smiled. 'Sure.'

She followed the smartly dressed young woman down a long hallway. She'd just arrived back at the *castillo* from the camera tests and was dressed in her own clothes again. Worn jeans and sneakers. A dusky pink long-sleeved cashmere top, which suddenly felt way too clingy.

The make-up artist had scrubbed her face clean and she'd left her hair down, so now she had no armour at all. She hated the impulse she had to check her reflection.

Lexie hadn't had much time yet to look around the *castillo* as she'd been busy since they'd arrived, doing rehearsals and fittings. It was massive, and very gothic. The overall impression was dark and forbidding. Oppressive. Not unlike its owner. Lexie smiled to herself but it was tight.

A stern housekeeper had shown her to her room when

she'd arrived: dressed in black, hair pulled back in a tight, unforgiving bun. She might have stepped straight out of an oil masterpiece depicting the Spanish Inquisition era.

Lexie's bedroom was part of an opulent suite of rooms complete with an elaborate four-poster bed. Reds and golds. Antique furniture. A chaise longue. While it wasn't her style, she had to admit that it was helping her get into character for the film. She was playing a courtesan from the nineteenth century, who was torn between leaving her profession for her illegitimate son and a villainous lover who didn't want to let her go.

It was a dark, tragic tale, and the director was acclaimed. This film was very important to her—and not just for professional and economic reasons. One scene in particular had compelled Lexie to say yes, as she had known it would be her own personal catharsis to act it out. But she didn't want to think of that now.

After a series of soulless but financially beneficial action movies, this was Lexie's first chance to remind people that she could actually act. And hopefully move away from that hideous *Luscious Lexie* image the tabloids had branded her with. Not entirely unjustly, she hated to admit.

The young woman stopped outside a massive door and knocked. Lexie's mind emptied. Her heart went *thump* and her throat felt dry.

She heard the deep and curt *'Sí?'* And then the woman was opening the door. Lexie felt as if she was nine again, being hauled up in front of the head nun at her school for some transgression.

But then Cesar Da Silva was standing in the doorway, filling it. The woman melted away. He'd changed. Washed. Lexie could smell his scent—that distinctive woodsy smell. But without the earthy musk of earlier. It was no less heady, though.

Wearing a white shirt and dark trousers should have

made him appear more urbane. It didn't. The material of his shirt was fine enough to see the darkness of his skin underneath. He stood back and held out an arm, stretching his shirt across his chest. Lexie saw defined hard muscles. Heat flooded between her legs.

'Come in.'

Lexie straightened her spine and walked past him into a massive office.

She was momentarily distracted by its sheer grandeur as he closed the door behind them. It was shaped like an oval, with a parquet floor, and it had an ante-room that looked like a library, with floor-to-ceiling shelves of books upon books.

Something very private and poignant gripped her inside.

'Please, take a seat.'

Da Silva had moved behind his desk, hands resting lightly on top, but not disguising his obvious tension. The desk was huge, awe-inspiring. A very serious affair, holding all sorts of computers and machines and phones.

And yet less than two hours ago she and this man had mutually combusted and she had been oblivious to who he was.

Feeling uncharacteristically awkward, she started, 'Look, Mr Da Silva—'

'I think we've gone beyond that, don't you?' His face was mirthless and hard.

Lexie wondered for a crazy moment what he would look like if he smiled. Genuinely smiled.

She burned inwardly at that rogue little thought, and in rejection of his autocratic tone. 'I...well, yes.'

Her big slouchy handbag was slung over her shoulder. She let it slip down now, and held it in front of her like a shield. Something was telling her this wouldn't be a quick meeting.

A bright colour caught her eye then, and she glanced

down to see a photo of herself on the ground. Frowning, she bent to pick it up. When she registered the image, her insides roiled. She'd been twenty-one. Completely naive. Cringing inside with embarrassment. Not that you'd know it from the picture. She'd been hiding behind a well-developed wall of confidence and nonchalance that hadn't come easily.

She held the picture between thumb and forefinger and looked at Cesar across the desk. He was totally unrepentant. Something hard settled into her gut. The awareness she had of his sheer masculine physicality made her feel like a fool. And very vulnerable—which she did not welcome. It had been a long time since she'd allowed anyone to make her feel that way.

Then she saw the open file and all the other cuttings and clippings and pictures. She didn't have to read the lurid headlines to know what the characters said even from here, upside down. *Luscious Lexie.*

She went icy. Her bag slipped to the floor unnoticed.

'What is this?'

'This,' Cesar da Silva offered tautly, 'is your life, I believe.'

Lexie looked at Cesar and right at that moment despised him. She'd barely exchanged more than twenty sentences with the man, and he'd displayed not an ounce of charm, yet she'd blithely allowed him to be more intimate with her than any other man had ever been.

Her conscience mocked her. That wasn't technically true, of course. But the other experience in her life hadn't been consensually intimate. It had been a horrifically brutal parody of intimacy.

Lexie forced her mind away from that and raged inwardly at the injustice of his evident blind belief in the lies spread before him. She hated that a part of her wanted to curl up and cringe at how all this *evidence* was laid out so starkly across his desk. Ugly.

She forced her voice to be light, to hide the raging tumult. 'And do you believe everything you read in the papers, Mr Da Silva?'

He gritted out, 'Call me Cesar.'

Lexie smiled prettily, hiding her ire, 'Well, when you ask so nicely...*Cesar.*'

'I don't care enough to give the time to believe or disbelieve. I couldn't really care less about your tawdry sex life with married men.'

Lexie saw red. She literally saw a flash of red. She forced air into her lungs. Clenching her jaw so tight it hurt, she bit out, 'Well, then, perhaps you'd be so kind as to let me know what you want to discuss so that I can get on with my *tawdry* life.'

Cesar had to force back the urge to smile for a second. She'd surprised him. Standing up to him so fiercely. Like a tiny virago. Or a pocket Venus.

It took an immense physical effort not to let his gaze drop and linger on the swell of her breasts under the clinging soft material of her top. Or to investigate just how snugly those worn jeans fitted her bottom.

When she'd walked in he'd taken in the slim, shapely legs. The very feminine swell of her hips. She was the perfect hourglass, all wrapped up in a petite, intoxicating package. Her hair was loose and wavy over her shoulders. Bright against the dark wood of his office. *Against the darkness of the castillo.* Something lanced him in a place that was buried, deep and secret. He didn't welcome it.

He didn't like that he'd also noticed her beauty spot was gone. The artifice of make-up. It mocked him for believing himself to have been in some sort of a dream earlier.

For thinking she was some sort of goddess siren straight out of a Greek myth.

But she was no less alluring now in modern clothes than she had been in a corset and petticoats. In fact, now that Cesar knew the flesh her clothes concealed, it was almost worse.

And he'd just been ruder to this woman than he'd ever been to another in his life.

He could actually be urbane. Charming. But as soon as he'd laid eyes on her again he'd felt animalistic. Feral. Even now his blood thundered, roared. For her. And she wasn't even remotely his type.

He ran a hand through his hair impatiently. His conscience demanded of him that he say, 'Look, maybe we can start again. Take a seat.'

Lexie oozed tension and quivering insult. And he couldn't blame her. Even if her less than pristine life *was* spread all over his desk.

'I'm fine standing, thank you. And where, might I ask, did you get your hands on what appears to be a veritable scrapbook of my finest moments?'

Her voice could have cut through steel it was so icy. Cesar almost winced.

'Someone working on the film compiled information on the cast and crew.' His eye caught another lurid shot of Lexie pouting over the bonnet of a car. His body tightened. He willed himself to cling on to some control. 'It would appear that person was a little over-zealous with the back catalogue of your work.'

Lexie flushed, her cheeks filling with dark colour, and Cesar felt his conscience twinge again. As if *he* was in the wrong. When this woman was standing there with her chin tilted up, defiant in the face of her less than stellar reputation.

She came forward and Cesar's gaze couldn't help but

drop to where her breasts swayed gently under her top. She stopped at the other side of the desk and put her hands on it and glared at him, her huge blue eyes sending out daggers of ice.

She plucked out the image of her on the car and held it up accusingly. '*This* is not a back catalogue of work. *This* is a naive young girl, trying to get on in a ruthless cut-throat business—a girl who didn't have the confidence or economic security to say no to bullying agents and photographers.'

She spat out the words.

'You might consider that the next time you find it so easy to judge someone you were only too happy to kiss without even knowing who she was.'

Before Cesar could respond to her spiky defence, not liking the rush of a very alien emotion within him, she'd gathered up all the cuttings and pictures, her CV and head-shots, and marched over to a nearby bin, dumping the lot.

She turned around, her hair shimmering as it moved over her shoulder. She crossed her arms. 'Now, what was it you wanted to discuss?'

Lexie hated that her body was humming with awareness for this man. Who was blissfully immune to the angry emotions he was arousing.

What a judgmental, supercilious, arrogant, small-minded—

'I owe you an apology,' he said tightly.

Lexie blinked. The anger inside her suffered a body-blow. 'Yes, you do.'

His mouth was a grim line. 'I had no right to judge you on the basis of those pictures.'

'No, you didn't,' Lexie snapped, but then she flushed again when she thought of another similar shoot she'd done relatively recently—albeit for a much more up-market publication and with a world-famous photographer. But still, she couldn't exactly claim the moral high ground either... 'It's fine,' she dismissed airily, 'let's forget about it.'

He sighed heavily then, and opened up the laptop that was on the desk in front of him. 'You should see this.'

Trepidation skittered over her skin. Warily Lexie walked around the desk until she could see the laptop, acutely conscious of her proximity to him. When she saw the images, though, her belly swooped alarmingly.

It was her, and him, locked in a clinch that looked positively X-rated. Both his hands were under her skirt, pulling it up, baring her legs. Her breasts seemed about to explode from her corset, crushed against his chest. Their mouths were locked together in a passionate kiss, their eyes closed. Lexie's hands gripped his shirt so tightly that her knuckles were white. And just like that it all came back in a rush: the desperation, the craving, the *aching*. The need.

Lexie could feel heat from behind her. She swallowed. There could be no mistaking that whatever had happened between them had consumed them both. It was not a comfort.

'Where is this?' she asked hoarsely, unable to stop looking away from the image with some kind of sick fascination.

'It's on a well-known internet gossip website. It's only a matter of time before it hits the papers.'

Lexie backed away from the laptop as if it might explode...retreating around the desk, feeling marginally safer once something solid was between them.

Cesar's eyes were glittering. His disdain was palpable. He might have just apologised, and surprised her by doing so, but there was no mistaking his disapproval of the entire situation.

Stung, Lexie said defensively, 'There were two of us there.'

He was grim. 'I'm aware of that, believe me.'

'So…' She swallowed painfully, thinking of the inevitable re-igniting of press interest and the weariness and fear of exposure that would provoke. 'What now?'

Cesar looked at her for a long moment and crossed his arms. 'We contain it.'

Lexie frowned. 'What do you mean…contain it?'

'We don't give it air to breathe. You're here in the *castillo* for the next four weeks. There should be no reason why it won't die a death if they have nothing to work with.'

Something icy touched Lexie's spine. 'What are you talking about exactly?'

A muscle pulsed in Cesar's jaw. 'What I'm talking about is that you don't leave this estate.'

Fire doused the ice. Lexie pointed at herself. '*I* don't leave the estate? What about you?'

Cesar shrugged minutely, arrogant. 'Well, of course I will have to leave. I have business to attend to.'

Lexie emitted a laugh that sounded far too close to panic for her liking. 'After a passionate embrace is plastered all over the world's press, you appear in public with me nowhere to be seen…do you know how that'll look?' She answered herself before he could. 'It'll look as if you're rejecting me and the press will be all over it like a rash.'

Cesar's jaw pulsed again. Clearly he was not used to having anyone question his motives. 'You will be protected in here from the press.'

'Oh, really?' asked Lexie. 'That paparazzo managed to get in, and I assume even a reclusive fossil like you has heard of camera phones?'

She was so angry right then at Cesar's preposterous plan that she barely noticed that he'd moved around the desk, or that his eyes flashed dangerously at her childish insult.

'What's to stop some enterprising crew member from snapping pictures of *poor jilted Lexie* on the set of her new film…?' Lexie was on a roll now, pacing back and forth. 'The press will love documenting *your* exploits while I'm the rejected fool, locked in the castle.'

Lexie stopped and rounded on Cesar, who was at the other side of the desk now and far too close and tall and dark. She took a step back.

She shook her head. 'No way. I'm not going to be incarcerated in this grim fortress just to make life easier for *you*. I'd planned to visit Lisbon, Salamanca…*Madrid!*' That last came out with more than a little desperation.

Lexie had dark memories of being all but locked up once before, and it wasn't going to happen again in her lifetime—not even on an estate as palatial as this one.

Cesar looked at Lexie and was momentarily distracted by her sheer vibrancy and beauty. Her cheeks were pink with indignation, her eyes huge and glittering. Her chest was heaving. As she'd paced back and forth energy had crackled around her like electricity.

Her words hit him then: *I'm not going to be incarcerated in this grim fortress…* He felt like cracking a bleak smile. He knew only too well what that was like. And he could sympathise with her rejection of the idea.

He rested back against his desk and crossed his arms, because right now they itched to reach out and grab her and pull her into him. So close to her like this he could smell her scent, all but feel those provocative curves pressed against him.

His body tightened, blood rushed south. He cursed silently.

'So…what would be *your* suggestion, then?'

Lexie blinked. Cesar marvelled that her every thought was mirrored on that expressive face and in those huge eyes. He'd never seen anything like it. He was used to women putting on a front, trying hard to be mysterious.

She bit her lip and that was even worse. *He* wanted to bite that lip.

She looked at him. 'We go public.'

Cesar's eyes snapped up from her mouth to her eyes. His crossed arms dropped. 'We go *what*?'

'We go public,' she repeated.

'As in...?'

Her eyes flashed brilliant blue, like fire. 'As in we are seen together. As in we go out in public. As in we let people think that we are having an affair.'

Cesar tensed for the inevitable rush of rejection at that proposition. He didn't *do* high publicity—especially not with women like Lexie, whose second home was among the tabloids. Whose life was laid out in a series of lurid pictures amid salacious headlines.

But it didn't come. The rejection. What did come was an intense spiking of anticipation in his already hot blood. His brain clicked and whirred at the thought of this audacious plan. The news of his half-brothers would be hitting the newsstands possibly as soon as tomorrow...

'Well?'

Lexie's voice cut through the snarl of thoughts in Cesar's head. Somehow, without analysing it fully right now, he knew that a news story featuring *them* would inevitably be more colourful and interesting than one about his family connections. That would be diminished in favour of a far more scandalous story: *Reclusive billionaire beds homewrecking Luscious Lexie.*

'I think,' Cesar said slowly, letting his eyes fill with Lexie again, 'that your idea has some merit.'

Some of the tension left her shoulders even as she crossed her arms, which pushed the swells of her breasts up. *Dios*, Cesar cursed again silently. Suddenly all rational thoughts of distracting the press via a story about him and Lexie fled, to be replaced with the very *real* urge to touch the woman in front of him.

'Good,' she said now. 'Because I really do think that's the best solution. And the fairest.' Her mouth firmed. 'I know the press, and sometimes you have to play them at their own game rather than fight them.'

She lifted her chin then, and something about the move was so endearingly spiky that Cesar had to stop himself from reaching out to trail his fingers across her jaw. Out of nowhere came a surge of something that felt almost like *protectiveness*.

His hands curled around the edge of his desk beside his hips. He forced his mind back to the conversation. 'I have a charity auction to attend in Salamanca next weekend. We can go to that.' The devil inside him compelled him to continue. 'And we'll have to be convincing, Lexie.'

Those big blue eyes narrowed. 'Convincing?'

Cesar smiled, the anticipation inside him tightening now. 'Convincing...as lovers.'

Lexie's arms tightened, pushing those firm swells up even more. 'Oh...well, yes. I mean, that's obvious...but that'll be easy enough... I mean...I'm an actress after all.'

Suddenly the confident woman of only a few moments ago was not at all sure of herself. Cesar was more intrigued than he liked to admit. He shifted on the desk, crossing one ankle over the other, and noted how Lexie's eyes dropped to his mid-section for a second before skittering away again.

But then the suggestion that she'd have to *act* with Cesar hit home and made something hot and dark pierce him inside. He tensed. 'So what happened earlier, Lexie? Were you just practising your *acting* skills on the nearest stable hand you could find?'

She looked at him. 'No. It wasn't like that.'

Cesar felt more exposed than he liked to. 'So what *was* it like?'

For a second he fancied that the turmoil he could see in those blue depths mirrored the part of him that still couldn't make sense of what had happened. But the very suggestion that it had been in any way within *her* control and not his made something snap inside him.

He straightened up and did what his hands had been itching to do ever since she'd walked into his study. He reached for her and pulled her into him, and something treacherous in his mind quietened as soon as those soft curves fell against him.

Her hands were pressed against his chest and a soft *oof* escaped her mouth: a sigh of shock. She looked up. 'What are you doing?'

Cesar's body was already hardening against hers. An automatic and helpless reaction to her proximity and touch. He hated this feeling of being out of control—it had been a long day of that very unwelcome sensation. He gritted out, 'I'm seeing how good you are at improvisation.'

And then he bent his head to hers, and her mouth was as firm and yet as soft as he remembered, and those lush contours sent his brain into a tailspin all over again.

Lexie was drowning. Her hands looked for purchase anywhere she could find it to try and cling on. Cesar's mouth was searing and hot. Hard. His arms were welded tight around her. She was off-balance and plastered against him, breasts crushed against rock-hard contours. One of his hands moved up to her head, angling it. Their mouths were open, tongues touching and tasting. Stroking, sucking.

Lexie wanted to wrap her arms around his neck and rub herself up and down his hard length, seeking to assuage the stinging in her nipples and the ache growing inside her.

She could feel a hard ridge against her belly and it caused a spasm of damp desire between her legs.

And then the haze lifted ever so slightly, when he took his mouth away for a moment and she remembered his grim look and what he'd said, *'I'm seeing how good you are at improvisation.'*

As if a cold bucket of water had been thrown over her Lexie jerked backwards, almost stumbling in an effort to right herself. She was shaky all over, breathing heavily. Cesar was resting on the edge of the desk, barely a hair out of place, even if his cheeks were flushed and eyes were glittering brightly.

Lexie wasn't ready for this onslaught of physical sensations and feelings. Barely able to get her head around articulating much, she asked, a little redundantly, 'What was that in aid of?'

'Proving that it will be no hardship to *act* out being lovers. In fact it's almost inevitable that we will *become* lovers.'

Lexie rebelled at that arrogant tone even as her body betrayed her spectacularly. 'Don't flatter yourself, Mr Da Silva.'

He smiled. 'It's Cesar, please.'

Lexie felt dizzy at how quickly this man was dismantling the bricks and mortar that had protected her for years. She couldn't analyse it now, but she knew that he must have connected with her on some very deep level for her to have allowed him to kiss her—not once, but twice. Without even putting up a fight.

Panic galvanised her and she reached down and picked up her bag, slung it over her shoulder. She forced herself to look at Cesar but it was hard. The air between them was saturated with electricity and tension and something else far more disturbing and new to Lexie: *Desire*.

She hated to admit that she was also stung to think

that he believed she was the kind of person who would just widen her eyes and say yes to such an autocratic announcement.

She bit out, 'I am *not* an easy lay, Cesar. Evidently you believe what you read in the papers, but I can assure you that I am perfectly capable of controlling myself. I am interested in putting forward a united front in order to get the press off our backs…that is all.'

Cesar stared at her for a long moment and then shrugged. He folded his arms across that wide chest, making the muscles of his arms bunch against the silk of his shirt.

'We'll see,' he said carelessly. As if he truly didn't care if she tumbled into his bed one way or the other. As if he knew that she would be helpless to resist him when the time came.

Curbing the urge to take her bag and swing it at his head, Lexie backed away to the door, her blood boiling— and not just from his words and that arrogance. She turned around and was reaching for the doorknob, relishing the prospect of removing herself from his orbit, when he called her name softly.

With the utmost reluctance Lexie gritted her jaw and turned around, keeping her hand on the door. He was still sitting there, eyes hooded, watching her.

'Don't forget…next weekend…Salamanca. That's if you still want us to proceed with *your* suggestion.'

For a second Lexie contemplated the alternative and saw herself pacing up and down the dark *castillo* corridors or in the grounds. Trapped. With the press digging her life up again. Speculating. She went cold at that prospect. There was no choice.

She managed to say icily, 'I won't forget.' And then she pulled the door open and left, with her dignity feeling badly battered.

CHAPTER THREE

WHEN LEXIE GOT to her room she paced. Full of pent-up energy. Hot and then cold at the same time when she reconsidered the equally disturbing prospects of appearing in public *with* Cesar and *not*. And the ramifications of the press's interest in her if that was the case.

There was no doubt about it: appearing with Cesar would be the better scenario. It was only in the last few weeks that the tabloids' interest in *'Luscious Lexie the homewrecker'* had let up. If she was going to become press fodder again so soon, then she would *not* be the victim.

Cesar was unmarried. A bachelor. An affair with him would be old news very fast. And, she realised with some cynicism, it couldn't hurt the film to be linked to this kind of publicity.

What she hadn't counted on was the attraction she felt for Cesar. She'd just kissed him back again, as passionately as she had earlier, with no qualms. No hesitation! It was as if as soon as he touched her some ever-vigilant switch in her brain turned to *off* and she became mute. Acquiescent.

She held out her hands and noted that even now they were trembling slightly. Disgusted, she shoved them under her arms and then spied her electronic tablet. She marched over and opened it up.

She hated herself for it, but she found herself searching for Cesar Da Silva Girlfriend. Predictably not much came up except a few photos of him at events with beautiful women. They were all tall, brunette. Sleek. Classy. One was a UN diplomat. The next an attaché to a world leader. Another was a human rights lawyer.

There were also pictures of Cesar with world leaders at economic summits.

Lexie put a hand to her mouth to stem a slight surge of hysteria. She was seriously out of her depth with this man, and she didn't like her feeling of insecurity when she was faced with the evidence of his previous lovers' undoubted intellectual accomplishments. The plan for them to appear as lovers mocked her now. Who would ever believe he'd choose *her*?

Feeling like a stalker, she looked up his background. To her surprise, a new news article popped up. And a picture of him from earlier that very day, taken at a wedding in Paris. Lexie frowned for a second, wondering how he could have come from Paris back to the *castillo* in such a short space of time—and then she recalled hearing a helicopter earlier. Of course—to a man like Cesar Da Silva travel between European bases was far removed from most people's more tedious, lengthy experiences.

She focused on the short piece again. It had been the wedding of Alexio Christakos and his very pretty bride— someone called Sidonie. The article seemed to be implying that a familial relationship existed between Alexio Christakos and Cesar Da Silva. And also another man: Rafaele Falcone.

Lexie frowned. She knew Christakos and Falcone were half-brothers. They'd been notoriously eligible bachelors before settling down. So…what? Cesar was related to these men? Lexie kept searching and found a very brief reference to his father. Joaquin Da Silva had been famously disinherited from his family after leaving to train as a bullfighter.

He'd achieved some fame early on, before dying tragically in a goring by a bull.

There wasn't much else apart from Cesar's current accomplishments, of which there seemed to be many. He was listed as one of the world's leading philanthropists.

The picture of Cesar at the wedding caught her eye again. She looked more closely. There was a definite resemblance between the two men. And Rafaele Falcone. She couldn't be sure, but it looked as if they all shared varying shades of green eyes. Unusual. *Too* unusual.

A suspicion slid into place inside Lexie. He'd agreed so quickly to appearing in public with her, when all the evidence pointed to a man who would find that kind of exposure anathema. *He wants me.* Lexie shivered at the thought. Was he prepared to court the press's attention just to get her into bed? That idea was both intoxicating and terrifying.

But perhaps Cesar had his own reasons for wanting to divert the press? If something was about to break about his family? She didn't like it, but a feeling of empathy gripped her. And curiosity…

Just then a knock sounded on her door. Lexie's heart jumped. She put the cover over her tablet's screen and went to the door, steeling herself. But when she opened it, it was Tom—the producer. An acute dart of disappointment made her want to scowl.

She forced a smile. 'Tom?'

He held up his own tablet to reveal the same picture of the kiss that Cesar had shown her just a short while before. Her insides tightened again at seeing herself in such an alien and lurid pose.

'Ah…' she said.

'Ah…' the older man echoed. 'I didn't realise you had history with Da Silva. You never mentioned anything…'

'I don't really want to discuss it, Tom, if that's all right.'

'Look,' he said quickly, mollifying her, 'I'm not complaining, Lexie—far from it. This is PR gold dust for the film. *If* you two are…together.'

Tom was obviously concerned that an affair between her and Cesar Da Silva might jeopardise filming if it wasn't all that it seemed. He could throw them off his estate at any moment if he so wished.

Lexie's jaw was tight. She imagined the press furore after they appeared in public next week. 'Yes…' she said reluctantly, as if not even wanting to give the words oxygen. 'We are…together.'

The relief that crossed the producer's face was almost comical. 'Okay, that's good. I mean, like I said, it's gold dust for the film. We could never have generated this much press just by—'

'Tom?' Lexie cut him off, forcing another smile. 'I'd appreciate an early night. I've a lot of prep to do this weekend before we start shooting on Monday.'

He backed away, putting a hand up. 'Of course. I'll leave you to it. Night, Lexie.'

When he was gone she sagged back against the door with relief. Out of the past, the words of her counsellor came back to her: *'Lexie, one day you'll meet someone and you'll feel desire. And you'll feel safe enough to explore it…and heal.'*

Lexie stifled a semi-hysterical giggle. She'd felt it today, all right, but she didn't feel safe right now. She felt in mortal danger. Especially when she thought of those distinctive green eyes and that hard-boned face…and that powerful body. That dark, brooding energy…

She felt anything but safe.

She thought again of Cesar's nonchalant assertion that they would become lovers. A dart of anger gripped her insides. He was obviously used to women falling at his feet if he could make such a declaration. He had no idea of the scars that scored her insides like tattoos. Not visible to the naked eye, but she felt them every day. Scars she'd fought hard to overcome so she could function and live and work.

She resented Cesar Da Silva right then for inserting himself so solidly and irrevocably into her life. And yet she had no one to blame but herself.

Sighing volubly, Lexie pushed off the door and vowed to do whatever it took to focus on the most important thing in her life right now: the job she had to fulfil for the next four weeks. Her *real* acting job, as opposed to the acting she'd be doing in a week's time. Although that filled her with a lot more trepidation because she was afraid that she wouldn't have to act at all.

Midway through the following week Lexie was pacing back and forth on the set while they set up the cameras for a new shot. She was listening to the script on her mp3 player and repeating her lines to herself.

They were shooting not far from the *castillo*, in a walled garden. Inevitably, though, her thoughts deviated yet again to the person who had dominated almost every waking and sleeping moment since she'd met him, in spite of her best efforts.

He'd appeared to watch the filming at various intervals, effortlessly unsettling Lexie in the process. If he was around she became acutely self-conscious. And being dressed in cleavage-revealing nineteenth-century garb didn't help.

Right then, just as she was sighing with relief that he *hadn't* appeared today, he did appear—as if conjured up from her overheated imagination—striding towards her on the narrow path. She had nowhere to go. Trapped. All of the crew were busy working, oblivious to the seismic physical reaction inside Lexie as Cesar bore down on her in a secluded part of the garden.

Her heart sped up. She went hot all over. Pinpricks of sensation moved across her skin. Nipples tightened against her bodice. The corset became even more constrictive. She pulled the long coat she wore to keep warm more closely around her, to try and hide some of her far too buxom cleavage. She took the earphones out of her ears and fought the urge to take several steps back.

Cesar came to a stop in front of her. It didn't help that he was dressed in much the same way as when she'd seen him for the first time, in a close-fitting polo shirt and jodhpurs. Hair mussed. Jaw stubbled. He'd obviously just been riding.

For a bizarre second Lexie actually couldn't speak. His eyes were hypnotic. When *he* spoke, it jarred her out of the daze she was in.

'I've arranged for my assistant to have some clothes delivered to you from a boutique in Salamanca.'

Lexie looked at him blankly. 'Clothes?'

'For the weekend…for future events.'

Suddenly Lexie realised what he meant, and immediately chafed at the implication that he had to buy clothes for her because she wasn't as classy or elegant as his other lovers. And she hated that she'd thought that.

Stiffly she said, 'You really don't need to do that.' Lexie knew she was out of his league; she didn't need a reminder.

Cesar was obdurate. 'Well, it's too late. They've been delivered to your suite.'

Lexie opened her mouth again, but Cesar put up a hand.

'If you don't want to use them, that's fine. See what's there and decide. It's no big deal.'

No, thought Lexie churlishly, because all it had taken was a mere snap of his fingers. She looked at him suspiciously. 'How did you know what size I was?' She immediately regretted asking the question when his gaze swept up and down her body. What he could see of it…

'I asked the costume designer, just to be safe, but my own estimation wasn't far off.'

Lexie burned with indignation and something much hotter to imagine Cesar guessing her vital statistics.

Just then a PA came close and hovered. When Lexie looked at her she made a signal that she was required. Lexie looked back at Cesar and said, with evident relief, 'I have to go. They're ready to shoot again.'

But he didn't get out of the way. And Lexie knew she wasn't supposed to step onto the manicured lawn.

She was about to open her mouth when he moved closer and put a hand around the back of her bare neck, exposed because her hair was up in a complicated chignon. He bent down and pressed a fleeting but hot kiss to her mouth, and then pulled back, letting her go.

Lexie tingled all over. Her head felt fuzzy. 'What was that for?'

Cesar smiled, but it didn't reach his eyes, and Lexie felt something tug inside her, wondering again what he'd look like if he *really* smiled.

'As you so memorably pointed out, there are camera phones around. I'm just being vigilant.'

Lexie flushed to recall what she'd said to him. There was nothing remotely fossil-like about this man. He was all bristling, virile energy.

Faintly she said, 'Celeste will have to retouch my lipstick.'

He smirked. 'Well, you'd better run along and let Celeste do that.'

For a second Lexie blinked at him. There was a tantalising glimmer of something lighter between them. But then he was turning and striding back the way he'd come, and as Lexie walked over to the main hub of the set she couldn't be unaware of several appreciative female *and* male glances that lingered in his direction and then on her with undisguised envy.

Cesar was waiting for Lexie in the main *castillo* drawing room three days later. Looking back on the last tumultuous week, he did not relish the twisting and turning of events since he'd taken one look at that woman and his brains had migrated to his pants.

Cesar was renowned for lots of things: his inestimable wealth; philanthropy; scarily incisive business acumen; a zealous desire for privacy; success. And control. Above all control over his emotions. He'd become a master of controlling them from a young age. Too young.

His usual choice of woman was tall and brunette. Elegant. Classic. Not blonde, petite and curvy, with blue eyes big enough to drown in. And with a dubious reputation splashed across the tabloids.

On some level he'd always sought to stay away from prying eyes, as if somehow they might see something in him that he couldn't articulate himself. A darkness that had clung to him for a long time. The stench of abandonment. The cruelty of neglect and a lack of care. It had been like an invisible stain on his skin.

Yet for someone who had spent his life largely on the periphery of the media glare, largely due to his very *non*-scandalous social life, the prospect of suddenly being thrust front and centre was not having the effect he might have expected.

Of course he didn't relish the idea. But at the same time it didn't fill him with repugnance.

Cesar poured himself a drink and smiled grimly. Right now though, all those concerns were receding and being replaced by something else. Some*one* else. Lexie Anderson. Cesar had been due to go to North Africa that week, to attend a meeting about aid, but had cancelled it on the flimsy pretext of wanting to make sure that the first week of filming went smoothly.

Cesar would be the first to admit that he had dismissed the film industry as flaky and narcissistic, but just one week had proved him wrong. The crew were tireless and worked twelve- and thirteen-hour days—if not longer. He was also surprised by how quickly and well they worked as a cohesive unit.

The producer had explained that most of them had worked together before, but there were lots of inexperienced locals in the mix and Cesar had witnessed more than one incident of a more experienced crew member patiently showing someone the ropes.

Lexie was one of the most tireless. Standing for long minutes on a mark while the lighting crew and cameraman worked around her. Her co-star would invariably go back to his trailer. Cesar had found out that she could have insisted they use a stand-in but had wanted to be there herself. He had to admit that he hadn't really expected her work ethic to be that strong.

She was popular. Especially with the male members of the crew. Cesar was more aware of that than he liked to admit. He'd never been jealous because of a woman before and he didn't welcome jealousy's appearance.

He heard a sound then, and with something whispering over his skin like a warning Cesar took a breath and turned around.

Bombshell. That was the only word that seemed to compute in his head when he saw the woman standing in the doorway. Her effect on him was like a bomb too—exploding out to every extremity and making his flesh surge as blood pumped south.

He took in details, as if he couldn't handle the full reality. Glossy blonde hair, trailing over one shoulder in classic screen siren waves. Pale skin. Slim bare arms. A sleeveless gold lamé dress that fell to the floor in a swirl of glamorous luxury.

She was poured into it, and the material highlighted her curves to almost indecent proportions. The deep, plunging vee of the neckline drew his eye to that abundant cleavage.

She was every inch the glittering movie star. And the most provocatively beautiful woman Cesar had ever seen in his life. He knew that if they hadn't already kissed, if he hadn't already seen her up close, he might have seen her like this and dismissed her as too garish. But right now he could no more dismiss her than recall his own name.

His hands clenched so tightly that he heard a crack, and he looked down stupidly to see his heavy Waterford crystal glass about to break in his hand.

He put it down on the sideboard with a clatter that jarred his ragged and sensitised nerve-endings.

She moved into the room, and the sinuous sway of her hips nearly undid him. Normally he had finesse. He could utter platitudes to women like *You look beautiful*. But right now all he could do was say gruffly, 'My driver is waiting outside—we should go.'

Lexie fought down a betraying quiver of insecurity as she preceded Cesar out of the room, and cursed herself for wanting his reassurance that she looked okay and not too over the top. Her dresses were normally fine—fairly standard designer fare, given to her after photo shoots or premieres—but when she'd compared them to the finery he'd ordered there had been no competition. She'd had to choose one of his.

She had not been prepared for his impact on her in a classic black tuxedo. It was obviously a bespoke suit, moulded to his powerful body in a way that most men's weren't. It should have made him appear civilised. Just like trousers and a shirt should make him look civilised. But the structured clothes only made him seem more raw. Untamed.

His hair was always on the slightly messy side, and Lexie didn't like the way that small detail already felt familiar. But his jaw was clean-shaven, and somehow it gave him a more youthful air.

He took her arm with one big hand and Lexie had to curb her response not to jump. She could feel slightly rough calluses. It made her think of how he'd looked swinging lithely from that huge horse the first time she'd seen him… muscles bunching and quivering. He was no mere soft-palmed money man. The very heart of her feminine core grew hot and damp.

She tried to pull her arm free but his hand was firm. She sent him a sharp glance, irritated at his effect on her, which quickly turned to something else when she saw him gazing at her intently. His hand slid down her arm and took her hand. It was a relatively chaste gesture, and yet it had an almost embarrassing effect on Lexie.

She let herself be led to the exclusive black car and Cesar let her go so she could slide into the back, with the driver holding the door open solicitously.

When he got in on the other side he sent her a look that made Lexie feel utterly exposed. As if he'd been toying with her, taking her hand like that.

Feeling unbearably prickly, Lexie stared out of the window. Anything to escape that dark green mocking gaze.

His voice was cool. 'This was your suggestion, you know. You don't have to look as if you're about to go to the gallows.'

Lexie tensed and felt angry. She turned back to Cesar. 'I don't regret my suggestion for a second. It's still the best option.'

The tinted windows gave the back of the car a disturbingly cocoon-like atmosphere. And since when had the privacy window gone up? Lexie's skin prickled. She could have sworn it had been down when they'd got in. And was it her or had the temperature in the back of the car just shot up by about a thousand degrees?

Cesar was lounging on the other side of the car like a pasha surveying his concubine. She almost wished he was glowering at her, as he had done that first day. She could handle that. She couldn't handle this far more ambiguous energy swirling between them.

Feeling a kind of desperation rising up, she said, 'What happened before…the kissing…it won't happen again.' *So why can't you stop thinking about what it would be like to be kissed again...and more?*

Something in Cesar's eyes flashed, but he said easily, 'We can't stand ten feet apart, Lexie. We'll have to… touch…display moments of affection. Surely it shouldn't be so hard for you to feign besotted devotion?'

That prickliness was lodging in Lexie's gut, and it made her say waspishly, 'Yes, well, I'm not the only one who has to be convincing.'

Before she could react, Cesar had reached for her hand and taken it in a firm grip. Lexie gasped as he brought it to his mouth and kissed her sensitive inner palm. It felt shockingly intimate, and a shard of pure sensation pulled at her belly and groin.

He took his mouth away, eyes glittering fiercely. 'Is that convincing enough for you?'

Lexie knew her eyes were wide, her breathing choppy. He'd just kissed her hand and she was a puddle. *Her hand!* She yanked it away before he could make a complete fool of her.

Cesar saw how Lexie shrank back and everything in him rejected that even as he saw the signs of mutual attraction: the hectic pulse at the base of her neck, flushed cheeks.

Almost accusingly she said, 'You don't look like the type of guy who relishes PDA.'

Cesar bit back the urge to clamp his hands around that tiny waist and haul her into him to show her *exactly* what he thought of PDA. Every time she moved her breasts moved with her, deepening that enticing line of cleavage. But a warning bell went off in his head. She was right, and it irked him that she'd read him so easily.

He *didn't* like public displays of affection *at all*. In fact he really wasn't a tactile person. He usually discouraged his lovers from touching him, preferring to keep their contact confined to the bedroom.

Human touch had been non-existent when he was growing up in the *castillo*. When it had come it had been rough, perfunctory. *Unloving*. A minute shove. A clip around the ear for some transgression. Worse after he'd been caught rolling around in the dirt with Juan Cortez, swinging punches at each other.

If a lover slipped her hand into his, or wound her arm through his, his first instinct was to flinch away. Except right now all he could do was see the wide chasm of distance between him and Lexie in the back of the car and resent it.

Salamanca wasn't far. And it was for *that* reason, Cesar told himself, that he said softly, 'Come closer.'

'*You* come closer,' Lexie responded spikily.

Unbidden, Cesar felt a burgeoning…lightness within him. He even felt a rare smile tip the corners of his mouth.

'I asked first.'

Lexie's expression turned mutinous and had a direct effect on Cesar's already raging blood. Arrowing directly to his groin.

'Lexie,' he growled, 'if you can't bring yourself to move

closer in the back of a car, with no one watching, how do you expect us to convince a wall of paparazzi?'

With palpable reluctance Lexie huffed a sigh and moved across the seat, still keeping a healthy few inches of space between them. Cesar was intrigued. She was spiky, confident. And yet she showed these tantalising glimpses of another side altogether…one less sure of herself.

Her faintly floral scent tickled his nostrils. He fought not to just grab her and haul her onto his lap.

'So, tell me something about yourself…'

'Like what?' Lexie's voice was almost sharp.

Even more intriguing. She was seriously unsettled.

'How did you get started as an actress?'

Lexie glanced at Cesar. The sensation that he was seeing a part of her that no one else cared to observe was acute and uncomfortable. Once again all of her deepest secrets and vulnerabilities felt very close to the surface, as if he might just peel a section of her skin back and see them all laid bare.

Right now, facing a barrage of photographers and pretending to be this man's lover would be infinitely preferable to this intimate cocoon in the back of the car. Then she remembered the awful, excoriating feeling of seeing her life spread across his desk in a series of lurid pictures and she said with faux sweetness, 'You mean you skipped the part about the casting couch in that extensive research file?'

That earned her a twitching muscle in his jaw that distracted Lexie momentarily. His jaw was so hard, so resolute. As if hewn from a lifetime of clenching it.

His voice was equally hard. Clearly he did not welcome her sarcasm. 'I'd like to know how you really got started.'

Lexie's belly dipped ominously and she looked at him suspiciously. He seemed to be genuinely interested. But that reminded her uncomfortably of how she'd once believed someone else had been *genuinely interested.* That experience had left her splashed all over the tabloids, with her reputation ground into the muck. Mocking her for how quickly she'd trusted the first person who had appeared to want to know the real her. After she'd lived a lifetime protecting herself.

The reminder was not welcome now.

In a desperate bid to avoid this, Lexie racked her brain for a pithy and superficial answer. But his gaze was too direct. Too…unforgiving.

'Well,' she started reluctantly, 'I was in a shop one day… I'd just moved to London from Ireland. I was sixteen.'

He frowned. 'You're Irish?'

She nodded, hiding the dart of pain. 'Originally, yes.' When he said nothing more, she continued. 'I was in this shop…and a young kid was in front of me. Suddenly, out of nowhere, the owner accused him of shoplifting—which he hadn't done. So I stepped in and defended him.'

Lexie shuddered slightly when she recalled the oily owner's eyes devouring her overly buxom curves. She'd developed early—another unwelcome reminder right now.

'The next thing I knew,' Lexie went on, eager not to think of that time, 'I was shouting at him. I told the kid to run…and then a woman arrived.' Lexie looked at Cesar, but he was just watching her. She felt silly. 'Look, this is a really boring story…'

'I want to hear it. Go on.'

Lexie glanced away and then looked back after a moment. His gaze was intent. She took a breath. 'The woman had heard me shouting and came to investigate. She stepped in and defused the situation. Afterwards she took me for a coffee. She told me she was a casting director and asked if I'd like to audition for a part in a short film.'

Lexie recalled how bleak those days in London had

been. How alone she'd felt. How impoverished. Vulnerable, but trying to be strong…optimistic…

'So I said yes…and I got a leading role in the film. It was shown in the fringe category at the Cannes Film Festival the following year, and it won an award.' She shrugged one slim shoulder, self-conscious all of a sudden, but determined not to let him see how easily he seemed to be able to unsettle her. 'That's it. That's how I got started. But it was a rocky road… I had an unscrupulous agent for a while… It takes time to realise who has your best interests at heart.'

For a long moment Cesar was silent, and then he said, 'I'd imagine if anyone had tried to lure you onto a casting couch you would have subjected them to the same treatment as that shop owner.'

A dart of unexpected warmth pierced Lexie—and then she thought of the lurid photo shoots she'd done and the warmth fizzled out. 'Unfortunately I wasn't always so sure of what to say no to…'

Something in the air shifted between them. Lexie couldn't look away from Cesar's gaze. It was hypnotic. He seemed a lot closer. For an awful churning moment she wondered if she had moved closer to him without even realising?

'You didn't say no when I kissed you in the stable.' His voice was deep, rough.

Breath was suddenly in very short supply to Lexie's lungs. 'Proof that my track record doesn't appear to be improving with age.'

Her brain was short-circuiting. Was it only a week since she'd first kissed this man? It felt as if aeons had passed. Cesar slid an arm around her waist, pulling her into him. She gasped, filled with a fatal but delicious hot lethargy that urged her not to think. Just to feel. He was going to kiss her, and all Lexie felt was intense anticipation. Her blood was sizzling.

His mouth touched hers. Soft, coaxing. Taking Lexie by surprise. Dismantling any feeble defences she had. His other arm pulled her in even closer and lust exploded deep in her solar plexus.

His mouth was firmer now—insisting, demanding that she respond. As the last shred of trepidation melted away Lexie's mouth opened, and Cesar's attack was brutally sensual and complete. His tongue was stroking hers, sucking it, forcing her to respond.

Without even being aware of it, Lexie touched his jaw, her fingers spreading, threading through his hair, gripping it. Learning the shape of his skull.

One of his hands cupped the weight of her breast and it sent no flares of danger into her brain. Only a desire for *more*. She arched into that hand and heard a low, feral growl of approval.

When his hand left her breast and his mouth left hers she let out a husky breath of disappointment. She opened heavy eyes to see two dark glittering pools of green and black, swirling with depths that reached inside her and tugged hard.

Cesar's fingers slid under the strap of her dress, dislodging it. Her heart-rate accelerated. The first tendrils of panic pierced the haze of heat.

'Cesar… I…'

'Shh…' he said, and that hand was busy peeling down the strap of her dress.

As if knowing just how to subdue those faint tendrils of panic, he kissed her again, pulling her under even more. Making her hot, making her *need*. Making something tight coil inside her until she had to move to try and alleviate it.

When air whistled over the bare slope of her breast Lexie tore her mouth away, breathing hard. Cesar was breathing harshly too. He was looking down, and she followed his gaze to see her breast, its nipple pink and tight and pouting. His hand seemed huge and dark against her pale skin.

'*Dios*...you are truly exquisite.'

His thumb moved back and forth over her nipple, making it pucker, grow harder. She bit her lip to stop from crying out at the exquisite feeling. The tightening sensation deep in her belly was sharper. She could feel wetness between her legs, against her panties.

She couldn't think...couldn't rationalise. She wanted to know how his mouth would feel on her. Tasting her... His tongue... But something was trying to break through. Sense, sanity...self-preservation?

Cesar pulled away from her abruptly, adjusting her dress at the same time, covering her up, and then Lexie heard it: the insistent knocking on the privacy window. A cold wind whistled over her skin.

She felt completely dazed, and could only watch as Cesar, who looked as if nothing had happened, pressed a button and said a few words in Spanish. He turned back to her, but already shame and embarrassment were clawing up inside Lexie.

An insidious image of his usual lovers inserted itself into her brain. She would bet that he didn't subject *those* cool beauties to such sensual attacks in the back of his car.

She pulled the strap of her dress up fully, covering her sensitised breast. Through the window behind Cesar's head she could see people milling, see the flashing pops of cameras. See security people waiting for them to emerge.

Realisation sank into her belly like a cold stone. Of *course* he didn't normally do this. He'd engineered that kiss purely because he'd known exactly how close to Salamanca they were. He'd known they were about to emerge from the car and had wanted to make things look as *authentic* as possible.

She couldn't meet his gaze, and tried to pull away

when his fingers caught her chin. 'What?' she spat out, livid with herself for the dart of hurt that she shouldn't be feeling. 'Do I not appear sufficiently dishevelled to make the paparazzi believe we've been making out like teenagers?'

He flushed angrily. His accent was stronger. 'That was not premeditated, Lexie. But now that you mention it...'

Eyes sparking, Cesar covered her lips with his mouth again and Lexie fought him, closing her mouth. But with expert precision and ruthless intent Cesar proceeded to show her just how pathetic her little outburst had been. Within seconds her mouth was open under his and he was bending her head back with the force of his kiss. And she was matching him, her anger heightening the tension between them.

Cesar was losing it. He knew he was losing it. But he couldn't take his mouth off Lexie's. He'd never tasted anything so sweet. Or so wicked. The way her lush mouth softened under his...the feel of that body under his hands. Her breast...that hard peak under his thumb... He'd wanted to taste it.

Dios.

Cesar finally pulled back, heart hammering. He did *not* ravish women in the back of his car. He was cool, calm, controlled.

Right now he felt anything but. He could hardly see straight. His body was on fire.

Lexie was looking at him with huge bruised eyes. She thought he'd done that on purpose. And he had—but not for the reasons she obviously suspected. He'd wanted to make sure there was no ambiguity about how he felt about her.

He cupped that delicate jaw, a little aghast that his hand shook minutely. Her mouth was pink, swollen. He couldn't help running his thumb across that pouting lower lip, feeling its fleshy softness.

'Make no mistake, Lexie, I want you…and not just to distract the crowds. You know the truth of what I said earlier. We will be lovers for real.'

CHAPTER FOUR

WE WILL BE lovers for real.

Lexie's hand was held tight in Cesar's. She hadn't had time to respond because the driver had opened the car door. And, as much as she wanted to pull free, right now she needed the support. They'd just run the gauntlet of the press outside. Lexie had felt so raw after those kisses that she'd probably looked as green as an *ingenue* at her first premiere.

Cesar had seemed as cool as a cucumber. He'd even rustled up a smile. It was galling. Shouldn't he be the one flinching and snarling?

Lexie finally managed to pull her hand free, once they were in the marble lobby of the very exclusive hotel that was hosting the event.

Cesar frowned. 'Are you all right?'

Lexie wanted to scream. She felt wild, dishevelled. Not herself. 'Not really,' she ground out. 'I need to freshen up before we go in.'

She spotted the powder room and made a beeline for it. Once inside she found it was mercifully empty and she let out a great shuddering sigh of relief. When she looked in the mirror she nearly lost the ability to breathe again.

Her hair was mussed. Cheeks bright pink, mouth swollen. Eyes huge and glittering far too brightly. Lexie pulled tissues out of the box and started to repair the damage.

Damn him. She cursed him roundly. Once again she was floored by how instantaneous his effect on her was and how her body betrayed her every time, jumping gleefully into the fire without any hesitation.

When Lexie was done she surveyed herself again and caught her own eyes in the reflection. There were shadows and secrets in their depths that only she could see. Someone like Cesar could never guess at them. She might be stronger now, but once she'd been utterly broken and had never thought she'd be whole again.

But when Cesar touched her it made her feel whole. It made her forget everything. Forget what had happened to her. There was none of the reflexive instinctive fear that had come when other men had kissed her—even if that had been in the safe environment of a film set.

We will be lovers.

Lexie couldn't seem to stem the tiny flicker of hope inside her. As inconceivable as it seemed…as unsuitable as Cesar Da Silva was…perhaps he was the one who could repair something in her that she had believed destroyed a long time ago? Just allowing that thought to enter her head made Lexie sway on her feet as a giddy mix of excitement and terror rushed up inside her.

There was a knock at the door, and then, 'Lexie, are you okay?'

Lexie's breath jammed in her throat. Her recent thoughts were too nebulous, too scary. She called out threadily, 'I'm fine. I'll be out in a second.'

When she did emerge she didn't like the spurt of emotion at seeing him leaning nonchalantly against a pillar, nor the way his gaze raked her face. He straightened up and just like that her mind started becoming fuzzy again.

She reined herself in with an effort. More people were milling around now, but to Lexie's relief he didn't take her hand again. He put it to her lower back instead, to guide her into the main ballroom where the dinner was being held. His touch burned like a brand through the back of her dress.

Lexie didn't like how aware she was of other women staring at Cesar, of the flurry of whispers that would stop as they grew close only to start up again after they'd passed. It reminded her uncomfortably of what it had been like to walk into a crowded room after the story had broken about her and Jonathan Saunders.

Cesar guided her to a seat and once she was sitting took his own, beside her. He stretched his arm out behind her, and his thumb was rubbing back and forth across the top of her bare back. Lexie almost closed her eyes as her body responded violently: nipples peaking, belly softening, warmth pooling and spreading.

His voice came close to her ear. Too close. 'Relax. You look as if you're about to shatter into pieces.'

Lexie opened her eyes and turned her head, and Cesar's face was so close she could see the darker flecks of green in his eyes. Green on green—an ocean. She had the bizarre urge to reach up and touch his face, and had to curl her hand into a fist to stop herself.

The line of his cheek was a blade, giving his features that edgy saturnine impression. Something came over her—perhaps the knowledge that she could touch him in public as it would be expected. She lifted her hand and touched his jaw. She felt it clench under her hand and looked at him. His eyes had darkened and something hard shone through their depths. Cynicism.

It made her snatch her hand back. But not before he caught it with lightning swiftness and captured it, pressing an open-mouthed kiss to the skin just as he had in the car. It was no less devastating this time.

'You are quite the actress…'

Before Lexie could respond with some acid retort that

might deflect from the fact that a scary poignancy had gripped her on seeing that cynicism, a menu was being handed to her by a waiter and she had to accept it. There was no room for poignancy; she didn't care if Cesar was cynical.

Lexie stared at the menu blankly for a moment as she regained her composure. Damn the man. *Again.*

But of course the menu still remained largely incomprehensible to her. Another kind of dismay filled her—especially when she was so keyed up. She didn't need this particular vulnerability right now.

'It helps if you turn the menu the right way up.'

His voice was low and gently mocking. Lexie's hands tightened on the thick vellum as embarrassment washed through her in waves, making her hot. She sent a glare to Cesar, who had that tantalising smile playing around his mouth again.

She turned the menu around but of course that made no difference. She could see the waiters taking orders now and started to panic. With the utmost reluctance she said to Cesar, in a low voice, 'What would you recommend?'

He glanced at her for a moment and then perused his own menu and said, 'Personally I'd recommend the quail starter—'

'Quail?' Lexie asked, feeling ill at the thought.

Cesar looked at her. 'Well, there's a brie starter too.'

'I'll have that,' Lexie said with relief.

Cesar glanced back at the menu. 'Then there's a choice of salmon risotto, beef carpaccio...'

'The beef,' Lexie said, too ashamed to look at Cesar. Especially when she thought of his multi-lingual lovers who would be well used to these situations.

He said from beside her, 'Not everyone is used to menus in French—it's nothing to be embarrassed about.'

Lexie's own mortification made her lash out. 'Don't patronise me, Cesar. I'm not stupid, I'm just—'

But before she could finish a waiter had arrived and Cesar was ordering for both of them. Lexie clamped her mouth shut. Did she *have* to let every tiny detail of her life out whenever she opened her mouth?

When the waiter moved on Cesar's attention was taken by someone sitting to his left, and Lexie was facing a table full of people looking at her with varying degrees of curiosity.

To her immediate right was an older woman who leaned into Lexie and said in an American accent, 'My dear, you've quite set the cat among the pigeons, arriving with one of the most eligible bachelors in the world.'

Lexie smiled weakly. To her relief, she discovered that the woman was as charming as she was obviously eccentric and rich, and she regaled Lexie with stories of her expat life in Spain.

Relieved to have an excuse to avoid that green-eyed scrutiny, Lexie conversed enthusiastically with the woman.

Cesar willed himself to relax for the umpteenth time. The food had been served and eaten. Lexie had managed to spend most if not all that time ignoring him. It was unprecedented. He'd never had this experience with a woman before. And certainly not with one he'd kissed.

When he'd noticed her struggling with the menu, and that she'd had it upside down, a lurch of emotion had tightened his gut. He remembered her story about how she'd got started in the industry, leaving home so young, and presumably leaving school. She hadn't gone to university. She obviously wasn't as sophisticated as the women he was used to. And yet there was something refreshing about that.

Just before they'd been interrupted she'd said angrily, *'I'm not stupid.'* But that was one thing that had never come into his mind. Lexie Anderson had more intelligence sparking out of those blue eyes than he'd ever seen in his life.

With some of his previous lovers Cesar had found himself calling things off purely because of mental exhaustion. It was as if they felt they had to prove to him what worthy candidates they were by conversing in three languages at once, about complicated political systems that he had no interest in. And in the bedroom more than one had been keen to initiate kinky scenarios that had felt anything but sexy.

But with Lexie…every time he looked at her he felt kinky. He wanted to tie her down to some flat soft surface and ravish her.

Perhaps it was due to the fact that when they'd stepped out of the car earlier, to face the press, his body had still been humming with an overload of sexual frustration, but the experience hadn't been half as painful as he'd imagined. Having Lexie by his side had seemed to mitigate his usual excoriating feeling that the lenses of the paparazzi had some kind of X-ray vision.

When he saw her dining companion get up to leave the table he felt a rush of satisfaction. Now she would have to turn back to *him*. Cesar wasn't unaware of the looks she'd been drawing all evening in that provocative dress. She outshone every other woman. Literally. Cesar couldn't even recall seeing another woman. It was as if she'd blinded him. *With lust.*

He didn't like the hot spokes of anger that lanced him every time he caught some man's gaze sliding to her abundant curves.

Lexie could sense Cesar beside her. Waiting… Mrs Carmichael had gone to the bathroom and she was ready for his gaze to be censorious for having avoided him so obviously.

Taking a breath, she turned back—and just like that a jolt of pure electricity shot through her belly. Cesar had his hand on the back of her chair again, far too close for comfort. He'd taken off his jacket and his shirt was pulled taut across his chest, doing little to hide that stunning musculature.

He spoke. 'What I said earlier…before you turned your back on me so comprehensively…'

Lexie flushed and was about to remonstrate, but she knew she couldn't. She felt like a child.

'Mrs Carmichael was interesting,' she supplied a touch defensively.

'I know Mrs Carmichael very well and she *is* interesting.' His lip curled slightly. 'About the most interesting person here.'

Lexie glanced around at the very important-looking men and women. 'But aren't these your friends?'

Cesar all but snorted, surprising Lexie.

'They pretend to be my friends because I come and bid an obscene amount of money at their auction and then go. The only reason I do it is because I believe in this particular charity and because the money goes directly to the source, rather than via a dozen government agencies.'

'Oh,' Lexie answered, a little taken aback at Cesar's words.

She'd have put him in the same category as many rich people who contributed to charity for far too cynical reasons. But this *was* a worthy charity; it was aimed at combatting sex trafficking—a cause close to Lexie's own heart. She knew it was not one that was especially 'trendy' in the media, so the fact that Cesar was endorsing it had to help.

'Mrs Carmichael told me about it.'

Cesar picked up a card with his free hand and held it out to her. 'Here's a list of items to be auctioned—see if anything takes your fancy.'

His insouciance and his air of almost bored expectation that she would expect to be indulged made Lexie feel bizarrely disappointed. Then the fact that she couldn't *read* the card sent a spurt of anger up her spine. Something bitter gripped her.

She whispered angrily, 'I might not be as intellectual as your usual lovers, Cesar, but you really don't have to treat me like some kind of bimbo just because I'm blonde and—'

'That's enough.' Cesar straightened up, his hand tensing across the back of her chair, his fingers touching her neck in a very light but subtle admonishment.

She tensed against her inevitable reaction and could have laughed. To all the world they must look besotted. Close together, staring at each other, intent…

She could see in his face that he was surprised at her response. She moved, dislodging his hand slightly. 'I'm sorry. I overreacted.'

Cesar grimaced faintly. 'I didn't mean for it to sound so dismissive or flippant.'

Lexie was once again taken aback by his ability to apologise. Slightly mollified, she said, 'Maybe I'll want to bid on something myself?'

To give Cesar his due, he didn't laugh before he said, 'Do you know how much the cheapest item is marked at?'

Lexie shook her head. He glanced down and then looked back up, naming a price. She paled and said faintly, 'I guess I won't be bidding, then.'

Cesar handed her the card and Lexie took it. She should really tell him—especially if he was going to have her so on edge—that even reading a menu would be a challenge for her.

'About the menu earlier…I should explain—'

'No.' He shook his head. 'I didn't mean to imply for a second that you're stupid.'

Now Lexie shook her head, regretting her defensive response. 'The reason I wasn't reading the menu very well was because I'm severely dyslexic.'

Lexie could feel her insides contracting, as if she were waiting for a look of disdain in Cesar's eyes. She'd seen it before.

But that didn't happen. He just said, 'And…?'

Lexie blanched. 'And…I can read perfectly well, but if I'm stressed…or under pressure…it becomes nearly impossible. I just need time.'

Cesar moved closer, his fingers whispering over her skin, under her hair. Lexie repressed a shiver of sensation.

'And are you?' he asked. 'Stressed? Under pressure?'

She wondered how it would be if she told him about the severe pressure and stress she felt under right now, with her body sparking and firing on levels she'd never even been aware of before.

Instead she said dryly, 'A little.'

He moved back slightly. 'You should have told me. A good friend of mine is dyslexic and he uses special software to help him. I'm sure I don't need to tell you of the renowned geniuses who had dyslexia but didn't let it hold them back.'

'Of course you don't,' Lexie said, almost feeling cross that Cesar was the one defending dyslexia and not her! 'I go to some of my local schools in London and talk to the kids about it—help them see that it won't limit them.'

He frowned, 'How do you manage with the scripts for your films?'

Lexie fiddled with her napkin self-consciously. 'I usually get an actor friend of mine to read them out. I record them, then I transfer them to my mp3 player…'

Someone sounded a gavel just then, and Lexie looked away with an effort. She was so engrossed in *him*. But people were sitting down again and she was glad of the interruption.

Not that long ago another man had duped her into thinking he was interested in her and she'd almost fallen for it. Now Cesar was coming perilously close to making her believe that *he* was interested but she knew that it was just lust. The spike of excitement in her gut was shameful, but she couldn't ignore it.

Cesar's attention had turned to the front. And then Lexie found herself distracted as with admirable nonchalance he made bids on the most expensive lots, only to get an assurance from the auctioneer that the lots he'd bought would be raffled for free at the charity for its workers.

When it was over, and Cesar had spent more money than Lexie had ever heard of, he turned to her and said brusquely, 'Are you ready to go?'

She nodded, too intimidated by what she'd seen to say a word. Lexie could see all the sycophants vying for his attention as they left, but he didn't stop for anyone, his hand on her back again.

His car and driver were waiting outside, as if psychically informed of his departure, but Lexie knew it must have been a series of frantic Chinese whispers from the staff, who had been watching his every move like a hawk.

Once they were in the back of the car, the darkness closed around them like a blanket, cutting out sounds, cutting out reality. It made Lexie exceedingly nervous and she scooted right over to her side of the car. The thought of Cesar kissing her again in this seductive gloom was far too scary to contemplate, even if the thought of his words *we will be lovers* tantalised her more than she cared to admit.

Through the tinted windows Lexie could see the lights of Salamanca glittering. It distracted her. She said on an awed breath, 'It's so beautiful…'

After a moment Lexie head Cesar say something to his driver in the front and then the car was turning around.

She looked at Cesar. 'Wait…what are you doing?'

A little gruffly he said, 'You should see the Plaza Mayor at night when it's lit up.'

After watching how generous he'd been to the charity, Lexie was mortified to think that he might feel the need to act as tour guide. 'It's fine,' she protested. 'I can come back again some evening.'

He ignored that and asked, 'Are you hungry for something sweet?'

Lexie blinked in the gloom. She hadn't had dessert. How did the man know she had a sweet tooth?

'A little…maybe…but really we don't—'

He cut her off. 'I know a place. We'll go there.'

The car parked on a street where couples strolled arm in arm. Cesar got out, and by the time Lexie had her door open he was standing waiting, holding out a hand for her to take. Muttering her thanks, she let him help her.

The early autumn air had a slight nip, and before Lexie could say anything she felt Cesar's dinner jacket being settled around her shoulders. His warmth and scent surrounded her like an intoxicating cloak.

When he took her hand Lexie had to battle the urge to pull it free again. The truth was she liked the way it felt to have her hand in his. She glanced up at Cesar and saw that his bow-tie was gone and the top button of his shirt was open. It made him appear rakish.

Lexie was attracting attention in her long gold dress. 'Do you think the photographers will be around here?'

Cesar looked down at her. 'They could be—they saw us leave.'

They rounded a corner then, and Lexie's mind blanked at the beauty before them. Salamanca's famous Plaza Mayor was lit up in golden lights. They spilled from everywhere and illuminated the huge ancient buildings. It was like the inside of a magical golden ornament. Lexie had known the old part of the city was a UNESCO heritage protected site and now she knew why. The square was huge…awe-inspiring.

Cesar led her across the airy space and she felt tiny in the midst of the baroque grandeur. When she was able to stop looking up and gaping at the beautifully ornate buildings, she saw that they'd stopped outside one of the cafés which was still open.

A small old man came rushing out, welcoming Cesar effusively and offering them a table under one of the massive arches that lined the square. They sat down. Lexie was relieved and disappointed in equal measure to get her hand back.

Cesar asked, 'What kind of dessert do you like?'

Feeling very bemused at being here with him, Lexie said, 'Anything…cakes…pastries.'

He arched a brow. 'Coffee?'

She nodded. 'Yes, please.'

Cesar said a few words to the proprietor, who looked as if he was about to burst with pride at having such an esteemed guest—clearly he knew who Cesar was.

A few people lingered over coffee, glasses of wine. Cesar's jacket swam on Lexie, but his warmth still tantalised her skin. It was incredibly seductive.

The owner bustled back out, with another young man following him. They set down coffee and a tray of different desserts. Lexie's mouth watered. When they'd left, Cesar explained what they were. There was an almond sponge cake, candied almonds, small fritters filled with cream, sweet puff pastry, small chocolate cakes…

Lexie groaned after she'd tasted some of the delicious pastry. 'If only I didn't have to worry about getting back into that corset in a couple of days.'

Cesar paused in the act of drinking his coffee and looked at her. Lexie looked back. The air between them sizzled. That moment in the back of the car earlier invaded her head like a lurid B movie.

He put his cup down. 'When I saw you for the first time I thought you were some kind of an apparition. That you weren't real.'

Lexie swallowed her dessert with difficulty. She remembered the transfixed expression on his face that day. She'd never forget it. While she hadn't thought he was an apparition, she'd felt something similar.

'I knew you were real...' she admitted. 'But I know what you mean. I wasn't meant to be there.'

Cesar grimaced. 'I was harsh on you.'

Lexie glanced down at her coffee and shrugged. 'Your privacy had been comprehensively invaded by hundreds of strangers...'

'I'd also just returned from my half-brother's wedding in Paris.'

He sounded so grim that Lexie looked up again. She recalled seeing the pictures on the internet of that wedding, the speculation.

Her curiosity piqued, she asked, 'So you *are* related, then?'

He frowned. 'Why do you ask?'

Lexie flushed, feeling like a stalker. 'I saw something on the internet when I went looking to see if there were any more pictures...of us.' It wasn't entirely untrue, she reassured herself.

Cesar's face was hard. 'Yes, it's true. He and Rafaele Falcone are my half-brothers.'

Lexie had the sense she was entering into a minefield. 'But this wasn't common knowledge?'

Cesar took a swift sip of his coffee and shook his head, putting the cup back down with a clatter. He was so tense all of a sudden that Lexie half expected him to jump up and stride away. But he didn't. Although for the first time his gaze was avoiding hers.

'We had the same mother but different fathers.'

'You didn't know them growing up?'

He shook his head and then speared her with a look that she couldn't read.

'No. I just knew of them. My mother was more interested in a life of opulence and luxury to think about cosy reunions, or to worry about the fact that she'd abandoned her eldest son.'

A multitude of questions hit Lexie. Why had his mother left him? But then that very first niggle of suspicion she'd had came back. 'Does that have anything to do with... *this*?' she asked carefully.

Cesar frowned. 'What do you mean?'

Lexie wasn't even sure herself. She only knew that she was feeling increasingly exposed on a level she didn't welcome.

'I mean, does the fact that it's come out about your brothers have anything to do with the fact that you were happy to agree for us to be seen together in public?'

His mouth tightened. 'I will admit that I saw an advantage in allowing another story to take precedence.'

Lexie had suspected that this might be a possibility. So why was a feeling of hurt blooming deep inside? A snide voice answered her—because she'd been seduced by his touch and his words into thinking his desire for her was his only motivation.

Of course someone like Cesar Da Silva would normally prefer to keep her tucked away out of sight, so that he could make it look as if that first kiss had been some crazy brief aberration. It had been his initial reaction.

Why hadn't she even questioned it properly at the time? His ready compliance? Because he'd turned her brain to mush exactly at the same time as he'd turned her insides molten.

She thought of the bathroom earlier—when she'd entertained the notion of their becoming lovers for a moment. The dizzying rush of exhilaration that had gripped her. *God*, she'd been so easily caught.

Lexie looked away from him and blindly picked up her cup again, not even noticing when some coffee sloshed over the rim to fall on her dress. Suddenly she couldn't stand it—being under his cool assessing scrutiny.

Almost knocking the small table over with her jerkiness, she stood up, any inherent ability to act deserting her. 'Would you mind if we left now? I'm quite tired…it's been a long week.'

She whirled away from the table and started to walk. Agitation was rising up from her gullet and also a kind of panic. Panic that she'd not thought more clearly that *obviously* he'd have an ulterior motive for wanting to be seen in public with her. He'd just been toying with her, while she'd been perilously close to proving how easily duped she could be—*again*.

She vaguely heard a muttered curse and some change being thrown on the table and just when she'd reached the middle of the golden square which by now was almost empty, her arm was caught in a big hand. She was spun around to face a familiar glowering expression. She welcomed it.

'What the hell was that about, Lexie?'

She wrenched her arm out of Cesar's grip, dislodging his coat from her shoulders. It fell to the ground, unnoticed by either of them. Words trembled on her lips, but if she uttered them she only risked exposing herself even more.

His lip curled. 'You find the fact that I have my own reasons to avoid the press digging into my life unpalatable?

That I was left behind like some unwanted luggage, with half-siblings who never even knew I existed?'

'What?' Lexie said, his words shocking her out of her own turmoil for a moment. 'No! Of course not... I didn't even know anything about your family.'

Cesar's mouth was tight. 'My mother hoped to get a good deal by bringing me back to the family home, but she hadn't banked on my grandparents giving her an ultimatum: just me or neither of us. So she left me behind.'

Lexie's agitation drained away. She put out a hand, 'Cesar...I had no idea.'

He stepped back. The huge magnificent square seemed to frame him in a leonine glow, making his masculinity even more impressive.

'That's what is about to hit the papers any day now. The full lurid story of Esperanza Christakos—née Falcone, née Da Silva—her rise from poverty to incalculable wealth and fame. And the gory details of the son she abandoned.'

Even as his words touched a painful nerve within Lexie she let out a tiny gasp of recognition at the name. She'd never put two and two together and realised that the world-famous beauty had been related to his brothers—*or him*.

She shook her head. 'I didn't know anything about her.'

Cesar, clearly angry at himself for letting all that spill out, said curtly, 'Well, *what*, then? If not that?'

Lexie's equilibrium was all over the place again. How could she articulate the fact that she was hurt because he evidently hadn't been motivated to appear with her in public simply out of sheer desire? When all along she'd protested vehemently at his arrogant assertion that they'd become lovers even as she'd pathetically melted whenever he touched her. And yet now that he clearly had another motivation it only highlighted her inner confusion and the tumultuous desires he evoked within her.

She searched his face for any hint of softness. But found

none. She realised then just how truly hard he was, and couldn't stop the tug of emotion at imagining a small child being left in that huge grim *castillo* without his mother.

Racking her brain for a way not to betray herself, she avoided his question and said weakly, 'We don't have to do this…if you don't want to.'

Right now even the prospect of staying in the *castillo* to avoid the press was more appealing than the thought of exposing herself like this again.

Cesar moved closer. His face wasn't so hard now. There was an explicit gleam in his eye that had a direct effect on Lexie's blood.

She spoke quickly, to hide her frayed nerves. 'Maybe this isn't such a good idea. If we stop now we can make it look like it was just a brief…fling.'

Cesar shook his head and said in that deep voice, 'We've gone too far to turn back now.'

Lexie's heart thumped hard. Her mouth dried. Treacherously, she didn't feel inclined to argue.

He said then, 'We both have our reasons for doing this, Lexie…and we're adults. This happened in the first place because we took one look at each other and couldn't keep our hands off each other.'

She thought of what he'd told her about his half-brothers. About his desire to avoid press intrusion around what was obviously a tender subject. Even though she didn't know the full story it resonated within her. She too had secrets to keep—dark ones. She found herself feeling a dangerous kinship with him. They were in this together.

He was sliding his hands and arms around her waist now, tugging her unresisting her body into his. All Lexie could feel was steel. Warmth and steel.

She put her hands on his chest. The moment felt slightly unreal. They were surrounded by the golden shimmering lights of the square.

Lexie's recent feelings of exposure and vulnerability were nowhere to be felt when Cesar's mouth touched hers. And they were certainly nowhere to be found in the almost shameless way she responded so quickly—opening her mouth, inviting him in, arching closer, demanding more.

There was a flash from nearby and it made her jerk in Cesar's arms. He pulled back, cursing. A photographer was feet away, snapping them. She felt Cesar tense but he made no move to stop the photographer, who was already walking away, checking his digital images.

Cesar turned back to Lexie and there was a distinctly satisfied gleam in his eyes. 'There goes any chance to protest that this was just a brief fling.' The satisfied gleam became something else—*hotter*. 'Whatever our reasons were, it's about *us* now. I want you. And you want me. It's that simple.'

CHAPTER FIVE

ABOUT AN HOUR later Lexie lay in bed with his words reverberating in her head. After that moment in the middle of that beautiful square Cesar had said nothing else. He'd just taken her by the hand and led her back to the car.

They'd remained in silence for the journey, as if both contemplating what lay ahead. Lexie's mind had been slightly numb, though. Too full to be able to tease out the different strands.

When they'd returned to the *castillo* the dour housekeeper had met them and told Cesar that he had some phone calls he must return. Lexie had welcomed the chance to escape, pleading tiredness, but she hadn't missed the intensity of Cesar's expression as he'd bade her goodnight. It had set a fire alight deep in her belly.

She could feel it now. As if she'd been awoken on some deep level. This hadn't happened with Jonathan Saunders, her *alleged* married lover... He'd appealed to an altogether less visceral side of her. Perhaps he'd appealed to the part of her that had finally been ready to trust again and she'd just chosen unwisely.

Suddenly that revelation made her heart beat fast. Perhaps she hadn't lost it completely. Perhaps she was still in control. This was totally different from what had happened before. There was no hint of scandal.

Cesar had not touched her innermost feelings and secrets. *He hadn't,* she told herself fiercely in the dark. He'd kissed her and she'd come alive. That was all. It was *physical*. And if anyone was long overdue their awakening it was her. She'd just got a little confused for a moment. Confused lust with feelings. Cesar was offering her a chance to explore this sexual attraction. And she realised with an almost desperate feeling that she wanted to. With *this* man.

What he'd revealed about his brothers and mother struck her again. That feeling of empathy. She knew exactly what it was like to want to avoid scrutiny of your most private self.

Cesar was a cynical being. It oozed from every part of him. Cynical and dark... She could appreciate why now. Lexie was cynical too—it had been branded onto her at an early age when she'd come face to face with the harshest side of life.

She'd prided herself on cultivating a sense of optimism over the years, but she knew that cynical shell hadn't really worn away completely. She could be as cynical as him now. More so. She had infinitely more to gain from this than he could ever realise.

And when the time came to walk away Cesar could go back to his classically coiffed intellectual lovers and Lexie would have achieved a personal emancipation she'd only ever dreamed about.

It was that simple.

'Thanks for a great day, everyone, that's a wrap.'

Lexie let out a sigh of relief. They'd finished shooting their scenes in the walled garden and would be moving further into the *castillo* estate for the rest of the week.

Cesar had been absent from the set all day, and Lexie had been glad of the space to try and get her bearings and remember that she was here to work. But her assertion to herself that she'd been glad of the space mocked her.

She hadn't seen Cesar since Saturday night, when he'd left her hot and bothered with that look. She'd felt so antsy on Sunday that she'd gone out for a long walk around the estate—and still no sign of Cesar.

After coming to the momentous personal decision that she would embark on an affair with him, she felt suddenly deflated now he'd disappeared into thin air. Without his unerring ability to distract her, and hypnotise her with his charisma and intensity, Lexie felt vulnerable.

She cursed herself for those weak feelings as she scrubbed her face clean in the empty make-up truck. It took her so long to get out of her costume that the base was usually quiet when she left. Only the wardrobe crew were still there, and the facility men who looked after the trailers. And the second assistant director, whose job it was to make sure Lexie was everywhere she needed to be and on time.

Lexie called goodnight and made her way back to the *castillo*. She didn't like the frisson of loneliness that assailed her and scowled at herself.

She was still scowling when she entered the *castillo* and ran straight into a wall. Except this wall was warm and it had hands that came around her arms, steadying her.

The singing rush of warmth and excitement made her scowl even more as she looked up into the elusive Cesar Da Silva's face. Damn him.

'I was just coming to find you.'

'Well, as you can see I'm here,' Lexie said testily, irritated at being irritated.

Cesar whistled softly. 'Bad day at the office, dear?'

His unexpected dry humour sparked something inside Lexie, but she pulled free of his hands before he could see it. She didn't want him to be flirty or endearing.

'I'm sorry,' she blurted out, avoiding his eye. 'It has been a long day.' *Liar,* her conscience mocked her.

She felt self-conscious in comfy leggings and a loose shirt. Face clean, hair pulled back into a messy knot. For all she knew he might have been wining and dining some dark beauty last night…

Cesar cut through her feverish thoughts.

'Those phone calls the other night…one of them resulted in me having to attend an urgent meeting in Paris early this morning, so I left yesterday.'

Lexie fought to repress the crazy lurch of relief. She shrugged a shoulder minutely and said airily, 'Really? I didn't notice.'

Cesar came close and tipped Lexie's jaw up so she had to look at him. She hated being small right now. If she'd been taller she could have eyeballed Cesar.

'Liar,' he said softly. 'Because I was aware of every minute I was away from this place.'

His words made air whoosh out of Lexie's lungs. An instantaneous bubble of lightness infused her blood. She couldn't help a rueful smile. 'Well, your meeting can't have been very exciting.'

Cesar shook his head. 'It was deadly dull.'

The air sizzled between them. And just like that all of Lexie's doubts and fears melted away again. His effect on her was ridiculous. But she couldn't resist.

He took his hand away. 'We hit the papers today…I thought you'd want to see.'

Lexie fought not to let him see how much he affected her. 'Of course.'

He stepped back. 'We can go to my apartment—it's more private.'

Lexie looked at him as he started to walk away. 'Your apartment?'

She walked quickly to keep up with him. He glanced at her and then took her hand, setting off a million butterflies.

'I have my own apartment here within the *castillo*.'

Curious as to what it might be like, in such a mausoleum of a castle, Lexie followed him down a warren of corridors, passing the study where she'd had that first cataclysmic conversation with him.

He stopped outside a door that had a keypad lock and entered a code. The door swung open. As he walked in and Lexie followed, her hand still in his, her jaw dropped. It was like stepping into another world.

The apartment was huge, cavernous. Like stepping into Narnia from behind the coats in the wardrobe. One side was dominated by a massive wall of windows. On the other side was a modern state-of-the-art kitchen. Steel and chrome with industrial lights.

The floor was wooden—parquet, like his office—and strewn with huge oriental rugs, softening it. One corner of the room was filled with three old battered leather couches and a low coffee table. A TV and music system. Along that wall was nothing but shelves and books—rows and rows of books.

Lexie felt that pang again. She loved books and reading, but for her it was a torturous process. Remembering how Cesar had responded to her dyslexia made her melt a little more.

'I have an office through here.'

As Lexie followed Cesar she saw another door, and glanced in as they passed to see a huge bedroom with a massive bed, sheets tangled on top. The image was incendiary and unbelievably intimate. She felt herself blushing. Would she be in that bed with him soon? Limbs entwined?

Her face was burning when he let her hand go inside the office. She was glad the lighting was dim and looked around. This was obviously a private study. Not as imposing as his other one, but somewhere he obviously spent a lot of time. Books were strewn around…papers. It was lived in. Comfortable. Messier than she would have imagined for someone who seemed so controlled.

He had some newspapers on the desk and turned one around to face her. Carefully keeping her expression neutral, she read the headline.

Hot! Hot! Hot! Luscious Lexie bags the world's most reclusive bachelor and richest man!

It was more or less what she had expected, but still a blow to her gut. She couldn't take her eyes off the pictures. One was of them arriving at the function the other night, her hand in his. She was practically welded to his body. She hadn't even realised that she'd been stuck to him like that. Her eyes were huge. Like a deer in headlights. Pathetic.

Another showed his head bending to hers. She couldn't remember what he'd said—something about going inside after another minute. But it looked as if he was whispering a sweet nothing. Her face was turned to his.

And one last one was a shot from inside the hotel; it must have been taken by a guest or a waiter on a camera phone. They were at the table, his arm around the back of her chair, heads close together.

Lexie felt horribly exposed, even though she was used to seeing her picture in the papers by now. But not like this. These showed just how enticing and fascinating she found this dark and difficult man. She was relieved that there didn't seem to be any pictures from the square. Even now those moments felt raw.

Cesar was perched on the edge of his desk, one powerful thigh in her eyeline, distracting her.

His voice sounding far too smug, he said, 'They look convincing…although you'd be more used to this sort of thing than me.'

Feeling prickly at his tone—obviously the experience

had been far more cataclysmic for her—and hating that he evidently believed in her guilt, Lexie stepped back and blurted out, 'I had nothing to do with ending up in the tabloids with that man.'

Cesar frowned. 'What do you mean?'

Lexie started to pace, agitated. Dammit, she didn't have to explain herself to this man. But…treacherously…she wanted to. Even if Cesar wasn't really interested.

She stopped pacing and faced him, crossing her arms in a classic defence pose. 'I didn't have an affair with that man.'

His eyes narrowed on her. 'So how did it come about?'

'Jonathan Saunders…' Lexie stopped for a moment. Even saying his name made her angry. 'We'd just done a small West End play together for a few weeks. I'd worked with him years before on my very first short film. He'd been nice to me at the time—kind of like a mentor. I considered us friends… During the play he made a point of hanging out with me. Making sure I got home okay. Stuff like that.'

Lexie felt queasy to think that his easy affection and hands-off attention had sneaked under her skin so that she'd believed she could trust him. And even though she hadn't really felt anything for him physically, she'd believed him to be a genuine friend. She'd been susceptible enough to consider that if he made a physical move she'd give him a chance. The thought made her skin crawl now.

'After we'd finished the play he called around one day and he was in a state, saying he needed somewhere to stay. He had some story about being chucked out of his house because he couldn't afford to pay the rent. I knew he wasn't that successful as an actor—it seemed believable. I had a spare room so I offered it to him and he moved in for about a week.'

'Did you sleep with him?'

Cesar's voice was sharp and Lexie glared at him, annoyed with herself for even bringing it up. It was only exposing her even more.

'I told you I didn't have an affair with him.'

'So what happened?'

'He left early one morning, and I only found out because there was banging on the door. I'd been asleep. I figured it was him—that he'd left something behind—he'd started rehearsals for a new play. I was half asleep, and when I opened the door the street was full of photographers.'

Lexie's face burned.

'I was dressed in night clothes…barely awake… I discovered later that Jonathan was actually married and had had a huge row with his wife because she'd found out he was having an affair and that his girlfriend was pregnant.'

Her mouth went tight.

'He'd known it was coming, because he'd been tipped off by his lover that the press suspected something, so he cultivated me. Made friends. Got me to trust him so that he could use me to be the fall guy when he wanted to protect his *real* girlfriend. He was terrified they'd track her down.'

Lexie sighed.

'His lover was the wife of a prominent Conservative cabinet minister; she wanted to avoid scandal at all costs. He figured *I* was a better prospect to throw to the ravenous press and he set me up well—living with me for a week, letting them believe we'd moved in together.'

Lexie looked at Cesar.

'I hadn't even known he was married. He'd said nothing at all about his wife. Or kids.'

'Why didn't you defend yourself once you knew the truth?'

Because she hadn't wanted to give the press any excuse to look into her background in case of what they might find.

A feeling of *déja vu* struck her. Here she was again, feeling the urge to *trust*, to believe. But if the last few minutes of rehashing the events of that unfortunate period told her anything it was that she couldn't trust. Not really. So she shrugged minutely. 'I didn't want to add fuel to the fire…attract even more attention. And I felt sorry for his wife and kids.'

She avoided his gaze. At least that was part of the truth.

There was something achingly vulnerable about Lexie as she stood in front of Cesar with her arms crossed so tight. He might have told himself before that he couldn't care less what she'd done, but right now he did care. And the fact that she hadn't slept with that guy made a tightness ease in him. Even as he wanted to find him and punch him. And that surprised him. Women didn't arouse feelings of protectiveness within him, a desire to avenge them. He shouldn't care.

A second too late Cesar saw that her eye had caught one of the other newspapers that had been delivered. A different headline: *Cesar Da Silva's long-lost family!*

Before he could stop her she'd reached out to pull the paper free. On the cover were recent photographs of all three men: Cesar, Rafaele and Alexio. And another of their beautiful mother. Shining out from all four photos was the undeniable genetic link of their green eyes.

Cesar stood up. Tense.

Lexie said slowly, 'That's where your green eyes come from. She was very beautiful, your mother.'

'Yes, she was,' Cesar said tightly, his skin prickling at having Lexie looking at the blatant evidence of his mother's lack of love for him. It made him feel raw again when he thought of the other night—how Lexie had all but run from the table in the square. When his irrational feeling had been that she'd seen the darkness in his soul and was repulsed by it.

Lexie gazed at him now and all he could see were those blue eyes. Something in him tightened when he saw the compassion in their depths, but it didn't make him want to run.

'Well,' she said a little awkwardly, dropping the paper down, 'I should go. I have an early start again tomorrow.'

When she turned to leave Cesar rejected it with every fibre of his being. 'Wait.'

He reached out and put his hands on her elbows, pulled her into him until their bodies were flush. The palms of her hands landed on his chest and his entire body thrummed with need.

His eyes roved over her face, as if learning every tiny detail.

'*Dios,*' he muttered. 'You are so beautiful.'

Lexie tried to duck her face. 'I'm not.'

'You are…' Cesar's ferocity made her look up. '…stunning. And I want you more than I've ever wanted anyone.'

Lexie felt the excitement in her blood obliterating the scary empathy that had come as soon as she'd seen the picture of Cesar and his half-brothers and mother. She'd *felt* the tension in his body.

Cesar's head dipped and his mouth found hers unerringly. She fell headlong into the flaming pit of the kiss. It burnt her up from the inside out, from the depths of her being.

This was *right*. She felt it in her bones. She trusted this, whether she liked to admit it or not. Her hands gripped his biceps in order to stay standing, and she came up on tiptoe, straining even closer.

Cesar undid her hair and she could feel it fall loose behind her shoulders. He was backing her towards something, and when she felt something solid behind her she realised dimly it must be his desk.

Still their mouths were clinging to one another, their

tongues tangling in a heady dance. Cesar lifted Lexie effortlessly until she was sitting on the desk. Instinctively she hooked a leg around one of his and heard his growl of approval as it brought his body into contact with hers.

The hard press of his arousal against her belly only set off another spasm of lust deep in her body. And between her legs. This was infinitely preferable to trying to rationalise her thoughts and feelings.

His hand was between them, unbuttoning her shirt. Lexie felt hot. Yearned for air, a breeze. His touch. When it fell open he pushed it off one shoulder, taking her bra strap with it, tugging it down her arm.

She wanted only one thing: *more*. When Cesar took his mouth from hers they were both breathing harshly. Somewhere she heard the ring of a phone—a mobile. She tensed.

He said gutturally, 'It doesn't matter.'

Lexie felt dazed, despite the intrusion of the phone. 'I want to see you.'

Standing up straight for a moment, Cesar undid his buttons and opened his shirt. Lexie closed her eyes when the intoxicating scent of man and musk hit her nostrils. Like when she'd first seen him.

When she opened them again they widened. He was magnificent. Broad and hard muscled. Dark blond hair dusted his chest, drawing her eye down to where it bisected the ridges of his abdomen muscles in a line and then disappeared into his pants.

And just like that Lexie became aware of being out of her depth. Overwhelmed. She knew that if they didn't stop now this would end in bed, and as much as she thought she wanted that she wasn't sure if she was really ready. And she realised a small part of her needed to know that he would stop.

She put a hand on his chest and felt him tense. It almost made her forget her intention.

'Wait…' Her voice felt rough, breathy. 'This is moving so fast…'

She looked up at him, wishing she could read what was in those green depths. Decipher that inscrutable expression.

Cesar stepped back and Lexie let her hand drop. It felt as if a chasm had opened between them. With a shaky hand she pulled her shirt and bra strap back up. She couldn't really think straight when Cesar was half clothed in front of her, and cringed as she realised it was only seconds ago that she'd been begging to *see* him.

Humiliation scored her insides. She was damaged. She couldn't just throw caution to the wind and do this. That was the problem.

She slid off the table, her legs unsteady. Between them she throbbed lightly. Mockingly.

Expecting Cesar to be irritated, put out, she caught her breath when she looked up at him and he smiled. Lexie nearly had to put her hands behind her to catch the desk. *Lord.* When he smiled something inside her ached because she hadn't really seen him smile before now.

He moved close again and rubbed his thumb across her bottom lip. His smile faded. 'We want each other.'

Lexie's heart thumped. Hard. 'Yes…' How could she deny it? God. She felt as gauche as a sixteen-year-old contemplating her first make-out session. But then she'd never had that experience.

'Next weekend there's a function in Madrid. You said you wanted to see the city?'

Her head felt fuzzy. Had she?

But Cesar didn't even bother to wait for her agreement, he just said, 'We'll go together. I have an apartment there so we can stay overnight.'

Lexie's heart nearly pounded out of her chest at the

thought but she managed to nod. 'It'll be good for us to be seen together. It'll be good for the press.'

'Yes,' Cesar agreed equably. 'But it's not just about that, Lexie. It's for *us*.'

When Lexie had left Cesar had to wait another few minutes for his body to cool down. He'd been ready to lift her up and carry her into his bedroom. His conscience mocked him—as if he could have held back from taking her right there on his desk.

When she'd pulled back, put her hand on his chest, everything within him had screamed with rejection. And then he'd come to his senses and realised just how close to the edge he was. So he'd welcomed a little space...sanity.

He was a civilised man, even though the last time he could remember feeling remotely civilised was over a week ago—just before he'd laid eyes on Lexie Anderson for the first time.

Cesar went to the window that looked out over a private section of the *castillo* gardens, tucking one arm under the other across his chest.

Something skated over his skin...a very old memory. A feeling. Vulnerability. He didn't like it. It harked back to a time before he'd made sure he was immune to such weaknesses.

He wanted Lexie, but she was dangerous. Because when he was near her he seemed to forget himself. His mouth tightened.

Everything in him had always urged him to trust nothing—and especially not women. After all, his mother and grandmother had taught him that lesson very well.

A memory came back, blindsiding him: his grandmother, dragging him painfully up to a first-floor window. Forcing him to sit down on the window seat. Every day, for hours on end. Before and after his lessons. Because she'd found him there one day. Watching…waiting.

'If you like it here so much then you'll do it every day. Watch, Cesar. *Watch*. See how she does not return for you. And when you tell me that you believe me we can stop playing this game.'

Cesar could remember glaring at his grandmother's thin, bitter face mulishly before she'd taken his ear painfully and pulled his face back to the window. Tears of pain had sprung into his eyes but he'd blinked them back. Loath to show her any emotion. Because even at that tender age of five he'd already known better.

And so he'd looked out of the window—fiercely—for hours on end, willing the figure of his mother to appear. Sometimes he'd thought he'd seen something, but it had only been a mirage. It had taken another full year before he'd finally told his grandmother what she wanted to hear.

His grandmother had made sure that he would see pictures of his mother enjoying her life in Paris. Becoming successful. Famous. A model. Having another son. His half-brother. Forgetting about *him*.

His mother *had* come back, with his younger brother, another year after that. The shattering pain of seeing his brother's hand in hers had been unbearable. He'd hated her—hated them both so much that he'd rejected her right back.

He'd lost his father before he'd even really known him. Then his mother had left him behind like a piece of unwanted luggage. Cesar's grandmother and grandfather had shown nothing but disdain and faint tolerance for their grandson. Their only motivation in making him heir had been their own greed and fanatical obsession with the family name.

The past finally receded from Cesar's head. He castigated himself for letting a woman, no matter how alluring, have this effect on him, for making him think about those things again. He *wanted* Lexie—pure and simple.

He was impervious to anything above and beyond sating himself with her. He would never want anything more with a woman than momentary satisfaction. And Lexie was no different.

CHAPTER SIX

TOWARDS THE END of that second week Lexie's nerves were jagged and fraying. It was almost certainly because of the constant presence of Cesar on the set. She felt his gaze on her like a physical touch sometimes.

She wasn't used to this. This excruciating build-up of sexual awareness and frustration. She hated Cesar for having done this to her, having this hold over her, while in the same breath she wished he would just stride across the set and take her in his arms and kiss her to make her head stop spinning.

But it wasn't just the physical sensations. He seemed to have snuck deeper. And she couldn't believe she was in danger of being gullible all over again even though this was infinitely different from what had happened with Jonathan Saunders.

Madrid and the weekend loomed large. The irony was not lost on Lexie—she was playing the part of a jaded sexual libertine and yet she had no idea of the reality of what that should feel like. She felt like a fraud, and gave thanks that no one seemed to have called her on it yet.

But after this weekend, a sly voice pointed out, *you'll know exactly what it feels like.*

When they finally called a wrap that day, and Lexie saw that it was Cesar waiting for her with a golf buggy to get her back to the unit base instead of one of the PAs, she snapped and said caustically, 'Don't you have a world leader to meet or something equally important to do?'

Cesar just looked incredibly sanguine and stepped out of the buggy to help her in, saying *sotto voce*, 'I'm your besotted lover, remember?'

Lexie stifled a snort and pulled the coat she wore to keep warm around her, hiding her voluptuous curves in the elaborate dress.

And then she felt churlish. She glanced at Cesar's patrician profile. He was even more gorgeous dressed down in faded jeans and a long-sleeved top. Workmanlike boots. He looked younger like this, less intimidating. Less a titan of industry.

As much as his presence on the set unnerved her, she'd come to expect it now. Two days ago she'd been waiting for the camera to be set up and had wandered behind one of the equipment trucks to find Cesar deep in conversation with one of the oldest members of the crew. A veteran who had worked on some of the biggest films ever made.

Cesar had been listening intently and asking him about his career. The effect this had had on Lexie was nothing short of pathetic. It had been akin to seeing Cesar cradle a small puppy. Inducing warmth, tenderness. *Danger.*

When they reached the base Cesar helped her from the buggy and opened the door of her trailer for her. Before she could go in, though, he caught her hand.

She looked at him warily.

'I have to go to London tomorrow morning for twenty-four hours. But I'll be back to take you to Madrid on Saturday. We'll leave after lunch.'

He let her hand go to cup the back of her neck, drawing her to him. Even though Lexie had a split second of realisation that he was going to kiss her the touch of his mouth to hers was still like an electric shock, infusing her blood with energy and heat. It was a chaste kiss, and he drew back almost as soon as it had started. But Lexie wanted more.

'Till then.' He let her go, stepped back.

Lexie's heart was beating fast. This was the moment. She could say something now—back out, not go through with it. *Stay safe.*

She opened her mouth. Cesar's green gaze was almost black. And, treacherously, she shut her mouth without saying anything. A recklessness within her was urging her to seize the moment.

Lexie saw other crew members arriving back from the set. Her dresser hurrying to help her out of her costume.

She took a breath. 'Fine, I'll be ready.'

Cesar smiled and it was distinctly predatory. 'I look forward to it. Don't miss me too much, will you?'

Lexie wanted to make a face but he was already turning to go. She really didn't like the impulse she felt to run after him and beg him to take her with him.

On Saturday Lexie was dressed casually, in a stripy long-sleeved top, a long, loose, gypsy-style skirt and soft boots. She had a weekend bag and was waiting for Cesar in the imposing reception hall of the *castillo*, trying not to think about the butterflies fluttering around in her belly at the prospect of seeing him again, or to think too much about what the weekend would bring.

So she thought of the difference between his private apartment and its soaring modern space and the rest of the *castillo*. So different. It made her wonder what it must have been like to grow up here…and why his mother had left him behind.

Something caught Lexie's eye through a doorway and she put down her bags for a moment to walk into a long formal room. It was filled with portraits and she shivered a little as she looked at them. They were all so stern and forbidding—much like the dour *castillo* housekeeper.

She walked around them and came to the most recent ones. Lexie figured they had to be of Cesar's grandparents. They appeared sterner than all the rest put together and she shivered again.

'Cold?'

Lexie jumped and put a hand to her heart, looking around to see Cesar lounging against the door frame, watching her. She took him in. He was wearing dark trousers and an open-necked shirt. He looked smart, yet casual. Gorgeous.

'You startled me.'

He straightened up and came in, hands in his pockets, which made her feel minutely safer. Her skin was hot. And an ache she'd not even been aware of noticing eased. *She'd missed him.* For one day.

Dragging her eyes away from him, she regarded the portraits again. 'Are these your grandparents?'

He stood beside her and a frisson of electricity shot straight to her groin.

He sounded grim. 'Yes, that's them.'

Lexie was curious. 'What were they like?'

He was clipped. 'Cold, cruel, snobbish. Obsessed with the family legacy.'

She looked at him and almost gasped at how hard his face had become. Stark. Pained.

'What did they do to you?'

He smiled, but it was hard. 'What *didn't* they do? My grandmother's particular favourite hobby was getting me to compile scrapbooks of newspaper cuttings featuring my mother and half-brothers, further driving home the message that they wanted nothing to do with me.'

Lexie stared at Cesar, too shocked to say anything for a moment. No wonder there was such tension in him when he mentioned his family. And yet he'd gone to that wedding… He glanced at her and she could see it in his eyes: *Not up for further discussion.* What surprised Lexie was the wave of rage she felt welling inside her at the horrific cruelty he'd endured.

'What happened to your father? Is it true that he was a bullfighter?'

Cesar looked away again and Lexie thought he would ignore her, but then he said, 'He rebelled. He wanted out and wanted nothing to do with his inheritance. So he did what he could to ensure that his family would disown him: he became a bullfighter. It was the worst insult to his parents he could think of. And they duly disinherited him.'

'Your mother…?'

Cesar kept his eyes on the portraits.

'My mother was from a small town down south, where my father went to train as a bullfighter. She was poor. He fell in love and they got married, had me.'

'Did she know who he was? Where he'd come from?'

Now Cesar looked at Lexie, and she almost took a step back at the cynicism etched on his face. He seemed older in that moment.

'Of course she did. That's why she targeted him. If he hadn't died she probably would have persuaded him to return home—especially once they'd had me.'

Lexie tried to hide her dismay at seeing this side of him. He seemed utterly unapproachable at that moment.

'You don't know that for sure, though…' she said, almost hopefully.

'Of course I know,' he dismissed coldly. 'As soon as my father died she brought me here, but my grandparents wanted nothing to do with her. Only me. They realised that their legacy would be secure with an heir. Once she knew there was nothing she could gain, she left.'

Lexie put a hand to her belly in a reflexive action as

the old pain flared inside her hearing his words. To think of the awful wrench it must have been for his mother to give him up. No matter what he said, she couldn't have been that cruel.

'But she came back…? You said that she came back some years later.'

A bleak look flashed across Cesar's face, but it was so fleeting that Lexie wasn't even sure she'd seen it.

'Yes, she did. Maybe she thought she could benefit then. But it was too late.'

'How old were you?'

'Almost seven.'

Lexie gasped. 'But that's so young…you were still so young. Why didn't you go with her?'

Even as she realised that Cesar wasn't going to answer her she had a moment of intuition. He'd been left here when he was so tiny, yet he had been old enough to remember. Remember his mother walking away. Lexie couldn't even begin to imagine what had broken inside him in those years after his mother had left him. Broken so badly that he'd let her walk away from him again.

Cesar stepped back and said, 'We should go. The plane is ready.'

After a short trip in a sleek Land Rover to a local airstrip, Lexie knew she shouldn't have been surprised to see a small private plane waiting for them—reminding her, as if she needed it, just who she was dealing with.

Except the man she was dealing with had just shown her a side of himself that was raw and bleak, and she couldn't stop her chest from aching. Even though she knew that he wouldn't thank her for it. He hadn't had to say a word for her to know that he would scorn the slightest hint of pity.

Cesar parked the car and swung out of the driver's seat

with lithe grace. He'd come around to help Lexie out before she could object, taking her hand in his firm grip.

An assistant took their bags to the plane. The pilot was waiting to greet them, and then they were stepping into the plush, luxurious world of the super-rich. Although Lexie was still a bit too shaken up by what Cesar had revealed to truly enjoy this novel experience.

A steward showed her to her seat solicitously, and Cesar took the seat opposite. There was no waiting for other people to arrive, to sit down. Once they were in they buckled up and the plane was moving.

In a bid to try and shake some of the residual melancholy she felt at hearing about Cesar's less than happy-sounding childhood, Lexie asked, 'So what's the function this evening?'

Cesar stretched out his long legs across the aisle. 'It's a dinner and Spanish music event at the Italian Ambassador's residence.'

Lexie felt her stomach plummet. 'Seriously? But I've never met an ambassador in my life…I won't know what to say—'

He leaned across and took one of her hands out of her lap and held it to his mouth, kissing it. Effectively shutting her up. The air in the cabin seemed to get hot and sultry.

'You don't have to worry about saying anything. They're not going to present you with an IQ questionnaire before dinner to see if you qualify.'

Lexie hated this insecurity that stemmed not only from her dyslexia but from having left school early. 'But they'll be talking about politics and the EU and economics…'

'And,' Cesar replied without hesitation, 'if they do I can't imagine that you wouldn't know just as much if not more than them. These are *people*, Lexie, they're not intellectual giants.'

'Well, you are…' She was being distracted by the hypnotic stroke of Cesar's thumb on the underside of her wrist. His thumb stopped and he frowned at her.

'Where on earth do you get that from?'

Lexie shrugged, feeling exposed again for having researched him in the beginning.

'You're one of the most successful men in the world… you go to economic forums…all those books in your study and apartment…'

Cesar's mouth twisted. 'All those books in my study belong to my family. The only reason I haven't ever got rid of them is in case I need them for reference and for reasons of pure vanity—because they look good.' Then he said, 'Me, though? The books I like reading are popular crime thrillers—nothing more intellectual than that, I assure you.'

Something shifted inside Lexie. An ominous feeling of tenderness welled up.

'And as for school…I was not a natural A student—far from it. I had to work for every one of my grades. Once my grandparents realised this they recruited the local swot— Juan Cortez, who is now the Mayor of Villaporto, the local town—to come and help me.'

The tenderness swelled. 'Are you still friends?'

Cesar smiled. Another rare, proper smile. Lexie had to stop herself from gripping his hand tighter.

'Yes, but only because we nearly killed each other when we were ten.'

Lexie asked impulsively, 'What happened?'

He looked rueful. 'I had issues with someone being smarter than me.' And then he said, 'I'm a hustler, Lexie. I go to these forums and meetings because I have inherited and manage a vast legacy. For a long time I thought I wanted to do what my father had done and turn my back on it, but then I realised that if I did and the fortune got carved up I'd be cutting off my nose to spite my face. I realised that I enjoyed being an entrepreneur—I was good at it. And once my grandparents died I could finally put the family's vast wealth to some good use.'

'How old were you when they died?'

Cesar's easiness vanished. 'Fifteen when my grandfather died and then eighteen when my grandmother died.'

Lexie squeezed his hand but said nothing. She could see the lack of grief for them in his eyes—it was almost defiant. Her own silly heart ached to think of him taking on all that responsibility at such a young age. And as a boy growing up with no love. The thing was, she knew what that felt like—albeit on a different level.

The lack of affection in her own family had come after shattering events and had never been repaired.

The steward appeared then, to offer them some refreshments, and Cesar let her hand go. To Lexie's relief the conversation turned to more neutral topics after that.

It felt like no time at all before they were descending into Madrid, and Lexie looked out of the window eagerly to catch her first glimpse of the capital city.

When they emerged from the plane after landing it was pleasantly warm with a hint of autumnal freshness. A car was waiting for them.

Cesar said in the back of the car, 'We'll go to the apartment and then I'm taking you out on a tour.'

'Okay,' Lexie answered. An incredibly light feeling was bubbling up inside her, and she was determined not to analyse it too carefully.

When Cesar put out his hand for her to come closer she didn't hesitate, sliding along the back seat until she was right beside him. His arm went around her, his fingers splaying provocatively just under Lexie's breast, making her toes curl in her shoes.

His apartment building was on a very grand, wide, tree-lined street. It was an old building, and his apartment was at the top. When he opened the door to let her in Lexie wasn't surprised to see that the same kind of modern design as was in his *castillo* apartment ran through this space too. The old building was the shell, but classic furniture and abstract paintings gave it a very contemporary and slightly eclectic Art Deco aesthetic. It oozed class and luxury. Good taste.

Lexie asked, as he led her down a corridor, 'Did you design this and your other apartment at the *castillo*?'

'Yes. A friend who is an architect helped me. Luc Sanchis. He oversaw the structural work and his team did the interiors.'

'Wow,' Lexie said, awed. Even she'd heard of the famous constructive architect.

Cesar stopped at a door. 'We've also come up with a plan to completely remodel the interior of the *castillo* but it's undergoing a lengthy planning permission process. As you can imagine it's protected because it's so old, and we have to incorporate that integrity with the new design.'

Lexie wrinkled her nose. 'I think it would be great… It's an amazing building, but…'

'Completely stuck in the Middle Ages and not in a good way?'

She smiled. 'If you say so. I couldn't possibly be so rude.'

He reached out and rubbed his thumb along her lower lip. Lexie's blood sizzled. And then, as if he had to make a physical effort to stop touching her, he gritted his jaw and let his hand drop.

He pushed open the door and let her precede him. It was a bedroom, with a massive en-suite bathroom and dressing room. The same Art Deco stamp on the furnishings. She loved it.

'This is your bedroom.'

She turned around, her heart speeding up. He was putting her bags at the bottom of the bed and turning around.

'I'm not even going to say it, Lexie… You know I want you. But this is your space.'

Beyond touched, and reassured in a very deep place that *needed* reassurance, Lexie got out a husky 'Thank you…'

A few hours later Cesar stood at the window in the reception room. He was waiting for Lexie, his hands stuck deep in the pockets of his black trousers. His hands had never itched so much in his life. The previous few hours had been both heaven and hell. Torture.

When he'd asked her how she'd like to see the city and she'd professed an interest in an open-top bus tour that was what they'd done.

He'd never done one of these tours in his life—it was completely alien to anything he'd normally do—but he had noticed them in various cities and always envied the kind of people who went on them.

Lexie had been like a child, her face lighting up to see the beautiful city. And Cesar had ended up inadvertently doing a better job of being tour guide than the actual tour guide. A small crowd had gathered around them on the top of the bus so they could hear his take on the various sites. It had helped that he spoke multiple languages.

Lexie had been laughing when they disembarked, because some of the American tourists had insisted on tipping him—one of the wealthiest men in the world!

In that moment, when Lexie had been laughing, Cesar had felt a dizzying rush of something that was also completely alien to him…it was only now that he could recognise it with a sort of incredulity. *Happiness.*

For a moment he'd felt pure, unadulterated ease. Joy. The blackness that seemed to be his constant companion had dissipated. And it had lasted even as Lexie had asked if they could walk back to the apartment because it wasn't far.

They'd stopped and had coffee and cakes on the way.

Cesar had never, ever spent such an enjoyable couple of hours with anyone.

The threads of that happiness lingered now, like a seductive caress. But Cesar was aware of something very strong inside him that refused to believe it. It was urging him to be vigilant, not to trust in this ephemeral feeling.

Anything that had felt vaguely like this had been ripped away from him at such an early age that now it seemed too…*easy*.

He heard a sound then, and turned around, and when he saw Lexie it was like a punch to his gut—it was that physical.

He couldn't have analysed what she was wearing in any kind of detail. All he knew was that it was black and seemed to cling to every curve she had with a precariousness that made Cesar's body stiffen in wanton reaction. Her shoulders were bare. Her hair was pulled back, revealing her long delicate neck.

She was a goddess.

Cesar walked over to her before he could melt into a pool of unrestrained lust and lock them both in this apartment until she finally gave in to him. He was actually afraid to touch her—afraid that if he did he'd turn into some feral being.

'My car is waiting outside.'

Lexie smiled, but Cesar could see a slight nervousness in her eyes. The thought of dinner? Was she feeling insecure? It made unwelcome protectiveness rise up, but lust was also rising, too high and fast for him to be able to focus on it or let it bother him.

He let her precede him, her scent light and fresh. Floral. Her long dress swung around her hips and legs, and Cesar all but closed his eyes and sent a prayer up to the God he hadn't consulted in a long time for the ability to show some restraint.

* * *

Lexie was finally relaxing. Although she knew it probably had as much to do with the second glass of wine she was on as the fact that the dinner was proving to be far less scary than she'd thought.

But the location was beyond intimidating in its grandeur. It was a very old palace in the centre of Madrid that had been turned into the Ambassador's residence. If everyone hadn't been in modern clothes it would have been hard to ascertain where the past ended and the present began under the soft, seductive lighting of hundreds of candles.

She'd imagined that people would be talking about complicated fiscal policies and the merits of a single currency, but they were actually far more interested in talking to her about the famous people she'd met and what they were really like.

She felt a large hand on her thigh and her lower body spasmed in pure need. She put her hand over his to remove it, but instead her fingers wound their way through his. Holding him there. Her body and her mind were in two different places...

She smiled brightly at the man beside her and took advantage of the lull in the conversation to turn and face Cesar on her other side.

He looked at her. 'Okay?'

She smiled wryly. 'I've been telling the esteemed Secretary to the Greek Ambassador exactly which celebrity tour he should take his kids on when they go to LA next month.'

Cesar smiled and leant forward to kiss her on the mouth. Lexie found herself wanting to cling to him, her fingers tightening on his on her thigh. *She was ready.* Her heart sped up at the thought even as old tendrils of fear made her trepidatious.

He drew back and his eyes were glowing dark green.

'There's a dance showpiece after dinner. We don't have to stay if you don't want to.'

Lexie shook her head, giving in to that fear like a coward, delaying the moment of inevitability. 'No, it's fine. I'd like to see it.'

As the dinner ended and they moved into the room where the showpiece was taking place Lexie seemed to be existing in a haze of shimmering heat. She was acutely aware of Cesar's every move.

Their afternoon on the bus had been delicious torture. Cesar had been dressed down, in jeans and a casual top and jacket. He'd pressed so close against her that she had barely taken in a word he'd said about any of the stunning monuments and squares they'd seen, all too aware of him.

He'd been so gracious and patient when the other tourists had wanted to listen to his explanations and she'd seen another side of him completely. He wasn't as misanthropic as first impressions would have led Lexie to believe—far from it. But she wondered if he even realised that himself.

They had front row seats for the dance performance— by a flamenco dancer. When the lights went down a hush went around the crowd and then a lone guitar started playing the most hauntingly beautiful Spanish music.

Lexie glanced at Cesar to find him staring at her with an intensity that made her insides liquefy. Only with extreme effort could she look away.

A spotlight lit up the small stage and a beautiful dark-haired woman with the lithe body of a dancer walked into the middle. She wore a long red dress, very plain and simple, red shoes, and a red flower in her hair.

She made the most exquisite shapes with her hands and body—typical flamenco postures. Then the hard soles and heels of her shoes started hitting the boards of the stage as the rhythm of the guitar picked up pace. Tiny hairs stood up on the back of Lexie's neck.

It was mesmerising. There was something so elemental and beautiful about this woman and the power in her body. It made a ball of emotion lodge in Lexie's chest and throat. She was acutely aware of the man beside her, of his sheer overwhelming masculinity. Something seemed to be flowing between them through the beat of the music, even though their thighs and arms were barely touching. It was carnal and earthy. Sexual.

The beat and power of the dancer's feet seemed to resonate with Lexie's heartbeat. Cesar had unlocked something powerful within her—something that she was finally connecting with herself after such a long time.

The beat of her own sexuality.

It was something she'd feared lost for ever, stolen from her too long ago ever to claim it back. Lexie wanted to look at Cesar again, but she was afraid that if she did, and he was looking at her, he'd see how raw her desire for him was.

She could see the sheen of exertion on the dancer's skin. The music and the dance were building and building. Lexie fancied she must have a similar sheen to *her* skin...she felt so hot. The expression on the woman's beautiful face was intense as her feet beat out the relentless passionate rhythm. Lexie felt it rise up through her body too.

As the music and the dance reached a crescendo, and as if he could sense how affected she was, Cesar's hand closed around Lexie's, his fingers twining through hers with an unmistakably possessive touch.

Her nipples pricked painfully. She was breathing harshly, every part of her body tingling with desire for the man beside her, as the music exploded and the woman came to a dead stop with her arms high in a proud and beautiful pose, her chest heaving with exertion. People started to clap rapturously. But still Lexie was almost afraid to look at Cesar.

'Lexie?'

She finally turned her head towards him and her world coalesced down to this moment and this man. She wanted him with a fierce drumbeat of need.

Another performer was coming on and she said impulsively, 'Would you mind if we left now?'

Cesar shook his head, a frankly explicit look coming into his eyes as if he could read what was on her mind, feel her desire. 'No—let's go before the next act starts.'

By the time they were walking out Lexie had taken deep breaths and regained some control. But she still trembled all over. Never had anything impacted her in such a deeply physical and visceral way as it had sitting beside this man and wanting him so badly that their very surroundings seemed to echo with it.

They were at the front of the residence now and Cesar's car was pulling up. The driver opened the door for her and Cesar got in on the other side. He reached for her almost immediately and Lexie went willingly.

Their mouths met and their kiss was hungry and desperate. Lexie's blood thundered and roared. She was still borne aloft on the sheer exhilaration of the dance. She drowned in the kiss, in the rough stroke of Cesar's tongue against hers and the feel of his arms around her.

By the time they reached the apartment she was half sitting on his lap, arms around his neck, mouth swollen, breathing fast.

Gently he took her arms down and opened his door before stepping out. He reached in and Lexie had one crazy moment of thinking she could just shut the door, instruct the driver to drive all the way back to the *castillo* and shut out the clamours of her body.

But she didn't. She'd already proved to herself that she was strong enough to withstand the worst things that could happen to a woman. She was certainly strong enough to withstand reclaiming her body and her right to sensual pleasure.

Lexie put her hand in Cesar's and let him pull her out. Keeping a tight grip on her hand, as if he was aware that a rogue part of her still wanted to escape, he greeted the concierge and led her to the lift. Once inside they didn't speak. But the air hummed with awareness and expectation. It was heavy.

When they entered his apartment and the door closed behind them the silence swirled around them. Lexie's heart was beating so hard she thought it had to be audible.

Cesar shrugged off his jacket and threw it over a chair haphazardly. Looking at Lexie, he pulled at his bow tie, undoing it. She was clutching her bag tightly, her eyes glued to his mouth, wanting it on hers again.

He reached down and took her bag, threw it aside to join his jacket. Then he put his hands on her arms.

'You're sure?'

After a moment Lexie nodded and said, 'I've never been more sure of anything in my life. Make love to me, Cesar.'

CHAPTER SEVEN

FOR A MOMENT Cesar did nothing, and a wave of cold clammy horror gripped Lexie as she imagined being rejected. But then he dipped, and she let out a little squeal when he lifted her into his arms against his chest.

He strode down the corridor, past her bedroom to another door on the opposite side. Lexie took in no details of the room he walked into beyond the fact that it was dark, palatial and had a massive bed.

He walked right over to it and let Lexie down, before reaching for a light and switching it on to put out a pool of golden light.

Light, Lexie thought. *Light is good.* The enormity of what she was doing was sinking in.

Reverently Cesar put his hands on Lexie's shoulders. She tried to calm her thundering pulse. Then he turned her around and it went haywire again.

He pulled the pins from her hair until it fell down. Then he brushed it aside over one shoulder. Lexie shivered when she felt him come close behind her, wrapping an arm around her midriff and pressing a kiss to her bare shoulder.

His fingers were on her zip at the back of her dress. Slowly, so slowly, he started to pull it down. The dress loosened around her chest and she curled her hands into fists to stop herself from impeding its progress as it fell forward and down.

Now she was bare from the waist up except for a strapless lace bra.

Cesar's hand had drawn the zip all the way to the top of her buttocks, where it ended. Then with both hands he pushed it over her hips so that it fell to the floor. She was aware of a rough indrawn breath, and then his hand was cupping her bottom in her silk French knickers, smoothing over her hip.

Her legs were losing their ability to hold her upright.

When he put his hands on her shoulders again, to turn her around, Lexie looked down. She felt hot, excited and scared. All at once. Cesar's hands were on her waist, pulling her into him.

'Lexie…look at me.'

She bit her lip, but looked up. His face was flushed, eyes glittering like dark jewels. His gaze dropped to her mouth, and then lower. Her skin went on fire.

He lifted a hand and cupped one breast. Her nipples were hard and stinging. Pushing against the lace of her bra. He brushed his thumb across one nipple, making Lexie gasp. Making her want more. *His mouth.*

Cesar sank back onto the bed and pulled her into him. Lexie nearly stumbled in her shoes and she kicked them off jerkily, steadying herself on his shoulders.

His hands closed around her waist again, and with her breasts at easy reaching distance for his mouth he explored her through the lace, his tongue laving the lace-covered tips, first one and then the other.

Lexie's hands were like claws gripping his shoulders. It was torture. The stinging chafing of the lace against those throbbing moist peaks. She almost sobbed with relief when he reached around to undo her bra and then cupped one breast before he encircled that aching naked tip with his wicked, hot mouth. It was exquisite.

Her hands moved to Cesar's head, fingers threading through silky strands of hair. When he tried to draw back she had to release him. She looked down, dazed, drunk. Instinctively she reached for his shirt, undoing his buttons, her breasts swaying with her movement.

He took over, emitting a soft growl of impatience when a button got caught, ripping it apart and off. Then his chest was bare. And gorgeous. Lexie had to sink down onto one thigh, unable to stand any more.

Cesar caught her to him with a strong arm, his other hand finding her chin and angling it so that he could plunder her mouth in a scorching hot kiss. He let that hand trail down to cup and massage her breast again, fingers pinching her stiff nipple.

Lexie squirmed. Between her legs she was stinging. Moist. Sensing her need even before she acknowledged it, Cesar moved his hand down over her waist. He pushed her legs open, his mouth still on hers, distracting her, until she felt those fingers exploring the delicate skin of her inner thigh. She held her breath as they trailed over her sex, hidden under the silk of her panties.

Lexie broke the kiss. Cesar's eyes were half lidded, hot with need. She was clinging to him and his hand was *there*, right where she felt swollen and needy. He was pressing against her flesh, moving rhythmically.

In a fast-moving world that had been reduced to all things physical Lexie tried to cling onto reality and the feeling that she could trust Cesar.

She put her hand on his wrist, stopping his movements, and said threadily, 'I don't want you to hurt me.'

He could never know the wealth of history behind that plea.

He frowned and removed his hand, bringing it up to touch her jaw again.

'I would never hurt you. We'll take this slow, okay?'

Lexie nodded. Relief flooded her. In a smooth move, Cesar lifted her from his lap and onto the bed. She sank back and looked up, watching him undo his trousers and push them down.

Her eyes widened on the bulge in his boxers, and they widened even more when he'd dispensed with the rest of his clothes and put his hands to the edges of those boxers. He pushed them down and his erection was freed.

Lexie waited for rejection, revulsion, fear…but it didn't come. She only felt intense excitement. And need. Euphoria bubbled up inside her. Lightness. When Cesar bent down and put his hands to her panties she lifted her hips to let him pull them down.

His body was awe-inspiring. He was a very masculine man in his prime. Broad through the chest and shoulders, slimming to lean hips, and down to powerful buttocks and thighs.

He came down on the bed beside her, on one arm, and looked at her. His gaze left scorching hot trails where it rested on her curves. 'You're more beautiful than anything I've ever seen.' He ran his hand up and down her body, barely skimming, teasing her.

Lexie touched his jaw reverently, feeling the tough line under her fingers, following the line of his cheek down to his mouth, tracing that sensual shape.

Her belly contracted when he caught her hand and sucked one finger deep. Then he took her finger out of his mouth and, not taking his eyes off her, trailed his hand down over her breasts to the curls protecting her sex.

Gently, he encouraged her to open her legs. Lexie held her breath. Keeping the heel of his hand against her, he explored her with his finger, seeking the seam of her body and parting it, releasing her desire to smooth his passage.

She was breathing again, but it was laboured as Cesar moved his fingers over her and pressed his palm against her. Without her even knowing it Lexie's body was moving, hips twitching, circling, seeking more.

He bent his head and took her mouth, and she almost sobbed into it when she felt him thrust one finger inside her. Her hands had to hold onto something and she found his arms, fingers digging into hard muscles. Cesar shifted and she could feel his erection against her hip.

She was too shy to reach out and touch it, but she wanted to. Wanted to explore what all that power would feel like encased in silken skin.

But right now his finger was moving in and out of her body and causing sensations such as Lexie had never experienced before. There was a delicious tightening feeling, building and building. An urgency. A desire for more.

When one finger became two, and Cesar's tongue thrust deep into her mouth, her hands tightened on him.

He broke away. '*Dios*…you're so responsive…I don't know how slow I can go…you're killing me.'

Lexie blinked. Cesar looked like a dark golden lion in the dim light. She whispered throatily, 'Don't go slow.'

He gazed at her, his breath coming sharp and fast. He was on the edges of his control…she could sense it. Right then Lexie felt invincible. Strong. In control.

Cesar disappeared for a moment and Lexie heard a drawer open and shut, then the sound of foil ripping. He came back and she saw him smoothing protection onto his erection.

A spurt of jealousy that he was touching himself so intimately caught her unawares, making her want to giggle with the sheer joy of discovering her own body again. Of being here and feeling *safe*.

Cesar came over her, careful not to crush her, but the weight of his naked body over hers was something Lexie craved. She reached for his body, clasping him, urging him down.

He cursed. 'I don't want to hurt you.'

'You won't,' she said, and meant it, feeling emotional.

Lexie felt him push her legs apart further with his hips, stretching her. Poised above her, he nearly undid her when he pushed some hair back off her hot cheek and pressed a kiss to her mouth. As if somehow…he *knew*.

And then she felt him—hard, forceful, pushing into her, seeking her acceptance. Her body resisted and Lexie sucked in a breath. She willed herself not to let the darkness of her past reach out to poison this moment. She willed her body to relax, to *trust*.

After several heart-stopping moments, punctuated only by their harsh breathing, she felt a shift and Cesar's body slid in a little more. Filling her.

'You're so small…so tight.'

She moved her hips experimentally and earned herself a long, low growl from Cesar that sounded feral.

She could see the cost of his restraint showing on his face, in his tense shoulders. He reached down a hand and moved it under her thigh, encouraging her to lift her leg around his waist.

The movement brought him deeper into her body, and now Lexie groaned as excitement built, a restless, surging yearning for a deeper connection between their bodies.

She lifted her other leg and Cesar pulled out before sliding back in, his body huge and powerful. He angled his body so that he was thrusting as deep as possible. He put a hand between them and found the cluster of cells at the juncture of her thighs. Lexie gasped out loud as that building excitement shot right through her core.

Her whole body was alive with a deep mystical energy, coiling and binding her to this man with an invisible weave. Cesar's chest touched hers, hair a delicious friction against her breasts. Lexie arched her back to ask mindlessly for *more*.

Cesar's movements were becoming more urgent, stronger. Faster. Her heels were digging into his muscular buttocks, driving his body deeper into hers, holding him to her.

She could feel wave after wave of ecstasy washing through her until they gathered such force that she begged Cesar to release her from the torture and let her fly. But she wasn't coherent.

He bent his head and kissed her. 'It's okay, *querida*, I'll catch you.'

Those words unlocked the tension and Lexie soared on a blissful plateau of pleasure so intense that it was almost painful. And as she fell, feeling the powerful contractions of her body around Cesar's, she bit his shoulder to stop herself from screaming out loud. His own body tensed powerfully before he let out a guttural shout, and he fell just behind her.

Cesar's brain was in meltdown. Even now he could still feel the ripples of Lexie's orgasm keeping his body hard, not letting him come down completely from the most intense climax he'd ever experienced.

It was the most difficult thing in the world to break the connection between their bodies, but Cesar gritted his jaw and moved, releasing them both. Lexie winced minutely. Her eyes were wide, cheeks flushed, hair in disarray around her head.

He moved so that he didn't crush her and came onto his side, pulling her into him so that they were face to face. Normally when Cesar made love to a woman he felt the overwhelming need to get away. Right now it was the last thing on his mind. She fitted him. One leg was still looped over his thigh. The centre of her body was still flush with his, doing little to help his arousal subside.

He could only look at her. The expression on her face was as stunned as he felt. A lock of hair was across one hot cheek, damp with her sweat. He raised a hand, noted vaguely that it was trembling, and tucked her hair behind her ear.

As his normal faculties returned Cesar was aware of feeling more and more vulnerable. But still he couldn't seem to move, to be able to unweld his arms from around her.

Then he saw a brightness in her gaze in the dim light. Her mouth wobbling even as she bit into her lower lip to disguise it. Cesar's belly dropped as if from a great height as something very cold lanced him. He'd just assumed... been so focused on how intense it had been for him... Even though he'd believed it had been the same for her, but she was so small...

He could feel tremors in Lexie's body now—as if she was experiencing a delayed reaction. Cesar moved and came up on one arm, cold terror trickling through him. 'Did I hurt you?'

Rapidly she shook her head and Cesar saw her eyes fill in earnest now, felt the tremors in her body getting stronger. Her cheeks paled. Was she going into some kind of shock?

Her body, which had felt so warm and languorous seconds before, now felt cold. Galvanised by increasing panic, Cesar gathered Lexie into his arms and stood up from the bed, taking her with him. She curled up against his chest, making something like bile fill him at the thought that he'd hurt her. She said nothing.

He walked into the bathroom and straight into the shower, where he turned on the powerful spray of hot water and stood them both under it. He felt Lexie gasp, her body curl even tighter into him, and he also felt those tremors increase as she started crying in earnest.

Her face was buried in his chest and her slim back was heaving with the force of her sobs as her hands pressed against him.

Cesar felt as if his chest was being ripped apart by bare hands. 'Lexie...*Dios*...please tell me...did I hurt you?'

She shook her head against him. The slimmest sliver of relief went through him. Cesar rested his back against the wall and wasn't even sure how long he stayed like that, under the powerful spray, while Lexie sobbed in his arms. He could still feel the power of the emotion running through her slim body.

Eventually the storm passed and she became still. They were surrounded in hot steam. She started to move, and then he heard a husky, rough-sounding, 'You can put me down. I'm okay.'

Reluctantly, even though his arms were stiff, Cesar let her down until she stood. She wouldn't look at him and he had to tip her chin up. When he saw those huge bruised eyes and her swollen mouth he had to curb his almost instantaneous reaction. *Again*. Already...

'Lexie...what...?'

She shook her head, came close, put her hands on his chest. 'You didn't hurt me...' Her voice sounded raw. 'The opposite. I promise.'

Cesar frowned as water ran in rivulets down their bodies, plastering their hair to their skulls. 'But...why?'

Lexie ducked her head, resting her forehead against him for a moment and making something incredibly alien flood through Cesar. Then she looked up again, 'I just... It's never been like that. That's all.'

Cesar had the distinct feeling that that *wasn't* all, but

something held him back from forcing her to explain. He hadn't hurt her. The relief was almost overwhelming.

'Come on,' he said gruffly. 'Let's get out.'

He turned off the water and stepped out, reaching back for Lexie. She emerged from the steam, taking his hand, and he couldn't stop his gaze from devouring those naked curves greedily. She was looking at him too, and Cesar had to stop himself from pressing her up against the shower wall and taking her there and then.

Instead he wrapped a towel around her and her hair. She stood as mute as a child and let him dry her off, and after he'd dried himself roughly he took her back into the bedroom.

He dropped his towel and gently took hers off and led her back to the bed. Her hair was damp but she didn't look inclined to dry it. He could see her eyes heavy with the need to sleep. Heavy after the outpouring of emotion that had left tentacles of panic inside him at the thought that he'd hurt her.

She crawled into the bed and lay down, and Cesar looked at her before getting in beside her. This was anathema to him—sharing a bed after lovemaking. But it was something he wasn't in a position to question right now.

Lexie burrowed straight into his arms, wrapping her legs around him, resting her head on his chest. Those soft abundant curves melted into him. His heart thudding unevenly, it was only when he could feel her body relax into sleep and her hold on him loosen that he was able to relax himself.

When Lexie woke up she opened her eyes and blinked at the dawn light coming in through long grand windows. She felt completely disorientated. Her body felt…different. Heavy. Lethargic. *Sated*. Hers…

She became aware of something moving steadily under

her cheek. *Cesar's chest.* She lifted her head and looked up to see him asleep. Dark stubble lined his jaw. And then her eye caught something else and she let out a small gasp of dismay.

A neat row of small teeth marks scored the flesh of his shoulder. And suddenly Lexie was back in that moment of such extreme pleasure that she'd had to bite him to keep from screaming.

She ducked her head again quickly, face burning. It all came back…every scorching moment. Taking him into her body had been far more momentous and emotional than she would ever have imagined it might be.

She'd cried like a baby.

Lexie cringed to think of how she'd curled up into his chest and sobbed. How he'd asked if he'd hurt her. Far from it. She felt almost guilty—as if she'd misled him by not telling him about herself. As if she'd taken something she only had half a right to. This man would never know the precious gift he'd unwittingly given her.

A sense of liberation from the dark past rushed up in a giddying sweep of emotion so physically acute that Lexie had to move or risk waking him. And she wasn't ready for that assessing gaze to land on her just yet.

Moving stealthily, she managed to extricate herself and climb out of the bed without disturbing Cesar, who lay in a louche, sexy sprawl. She couldn't help stopping for a moment and looking at him covetously. He was so beautiful…his skin a deep olive, his chest broad and powerful, and lower… Her face burned even hotter at the thought of how he'd felt moving inside her. So gentle but so powerful.

Emotion tightened like a fist around her heart. On first acquaintance with this man, she never could have imagined he'd have so many hidden depths, or have the capacity to be so…*considerate.*

Lexie immediately dismissed the direction of her

thoughts when a kind of panic seized her guts. She had to lock off her emotions. This was purely physical. She'd gone into this with eyes wide open. It was an affair. And when the time came she would walk away with her head held high.

Lexie grabbed up her things and crept out of the room. Once she was in her own room she had a shower, before donning faded comfy jeans and a V-necked cashmere top. She pulled her hair back into a ponytail and went to find the kitchen.

Lexie had found a radio station playing classical Spanish music and was blissfully unaware of the tall man resting his shoulder against the door, arms crossed, as she made breakfast.

It was only when she turned around to find some salt and pepper that she saw him and nearly jumped out of her skin.

He straightened. 'Sorry, I didn't mean to startle you.'

Lexie flushed, still not ready to see him. Already a hum was starting in her blood. 'You didn't…' She flushed some more. 'I mean, you did—but it's okay.'

He was bare-chested and wearing jeans with the top button open. Lexie nearly melted. Her body was unaccustomed to this overload of sensations and desires.

He came into the kitchen, right up to her, and growled softly, 'I woke up alone.'

'I just…I woke up and you were asleep,' Lexie stammered. 'I didn't want to disturb you.'

A look she couldn't identify came into his eyes and he said, 'You didn't.'

He bent then, and pressed his mouth to hers. In an instant she was on fire, her mouth opening under his, seeking more. When he pulled back she was breathing fast.

She was out of her depth. This whole morning-after thing was totally alien to her.

In a bid to try and disguise her discomfiture Lexie turned back to where she was frying some eggs and bacon, glancing over her shoulder. 'I hope you don't mind... I found some food in the fridge. Are you hungry?'

She was babbling now.

Cesar just leant back against the island in the kitchen and said huskily, 'I'm starving.'

But the look he sent up and down Lexie's body told her he didn't mean for food. She bit her lip and tried to ignore her body's reaction. Was this even normal?

Somehow she managed to make something resembling breakfast and coffee, and to serve it up without it ending up all over the floor.

The state-of-the-art kitchen in Cesar's apartment led into a large open-plan dining/living space. She sat down at the table there and noticed that there were Sunday papers, and—thankfully—that Cesar had put a top on.

He saw her glance at the papers and explained, 'The concierge drops them in if I'm here.'

Lexie spotted something that piqued her interest and pulled one of the more tabloid-looking papers out of the pile—only to realise that the press had managed to catch her and Cesar on their open-top bus tour.

There were also pictures of them walking hand in hand back to the apartment.

Something about that sent acute disappointment to her gut. It had been a spontaneous moment. This tainted the memory. She said faintly, 'I never imagined they could have known that we'd be doing that.'

Cesar took a sip of coffee and said, almost absent-mindedly, 'I called my assistant—told her to tip them off anonymously.'

Something cold slithered into Lexie's gut. She put down

her fork and looked at Cesar and brought up a dim recollection of him on his phone briefly at one stage on the bus.

'But....' Lexie was about to ask him *why* when she stopped herself. Of *course* he'd wanted to tip them off. They were meant to be courting the press—for both their benefits. Why waste an opportunity to document it?

'But...?' he asked.

She hated to think it, even to acknowledge it, but she felt betrayed. And she shouldn't be feeling that. Because if she did then it meant that Cesar had attained a significance for her that she had no control over.

She forced a smile and shook her head. 'But nothing. Of course you should have tipped them off. It was a good opportunity to let them see us.'

Cesar watched Lexie continuing to eat her breakfast and something twisted inside him. She looked so young, so innocent.

When he'd woken up alone in the bed his immediate reaction had been irritation that she'd left. He'd been about to go and find her when he'd remembered her tears, that incredible outpouring of emotion, and like a coward he'd stopped. Not sure if he was ready to face that searing blue gaze in the morning light.

The look in her eyes just now, though, made him feel like a heel. His own conscience mocked him. Making that call to his assistant yesterday had come out of a gut reaction to how Lexie's lit-up face and smile had made him feel. A gut reaction to doing something so out of his comfort zone. Cesar didn't *do* quirky, fun sightseeing tours with lovers. He didn't engage with the public. But he had— and moreover he'd found himself enjoying it.

He was dark and brooding, and most people ran a mile when they saw him. But not when he was with Lexie.

And that, frankly, had terrified him. So he'd called Mercedes and once he'd instructed her to alert the press he'd felt that he *hadn't* lost his mind completely.

Now, absurdly, he felt guilty.

Lexie was taking a sip of coffee, wiping her mouth, avoiding his eyes. Cesar reached out and took her hand. He saw her tense and that guilt intensified. *Damn her.*

Warily she looked at him.

Carefully Cesar said, 'Our becoming lovers was inevitable. Diverting the media is a beneficial consequence for both of us.'

Lexie blinked. Cesar saw how her expression became inscrutable, hidden.

'Of course. I know that. Don't worry, Cesar, I'm not some soft-hearted teenager who is weaving fantasies around a happy-ever-after scenario. I know that doesn't exist. Believe me.'

Something about the harshness of her tone caught at Cesar's chest, making it ache even as everything within him urged him to agree with her, to feel relieved.

She stood up to take their plates and Cesar caught her wrist, said gruffly, 'Leave it. My housekeeper will attend to it later, when we're gone.'

He tugged her towards him until she put down the plates and fell, resisting, into his lap.

She huffed out, 'What are you doing?'

The feel of her soft, lithe body against his made a lie of every one of Cesar's last words. All he could think about was how much he wanted this woman. But Lexie was stiff in his arms and that made him feel slightly desperate.

His hand was on her waist and he could feel a sliver of silky skin under her top. He explored underneath, over the indent of her naked waist and higher. Already he could feel the effect, the softening and relaxing of her body into his.

'Lexie…'

Slowly she turned her head to his, and for a moment

there was something unguarded in the depths of her eyes. Something very raw and pained. But it didn't make Cesar want to run.

His exploring hand came into contact with the bare swell of her breast. *No bra.* And just like that lust surged between them, red-hot and powerful. Their mouths connected, their kiss deepened, Lexie groaned softly and Cesar cupped the full weight of that breast in his hand.

Weakly he drowned out the clamouring voices in his head that told him he was deluding himself if he believed that he was half as in control of this as he would have Lexie believe.

CHAPTER EIGHT

'*LET'S GO AGAIN,* folks.'

Lexie clenched her jaw. This was the thirteenth take, and if she fluffed her lines one more time more than one crew member would want to wring her neck. Including herself. The director called *action* and by some miracle Lexie managed to get through the dialogue with no mishaps.

There was an audible sigh of relief around the set. Everyone was tired. It was the end of the third week and fatigue was setting in. The prospect of another week here and then two weeks in London stretched like a never-ending horizon line.

As they called that scene complete and started to set up for the next one Lexie was whisked back to the unit base for a costume-change. She relished the time to try and gather her scattered and fragmented thoughts.

Since the previous cataclysmic weekend, and their return to the *castillo* from Madrid on Sunday, Lexie had been avoiding Cesar at every opportunity. It didn't help that he was almost constantly on set—hence her fluffed lines and general state of being flustered. But today he hadn't shown up, and that had nearly been worse.

Lexie was terrified that she'd gone and fallen for the first man who had come along and kissed her whole body awake—much like Sleeping Beauty in the fairy tale.

That was why she'd been avoiding Cesar all week. She

felt as if she wasn't in control of these new and overwhelming desires. It was like having a car and not really knowing how to drive it—being afraid that if she got behind the wheel it would career off the road and cause mayhem and destruction.

She felt feverish, excited. Exactly like the soft-hearted teenager she'd mocked only days ago.

That weekend he'd only had to pull her onto his lap and kiss her before she'd been reduced to a puddle of lust, letting him take her back to bed and make love to her again and again. Showing her the heights her body could attain with just the barest sweep of his clever fingers against her body's core.

He had no idea who he was dealing with. The dark secrets Lexie harboured. But every time Cesar touched her she felt more and more exposed—as if sooner or later she wouldn't be able to stop it all tumbling out. Baring her soul to him.

So she'd been avoiding him. Like a coward. Even though all she could think about and dream about and yearn for was him.

It was affecting her work. And it didn't help that one scene in particular was due to be shot at the beginning of the following week and Lexie was dreading it, but unable to say anything to anyone about it.

After her dresser had left Lexie waited for the call to go back to set, pacing up and down her trailer, repeating her lines, trying to force all other thoughts out of her head.

When a knock came on her trailer door she said distractedly, 'I'll be out in a minute,' assuming that it was the call for set. But then the door opened and Lexie whirled around, copious amounts of silken layers rustling as she did so, only to see Cesar coming up the steps and entering.

Immediately the relatively big space was tiny. He closed the door behind him. He looked dark, gorgeous. Intent.

Lexie was breathless, and it only had a little to do with her costume. 'You shouldn't be here—they'll be calling for me in a minute.'

Cesar crossed his arms. '*Here* seems to be the only place I can find you without you avoiding me or hiding in your room.'

Lexie flushed, her whole body tingling just to be near him. She couldn't deny the sheer excitement that gripped her, the anticipation at the look in Cesar's eye. Especially when his gaze dropped to the swells of her breasts, made even more provocative than usual in the dress.

Lord, she wanted him right now. *Here*. Like some lurid parody of the stories she'd heard of actors and actresses behaving badly while shooting on location.

Cesar came towards her and Lexie had nowhere to escape to. He wrapped an arm around her waist and pulled her into him. Her body sang and, bizarrely, something inside her calmed. She felt more centred.

'Why have you been avoiding me all week?' he growled.

'Work…I need to concentrate on my work,' Lexie blurted out weakly.

His eyes flashed. 'Well, you're singularly to blame for *me* not being able to concentrate on a single thing.'

'Really?' Inordinate pleasure snaked through Lexie to hear that. To imagine this stern, unflappable man being distracted because of her. She felt like smiling.

'I don't play games, Lexie.'

She blanched. 'You think…you think I'm playing some *game*?'

His jaw was set, stern. Her belly swooped.

'Cesar…I'm not playing a game… I was avoiding you because last weekend… It's just been a long time for me.' *Try for ever,* said a small voice, but she blocked it out. 'I'm not used to this—I don't have *affairs*.'

Flustered, she ducked her head. Cesar put a finger to her chin to tip her face back up.

His gaze dropped to her cleavage and his voice was rough. '*Dios*...do you know what it does to me to see you in these dresses?' His eyes met hers again and his arm tightened around her. 'Come to my apartment this evening.'

Resistance was futile. Lexie felt herself dissolving, aching to say *yes*, let him take control so she didn't have to think or analyse. Just *be*.

'Okay.' She smiled, unable to keep it in.

Cesar was about to kiss her when a knock came on the door and a PA called out, 'Lexie, they're ready for you.'

Cesar stopped and Lexie almost groaned. 'Okay, thanks,' she called back.

Then he smiled, and it was wicked. 'I'll cook dinner. Come by when you've wrapped. Bring a weekend bag.'

Lexie almost rolled her eyes, 'My room is in the *castillo*. If I need anything surely I can just—?'

Cesar cut her off. 'Just...do it.'

'Okay,' Lexie said again, her smile turning wry at his autocratic tone.

She let Cesar lead her out to where her driver was waiting in the car to take her back to the set.

The following day Lexie grumbled good-naturedly, '*Why* can't you tell me where we're going?'

Cesar stopped abruptly and Lexie almost careened into him. He caught her hands and held them. The breeze had mussed up his hair. He looked vital, and so gorgeous that she sighed with pure appreciation. He looked darker too, all dressed in black.

He was mock stern. 'Just do as you're told.'

Lexie saw a staff member carrying their bags to a waiting helicopter. It was sitting on a landing pad at the back of the *castillo*.

Cesar had woken her early that morning and she'd stretched like a satisfied cat amongst his very tousled sheets before she'd even really realised the enormity of where she was.

In Cesar's bed, in his private apartment. After a night of lovemaking that had almost brought her to tears again. She'd only held them back with gritted teeth, determined not to let him see her get so emotional again.

But she couldn't help it. With every touch, every kiss, this man was rebuilding the very fabric of her soul. A fabric that had been torn apart brutally years before.

As instructed, she'd packed some things the previous evening and had gone to his apartment after work to find him waiting for her, busy in his kitchen making dinner. The sight had been so incongruous and so…*sexy* that Lexie had struggled to affect a nonchalance she hadn't felt.

Before she could say anything else Cesar took her by the hand and led her to the helicopter, bundling her inside. Lexie gave up trying to figure out where they were going and did as she was told, putting on earphones and buckling up.

Cesar leant over from his seat to help her just as the rotor blades started up outside, and adrenalin and excitement kicked in her belly.

He grinned at her. 'Don't worry—you'll like it, I promise.' And then he pressed a swift kiss to her mouth and sat back.

Lexie scowled at him, hating that his grin made her heart clench and that he could so easily affect her. But then her mind emptied as the chopper rose smoothly into the air and she saw the *castillo* drop away underneath them.

Cesar had obviously asked the pilot to take a tour of the estate, and he pointed out vineyards and more land than she had ever realised belonged to him. It was truly mind-boggling. And sobering to realise the extent of his responsibilities.

Then they were banking and heading away from where the sun had risen only a short while before. Lexie was transfixed by the changing landscape underneath them as they passed over low mountains and rivers.

Eventually she could see that the sparse countryside was making way for more built-up areas. Cesar took her hand and pointed out of the main window of the helicopter. She could make out a smudge of blue...*the sea*?

She glanced at him and he smiled. One of those rare smiles that made her want to smile back like a loon. She could see that they were flying over what had to be a city. The rooftops were terra-cotta, glinting in the sun. She saw a very majestic-looking castle on a hill.

They seemed, impossibly, to be heading right for the city centre. Lexie could see a bridge spanning a huge river, and the way the city was spread out on hills. It didn't look especially modern. There were trams and beautiful old crumbling buildings covered in coloured tiles.

She gasped and turned to Cesar and shouted over the noise, 'Lisbon?'

He nodded. So that's why he'd told her to pack her passport. A rush of incredible emotion and gratitude filled Lexie. She remembered standing in his study that day and exclaiming with a feeling of panic that she wanted to visit Madrid, Salamanca and Lisbon.

So far he'd taken her to all of them.

The helicopter set down on the rooftop of a building and Cesar helped her out. Lexie realised it was a hotel when the staff greeted them and led them inside where solicitous customs officials were waiting for them to check their passports. Cesar took her hand once they were done and she sent him a quick, dry look. 'No queues for you?'

Cesar smiled. 'My name, Da Silva, isn't strictly Spanish in origin. It comes from a very distant Portuguese ancestor. So I'm allowed…certain liberties…'

Lexie all but rolled her eyes as one of the staff got Cesar's attention. She'd just bet he was allowed untold liberties for the promise of his favour and business opportunities. The fact that he was obviously a regular visitor to Lisbon told her that he didn't take advantage of their respect and that made her feel soft inside.

They went one floor down and were shown into the most sumptuous suite of rooms Lexie had ever seen.

She explored on her own and found a terrace outside the bedroom's French doors. She went out. The view was astounding. She could see the huge imposing castle up on a nearby hill, lots of steep streets with distinctive yellow trams. And then what had to be the River Tagus, spanned by a massive bridge.

She felt a presence behind her and then arms came around her, hands resting by hers on the rail. Lexie shut her eyes for a second at the way her body wanted to melt, and when Cesar pressed close behind her she *did* melt into him, blocking out the voices screaming *Danger! Danger!*

One of his hands disappeared and she felt her hair being tugged back gently, so her neck was bared. Breath feathered there and then she felt his mouth, warm and firm. Lexie's hands tightened on the rail and the view became blurry.

She turned around to face him and looked up. His eyes were heavy-lidded, full of something dark and hot. A pulse throbbed between Lexie's legs.

'I have a whole agenda laid out for you today, Miss Anderson.'

Lexie arched a brow and tried to be cool. 'Oh, you do?'

Cesar nodded, and took some of her bright hair between two fingers. He tugged gently again and his eyes rose to hers.

'And right now I have something very specific in mind.'

Lexie was already breathless. 'You do…?'

'Yes.'

And then, with devastating precision, Cesar's mouth closed over hers and Lexie didn't care where she was in the world as long as she was right in this moment.

'A nightcap?'

Lexie looked at Cesar and nodded. 'That'd be nice, thanks.'

She watched as he turned and went to the drinks cabinet, her eyes devouring his tall, lean form sheathed in a dark trousers and a light shirt. He'd already shrugged off his jacket.

Lexie was reeling after the day. Not wanting Cesar to see how overwhelmed she was, she made her way out to the terrace that was accessible through the living room too. She heard the faint sound of a mobile and Cesar's deep tones as he answered.

A quiver of relief went through her—a moment alone, to try and assimilate everything. She sucked in the evening air, hoping it might cool her hot cheeks. They'd felt permanently hot since Cesar had made love to her that morning.

Afterwards, when she'd been sated and replete, he hadn't let her burrow back under the covers as she'd wanted to. He'd all but washed and dressed her, picking out a pretty shirt and jeans, sneakers.

They'd left the hotel and a car had taken them up to the impressive St George's castle, with its breathtaking views of the city. Peacocks had strutted on the paths, fanning their colourful tails much to the delight of the tourists.

Then, as if reading Lexie's mind, he'd taken her on one of the old yellow trams down a steep hill. It had been so packed that Cesar had pulled her into his body in front of him, arms wrapped tight around her. By the time he'd pulled her out at another stop she had been thoroughly turned on.

She'd found herself being led though a dizzying labyrinth of ancient streets. Cesar had explained that it was the Alfama—the old Arabic quarter.

Beautiful murals decorated walls at the ends of alleyways, little children darted dark heads out of tiny windows and called, *'Bom dia!'* Washing hung on lines between houses.

They'd had lunch there, on a tiny terrace overlooking the river. Afterwards they'd wandered some more, Lexie's hand tightly in Cesar's. At one point she had tugged gently, and when he'd looked at her she'd asked, 'No paparazzi?'

Something had flashed across his face but he'd smiled and said, 'No. Not here.'

Something very dangerous had infused Lexie's blood to think that here they were truly anonymous. That Cesar hadn't automatically thought of the bigger agenda.

Dangerous.

The car had reappeared then, as if by magic, and had taken them to see the stunning sixteenth-century monastery where Vasco Da Gama was buried in Belem. Afterwards Cesar had pointed to a blue-canopied shop nearby, where a queue literally about a mile long waited patiently.

They'd joined the back of it. Lexie had looked at Cesar, but he'd said enigmatically, 'Wait and see. Then you'll understand why all these people are here.'

Eventually, when they'd reached the shop itself, Cesar had spoken in flawless Portuguese. He'd handed Lexie what looked like a small custard tart.

'Taste it,' Cesar had urged as they'd found stools in the heaving shop with its beautiful ornate interior.

Lexie had obediently bitten into the flaky pastry and the smooth warm custard had melted on her tongue. She'd groaned her appreciation, much as everyone else had.

When she'd been able to speak again she'd said, 'That was probably one of the best tarts I've ever tasted in my life.'

A smug Cesar had just said, 'See?'

And then they'd queued again for more.

After they'd taken a circuitous sightseeing route back to the hotel, instead of leading her up to the suite Cesar had taken Lexie down to the spa, where he'd consulted in Portuguese with the receptionist, who had gone bright pink and giggly. Lexie might almost have felt sorry for her if she hadn't been feeling a disturbing rise of something else. *Jealousy.*

Cesar had turned to her. 'See you in a couple of hours.' And after pressing a swift kiss to her mouth he'd left Lexie there, gaping at his retreating form.

Two women had emerged and Lexie had been taken in hand—literally. The full works of an all-over beauty treatment, followed by a full body massage.

Then, when she'd floated back to the suite, Cesar had been waiting with champagne, and once Lexie had changed into the dark pink off-the-shoulder dress she'd brought with her they'd gone to dinner.

And now…now…Lexie took in the sparkling view of one of the oldest cities in Europe and felt overwhelmed. No more in control of her emotions than she had been ever since they'd queued a second time for the glorious *pasteis de natas* in Belem. When Cesar had looked so carefree and years younger.

Conversely, it had reminded Lexie that she harboured dark secrets, and they were rising up within her now—because she was going to be coming face to face with a very personal old scar on set the following week. The thought of it terrified her, and she knew she was feeling more vulnerable about it because being with Cesar…being intimate for the first time…had ripped away some vital layer of protection.

'Sorry, I had to take that call.'

Lexie tensed at Cesar's deep voice. He came alongside her and handed her a small glass of port. She forced a smile and tipped it towards him after sniffing it appreciatively. 'Appropriate—given we're in the land where port is made.'

Cesar inclined his head. He looked absurdly suave and gorgeous this evening. Tall and imposing. Yet with that very definite edge of virile masculine energy.

Lexie took a quick sip of her drink. It was smooth and luxurious. Her feeling of vulnerability and the darkness on her soul made her want to avoid Cesar's far too incisive gaze. Even now he was regarding her speculatively. She felt raw after the day, and on some perverse level she almost felt angry with him—for charming her, for making her fall for him.

A rogue desire to crack that impenetrable façade he wore so well made her ask, 'So how come you're not married…?'

Lexie immediately wanted to claw the words back. Regretting the impulse.

Cesar's gaze narrowed predictably and Lexie squirmed, cursing herself. Thinking frantically of a way to save herself, she sought to mitigate it by saying lightly, 'You're a catch. I mean you have all your own teeth, your breath isn't bad. You own property…'

Somehow Lexie was afraid she hadn't fooled him. Her voice had sounded too breathy, slightly desperate. She took another sip of the port.

But when she looked back at him he was smiling wryly. 'No one's ever mentioned the boon of having my own teeth before.'

No, thought Lexie, she'd bet they hadn't. They'd probably looked at him and seen a walking, talking dollar sign.

Inexplicable anger rose up within her to think of women seeing him as a target, and then just as quickly dissolved. Cesar was so cynical that he would never be taken for that kind of a fool.

Suddenly loath to think that he might consider *her* a vulture like that, she said quietly, 'Thank you. Seriously, this day has been…amazing. I never expected it.'

Something painful gripped her inside. Their time was finite.

Not wanting to think about that, she figured she had nothing to lose so she dived in, telling herself she wasn't genuinely curious. 'Have you ever come close? To being married?'

Cesar tensed. His fingers tightened fractionally on his glass. Then the line of his mouth flattened. 'I was abandoned at an early age and then left in the hands of two people who were little better than uninterested caretakers. They resented the fact that my blood was not pure. That experience hardly left me with the qualifications to create a warm, inviting atmosphere conducive to family and such frivolous things.'

Lexie's insides clenched in rejection of that. Creating a family, a home, was not frivolous. Cesar's words, however, had been emphatic. She realised something about herself then, in a blinding flash of clarity: on some fundamental level she hadn't given up hope for herself. She hoped that some day she might have a second chance and her own rather dismal experience of what a family was could be proved to be the exception rather than the rule.

'Your half-brothers…' she offered huskily. 'They looked happy in the wedding pictures.'

Cesar's jaw tightened. 'They're different. They had a different upbringing, different perspectives.'

Lexie thought of his grandmother, cruelly making him

cut out and paste pictures of them growing up with their mother—*his* mother. Together.

'They had your mother… But I wonder if it was any easier or better for them just because she was there?'

'Perhaps—perhaps not,' Cesar said, but it rang hollow.

Lexie wanted to slide her arm around him but didn't. 'Are you going to see them again?'

He glanced at her and his face was hard. As it had been when he'd looked at the portraits of his grandparents.

'I have nothing in common with them. Especially not now.'

He turned to face her more fully and Lexie almost shivered at the frost in his eyes.

'I made a decision a long time ago never to marry and have children.'

'Why?' Lexie breathed, not liking how that declaration seemed to affect her physically. How it felt as if he was giving her a distinct message.

'Because I vowed that the *castillo* is no place for a child. The legacy of my family is tainted, built on obsessive greed. Snobbery. When I die the *castillo* will be left to the local town and they can do what they like with it. And all the money will go to various charities and trusts. That's what I'm building it up for now.'

'But…' Lexie searched wildly for a way to penetrate the cool shell that surrounded Cesar. 'You said yourself that you wanted to renovate the *castillo*, but…why bother? Why not just leave it behind now?'

Cesar looked at her then, and for a second Lexie saw bleakness in those green depths. A bleakness that resonated in her because she knew what it felt like herself.

'Because…' he was grim '…it's in my damn blood like some kind of poison.'

Lexie was stunned into silence. She didn't like the way she wanted to do something to comfort Cesar. Touch him.

And even though he was only inches away it felt as if a chasm yawned between them.

Huskily she said, 'I'm sorry. I shouldn't have said anything.'

His mouth tipped up but it was a parody of a smile, a million miles away from the smiles she'd seen earlier.

'What about you, Lexie? Do you wish for a cottage with a white picket fence and a gaggle of cherubic children?'

For a second Lexie felt nothing. The words seemed to hang suspended in the air between them. But then it was as if a roaring flood was approaching and gathering speed from a long way off. *Pain*. Incredible pain.

A kaleidoscope of images bombarded her—a tiny baby, crying lustily. Nurses with rough hands and judgemental looks. Officials. And then...nothing. Silence. More pain.

'Lexie?'

She blinked. Cesar was watching her, his eyes narrowing. Face stark. From somewhere she found a brittle smile and said through the ball of emotion growing in her chest, 'You forgot the dog...there's a dog there too.'

'Ah...yes, of course. No idyllic picture would be complete without a dog.'

Cesar put down his glass and took Lexie's from her too. He reached for her with both hands and pulled her into his body. Lexie felt cold, and she shivered lightly. She desperately wanted to drive away the chill and feel warm again. She desperately wanted to blank out the dark images she'd just seen.

Coming up on her tiptoes, Lexie reached up and brought her arms around Cesar's neck, pressing her whole body against his. She saw the flare in his eyes and felt herself start to thaw from the inside out.

'Kiss me, Cesar.'

Cesar smiled briefly before a look of almost feral intent crossed his face. He moved his hands up to Lexie's face.

The kiss was fierce and passionate, and before Lexie lost all ability to think clearly she knew that they were both running away from the demons nipping at their heels. This time, though, it didn't feel like kinship—it felt bleak.

Much later Cesar lay awake in the dark room. Traces of the constriction in his chest brought on by Lexie's questions were still there, faintly. Even though his body hummed with much more pleasurable sensations.

She was curled into him now, her naked curves keeping him at a level of near constant arousal. If it wasn't so damned intoxicating he could almost resent her for her effect on him.

Her breath was feathering softly across his chest, light and even, and her hair was soft and silky. One hand lay right over the centre of his chest, where he'd felt the constriction most keenly earlier.

'So how come you're not married?'

Other women had asked him that question with a definite look in their eyes. Lexie hadn't had that look. He never talked to anyone about his upbringing, but he seemed to be incapable of holding it in whenever those huge blue eyes were trained on him.

He'd told her…*everything*. He'd never even articulated his plans for the *castillo* to his friend Juan. He'd never told another soul. And when he'd told her something incredibly bleak had hit him. Bleak enough to drive him to taunt her, ask her if she pictured herself in that idyllic scenario.

And she'd looked for a moment as if he'd run a knife right through her belly. Pale. Stricken. Shocked. Clearly the thought was anathema to her, even though she'd joked about a dog.

Cesar went cold in the bed beside Lexie as something slid home inside him. The joke was on him, because for the first time in his life he was aware of a yearning sensation, a yearning for something he'd always believed to be utterly beyond his reach.

The following morning Lexie woke up alone in the bed. She sagged back against the pillows with not a little relief. Images from the night flooded her head and her cheeks reddened even as a tight knot of tension made her belly cramp.

She'd been able to drive away the demons for the night, but now they were back. The conversation with Cesar replayed in her head. The bleakness she'd felt when he'd spoken about the *castillo*, about leaving it behind so no child would have to endure what he had.

It shouldn't be affecting Lexie like this. If anything it should be inciting a sense of protection within her. A sense that as long as she could count on Cesar's obviously deeply rooted cynicism then she would be okay too.

But she couldn't keep fooling herself. That discussion with Cesar had told Lexie that she wasn't half as cynical as she'd always believed she was. It had told her that at a very deep core level she *did* harbour a fantasy. A fantasy of family and security and happiness. Fulfilment. It might not be dressed up in a vision of a cute cottage with a white picket fence and a dog and children, but it wasn't far off.

And it made Lexie feel physically ill, almost as if she'd betrayed herself, to realise that. She'd been betrayed in the worst way possible by the very people who should have loved and protected her. And she'd always vowed to herself that she'd never allow that to happen again.

She'd vowed it. But deep down she hadn't wanted to become that hard inside.

Lexie could see now that that was why she'd allowed herself to believe she could trust Jonathan Saunders, even briefly. Even then she'd been trying to prove to herself that she could trust again. That she could believe that she wouldn't be betrayed. But he *had* betrayed her. And that should have proved to her that she'd been right all along not to trust. It should have shored up her defences. Made her even stronger.

But it hadn't.

Because Lexie knew that any illusion of feeling in control of what was happening between her and Cesar Da Silva was exactly that. An illusion. And this man had the power to show her the true extent of how flimsy her defences had always been.

CHAPTER NINE

'WOULD YOU MIND if we returned to the *castillo* this morning? Something's come up that I have to attend to in the vineyards.'

Lexie was in the bedroom and had just finished dressing in the jeans she'd worn the day before and a stripy Breton top. For a second Cesar's words didn't even compute because she was just drinking him in, looking impossibly handsome in jeans and a light wool sweater.

Then the words registered and relief rocked through her. She'd been dreading facing Cesar so soon after her recent revelations.

'No,' she said quickly—too quickly. 'I don't mind at all. There's some heavy scenes next week so I'd appreciate some time to prepare…'

Anxiety at the prospect of what lay ahead for her gripped her again.

Cesar crossed his arms and lounged against the door. Instantly Lexie's skin prickled with awareness. She could feel her nipples drawing into tight buds. Even more reason why she would relish some space from this man…

'You don't have to sound so eager.'

She blushed and glanced away for a second, feeling churlish. 'It's not that I want to leave…you've been so generous…'

Cesar closed the distance between them so fast her head spun. He looked stern. 'You don't have to thank me.'

Lexie said weakly, 'Yes, I do… It's polite.'

'I don't want your politeness,' Cesar growled softly. 'I want you.'

He cupped the back of her head and kissed her. Lexie clung to his arms to stop her legs from buckling.

When he drew back she opened her eyes. *Lord,* she could barely breathe.

'Maybe I can convince them they don't need me,' Cesar said roughly.

It took a second for his meaning to sink in and then, despite the lurch in her chest, Lexie said hurriedly, 'No, you should go back. And I *do* need to prepare for next week.'

'You're staying with me in my apartment, though.'

She opened her mouth to object and saw the glint of determination in Cesar's eyes. She sighed, feeling weak. 'Okay.'

Much later that night Cesar finally returned to his apartment in the *castillo*. He was irritated and frustrated. The problem in the vineyards had been more complicated than he'd thought, and then he'd been waylaid by his house manager and that had evolved into a long impromptu meeting about the renovations Cesar was embarking on. Renovations that were now taking on a new resonance—as if something had shifted inside him with regards to his long-term plans for the *castillo*.

But he didn't want to think of that. All he wanted *was to see Lexie.* His apartment was quiet. Empty. When he considered for a second that she might well have gone back to her own rooms the rise of an even deeper frustration made him clench his jaw.

But, no… He saw her sneakers, thrown off near the couch where a low light was burning. Cesar walked over and his chest grew tight when he saw Lexie fast asleep. Her top had risen up, revealing a sliver of pale soft belly. One arm was flung over her head, the other was just below her breasts.

He came closer and wasn't even really aware of the way the irritation and frustration he'd been feeling moments before had just dissolved away. To be replaced by a different kind of frustration. A hunger.

He spotted the earphones of her mp3 player in her ears, the wires leading to the device. And that tightness was more acute as he thought of her dyslexia and how hard it must have been for her to overcome its challenges along the way.

As if aware of his intense scrutiny, she opened those huge blue eyes. It took a second for them to focus and then Lexie scrambled up, her cheeks pink.

'Oh, my God, what time is it?'

Cesar came down on the edge of the couch and pinned her with his arms. She lay back. She looked tousled and delicious and sexy as hell.

'It's way past your bedtime.'

She smiled and an incredible lightness infused Cesar. Addictive, seductive...

'Is it now? What are you going to do about it?'

Cesar said sternly, 'I'm going to make sure you go to bed right now and tuck you in myself.'

He stood up and reached for Lexie, swinging her into his arms, relishing the way she snuggled into his chest. Relishing even more the way her mouth unerringly found his neck and started pressing kisses there. Open-mouthed kisses, so that he could feel the tip of that wicked tongue.

Lexie sank back onto the bed and Cesar loomed over her, pulling off his top with one graceful move. She was still in a delicious half-dream haze. She didn't even have to be awake for him to have an effect on her.

But then, like a dream that became clearer on waking, the darkness of the material she'd been studying in the script came back to her. It made her mood change in an instant, dousing desire. She recalled too that just before she'd woken she'd been having disturbing dreams. Almost nightmares. And it was no wonder.

Cesar came down over her on his arms and just like that Lexie froze under him. In that instant she felt tainted, *damaged*. She could see now that the exhilaration of becoming more intimate with Cesar had helped her to forget for a moment who she really was. What had happened to her. The sheer extent of the dark secrets she harboured.

Right then it felt as if a chasm yawned between them. He wouldn't ever want to know who she really was. Why would he? This was just an affair. Fun. Lighthearted. Lexie felt anything *but* lighthearted. She felt acutely alone. As if she carried the weight of the world on her shoulders.

Cesar lifted a hand as if to touch her and Lexie flinched violently. Everything in her was screaming to get away *now*—before he could seduce her so much that she found herself spilling out all the awful ugliness that had no place here.

He stopped. 'Lexie…?'

Lexie scrambled out from under Cesar's arms and stood up by the bed, her whole body cold. Numb. Cesar was looking at her as if she'd grown two heads. Galvanised by panic, Lexie found her bag and started throwing things in.

'What are you doing?'

She shoved the blouse she'd worn the previous day into the bag, her belly swooping at the thought of that day. How perfect it had been. It felt as if it had happened to another person now. A person who *didn't* have the awful memories that were bombarding her right now.

'I'm going back to my own room.'

She picked up her bag but Cesar caught her arm. He was shaking his head, incredulous. 'What on earth is going on?'

She pulled her arm free and backed away, torn by the sense of increasing panic she felt and also by something much more disturbing: the desire to throw down the bag and launch herself into Cesar's arms, ask him just to hold her, to reassure her that she could feel safe with him. But that was not what he was interested in—Lexie being vulnerable. He'd run a mile.

Then he stopped looking incredulous. He folded his arms. 'I told you before that I don't play games, Lexie.'

Lexie felt sad. 'I'm not playing a game. I just can't do this right now. I need…some space.'

For a long second Cesar just regarded her, and then his face became unreadable. He stepped back and said coolly, 'By all means, Lexie, take all the space you need.'

Lexie gripped her bag and turned and walked out of the bedroom, and out of Cesar's apartment, adrenalin coursing through her system. When she got back to her own room it felt desolate. And then she realised with a sense of dread that *she* felt desolate.

The truth was that she was damaged and broken inside. For a brief moment in time she'd believed that she had somehow been miraculously cured. But she hadn't really. And this minor meltdown had just proved it to her.

'I need some space.' Cesar glowered so fiercely that his house manager saw him coming and scuttled out of sight. Those words had been eating away at him like poison for two days now.

One minute Lexie had been supine on his bed, flushed and sexy, huge eyes all but eating him up…and the next she'd become a different person. Cold. Stark. *Dios*, she'd flinched as if he might hurt her.

His skin prickled. He hadn't liked that feeling. And he

hadn't liked to acknowledge how feral she'd made him feel. When she'd said she needed space it had been like a punch to his gut.

The thought that she might have even glimpsed a tiny part of how ravenous she made him feel had made him go cold all over. He'd had to step back to stop himself from acting on the visceral impulse to prove her words to be a lie.

But even now he could remember the look in her eyes. It had been panicked. And he couldn't understand why.

The film unit was due to head back to London at the end of the week and Cesar was acutely aware of the fact— much to his chagrin. Especially when he'd set out at the very beginning to avoid getting involved at all costs.

For two days he'd deliberately avoided going near where they were shooting, in an old abandoned wing of the *castillo*. But today he found himself heading there even before he'd consciously taken the decision. The fact that he *needed* to see Lexie only put him into an even more foul humour.

Cesar saw the usual cluster of people as he got closer to the set—crew hanging around, waiting for someone to call for them urgently.

They nodded to him now. Said hello. He managed some civil responses. When he got closer he saw that the door to the set was closed. And there was a hushed air. He asked the third assistant director if they were shooting.

The young man shook his head and Cesar made to go onto the set, but the man stopped him. 'You can't go in there, Mr Da Silva.'

Cesar chafed at the obstruction. His need to see Lexie was like a burr under his skin now. 'Why not?' he demanded.

'It's a closed set. They're doing the rape scene. Essential crew only.'

The rape scene.

Cesar didn't know why, but he suddenly felt a chill in his blood. He looked around and saw the video assistant in the corner, with his wall of monitors which showed whatever the camera was seeing inside the room. Usually there would be a couple of producers or some crew watching the scenes, but today there was no one.

He went over and sat down. Just as he realised that he couldn't hear what they were saying the video assistant handed him some earphones. Cesar put them on and hunched forward.

They were about to shoot. The director was talking to Lexie and to Rogan, the male lead. Cesar's breath hitched when he saw her. Her hair was down, tousled, and she was wearing some kind of diaphanous white gown. It was open at the front, as if it had been ripped, and he could see the ripe curve of her breast.

And then the director disappeared, leaving Lexie and Rogan on the screen. The first assistant director called out the instructions to shoot and then the director called *action*.

Rogan grabbed Lexie by the arms and shook her, spittle flying from his mouth as he said crude, horrific things. She looked tiny and vulnerable. She was pleading with him. But he wouldn't listen. Then he brutally turned her and shoved her down on the bed, pulling her gown up over her thighs, undoing himself before he pressed himself into her, grunting like an animal.

The camera went close in on Lexie's face, pushed down onto the bed. Rogan's big hand was on the back of her head, holding her down. Her eyes were blank.

Cesar heard *cut*. But all he could really hear was the roaring of blood in his head. He wanted to move but he was paralysed.

On some rational level he knew it wasn't real. That it was just acting. He could see Rogan helping Lexie up. The actor looked faintly traumatised. Lexie looked impossibly pale, and sort of glassy-eyed. A shiver of foreboding went down Cesar's spine. He knew that it had obviously been a traumatic scene to shoot, but there was something else going on—he could feel it.

But then they were going again, and he heard the camera assistant say, 'Scene One Hundred, Take Twenty.'

Cesar pulled off the earphones and looked at the video guy incredulously. 'They've done this *nineteen* times?'

The man gulped. 'Yes, sir. We've been doing this scene all day from different angles. This is the last shot, but he's milking it.'

Cesar felt rage building inside him. The camera was close up on Lexie's face again and he saw a tear roll out of her eye and down one cheek. She hadn't cried last time.

Something rose up inside Cesar—something he couldn't even articulate. An overwhelming need to get to her. He surged to his feet, almost knocking over the wall of monitors. He stormed to the door of the set, swatting the protesting third AD aside.

He opened the door just as the camera assistant was saying, 'Scene One Hundred, Take Twenty-One.'

'Enough.' Cesar's voice cracked out like a whip.

Lexie turned her head and looked at Cesar. He saw only those huge bruised blue eyes, and something in their depths…a mute appeal. She wasn't acting any more. He knew it without even knowing how.

He walked straight over and scooped her up into his arms, and for the first time in two days he felt slightly sane again.

The director was standing up now, blustering. 'What the hell are you doing, Da Silva? You can't just barge in here like this.'

Cesar stopped in the act of turning around. Lexie was

far too slight a weight in his arms as he said coldly, 'You're on my property. I can do whatever the hell I want.'

'But we haven't got the shot yet.'

Even icier now, Cesar said, 'If you haven't managed to get it yet then perhaps you shouldn't be directing.'

He was barely aware of a suppressed snigger from one of the crew as he strode out of the room, Lexie curled into his chest, her head tucked down. It reminded him of how she'd curled into his chest after making love that first time. When she'd cried like a baby.

He carried her all the way to his apartment and took her into his bedroom. He sat down on the edge of the bed, still holding her. He was shaking from the adrenalin and anger coursing through his system.

After a long time, she moved in his arms. But she wouldn't look at him. She just said, in a quiet voice, 'I need to have a shower.'

Cesar got up and deposited her gently on the side of the bed, crouching down. Finally she met his gaze but her eyes were flat. As if she didn't see him. A shard of ice pierced him inside.

Reluctantly he left her to go and turn on the shower. When he came out she was standing, albeit shakily. 'Do you need help?' he asked.

She shook her head and went in, closing the door behind her. Cesar restrained himself from following her, making sure she was all right. The shower ran for long minutes.

Eventually it stopped. Lexie was so long coming out that Cesar was about to knock on the door when it opened. She was wrapped in his towelling robe. It swamped her. Her hair was damp and hung in long golden tendrils over her shoulders.

He handed her a glass of brandy. 'Here—you should drink some of this.'

Lexie wrinkled her nose, but she took it and sipped at it before handing it back. Cesar put it down on a nearby table. He felt unaccountably ill-equipped to know what to do. What to say.

'You shouldn't have done that.'

She was looking at him with her chin tilted up and Cesar arched a brow. 'Would you prefer to be back there doing Take Thirty right now?'

She paled so dramatically that Cesar reached out and put his hands on her arms.

'No,' he said grimly, leading her out to the living area and guiding her to sit down on the couch. 'I didn't think so.'

Lexie seemed impossibly tiny and fragile sitting on the big couch. Cesar stood over her and crossed his arms, because even now all he wanted to do was touch her. *I need space.* He cursed silently.

'So, are you going to tell me what's going on?'

Lexie glanced up at Cesar and then away again quickly. He was so…implacable. Determined. Stern. The numb shell that had surrounded her for the past two days was finally breaking apart.

When Cesar had burst onto the set and she'd seen him… He would never know the depth of the gratitude she'd felt. Because on some level she'd always needed to know that someone might have saved her.

She forced herself to look at him. 'Why did you do that?'

Cesar paced back and forth now, energy sparking off his tall, lean body. His mouth was tight. 'I don't know, to be honest. But when I saw you…I could tell something was wrong.' He shook his head, stopped pacing. 'You weren't acting, Lexie.'

Something huge inside her shifted to know that he'd

intuited something was wrong. 'No, I wasn't acting…not by the end.'

Cesar pulled a chair over to sit in front of her. Lexie gazed at him. Remembered how good it had felt when he'd swept her up into his arms. *Too good*. As if she'd been running for a long time and someone had finally allowed her to stop and rest.

She found that she wanted to tell him. She wanted to explain about the other night.

'Lexie…*what*?'

She took a breath and then said starkly, 'I was raped when I was fourteen.'

Cesar went white in an instant. His whole body tensed. 'What did you say?' His voice was hoarse.

Lexie bit her lip. She couldn't go back now.

'I was raped by my aunt's husband. One night my parents and my aunt had gone out—he said he'd babysit. He brought me into my parents' room when the others were in bed and raped me.'

'The others…?'

'My five younger brothers and sisters.'

'*Dios mio*… Lexie…that animal…' Cesar looked sick. 'You looked at me the other night like I was going to hurt you—you were scared…'

Lexie leant forward and touched his arm. 'No…'

But Cesar was almost recoiling now, and she could see the horror on his face that she might have thought for a second he was capable of something so heinous.

She shook her head, '*No*, Cesar. I wasn't afraid of you. I knew this scene was coming up… I was apprehensive about it… It's the first time I've ever had to do a scene like this and it was just too close to the bone.'

Cesar pulled free of her touch and stood up, pacing again. Lexie was tense, her hands forming fists in her lap.

He faced her, eyes flinty green. 'My God,' he said again—in English this time.

Suddenly a kind of hurt bloomed inside her. He was looking at her as if she was a stranger. A damaged stranger. The guilt that she had worked long and hard to believe wasn't hers reared its ugly head again. Her rapist's accusations were as clear today as they had been then. *'You were asking for it, you know. Always prancing around under my nose dressed in that uniform.'*

She felt cold and said tightly, 'I'm sorry. I shouldn't have told you.'

She stood up from the couch, hating that she'd been weak enough to confide in Cesar. Hating that she'd thought his intuition made her feel as if he deserved to know.

'Where are you going?'

She looked at him. 'Back to my room.'

She turned and headed for the bedroom, but Cesar caught her hand. This time when she looked at him his eyes were blazing. 'Dammit, Lexie, you're staying here.'

Hot tears pricked the back of her eyes, galling her. She hadn't even cried after she'd been raped—too shocked and traumatised—and yet with one touch, one look, this man could reduce her to tears and make her want to lean on him when she'd fended for herself for so long now…

'Damn *you*, Cesar.' She pulled her hand free and faced him. 'Just let me go.'

He shook his head. 'You shouldn't be alone right now.'

More hurt bloomed inside Lexie to think that he was acting out of a sense of duty. 'I've done my therapy, Cesar, years of it,' she sneered. 'You really don't have to act as my babysitter just because it turns out that your lover is damaged goods.'

Now Cesar was angry. He took her arms in his hands, gripping her. 'Don't you *dare* put words in my mouth. I don't think any such thing. And you are *not* damaged. You're perfect.'

Lexie's anger drained away, leaving her feeling shaky. 'I'm sorry. I just…I shouldn't have told you.'

'I'm glad you told me. It's just a lot to take in.'

He let go of her arms and stepped back, raking a hand through his hair. Lexie felt bereft.

'Look,' she offered, 'I'm fine—really. I always suspected this scene would be difficult. But it's one of the reasons I took the job in the first place. Initially I wanted to say no, but I knew I couldn't let it stop me. I dealt with what happened a long time ago, Cesar. But something like this would be difficult even under the best of circumstances.'

Cesar shook his head lightly. He came close again, touched Lexie's jaw.

'You shouldn't have had to face it alone.'

Lexie felt emotion building inside her. Terrified of it, she said simply, 'I've always been alone.'

Cesar looked at her with a burning intensity. Desire, pure and hot, sparked to life within her, mixing with the emotion to produce something volatile. She brought her hand up to cover his and saw his eyes widen slightly.

'*Please…*'

One word. She could see that he understood, and she trembled inwardly in case he might balk. He could never know the depth of how badly she needed him right now—for myriad reasons.

His voice was gruff. 'Lexie…are you sure? The other night…'

She nodded. 'I'm sure. The other night…it wasn't about you. It was about me.'

'I don't want to hurt you.'

'You won't…'

He didn't move, though. Frustration welled inside her. Maybe Cesar couldn't deal with the ugly truth of what had happened to her. She took her hand down, stepped back, dislodging his hand. She'd just exposed herself spectacularly.

'It's okay… If you don't want me any more because of—'

His hand shot out, caught her. She looked at him.

'Of *course* I want you.' He sounded fierce. 'I just have to look at you to want you.'

He came closer. Held her face with both hands. 'You're in my blood. I need you.'

Lexie's own blood sang. She needed him too. Her whole being came alive as he drew her close and lowered his mouth to hers. The kiss was so tender and gentle that she almost emitted a sob of emotion, but held it back.

When he drew back he took her by the hand and led her into his bedroom. There was no sense of hesitation within Lexie. No sense of that same panic that had gripped her the other evening. She knew now that that had been largely because of her apprehension of acting out being raped. And it was over.

Cesar stopped by the bed and she faced him. He said, 'If you want to stop…'

Something melted inside her. She shook her head, her hands going to the buttons on his shirt, her voice husky with need. 'I won't want to stop.'

Her hands were clumsy on his buttons and he gently took them away to undo them himself. Lexie sucked in a breath to see his chest revealed. She opened the knot on her robe.

Cesar looked down and she saw a dark flush slash across his cheekbones. He slid his hands under the shoulders of her robe and pushed it till it fell to the floor.

Lexie ran her hands over his pectorals, her nails grazing his nipples, making them stand up into hard little points. She reached forward and put her mouth there, swirling her tongue around one hard tip, feeling her core moisten with desire.

As she lavished kisses on his chest and nipples her hands were on his jeans, flipping open the buttons, feeling the hard ridge of his arousal brushing her fingers. She drew back and pushed his jeans down, taking his underwear with them, her breath disappearing when his erection was freed.

She wrapped a hand around him, awed by his sheer size and strength and the knowledge that he would never use it to hurt her. Cesar was kicking his feet free of his clothes and then he put his hands on Lexie's arms.

She looked up.

He sounded rough. 'I need you. I need to taste you.'

Her hand stalled on the thick column of flesh and gently Cesar removed it, pushing her down onto the bed. He came down beside her and his mouth was on hers, and Lexie moaned as she tasted him hungrily, sucked him deep. Wrapped her legs and arms around him as if she could bind him to her for ever.

Gently Cesar unbound her, spreading her arms out, his mouth leaving hers to explore over her jaw and neck. Over the tops of her heaving breasts. Taking each tight bud of her nipples into his mouth, making her moan even louder and her hips writhe against him.

But he kept moving down, over her belly. An arm came under her back, arching her into him, his other hand pushed her legs apart.

She felt dizzy. 'Cesar...'

His green gaze was blistering. 'Trust me.'

Trust me. Lexie sank back. She did trust him. She always had—from the moment she'd met him and let him kiss her. *Her*—with her history. The knowledge rushed through her. Wiping aside any trepidation or lingering hurt.

His mouth was moving down, kissing the top of her

thigh. Moving in. A big hand was splayed under her buttocks, tipping her towards his face. Lexie's breaths were coming so hard and fast she had to consciously slow down for fear of passing out.

And then his tongue touched her *there*. He licked her with explicit skill. All the way up the seam of her body, his tongue delving into her secret folds, opening her up to him, baring every part of her.

Lexie's hands gripped the sheet. Legs bent, back arched. Cesar licked and sucked and drove her more and more mindless. His tongue swirled with maddening strokes against her clitoris before leaving it to lavish attention elsewhere and then returning just when those cells were screaming for release.

When it came it was so huge…so all-encompassing…that Lexie thought she'd passed out. Because the next thing she was aware of was Cesar sliding into her, so deeply and thoroughly, and with such a fierce look of concentration on his face that it was all she could do to wrap her legs around him as far as they'd go and tilt her hips to take him even deeper.

They were locked in a dance that was as old as time and as profound. Lexie couldn't look away from Cesar even though she felt as though her soul was being turned inside out and he'd see it as clear as day. *She loved him.* And it went deeper than just loving him because he was the first man she'd allowed herself to be intimate with. He was the *only* man she could imagine being intimate with. The only man she *wanted* to be intimate with.

That revelation came just as bliss split her body in two, throwing her high into the air, where she seemed to hang suspended on the crest of a huge wave until it finally dropped her again. Cesar caught her in his arms and rolled them both so that she went limp across his heaving chest, their hearts thundering in unison, their skin slick with perspiration.

* * *

In the aftermath of her shattering climax and revelation Lexie felt as wobbly and vulnerable as a new foal trying to stand on spindly legs. So much had happened, and in the past couple of days since leaving Cesar's apartment she'd deliberately cut herself off from the people around her, dreading the upcoming rape scene.

It had reminded her of when she'd arrived in London for the first time, when she'd been completely alone and unsupported.

Cesar shifted now and she winced minutely as the connection between their bodies was broken.

He asked with obvious concern, 'Are you okay?'

Lexie nodded and looked at him. He was on one elbow, some hair flopping into his forehead, his face dark, eyes glowing like dark green gems. *She loved him.*

But even as she knew that she also knew, with a feeling of desolation, that he didn't feel anything for her other than desire…and maybe worst of all pity.

Cutting into her thoughts, Cesar asked, 'What happened to him?'

Lexie went cold inside. 'My uncle?'

Cesar nodded.

She braced herself for the pain that inevitably came whenever he was mentioned or she thought about him, but it wasn't as sharp. Lexie's mouth became bitter. 'Nothing. My parents didn't want to know when I told them. They were very religious—pillars of the community. My father was a salesman; he travelled a lot. The thought of the scandal was too much for them.'

Cesar was incredulous. 'You mean he just got away with it?'

She pulled the sheet around her and sat up against the pillows. 'He died in a car crash about a year after it happened. But, no, he never got prosecuted or punished.'

'How could they have done that to you? Just ignored it?'

Lexie glanced away from Cesar. There was an even darker stain on her soul than he could imagine. She suddenly felt jaded and weary. Knowing that she loved him, but that it would end when she left the *castillo* for London at the end of that week, she felt reckless. As if she had nothing more to lose.

'That wasn't all,' she said now in a quiet voice.

'What do you mean?' Cesar moved, sitting up too.

She looked at him. 'The rape resulted in me becoming pregnant.'

He frowned. 'Pregnant? You had a baby?'

Lexie nodded, suppressing the inevitable spasm of emotion. 'A baby boy. I named him Connor.'

Cesar shook his head, clearly finding this hard to digest. 'But…you don't… Where is he now?'

'I had just turned fifteen when I had him. My family sent me away to a distant relative down the country for the duration of the pregnancy, where I was pretty much kept a prisoner for nine months. He was adopted two days after the birth, and is growing up somewhere in the greater Dublin area—that's all I know. And that they kept Connor as his middle name.'

Lexie watched as Cesar, looking slightly stunned, blindly pushed back the covers and got out of the bed. A sinking feeling gripped her. This was it. Her ugly truth bared. She'd known on some deep level that it would be too much to take in. This relationship was about a flirty affair while they were filming—not about dark secrets.

She knew with a sick feeling that she had just ended it.

CHAPTER TEN

CESAR PULLED ON his jeans and then he faced Lexie again. She looked impossibly young against the sheets, eyes huge. He was literally speechless. Didn't know what to say. The knowledge of what she'd been through was…enormous. And it was making all of his own dark demons rear their ugly heads.

He felt tight inside. As if a hand was closing around his chest and heart and squeezing with remorseless pressure. He thought of her reaction when he'd first presented her with the option of staying in the *castillo* for the duration of the shoot. No wonder she'd looked panicked.

Lexie was a mother. She'd had to give up her baby. He knew rationally that she'd had no choice, but it impacted on him in a deeply raw place. He couldn't breathe.

'Why did you tell me this?'

Lexie's eyes widened. Her face paled. And then something in her features hardened, as if in response to Cesar's stoniness.

'I told you because I felt I could… But I can see I shouldn't have.'

Cesar watched as if slightly removed from his own body as Lexie reached for her robe and pulled it on, getting out of bed too. Belting the robe tightly around her.

So many different emotions were impacting on him that it was almost overwhelming. Among them was anger—

which he knew was directed at himself, for his less than coherent response, and at Lexie for bringing him face to face with things he didn't want to look at in himself.

'I don't know what you want me to say.'

Lexie stared at him, her hair tumbled around her shoulders. Right then she seemed like a tiny warrior queen. Majestic.

'You don't have to say anything, Cesar. I'm not looking for therapy. I had years of that. I told you…'

She stopped for a second and that tightening sensation in Cesar's chest grew stronger. He almost put a hand there, as if that could alleviate the pain.

'I told you because I've never been with another man.'

Cesar stepped back. Stunned. 'Since you were…?'

Lexie snapped. 'Since I was raped, yes. You were my first lover.'

Faintly, Cesar said, 'Why me?'

She crossed her arms. 'You were the first man I desired.'

Lexie had never regretted anything more than opening her mouth to Cesar. Self-disgust ripped her insides to shreds. She'd truly learnt nothing. For a long time she'd felt ashamed, dirty. That she was some kind of damaged goods. And then therapy had helped her make sense of what had happened and she'd begun the long process of healing and forgiving herself.

Healing. The physical process of that, which had started with Cesar's incendiary kiss in the stable, mocked her now. She'd confused physical intimacy with something deeper. Clearly it had never been about anything else for him.

Her own family had shunned her a long time ago, and she was damned if she was going to let that happen again.

Lexie stalked around the bed and into the bathroom, aware of Cesar's eyes on her. The fact that he was so silent, not making any attempt to touch her, said it all. She closed the door and with shaking hands that told her of the heightened emotion she was barely reining in, she took off the robe and put on the costume nightshirt she'd been wearing for the rape scene.

When she emerged Cesar had put on a top. He looked serious.

Lexie hated that even now she was acutely aware of her sensitised naked body under the voluminous robe.

She was brisk. 'I shouldn't have said anything.' From somewhere, Lexie even managed to force a smile—as if this *hadn't* just cost her everything.

'Lexie—'

She cut him off, dreading hearing some platitude, and a spurt of anger made her say, 'Cesar, we're wrapping here on Friday. It's not as if this was ever going to go further. The papers have already lost interest in us—we've done what we set out to do in the first place.'

'We have.' His voice was flat.

'Yes,' Lexie insisted, forcing herself to look at him even though it was hard. 'I wanted to salvage my reputation and avoid being dragged through the tabloids again as some kind of victim. You wanted to avoid unnecessary scrutiny into your family. It was a mutually beneficial affair—isn't that what you called it?'

Everything within Cesar rejected Lexie's terse words but something was holding him back. The feeling that the very walls around him were about to start crumbling—as if some sort of invisible earthquake was happening below ground.

Right at that moment the full impact of just how different Lexie was from any other lover he'd had hit him with the force of a blunt object. She'd turned him upside down and inside out.

'Yes,' he agreed, 'it was.'

Just then there was a knock on the main door of Cesar's

apartment. He cursed even as a very weak part of him welcomed the interruption. He strode through the main living space to get to the door, and opened it to see one of the film's PAs.

'Sorry to disturb you, Mr Da Silva, but the director is looking for Lexie.'

Cesar knew Lexie was behind him without turning around. His skin prickled. He felt disorientated, dizzy. Even now he had to battle an absurd urge to protect her and snarl at the young guy to leave.

Lexie was oblivious to the messy tumult in Cesar's gut. She stepped around him, didn't look at him, and spoke to the PA. 'Tell Richard I'll just change before I come to him.'

The PA hurried off, clearly relieved to have delivered his message. Cesar watched Lexie. She was avoiding his eye. He wanted to tip her chin up, force her to meet his gaze, but at the same time he didn't want to see what was in those blue depths.

'I should go and talk to Richard.' Lexie's voice was husky, her almost belligerent stance of moments ago less evident.

She looked at him then and Cesar tensed, but her eyes were clear. Unreadable. It irritated him—which irritated him even more.

'The next few days are heavily scheduled so that we get out of here on time. I think it's best if we just…let this be finished now.'

Cesar felt slightly numb. This was a novel situation: a woman who was ready to walk away before he was ready to let her go.

Humiliation scored at his insides. Lexie was right—this had only ever been about the short term. The thought of anything beyond this place was not an option. He did not chase women around the world. Whatever desire he felt would dissipate. He could not want her so badly that he was unable to let her go.

He was tight-lipped as he reached for the door and held it open. 'Goodbye, Lexie.'

Something flared in her eyes for a second, and then it disappeared. She didn't speak again, just turned and walked out, and as Cesar watched her go he thought numbly that she could be a ghost in the long white gown and in her bare feet.

He closed the door on her, on that evocative image, and pushed down the chilling sensation that she would haunt him for ever. Everything he'd been holding in since she'd told him about the rape, and then the baby, surged up in a tangled black mess of emotion.

He went to his drinks cabinet and took out a glass, poured himself a drink. Taking a swift gulp, he felt the liquid jolt him back to life. His hand tightened on the glass as he stared unseeingly at the wall in front of him.

His own mother had abandoned him and left him at the mercy of his grandparents. Lexie had given up her own son. For a moment pure unadulterated rage rose up within Cesar as he acknowledged what she'd done —but it was an old, reflexive anger that had more to do with his mother than with Lexie.

His rage dimmed when he thought of Lexie aged fifteen, a terrified and traumatised schoolgirl. What choice had she had? None.

For the first time in his life Cesar had to concede that by the time his mother had come back for him his grandparents had done such a number on him that he'd had no choice but to reject her.

And he had to concede too that perhaps there had been more to his mother's motives than pure greed and selfishness. Her distress when she'd said goodbye both times stung him now—hard. Like a slap across the face. This unwelcome revelation brought with it an even stronger feeling that everything he'd always counted on was falling apart at the seams.

Cesar pinched the bridge of his nose. All he could see was Lexie's face and those huge eyes.

Anger surged again. What had she wanted from him? Damn her! Had she expected him to take her in his arms and soothe her? Promise her that everything would be all right?

Cesar wasn't gentle. Or sensitive. Or kind. He was black all the way through, and he resented Lexie right then for making him see just how black he was. For showing him how little he could offer comfort. And for making him think of the bleak reality of his childhood, filled with a lifetime of resentment for his two half-brothers. How powerless he'd been under the influence of his bitter grandparents, intent on punishment and revenge.

Rage and a feeling of impotence wound up inside him so tightly that he exploded. He turned and raised the hand holding that heavy crystal glass and with an inarticulate roar of pain and rage flung it with all his might across the room at his stainless steel kitchen. He watched it shatter into a million pieces, amber liquid spraying everywhere.

An echo from a long time ago whispered across his soul, bringing a chill wind. It reminded him that no good came out of this dark, gothic place. And to have imagined otherwise, even for a second, was to have become weak.

Lexie Anderson would be gone in a few days, and right in that moment Cesar hoped he'd never set eyes on her again. Because she'd done the worst thing in the world: she'd made him forget who he really was.

Lexie was sitting in her chair on the set, waiting while they set up for a new camera shot. People milled around her, working, chatting. But she felt removed. She'd heard the helicopter leaving early that morning.

She'd known that Cesar had left the *castillo* even before she'd heard one of the producers say something about him having business to attend to in America.

She'd been awake for most of the night, alternating between seething resentment directed at Cesar for having awoken her body from a lifetime of numbness and anger at herself for being so stupid as to fall for him. She'd tried to tell herself that she hadn't fallen so hard…but the hurt was too real and too deep for feelings not to be involved.

She'd never forget the look on his face when she'd told him about her baby. He'd shut down. Lexie had only ever talked about her baby to her counsellor. No one else knew. It was one of the reasons she was paranoid about press intrusion—in case anyone ever dug deep enough to find out.

Her son would be thirteen now, and every day Lexie wondered about him—wondered how she would cope if he ever came looking for her, asking for information. Sometimes the thought was overwhelming. She went cold inside as something struck her. Had she, on some level, put Cesar in the role of confidante because she'd been so desperate for support?

Even as Lexie felt anger for being so weak she had to acknowledge that she could have asked for help before. She'd just been too stubborn. That had been borne out the previous evening, when she'd gone to find the director to try and explain to him why she'd reacted the way she had.

She'd told him about the rape, knowing instinctively that she could trust him.

He'd shaken his head and taken her hand, his eyes full of compassion. 'Lexie, you should have told me. If I'd had any idea of how huge that scene was for you I'd have approached it differently. We could even have got it out of the way in the first week…'

He'd humbled her, apologising for unwittingly causing her distress. It was as if another weight had lifted from her shoulders, and Lexie knew that if she hadn't already told Cesar there was no way she could have confided in anyone else.

That only made her angry with him all over again. He hadn't been able to get rid of her fast enough yesterday. His face had been hard. Clearly he'd rejected her unwelcome confidences. No doubt his other lovers didn't come with messy histories, or weep all over him after making love.

She was glad Cesar was gone because she knew all her bravado was very shaky and that if she saw him again her heart would splinter into a million pieces.

Over a week later Cesar returned to the *castillo*. It was as if there had never been a film unit on the estate. Apart from the flattened bit of grass where the extras' marquee had stood everything had been restored to its pristine state— and, perversely, it annoyed Cesar intensely.

For the past week he'd put in long days at board meetings he'd been neglecting. Because of a blonde-haired, blue-eyed temptress. Damn her. Those were his favourite words at the moment, and they beat a constant refrain in his head.

Damn her for coming into his life. Damn her for making him want her so badly that he seemed to have a constant ache in his gut. Damn her for being so light in spite of the horrific things she'd endured.

Just…*damn her*.

For making him think of things like his brother Alexio's wedding and how happy both his half-brothers had looked with their wives. And damn her for making him come to the uncomfortable realisation that he had to stop blaming his brothers for living their lives oblivious of his presence.

That realisation had hit him as he'd looked blearily into

the bottom of an empty bottle of whiskey in a dingy bar on the Lower East Side of Manhattan about two days ago.

Cesar stopped at the entrance of the *castillo*. It sat there, as forbidding and dark as it ever had been. But for the first time in his life it didn't feel quite so…oppressive.

It was quiet, though. And that quiet, which had never really bothered him before, seemed to reach around him and squeeze, bringing with it restlessness. Dissatisfaction.

Without even being aware of making the decision, Cesar found himself walking up the main staircase to the first-floor landing. He went and stood at the window where his grandmother had found him waiting, looking for his mother.

He felt the old pain like a bruise that would never fade. But it didn't bring with it that futile sense of anger. It only brought a sense of melancholy and a growing sense of something else. *Loss*. Acute, aching loss. Worse than anything he'd ever felt before—worse even the loss he could remember feeling as a child for his mother.

Cesar knew then that as much as his grandparents had all but imprisoned him in this *castillo* when he was a child, since he'd become an adult he'd happily inflicted the same punishment on himself, and self-disgust filled him.

Lexie's face and eyes filled his vision. How she'd looked that last time he'd seen her, in the ridiculous period nightgown. Pale. Yet strong. Defiant in the face of his frankly pathetic response to her pain and trauma.

Something had shut down inside him that day, as if to protect him from feeling the pain too acutely. But now that was breaking apart inside him as he stared out at a bleak view that was seared into his consciousness.

He was sick of bleak. He was sick of darkness. He was sick of himself.

Damn Lexie, indeed. Because she hadn't made him

forget who he was at all. She'd shown him *exactly* who he was and who he could be. If he was brave enough.

The street was stinking, narrow. Beggars lined it, calling out for mercy or money. Small children darted under people's feet. Lexie stepped out of the path of a horse and carriage only at the last moment and gasped as it whistled past. Her long skirts were splashed with mud. People jostled her. She was going against the tide. And all she could think about, even as the cameras were running, was *him*. Cesar.

She cursed him for about the hundredth time that day and hoped that her expression conveyed anger at her co-star, who followed her through the streets, tracking her like a hunted animal.

'Cut!'

Immediately Lexie stopped. All of the extras turned and went back to their first positions on the enormous set that had been built for the film on a back lot in the London studios. A swarm of crew moved in to rearrange things, fix focus marks, touch up hair and make-up.

Lexie felt removed, though. The director approached her and she smiled brightly.

He took her arm and said in a low voice, 'Lexie, are you all right? You just seem…not that focused.'

She grimaced inwardly, regretting having ever told him what had happened to her. He'd been overly solicitous ever since. 'Sorry, Richard… I'm fine. It's just—'

'Oh, my God.'

'Sir! *Sir!* You can't go onto the set without a pass!'

Richard frowned and looked past Lexie. 'What on earth is *he* doing here?' he said incredulously.

Lexie felt a prickling sensation and turned around to see a tall figure approaching them. But even now she couldn't really compute that it was *him*.

Cesar. Dressed in dark worn jeans. A jumper and a battered brown leather jacket. Dark golden hair glinting in the
London sunshine. He was almost too gorgeous to be real.

She even heard one of the extras nearby say in an awe-
struck voice, 'Who *is* that?' and Lexie could almost sympathise with the inevitable impact he would be having on
some poor unsuspecting person's senses.

He looked as intense as she'd ever seen him. A security
guard caught up with him and took his arm. Cesar shook
him off and kept coming.

Her mouth had gone bone-dry. She wondered if she
was seeing things. Damn this corset that constricted her
breath…

Cesar stopped just feet away and the security guard
came panting up behind him. 'Now, look here—'

Lexie put out a shaky hand. 'It's all right, we know
him. I…know him.'

Then all the anger and pain that had been her constant
companion for a week now came flooding up, boiling over.
She hissed at Cesar, 'What are you doing here? We're in
the middle of a scene.'

'So I see,' he remarked dryly, taking in all the gawping
extras and the crew, who were loving the interruption. He
looked back at Lexie, and then spoke as if they were continuing a conversation that had stopped only moments ago.
'The thing is I should never have agreed with you when
you said we should end the affair.'

Lexie gulped and darted a look at the avid crowd.
'Cesar, do we really have to do this here?'

Just then Richard stepped forward. 'Now, listen, Da
Silva—interrupting my set once was—'

Cesar took his eyes off Lexie to stare at the man, and Lexie
shivered when she saw the familiar steel in his expression.

'How much will it cost to shut down production for the
rest of the day?'

Lexie blinked. Richard spluttered. 'I'd have to ask the producer...'

'Well, why don't you find him and ask him, and whatever amount he gives you tell him I'll double it.'

A murmur started through the crew and the extras. Lexie could see the PAs galvanised into action at the thought of an early wrap and a day off. The set started to clear.

Cesar stepped right up to Lexie and she was rooted to the spot. Terrified of the flutters that had started in her belly. Her heart squeezed. She loved this man so much, but he'd hurt her, and if all he wanted was to continue their affair...

'Cesar, if you've come just because you're not ready to end the affair then I'm not interested.'

His gaze on hers became assessing. Lexie's body hummed with awareness. With hunger.

'So what *are* you interested in?'

She blinked, confused. Fear gripped her... *What had she just said?* 'I just told you—I'm not interested in an affair.'

A ghost of a smile touched Cesar's mouth and she realised very belatedly how dishevelled he was, with stubble lining his jaw.

'One thing I do know is that I am not ready to end the affair—and I don't think you are either.'

A ball of pain lodged in her gut. She didn't have it in her to keep seeing Cesar knowing that it would end. Even one night with this man would kill her, even though every cell in her body was crying out for his touch.

She stepped back, her movement slightly hampered by her long dress. 'Yes, I am. And you should go and tell Richard you were joking about shutting down the production before too many people leave. You've caused enough disruption in my life as it is.'

Lexie went to walk around him, cursing her costume when she couldn't move more freely.

Cesar caught her and whirled her around, eyes flashing. 'I've caused disruption in *your* life? What about the disruption you've caused *me*?' He pointed a finger at his chest and glared at her.

Lexie pulled free, her anger matching his, boiling over when she thought of how naive she'd been, baring her soul to him.

'I did nothing but warm your bed for a few weeks! I was a convenient lover who also handily deflected some heat from the press about your family issues, and you were quite happy to take advantage of that.'

'On the contrary—you weren't *convenient* at all! The fact is, Lexie Anderson, you have been the most singularly *in*convenient lover I've ever known.'

Cesar was practically roaring now, and Lexie's eyes stung with tears. She bit back the lump in her throat to hear Cesar declare so baldly just how much he resented his desire for her.

Her voice was thick. 'Well, then, what are you waiting for? Leave me be.'

She went to walk away before Cesar could see the extent of her distress, but he caught her again. She cursed out loud, but he had both hands on her arms now.

Lexie felt a tear slip down one cheek and cursed again, struggling against his hold. She stopped and looked up. 'Just…let me go, Cesar. Please. I can't do this.'

He paled under his dark skin. 'I didn't want to make you cry.' His hands tightened. 'The reason you were an inconvenient lover is because you made me face up to myself in a way no one ever has before. Or will again.'

Now Cesar looked almost angry, but something in Lexie went very still.

'I was doing just fine without anyone challenging my

emotionally barren life. And then *you* appeared, literally like some kind of vision, and from that moment on something broke inside me. Something that needed to be broken.'

Cesar moved his hands up to cup Lexie's jaw.

'The truth is that you were...you *are*...the most beautifully *necessary* inconvenience, because you've brought me back to life. I don't want to end the affair, Lexie—*ever*. I want it to last for the rest of our lives.'

Lexie tried to shake her head, as if that might improve her hearing. But Cesar's hands held her immobile. She had to put her hands out to touch him, barely able to breathe. 'What are you saying?'

The tendrils of something impossibly light and effervescent were scaring her, beckoning her to a place where surely she would face the most epic fall of all if she was dreaming this.

'What I'm saying is that I'm in love with you. I think I have been from the moment I saw you. And I want to spend the rest of my life with you. I want it all—the picket fence, children, even the damn dog. *Everything.*'

His mouth twisted.

'When you asked me about getting married I taunted you because I couldn't bear the fact that you'd put a seed of something incredibly fragile in my head. A hope for the future I'd never even allowed myself to think about or imagine.'

Emotion was blooming inside Lexie's chest, making it expand, making her dizzy. She wanted to laugh and cry at the same time. But then she remembered his stark non-reaction that day at the *castillo*. The way he'd let her go so easily.

One of her hands on Cesar's chest curled into a fist and she hit him ineffectually. Her voice was choked. 'You hurt me. I thought you didn't care.'

Cesar looked pained. 'I'm so sorry—my response was… pathetic. I cared so much I shut down. I literally didn't know what to do or say. You were telling me those things… and all I could feel was my own pain. I couldn't begin to understand the horror of what had happened to you. I wanted to go out and find that man and kill him with my bare hands.'

Lexie paled.

'For the last week I've kept imagining you as a young girl, alone and scared, going through pregnancy and birth without any support.' He shook his head, his eyes glittering a little too brightly. 'You're the bravest person I know. You humble me.'

'I thought…' Lexie was whispering now '…that you hated what I'd told you because it was too personal. And that you didn't understand why I had to do what I did. I thought afterwards that it must have reminded you of your mother.'

Cesar's thumb caressed her cheek. 'If anything it's helped me to understand her a little better, because it's not so black and white any more. She wouldn't have been human if she hadn't felt some pain on leaving me behind— and God knows what nefarious bargain my grandparents struck with her to make her stay away.'

Feeling absurdly shy, Lexie said, 'I thought you resented the fact that I'd told you those things because our relationship wasn't about anything but…sex.'

Cesar grimaced. 'At first I did. I was angry because you'd forced me to acknowledge that what I felt for you went a lot deeper than I'd admitted to myself.'

Lexie could see it on his face now—in his eyes. Love. Blasting her doubts and fears. But it was huge. She was scared.

As if he could tell, he moved even closer and said throatily, 'What is it?'

'I'm scared,' she whispered, baring herself in a way she'd never done with anyone before. 'I'm scared because my own family turned their backs on me. Betrayed me in the worst possible way. I couldn't survive that again.'

Lexie could feel the tension in Cesar's body, see the ferocity in his expression.

'I vow to you with every breath in my body that I will spend my life protecting you from hurt and harm. I love you, Lexie. You're as much a part of my soul as I am myself. A betrayal of you is a betrayal of me…and whatever the future brings I'm going to be right by your side to deal with it. Including Connor.'

Lexie's eyes filled with tears. The fact that he'd acknowledged her son dissolved the last of her defences.

Cesar was blurry in her vision as she came up on tiptoe and slid her arms around his neck. 'I love you, Cesar… so much.'

He groaned softly and covered her mouth with his. The kiss was searing and passionate.

Lexie broke free and looked up. 'Take me home, please?'

Cesar smiled and his thumbs wiped away the tracks of her tears on her cheeks. '*Espere querida*…wait… There's just one thing I have to do first.'

Suddenly Cesar disappeared, and Lexie gave a little surprised yelp to see him kneeling at her feet, her huge skirt between them. He was holding out a black box which he then opened. He looked up, his slightly nervous smile making Lexie's heart flip-flop.

'Lexie Anderson…will you marry me?'

More tears filled Lexie's eyes. Pure joy bubbled up inside her. Her heart was in her voice when she said simply, 'Yes!'

Cesar took her hand and slid a stunning antique gold and diamond ring on her finger. The fact that she'd barely looked at it didn't seem to bother either of them, because he stood up and swept her and her voluminous dress into his arms before kissing her senseless—much to the entertainment of the security guards, who were the only people left on the set.

A week later Cesar had arranged to have his private jet standing by at a nearby private airfield. As soon as Lexie was wrapped after her final scene later that day they were going back to Spain.

Cesar's mobile phone beeped with a message and he read it.

Congratulations on your engagement. Alexio and I would like to meet you, if you're ready. Call me any time. Rafaele.

Cesar showed the message to Lexie later, when they were on the plane, and she was sitting in his lap. She looked at him and he saw the way her eyes grew suspiciously bright.

She pressed a kiss to his cheek and said, 'I'm ready when you are.'

Incredible joy gripped him—there wasn't a hint of the old darkness and pain. Cesar grinned and threw his phone down, and then got busy showing his fiancée just how ready he was.

EPILOGUE

Eighteen months later

'I MEAN...THEY look so innocent, don't they?'

Cesar smiled at Alexio's almost incredulous tone. Rafaele sighed deeply on his other side. They'd been standing and talking and were now watching the three women who were sitting around a picnic table under a huge tree, a few yards away. They were on Cesar's lawn, at the back of the *castillo*, where a new outdoor pool twinkled invitingly through some small trees.

The *castillo* looked the same on the outside but it had been almost completely remodelled on the inside, so that very few vestiges of the past remained apart from the parts that had to be preserved. It was light and airy, with vast spaces, and decorated with a sumptuous yet understated luxury. Lexie had personally supervised the storage of the portraits of Cesar's grandparents in a special airtight room deep in the cellars.

'I know,' Rafaele said now. 'And yet in spite of that innocence they all—

'Brought us down,' Cesar chipped in, sounding the happiest out of all of them.

Just then the three women's heads drew closer together: one dark, one bright blonde and the other reddish blonde. There came a very distinctive peal of laughter from Samantha Falcone, and then they were all guffawing inelegantly, heads thrown back.

Rafaele shifted uncomfortably. 'Why does that always make me nervous? As if they're talking—

'About us?' Alexio cut in.

'Because they probably are,' Cesar said equably, once again sounding like a Zen Buddha.

His younger half-brothers turned towards him and folded their arms, two versions of his own green eyes narrowed on him.

Alexio remarked dryly, 'I could take a photo of you right now and Tweet it and you'd lose your well-honed mystique in seconds.'

Cesar smiled and said ruefully, 'Be my guest. I think I lost that mystique somewhere around the first nappy-change, when my sense of smell got scarred for life.'

The tiny bundle wriggled against his chest and he looked down at the small downy head of his two-month-old daughter, Lucita, where she was burrowing into a more comfortable position. His hand supported her bottom in the baby sling protectively.

Just then a small toddler in a bright dress broke free of the women at the table and tottered towards the men with a determined expression on her face. A halo of strawberry-blond ringlets framed a heart-stoppingly cherubic face dominated by huge green eyes.

She'd already wrapped everyone within a ten-mile radius around her tiny finger—even Cesar's normally very taciturn housekeeper.

Cesar's chest grew tight as he imagined Lucita at that age. And growing older in a vastly different *castillo* from the one he'd experienced. One filled with light and love.

Alexio bent down and encouraged his daughter Belle the last few yards, until she fell into his arms with a squeal of excitement. Lifting her up, he settled her high against his chest, a distinctly soppy expression on his face as she rested her head between his neck and shoulder, thumb firmly in her mouth.

'How the mighty are fallen indeed,' Rafaele remarked wryly, observing this just as Milo, his almost five-year-old son, streaked by with his armbands on, ready to jump into the pool, followed swiftly by Juan Cortez's similarly aged son—Milo's new best friend.

Belle immediately straightened up to take her thumb from her mouth and pointed a clutching hand at where Milo was, exclaiming urgently in baby gibberish.

But Alexio's attention was fixated on his wife, Sidonie, who had followed her daughter and was sliding an arm around her husband's waist. She wore a long colourful kaftan over a bikini.

Cesar knew that they were sitting on the news that they were expecting again until Sidonie had passed three months. But Sid had already told Lexie, and Lexie had told Cesar, and he was pretty sure that Sam must know too—which meant Rafaele knew, which meant it was an open secret. But of course no one would acknowledge it till they did.

The look between Alexio and Sidonie was definitely carnal and very private.

She smiled as Belle wriggled to be put down. 'You know that now she's seen Milo she won't rest until she can play with him.'

Alexio scowled in Rafaele's direction and Rafaele raised a brow. 'What? It's not *my* fault she's hero-worshipping her cousin. She's displaying remarkably good taste in men already. That's a *good* thing!'

Sidonie just shook her head at the men's ribbing and took Belle's hand when Alexio let her down. She glanced fondly at where her new niece was cuddled against Cesar's chest. 'Lucita's due a feed, and Sam wants to take a nap, so I said I'd watch the kids. I'll take Belle to the pool.'

Alexio immediately declared, 'I'll come too,' and another hot, private look passed between them.

Samantha Falcone was walking towards them now, still graceful despite her seven months pregnant belly, evident under a stretchy dress. When she came near Rafaele drew her close and asked throatily, 'You're taking a nap?'

She looked up at him and nodded, and then said, far too innocently, 'You didn't sleep very well last night, did you? Maybe you should take a nap too?'

Cesar almost laughed out loud at the way Rafaele muttered something unintelligble and all but dragged his pregnant wife into the *castillo*. Rafaele had confided that this time was very poignant for him, because he'd missed Sam's pregnancy with Milo.

Alexio and Sidonie were now wandering off hand in hand, with Belle toddling in front of them, towards the pool.

Cesar looked over to where Lexie sat on the love seat beneath the tree, watching him. She smiled and crooked her finger. As if he needed any encouragement...

When he sat down beside her Lucita was already raising her head and mewling softly, clearly ready for her feed.

Deftly Cesar unhooked the sling and lifted his daughter out, holding her head securely as her huge blue eyes opened wide and she gazed back at him guilelessly. His heart clenched. Was it possible to fall even more deeply in love every time he looked at her? And then she smiled and the question became moot, because he fell fathoms deeper in a nanosecond.

'Look!' Cesar declared proudly, angling her for Lexie's inspection. 'She smiled at me.'

Lexie grinned and took their daughter from his safe

hands, settling her against the breast she'd bared, helping that seeking mouth to find her nipple.

As Lucita latched on, Lexie said wryly, 'I hate to burst your bubble but it's probably just wind.'

Cesar said nothing and when she peeked at him he was just smiling at her, a very private smile. He put his arm around her and said throatily, 'I could watch you nurse Lucita all day.'

Lexie rested her head back against him and smiled. 'Happy?'

Cesar looked down at her and felt his heart swell so much it might explode. Those huge blue eyes sucked him in as they had that very first time.

He shook his head and said quickly, '*Happy* doesn't even come close to how I'm feeling.'

He took Lexie's free hand—the hand on which she wore his rings. He brought it up and pressed his mouth there, over the rings that bound them together for ever.

He found himself admitting something he'd been too ashamed to admit before. 'Do you know…just before Lucita was born I was afraid…afraid that I couldn't possibly love any more than I already loved you?'

Lexie's eyes grew bright.

'But as soon as she was born I realised it's infinite. Love can't be bound to one person.'

'I know,' Lexie whispered. 'I felt it too.'

The pregnancy and birth had been incredibly emotional for them both, but especially poignant for Lexie, considering it had brought back everything she'd been through with her first baby. But Cesar had been with her every step of the way, and more supportive than she might have dared to imagine. With his encouragement she'd even been in touch with the adoption agency to leave word as to where she could be contacted should her son ever feel the desire.

A deep sense of peace and security pervaded her life now. And love.

Lexie huffed a small laugh then, even as emotional tears made her eyes glitter. 'You know, for someone who was deprived of love growing up you're remarkably good at it.'

Cesar smiled back and said, with not a little sadness, 'I can feel sorry for my grandparents now. They were so bitter and caught up in anger.'

Predictably, at the mention of his grandparents, Lexie's eyes flashed with emotion. But before it could rise Cesar pressed a kiss to Lexie's mouth, long and lingering, full of love.

When he drew back the fire of anger had gone out of Lexie's eyes to be replaced by another kind of fire, and she said, almost grumpily, 'That was blatant distraction.'

Lucita's mouth popped free and Lexie handed her back to Cesar while she prepared her other breast for feeding.

When their daughter had emitted a gratifyingly robust burp Cesar handed her back. With Lucita settled again, Lexie looked at her husband. 'Are you ready for tomorrow?'

'Tomorrow?' he asked disingenuously, clearly much more interested in his wife and baby. 'Tell me what's happening tomorrow again?'

Lexie smiled. He knew exactly what was happening. Even so, she reminded him. 'Sidonie's aunt is arriving and it's her first time out of France, so we all have to be very mindful of her. Alexio is going to Paris to meet her and bring her here so she won't be nervous. Rafaele's father and his new wife Bridie are coming from Milan. And Juan Cortez and Maria are coming to pick up Miguel— although you know they'll probably end up spending the night because it'd be rude not to ask them to stay for the barbecue...'

'And,' added Cesar dryly, 'because Maria is as thick as thieves with you and Sid and Sam.'

Lexie smiled, but couldn't stem a niggle of anxiety for Cesar. This was their biggest family get-together yet. And it would getting bigger all the time—especially as Sam's new baby would be born soon and added to the mix. And then Sid's.

It had been easier for Lexie, knowing what it was to come from a sizeable family, in spite of their estrangement. And also because she and Sam and Sidonie had formed a solid and genuine friendship almost within the first ten minutes of meeting each other.

She knew that even though Cesar's relationship with his half-brothers had taken a quantum leap ever since that first meeting in Rome, when she'd gone with him to meet them properly for the first time, it was still a novel experience for him to play at happy families having come from the exact opposite experience.

But then, it had been healing for Cesar to hear how Rafaele and Alexio had suffered at the hands of their unhappy mother in their own lives. Happy families didn't come naturally to them either. Once he'd seen they could empathise with him he hadn't felt so alone in his experiences.

Lexie saw the glint of determination in Cesar's eyes and castigated herself for underestimating how he might deal with this. He pressed another lingering kiss to her mouth and then pulled back, saying with a grin that transformed him into someone infinitely younger and even more gorgeous, 'Am I ready? As long as you're with me I'm ready for anything.'

Lexie answered huskily, with her heart in her voice, 'Well, that's easy—because I'm not going anywhere.'

* * * * *

COMING SOON!

We really hope you enjoyed reading this book.
If you're looking for more romance
be sure to head to the shops when
new books are available on

Thursday 23rd October

To see which titles are coming soon, please visit
millsandboon.co.uk/nextmonth

MILLS & BOON

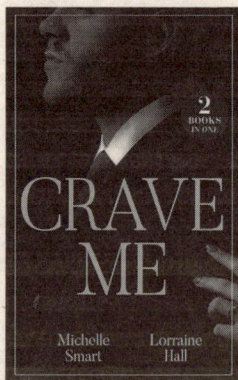

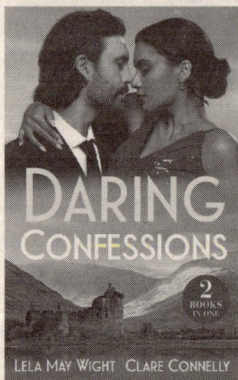

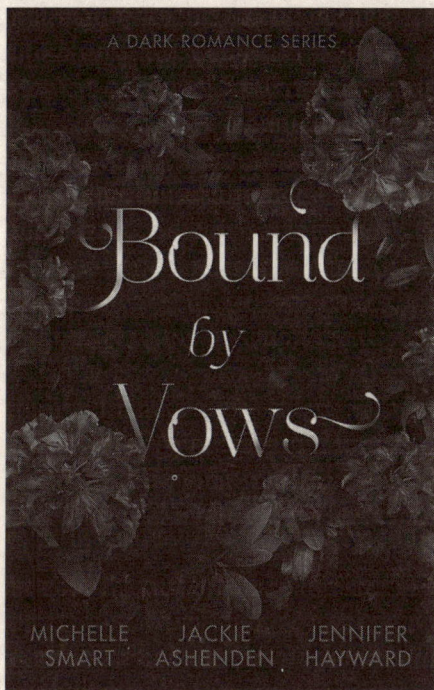

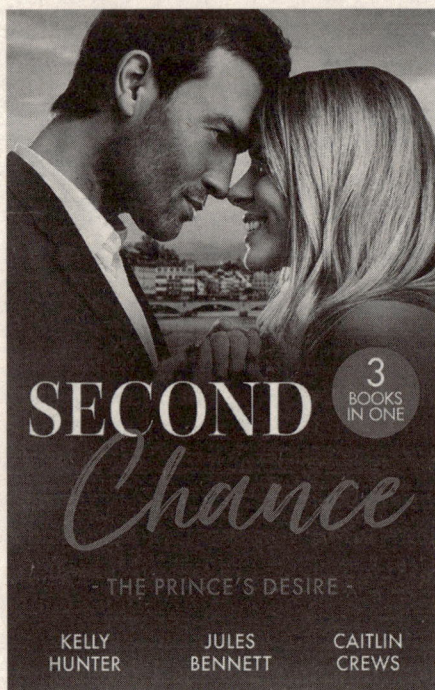

MILLS & BOON

THE HEART OF ROMANCE

A ROMANCE FOR EVERY READER

MODERN

Prepare to be swept off your feet by sophisticated, sexy and seductive heroes, in some of the world's most glamourous and romantic locations, where power and passion collide.

HISTORICAL

Escape with historical heroes from time gone by. Whether your passion is for wicked Regency Rakes, muscled Vikings or rugged Highlanders, awaken the romance of the past.

MEDICAL

Set your pulse racing with dedicated, delectable doctors in the high-pressure world of medicine, where emotions run high and passion, comfort and love are the best medicine.

Love Always

Celebrate true love with tender stories of heartfelt romance, from the rush of falling in love to the joy a new baby can bring, and a focus on the emotional heart of a relationship.

HEROES

The excitement of a gripping thriller, with intense romance at its heart. Resourceful, true-to-life women and strong, fearless men face danger and desire - a killer combination!

afterglow BOOKS

From showing up to glowing up, these characters are on the path to leading their best lives and finding romance along the way – with plenty of sizzling spice!

To see which titles are coming soon, please visit

millsandboon.co.uk/nextmonth

afterglow BOOKS

Afterglow Books is a trend-led, trope-filled list of books with diverse, authentic and relatable characters, a wide array of voices and representations, plus real world trials and tribulations. Featuring all the tropes you could possibly want (think small-town settings, fake relationships, grumpy vs sunshine, enemies to lovers) and all with a generous dose of spice in every story.

♪ @millsandboonuk
⊙ @millsandboonuk
afterglowbooks.co.uk

#AfterglowBooks

For all the latest book news, exclusive content and giveaways scan the QR code below to sign up to the Afterglow newsletter:

SCAN ME

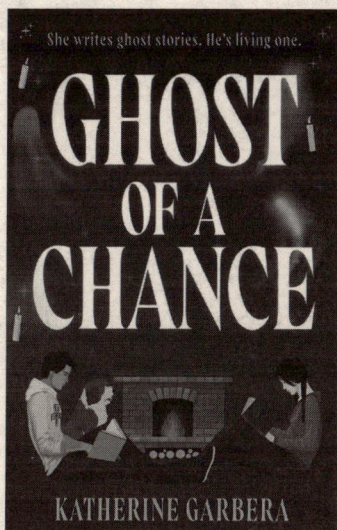

LET'S TALK

Romance

For exclusive extracts, competitions and special offers, find us online:

f MillsandBoon

X @MillsandBoon

⊙ @MillsandBoonUK

♪ @MillsandBoonUK

Get in touch on 01413 063 232